PRAISE FOR *RECURSION*

"An exceptional first novel. A new British star has arrived to join the likes of Hamilton, Reynolds and Banks."

—*Vector*

"An ingenious novel, positively bristling with ideas, memorable characters and gripping storylines that do indeed manage to meet most memorably before the novel is complete...This is a mystery of epic proportions, a mystery that sums up the appeal of great science fiction; it can ask how our world came to be, then answer the question with verve and imagination."

—*Agony Column*

RECURSION

TONY BALLANTYNE

BANTAM BOOKS

RECURSION
A Bantam Spectra Book / September 2006

Published by
Bantam Dell
A Division of Random House, Inc.
New York, New York

ISBN-10: 0-553-58928-8
ISBN-13: 978-0-553-58928-3
Printed in the United States of America
Published simultaneously in Canada

www.bantamdell.com

OPM   10 9 8 7 6 5 4 3 2 1

For Barbara

RECURSION

Herb looked at the viewing field and felt his stomach tighten in horror. He had been expecting to see a neat cityscape: line after line of silver needles linked by lacy bridges, cool silver skyscrapers shot through with pink-tinted crystal windows; artfully designed to resemble the spread of colors on a petal. Instead he saw... bleak nothingness. Cold, featureless, gently undulating wasteland spreading in all directions.

Something had gone badly wrong. Suddenly the cozy white leather and polished yellow wood lounge of his spaceship was not the safe cocoon he had grown used to over the past few months. Now they would be coming to prize him from this warm, cushioned shell to cast him shivering into the real world, all because he had made one tiny mistake.

Somehow he had made a mess of the code that should have told the Von Neumann Machines to stop reproducing and start building.

Herb's machines had eaten up an entire planet.

• • • •

But there was nothing to be gained now by crying about it. Herb had known he was on his own when he embarked upon this project. It was up to him to figure out what had gone wrong, and then to extract himself from the situation.

He opened a second viewing field next to the first and called up an image of his prototype Von Neumann Machine. A cylinder, nine centimeters long, with eight silver legs spaced along its body, giving it an insectile appearance. Six months ago Herb had dropped out of warp right over this planet, opened the hatch of his spaceship, and stood in solemn silence for a moment before dropping that same machine onto the desolate, rocky surface below.

What had happened next?

Herb liked to pace when he was thinking, and he had arranged his spaceship lounge to allow him room to do so. Two white sofas facing each other occupied the center of the room. A wide moat of parquet flooring filled the space between the sofas and the surrounding furniture that lined the walls of the room. The smell of beeswax polish and fresh coffee filled the cabin. Herb closed his eyes and ran through the order of events after he had released the Von Neumann Machine.

He imagined that first VNM turning on six of its spindly legs, lifting them in a high stepping motion as it sought to orient itself. The remaining two legs would be extended forward, acting as antennae, vibrating slightly as they read the little machine's surroundings. It would have walked a few paces, tiny grains of sand sticking to its silver-grey limbs, then maybe changed direction and moved again, executing a random path until it found a patch of rock of just the right composition, then settled itself down, folding its legs around itself to bring its osmotic shell in contact with the surface.

His thoughts on track, Herb began to pace, soft ships' slippers padding on the wooden floor. He was naked except for a pair of paper shorts. *Okay, what next?*

In his imagination he saw the first machine absorbing matter from the planet, converting it, working it, and sending it around that half-twisted loop that no human mind could comprehend. Soon there would be two identical machines standing on the rock, their legs waving in an explorative fashion. And then four of them, then eight...

The program was perfect, or so the simulations had told him. When they reached the optimum number, the machines should have begun constructing his city out of their own bodies, clamberering on top of each other using the sticky pads on the ends of their feet. Herb was proud of the design of those pads: each seemingly smooth foot ended in a chaotic branching of millions upon millions of tiny strands. Press one foot down and the hairs would spread out, reaching down and around to follow the contours of the surface beneath them so perfectly that they were attracted to it at a molecular level.

Not that any of that mattered now. This was the point where the error lay. The machines hadn't paused to build his city. They'd just gone on reproducing, continued eating up the planet to make copies of themselves until there was nothing left. He opened his eyes again to look at the viewing field. Maybe he had only imagined it.

Herb groaned as the view zoomed in on the cold grey shifting sea beneath. He could make out the busy motion of millions of VNMs walking over and under each other, struggling to climb upwards to the surface only to be trodden on and forced down by other VNMs, each equally determined about seeking the light. Wasn't that part of the end program? City spires, growing upwards, seeking the light in the manner of plants? Everywhere he looked, everywhere the ship's senses could reach— out to the horizon, down to the submerged layers of machines—it was the same: frenzied, pointless activity.

He paused and felt a sudden thrill of horror. That wasn't quite true. Something was happening directly below. He could see a wave building beneath him: a swelling in the grey, rolling surface. Thousands of pairs of tiny silver antennae were now waving in his direction. They sensed the ship hanging there. They sensed raw materials that could be converted into yet more silver VNMs. Herb felt a peculiar mix of horror and betrayal.

He croaked out a command. "Ship. Up one hundred meters!"

The ship smoothly gained altitude and Herb began to pace again. He needed to think, to isolate the error, but he couldn't concentrate because one thought kept jumping in front of all the others.

He was in serious trouble.

Herb didn't exactly fear the EA. Why should he? The EA was like a parent: it cared for and nurtured all its human charges. The EA wanted Herb to become the best that he could be. No, Herb did not fear the EA: he *respected* it. After all, it watched everyone, constantly monitoring their slightest action.

And it acted to correct the behavior of those who transgressed its boundaries.

The EA would have been upset enough by the thought of a private city being built on an unapproved planet. Never mind the fact that the planet was sterile and uninhabited, they would still point out the fact that a city wasn't part of this planet's natural environmental vectors.

"We are uniquely placed to manipulate not only our environment, but also that of other races as yet unborn. It is our responsibility not to abuse that privilege."

The message was as much part of Herb's childhood as the smell of damp grass, the dull brown tedium of Cultural Appreciation lessons, and the gentle but growing certainty that whatever he wanted was his for the asking. Everything, that is, but this. Everyone knew the EA's philosophy.

So what would the EA think when they discovered that in failing to build his illegal city he had accidentally destroyed an entire planet instead? Did they know already? Had something in his behavior been picked up by the EA's monitoring routines? Was someone already on their way here to arrest him?

Herb didn't remember setting out a bottle of vanilla whisky on the carved glass slab that served as a side table. Nonetheless, he poured a drink and felt himself relax a little. His next moves began to fall into place.

First he had to try and destroy any evidence linking this planet with himself.

Next he had to get away from here undetected.

Then he had to slot back into normal life as if nothing had happened.

Then, and only then, could he pause to think about what had gone wrong with his prototype.

The first objective should be quite straightforward. The original VNM had been designed with anonymity in mind: standard parts, modular pieces of code taken from public libraries. The thought that someone might accidentally stumble across his planet had always been at the back of his mind. He gulped down some more whisky and an idea seemed to crystallize from the alcohol. He prodded it gently.

As far as Herb knew, no one else even knew that this planet existed. He had jumped across space at random and set his ship's senses wide to find a suitable location. What if this planet were just to disappear? What if he dropped a second VNM onto it—one with a warp drive and access to a supply of exotic matter? Set it loose converting all the original machines, and then, when that work was done, just jump them all into the heart of a star?

Could he do it?

Getting hold of enough exotic matter to build the warp drives of the modified VNMs would be a problem, but his father had contacts, so that could come later. He had to get away first.

He could do that. A random series of jumps around the galaxy, eventually returning to Earth. Enough jumps, executed quickly enough, and nothing would be able to retrace his course.

Good. Now, how about slotting back into normal life? Would anyone suspect him? More to the point, would the EA suspect anything? Their senses were everywhere. They said the EA could look into someone's soul and weigh the good and evil contained therein to twenty decimal places, and yet . . . and yet . . .

Herb was different. He had known it since he was a child. Sometimes it was as if he was merely a silhouette. Like he was there in outline, but they couldn't fill in any of the specific details.

If anyone could get away with it, it was Herb.

A gentle breeze brushed his face and he felt his spirits

lift. He took another gulp of whisky and felt a flood of warm relief as he swallowed. The plan was good. He could get away with it.

"I can get away with it," he whispered to himself, his confidence growing. Another sip of whisky and that familiar sense of his own invulnerability swung slowly back into place. Get back home, and he would be able to examine the design of his VNM and discover what had gone wrong with it. He drained the glass and began to stride around the room, feet padding on the wooden floor, energy suddenly bubbling inside him.

"I'm going to get away with it!" he said out loud, punching at the air with a fist. And then, once he was home, once he had found the error in his design, he could find himself another planet. Build his city there instead.

"I will get away with it!" he cried triumphantly.

"No you won't."

The glass slipped from Herb's fingers. He spun around and fell into a crouch position, ready to run or fight, though where he would run to in a three-room spaceship his body hadn't yet decided.

A slight, dark-haired man with a wide, white, beaming smile and midnight-black skin stood on the sheepskin rug between the facing sofas. He wore an immaculately tailored suit in dark cloth with a pearl grey pinstripe. Snowy white cuffs peeped from the edge of his sleeves; gleaming patent leather shoes were half hidden by the razor-sharp creases of his trousers. The man raised his hat to Herb, a dark fedora with a spearmint green band.

"Good afternoon, Henry Jeremiah Kirkham. My name is Robert Johnston. I work for the Environment Agency."

Herb slowly straightened up. He felt naked and exposed.

"What are you doing on my ship?" he said, the faintest tremor in his voice.

Robert Johnston gave a sad little shrug of his shoulders.

"Oh Herb, I don't like this any more than you do, but, well, I have no choice. You have put me in this position; your actions have led me to this juncture. I'm afraid that I am going to have to punish you for the destruction of this planet." He shook his head in regret.

Herb frowned back at him. "No, that's not what I meant. I meant, how did you get on my ship? You can't have stowed away; it's too small. I'd have heard the alarms if you tried to come through the airlock."

Herb bit his lip in thought. "Ergo, you can't be here," he murmured. "What are you? Externally projected V-R?"

"Sorry, Herb, no." He suddenly became more animated. "I'm as real as the next man. I'm here in person, in the flesh. Accept no substitutes, the One and Only, the real McCoy, the Cat in the Hat." At this he skimmed his broad-brimmed hat across the room toward Herb, who ducked quickly to avoid it. The hat spun over Herb's head and hit one of the glass ornaments on the sideboard, knocking it over. It fell to the floor and shattered. Herb ignored the noise. His anger was building, his arrogance asserting itself. He fanned it, forced himself to hold Johnston's gaze and speak with a level voice that belied the tension that was building in his stomach.

"Okay, if you're real, how did you get in here? The ship's integrity has not been breached since we left Earth, or I would have known about it. Every particle of onboard matter will have been tracked by the ship's AI since it was loaded, and you are to be found nowhere on the manifest. You cannot be here. I can only surmise that I am hallucinating." He looked thoughtfully for a moment at the bottle that sat on the floor near his feet and murmured to himself, "Possibly drugged by this vanilla whisky that I don't remember putting out here on the table..."

He frowned. Robert Johnston tilted his head back and laughed. His neatly knotted green-and-pearl tie shimmered in the light.

"The lengths some people will go to to avoid the simple truth! The whisky has been tampered with, but only to the extent of adding a mild sedative. That is what allows you to stand there arguing rationally with me, rather than following the more natural urge to crouch shivering in the corner. Anyway, if I'm a hallucination, how could I have put the whisky bottle there in the first place?"

Herb frowned thoughtfully. He did feel a lot calmer than he would have expected to under the circumstances.

"Why have you drugged me?" asked Herb, after a pause.

"The EA is concerned about your health. The shock of me suddenly appearing in your ship could have had severe consequences."

"Good for the EA. So how did you get here? Matter displacement?"

"No. Nothing so exotic. I came down the secret passage."

Herb was silent for a moment as he considered the statement. When he spoke, it was with icy calm.

"You don't have secret passages on spaceships."

"Yes, you do. There's one underneath that armchair. Look."

At that, Johnston walked across the room, the heels of his shoes clicking on the polished wooden floor. He seized the armchair by its back, his fingers making deep dimples in the soft white leather, and pulled it to one side. The outline of a trapdoor could be seen, a knife line through the contrasting colors of the parquetry. Johnston pressed one corner of the outline with an elegantly manicured finger and the trapdoor popped up with a soft sigh. He pulled it back to reveal a long metal tube dropping away into the distance. Herb felt the gentle pull of air leaving his lounge, sighing its way down the dark, yawning passageway.

"I don't believe it," whispered Herb softly. "Are you sure you're not a hallucination?"

"I feel it in my bones," said Robert Johnston.

They both crouched down by the edge of the secret passageway, staring into its depths.

Johnston stroked his chin. "The floor of your lounge is built into the port wall of your ship. I attached my ship to yours just after you completed your first jump from Earth. The pipe you can see is the connection between us. A simple deep scan ensured that the hatch was located beneath your armchair for concealment."

Herb gazed at Johnston in disgust. He hated being patronized. "What are you talking about? How could you attach your ship to mine without me noticing it? I'd have picked it up the first time I scanned any system on reinsertion from warp."

Johnston shook his head sadly. "Oh, Herb. And you're supposed to be quite intelligent."

"What do you mean, *quite* intelligent?" snapped Herb.

"Do you find that offensive? I'm sorry." Johnston gazed at the tips of his fingers for a moment, an enigmatic smile playing around his lips, then continued.

"What I mean is that I'm surprised you haven't worked it out. Surely you have heard of stealth technology?"

"I have. I don't believe it is sophisticated enough to fool my scanners," replied Herb shortly.

"Oh, it is," Robert Johnston said softly. "It is."

They crouched by the hole for another moment in silence. Herb's pale blue eyes locked with Johnston's dark brown gaze. Herb was used to playing this game, and usually he was the last to look away. Not this time. He blinked and looked back down into the shadows.

"Okay," he muttered softly, "I believe you. You attached a stealth ship to mine."

"I didn't say that," said Johnston.

Herb jumped to his feet in anger. "Hell's teeth!" he shouted. "What is your problem? Why do you keep playing games with me?"

The smile vanished from Johnston's face, and Herb found a very different person looking at him. There was no emotion in his face, just the cold certainty that Robert Johnston—and only Robert Johnston—was in charge of the situation.

Johnston spoke in the softest of tones. "I just wanted to establish, right at the beginning of our relationship, that I could. I'm not one of your father's lackeys, paid to be pushed around."

The smile snapped back onto his face, and Herb felt a rush of relief.

"However, let me explain. I did not say that I used a stealth ship, I merely pointed that out as a possible solution to the problem: namely, how did I attach my ship to yours without you noticing?"

Johnston rose to his feet and walked across to the sofa facing the viewing field that Herb had opened earlier.

Herb paused to run his finger along the rim of the hatch Johnston had opened in his ship. The parquetry was joined to the metal of the hatch like the crust on a loaf of bread: one material faded into another without any definable boundary. However the join was achieved, Herb had not seen the effect before. Reluctantly, because Johnston was waiting, he pulled the hatch shut and went to sit on the sofa opposite him.

When Herb had designed the lounge of his spaceship, he had intended it to be light and airy. White leather furniture and slabs of glass sat above the nonrepeating, tessellating pattern of the parquet floor. The walls were left quite plain, only the occasional tall ornament or sculpture set out around the perimeter of the room acted to relieve their blankness. The ceiling was hung with the fragile white balls of paper lanterns that gently illuminated the room. To Herb's eyes, Robert Johnston, sitting on the white sofa, stood out like a turd in cotton wool. His dark suit may have been immaculately tailored, his sharp starched cuffs may have slid from the sleeves of his jacket as he smoothed a crease on his trousers, but as far as Herb was concerned, there was something jarringly wrong about the man sitting opposite. As he was thinking this, the answer to the problem occurred to him.

"You suppressed my ship's AI, didn't you?" Herb said. "My ship is completely under the control of your ship's AI. Your ship has processed every command I've made and filtered out any information it didn't want me to see."

"Very good. You *are* intelligent, but I knew that. However...I want you to understand that everything

you have done over the past six months has been cata-
logued by the EA. We have the proof you destroyed this
planet."

"It was an accident." Herb narrowed his eyes. "If
you've monitored everything that I've done, you will realize that."

Johnston smiled sadly.

"Oh, I realize that. But Herb . . . it's not an excuse.
You've still destroyed a planet."

"It was completely lifeless. I checked first."

Herb knew that it was the wrong thing to say as soon
as the words left his lips. Johnston's eyes darkened and
the smile snapped away again to be replaced by an expression of pure anger.

"You checked, did you? Ran a full spectroscopic
analysis of the atmosphere for airborne plankton? Per-
formed a high-resolution deep scan in case microbes
were clinging onto life beside hot vents deep at the
heart of the planet?" He flicked his right hand in a dismissive fashion. "Or did you just run a five-minute local sweep for Earthlike life-forms?"

Herb opened his mouth to speak but Johnston interrupted.

"Don't!" he shouted, holding up a hand. "We both
know the answer to that, don't we?"

Herb cringed. Johnston remained perfectly still, his
arm raised as if to strike, the edge of one perfectly pressed
and gleaming white cuff emerging from the sleeve of his
jacket, the tide line between the pale and the midnight
black skin that traveled around his hand, dead center in
Herb's vision.

Johnston held that position, held it and held it, then
his eyes moved slowly to the left to gaze at his own

hand. His mouth creased back into a wide smile and he relaxed. The upraised hand was dropped.

"...but that's all in the past now. A crime has been committed, and now we must decide upon the punishment."

Herb felt his stomach tighten again. Maybe the effect of the drugged whisky was wearing off, because he felt more panicky than before.

He began to babble. "We don't have to do this, you know. My father is a very important man. I'm sure we can come to some arrangement. Besides, I'm sorry. I've learned my lesson. I won't do anything like this again. Look, face it, I've got a lot to offer society. I put together those VNMs to my own design. My technical skills have got to be worth something; it would be a real waste to lock me away where I couldn't achieve anything worthwhile..."

"Preemptive Multitasking?" said Johnston, innocently.

Herb paused in mid flow, his mouth moving soundlessly.

Johnston began to adjust the viewing field. The greyish square hanging in the air above the coffee table began to grow.

"I mean, I know that it reduces the overall intelligence slightly, but it does mean that a perfectly good brain can work on five or six different jobs at the same time."

The viewing field had now expanded to a square about three meters across the diagonal. Johnston began to apply a slight curve across its surface, continuing to speak as he did so.

"So, we could have your body locked up in a nutrient vat in a station in the Oort cloud, while we apply your

intelligence to controlling five or six different maintenance craft."

The viewing field darkened and a few stars began to
appear.

"We could leave you a time slice of consciousness for
your own use: a time for you to think and dream, to be
yourself. Depending on how you cooperate, we could locate that consciousness inside your body, in the vat . . .
though that would be very boring—" Johnston turned
from the viewing field to smile at Herb "—or maybe controlling a robot with the run of the station. That way you
could get to mix with some members of the crew."

Depth was added to the picture in the viewing field.
A section of a black sphere grew in the lounge, diamond
stars winking into existence inside it. Herb was looking
at a star field. His mind, however, was far away across
the galaxy, trapped in a tight-fitting metal coffin filled
with lukewarm nutrient soup, while his eyes stared into
infrared and the empty drones under his control crept
and crawled beneath the cold remnants of starlight.

"I don't want that," Herb said softly. His eyes were
filling with tears.

"What makes you think you have a choice?" Johnston
asked. "You're not a child anymore; your father isn't
going to come along and say, 'Okay, maybe not this time
if you really, really promise not to do it again.' We're
dealing with cause and effect here. You do the crime,
you do the time. That's it; you can't go back, any more
than we can restore the life to this planet that your self-
replicating machines have just spent the last few months
destroying."

"Oh." Herb couldn't think of anything else to say. He
looked around the lounge of his spaceship and already
it seemed to belong to someone else. He had passed

from one world to another. He sat down heavily on one of the sofas and put his head into his hands.

"Will you tell my father?"

"You will have the opportunity to do that yourself. You will have access to a public comm channel. That's a basic right of any intelligent being."

Johnston continued to manipulate the viewing field. Stars began to move across it. He appeared to be searching for something. Herb said nothing. He began to run his fingers over the soft white leather of the sofa, enjoying the sensation of luxury while he still could.

Johnston paused in his search and glanced toward him. "Don't you want to know how long your sentence is?"

The thought that a finite sentence made any difference to his current circumstances hadn't occurred to Herb. The thought of going to the Oort cloud was too big. Coming back was too remote a possibility, be it in ten or a hundred years' time. He just shrugged.

Johnston grinned as he brought the stars' movement to a halt.

"That's an unfair question, of course. We don't know the answer. How long will it take for you to atone? Only the EA knows. We don't get that many cases of planetcide—one a year, if that. I'd guess your sentence would probably be more than your natural lifespan. We'd probably have to take an e-print of your consciousness."

"Are you deliberately tormenting me?" asked Herb, a feeble twist of anger gently uncurling in his stomach. Johnston turned toward him again with an approving smile.

"Good. You do have some spirit, don't you? No,

Herb, I'm not tormenting you. I'm just trying to impress upon you the seriousness of your predicament."

There was a silence, and Herb had the first inkling that maybe his fate wasn't yet decided. He paused, wondering if he dared hope otherwise.

Eventually he had to speak. "Why?" he asked.

Johnston grinned in response. If Herb hadn't known better, he would have thought the other man was pleased with him.

Johnston had finally found what he was looking for. He set the viewing field to full locale. Herb was floating in interstellar space on a white leather sofa. A star rushed toward his face, growing in size. It veered to one side just before hitting him and a smaller, darker object swam into view. A planet with the size, and the apparent intent, of a fist now hung in front of Herb's nose.

"Take a look at it," said Johnston. 'I've enabled the tactiles.'

Herb reached for the planet and turned it around in his hand, the rest of the universe spinning around the room in a dizzying pattern of lights as it maintained the correct orientation with Herb's viewpoint. The planet was a grey featureless sphere, like an old ball bearing Herb had once seen in a museum.

"What is it?" he asked, fascinated. As he stared at the object in his hand, the surface of the planet seemed to ripple slightly.

Herb frowned. "Those ripples must be hundreds of kilometers high. What's going on?" As he spoke, an answer occurred to him. For a moment he had thought he was looking at his own planet, the one that seethed just outside the door of his ship. Then he had noticed the patterns of the star field.

"It's the remains of another planet, isn't it? Someone else has done what I've done here."

Johnston's smile loomed in the blackness of space, his teeth glowing blue in the reflected starlight.

"A few people, actually. Oh, don't look so disappointed, Herb. I thought you were sorry for what you've done. Look at that planet, though. Look at the way it's writhing in your hands. Think about the sheer power behind those machines. Just compare them to yours."

"Mine were designed to build a city. Raw power is all very well—"

"Oh, Herb. Don't be so sensitive. I was only making a point."

Herb bristled. "Not necessarily. As I was trying to say, power isn't everything. It all comes down to the design of the original machine. If that hasn't been thought through properly, all the power in the world won't insure its integrity."

Johnston was silent. Herb let go of the planet and tried to see the man through the darkness, without success. He started at a sudden movement beside him. It was Robert Johnston, sitting down beside him.

He leaned close to Herb's ear and spoke softly. "So what you're saying is that you're not worried by what you can see before you? If I asked you to, you could neutralize those machines?"

Herb said nothing. He breathed in and out slowly, gazing at the planet. So that was the deal.

"Yes . . ." He hesitated. Johnston was staring at him intently. Herb took another breath, and his habitual confidence rekindled.

"Yes," he said again. "Yes, I could do it. I'm sure I could. I know I could."

"Excellent," said Johnston, slouching back in the

sofa. "I hoped you could. I knew you could. Set a thief to catch a thief, that's what I said to them." He crossed his legs, his left ankle resting on his right knee, and began to tap out a rhythm on his thigh.

Herb stared at him. "So?" he said.

"So what?"

"So we have a deal. I neutralize those VNMs that have converted the planet, and you let me off?"

"Oh, Herb." Johnston shook his head sadly. "I can't let you off. Your crime is much too great for that."

Again, Herb felt a great weight descend upon him. He slumped forward, all energy draining from his body. Johnston leaned forward quickly and placed a hand on Herb's knee.

"That doesn't mean that we couldn't cut a deal, though." I could have you transferred to an Earth prison, instead. Get your sentence cut to about a year. Even arrange for some remedial training in the responsible applications of self-replicating machines."

Herb sat up straighter, though without as much enthusiasm as he would have expected. His constantly changing fate was making him feel drained and passive.

As it was supposed to.

He gave a weak smile. "Would you?" he said.

"Oh, yes," said Johnston. "If it was anyone else but you."

He rolled out of the chair easily before Herb could seize him by the throat and then backed casually around the room, ducking and dodging as Herb tried to catch him. Herb was incoherent with rage: shouting and swearing as he tried to punch, kick, scratch and bite his tormentor. Eventually Johnston tripped him up with one elegantly shod foot. Herb curled up on the floor and began to cry.

"Why are you doing this to me? Why are you playing with my life?" he sobbed.

Johnston looked puzzled. "I'm not. I'm sorry. I'm not explaining myself very well. Come here." He reached out and took hold of Herb by the hand. Gently, he led him back to the sofa and sat him down.

"I think you need some more vanilla whisky." He filled a new glass and pressed it into Herb's hand. Herb gulped it down, staring into the star field that filled the room.

Robert Johnston's voice was low and comforting. "You see, Herb, I didn't mean that I wouldn't cut a deal with you. No. Any time you want me to cut a deal, just say so, and it's cut. You can trust me. But Herb, I have your best interests at heart and I don't think you could handle this. You have to believe me: there is more to that planet than you think; a lot more. If you agree to make a deal with me, there is no going back. You can't change your mind. You have to see this through. Do you understand?"

Herb nodded.

"I don't want to go to the Oort cloud," he said.

"I know that," said Johnston, patting his hand. "But there are even worse things than service in the Oort cloud. Are you sure you want me to go on?"

"Yes."

"Very well."

Johnston sat back in the other white sofa, facing Herb, the converted planet they had been looking at still hanging between them. He placed the tips of his fingers together, gazing at Herb over them. The universe wrapped itself around him in trails of brilliant stars and black depths. His voice was rich and low.

"Herb, listen to me. You, me, this planet we see before

us, the planet below us, we are all linked together. The roots of the events that bring us together here today run deeper than you might guess. You are at the end of a process that started when an ape first picked up a bone to use as a weapon. When humans began to bury their dead and to raise ziggurats so that they could speak to their gods, they hastened this process. When the first electronic counting engine was built, humankind knew that someday they would end up in this situation, with people like you and me sitting together in a room looking at a planet like that one before us in the viewing field."

Herb looked at Johnston suspiciously. The whisky was calming the dull edge of his fear, helping him to think clearly.

"Are you sure?" he said carefully, expecting Johnston to flare up in anger. To his surprise, Johnston remained calm.

"Trust me, Herb. If we get to the end of this you will see that I am right."

"If?"

"Yes, if. Were you not listening? This goes deeper than first impressions would suggest. This planet we see before us is just the first pebble skittering over the scree at the foot of the cliff. Bouncing down behind, you may hear the clattering of other pebbles and rocks, and you may be fooled into thinking that this is just a minor slippage, and that soon everything will come to a halt and the balance will be restored. Don't think that. That silence you can hear will just make the ensuing avalanche sound that much louder."

Herb licked his lips, trying to understand what Johnston was saying.

"You mean there are other planets like that one?"

"Oh, yes. Something in that region of space has begun reproducing. We don't know what it is, but it has taken root and is growing fast; faster than anything we have so far encountered, faster even than us. Just as your VNM destroyed this planet, whatever is at work in there is viciously converting whole systems. If we live in the Earth Domain, then that region of space is the Enemy Domain. In a very short time it has grown from nothing to something that threatens to totally engulf us and everything we know."

Johnston leaned closer. "I'm putting together a team to do something about it and I want you to be part of that team. Do you think you will be useful? Could you help us fight it?"

"I can fight it," said Herb. "Yes. No problem." He paused, gazing contemplatively at the glass in his hand.

"Are you sure? Because I want you to understand, I cannot guarantee that you will return to Earth at the end of this."

Herb sighed. Pushing through the smothering wall of the whisky that he had drunk, Johnston's words had a sobering effect. Following them came the thought of the Oort cloud: years spent living as multiple copies of himself at the edge of nothingness, cold and forgotten. Better that he should take his chances out here.

"I understand," he said.

"Again, I ask, are you sure? The EA picked you for this team because of certain qualities that you possess. Those qualities may enable you to complete your role as a team member, but nothing more. Are you willing to take that risk?"

"I am," said Herb.

"Excellent." Johnston proffered his hand. "We are

about to shake on a contract. There will be no going back."

"No going back," echoed Herb. He placed his whisky glass on the floor and shook Johnston's hand firmly.

Robert Johnston beamed widely. "We've got a deal."

Herb felt himself relax a little. It was going to be all right, he thought. Anything was better than the Oort cloud. Anything.

The feeling of relief that welled up inside him was so intense that he went quite limp. Johnston switched off the viewing field and set some gentle music playing. Herb listened and drank more whisky. It helped to kill the growing feeling of unease.

For Herb was dimly aware of how expertly he had been distracted by Robert's entrance; he had a vague appreciation of how he had been kept off balance by the rapid pace of events and the constant changes of direction in Robert's approach.

He refilled his glass and gulped down some more of the sweet alcohol, wondering at how carefully Robert had worded the terms of his agreement.

Herb was beginning to suspect that he had been suckered.

Eva had a headache. This was the day she had
been working toward for the last three months and she
had awoken with a headache.

Sitting at the tiny kitchen table, she forced herself to
drink a glass and a half of water, then rested her head in
her hands, elbows propped on the daisy-patterned surface of the tabletop, and tried to think. Her stomach
was bloated with stale water, she felt sick and hung
over, this despite the fact that she hadn't had a drink in
months. Maybe if she ate something, filled her stomach
with something solid, she would feel better? There were
plenty of things to eat in the flat: the fridge even held a
convector burger she had brought home from work last
night. She had had to buy food to maintain the pre-
tense. Any deviation from her routine and *they* would
come around, tapping politely at the door. All those
professionally friendly people with their sincere smiles
and concerned frowns and their "Could we come in for
coffee? Just passing, you understand. Saw your light was
on and thought we'd pop in for a chat."

Still, if things went according to plan, by this evening she would be free of them. They would be left tapping at the door, stretching up on tiptoes to peep through the windows, stooping to peer through her old letterbox, and Eva would be hundreds of miles away...

But first she needed to get rid of this headache. The next few hours were the most crucial, and it was vitally important that she be able to think clearly. So, first something to eat, then get dressed, then down to the garage shop to buy some Somaspirin or Panacetamol.

She took the burger out of the fridge and set it spinning in the convector, the smell of strawberry-flavored meat quickly filling the room. After watching it turn a few times, she decided to get dressed while her breakfast cooked.

The sun was shining through the faded yellow curtains of her bedroom. Eva sometimes wondered who had hung them there originally, all those years ago. When the next tenant came to the flat, would there be anything left behind to remember Eva by? She doubted it. The white paper ball of the light shade caught her eye and cheered her up slightly. She had bought it seven years ago, just after she had moved in, to replace a glass shade that had filled the room with red light. Maybe one day someone would lie on the bed and gaze up at her paper lantern and wonder about the person who had hung it there. Brewster, her threadbare teddy bear, sat on the bed, gazing at her with a glassy-eyed stare that reminded her she still had things to do.

She opened the wardrobe door. Three outfits in burger bar colors. It was tempting to put one on: she got extra credit in her pay for every hour she was seen wearing the uniform outside the firm's time. She flipped past her good dress and some not-so-good skirts and trousers, all hung neatly on their hangers. She paused as she reached DeForest's forgotten suit, still hanging in its expensive blue storage bag, left behind when he had been recalled from her life and relocated to who knows where. She gazed at it for a moment, lost in thought.

The convector chimed and her head throbbed in time to the notes. She pulled out one of the burger bar suits and quickly got dressed. She found a purple-and-red uniform baseball cap rolled up in the trouser pocket. Eva threaded her prematurely grey-white hair through the hole in the back to make a little ponytail as she walked back into the kitchen/lounge.

Her burger sat steaming in front of the convector.

Two bites and a swallow and her headache was getting worse. She forced herself to eat the whole of the burger slowly and finished the remaining half glass of water. Then Eva picked up her purse and keys and walked out of the flat, down to the garage.

Reasons for escaping:

I couldn't even get myself promoted at the burger bar.

The greyness of South Street is seeping into my soul.

I have no friends to speak of.

They killed my brother.

Eva ran through the list in her mind as she stepped out into the unpleasant morning air. She didn't dare write down her reasons. *They* would see, as *they* saw everything. Then they would be around to visit her with their professional concern, something they learned in the second year of the Social Care course.

"Eva, why are you unhappy?" they would ask. "Why is promotion so important to you? What do you mean by the greyness of South Street? Why do you want to leave? But where would you go? Your problems will just come along with you, Eva; you must know that. You'll never solve anything just by running."

But there were still places *they* didn't control. Places *they* couldn't see. Eva had heard the rumors like everyone else. Eva knew one such place, and she had planned her flight there with meticulous care.

The late morning rush hour was easing off. All those people who paid good money to live in the supposedly clean air of the country were helping to make each breath Eva took just that little bit more unpleasant as they drove past to their city center jobs. Across the road, the garage was a brightly colored plastic blancmange mired in a grey sea of cracked and crumbling concrete. She dodged through the traffic to reach it, stepping gratefully from the hot air reeking of raspberry-scented gasoline into the cool antiseptic atmosphere of the retail area. She thought it was funny, the way the cleanest places in the city were responsible for the greatest proportion of its pollution. She staggered to the pharmacy shelf and looked for something to take the throbbing pain from her head. It was all that she could do not to laugh at the irony of her purchase.

Eva found a yellow-and-red-striped pack of tablets and took it to the counter, along with a pink can of cola. She felt in her pocket for her e-card as the young man behind the counter scanned the pack of pills. He frowned at his screen.

"It says here you've been going through quite a few of these lately. I've got to ask you when you finished the last pack." He blushed as he spoke, the flesh-toned cream he used to hide his acne contrasting nicely with his reddening skin. Eva reckoned he couldn't be aged more than thirteen. Only just old enough to hold down a part-time job.

"I finished the last pack last weekend. I was having a very heavy period. Does it mention that there, too?" The boy turned a deeper crimson and tapped at a button.

"I've got to ask if you have any alcohol at home."

"I gave that up months ago. The computer must know that. It monitors everything that goes into my apartment, and it counts every empty package and bottle that comes out."

"Sorry, Eva," apologized the boy.

"Call me Ms. Rye. You don't know me."

"Sorry, Ms. Rye." He placed her e-card on the counter and held out the painkillers. "Your account has been debited."

Eva snatched the package from his hand, popped the top of the cola can and took a deep swallow. She slid two pills from the package into her mouth and then chased them down with another gulp of cola.

"That's better," she said.

"Good morning, Ms. Rye."

She ignored him and pushed her way back out into the raspberry-stinking air. As she strode toward the middle of South Street, she ran over what she had to do in the next few hours.

The most important thing was to continue acting normally. If there were any hints that she was deviating from her normal routine, *they* would spot it. She had learned that lesson the hard way, when they had killed her brother. Her phone vibrated in her back pocket.

She hit the answer button. "Hello."

"Hello there, Eva. What would you think about one hundred and fifty credits for ten minutes' work?"

The voice was colorless and sexless. Their voices

always were. She thought quickly: she couldn't afford to lose time from her schedule on this day of all days; at the same time she didn't want to attract suspicion. She made her voice sound tired and listless.

"I've got a splitting headache. Ask someone else."

"Three hundred credits, Eva. All we're asking is that you take a detour down Keppel Road on your way to the shops. Three hundred credits could pay for a new washing machine."

"I don't need a new washing machine."

"You will in about three weeks. Built-in obsolescence is a pretty exact science these days."

Eva was about to agree, she didn't have time to argue. But she stopped herself. She had to act normally. What would the normal Eva have done? Bargain, of course.

"Five hundred credits," she said.

"Done," said the voice. "Near the station end of Keppel Road there is a hawthorn tree. Hawthorn trees have twisty brown trunks and small ragged green—"

"I know what a hawthorn tree looks like."

"Of course you do. There may be some small pieces of metal stuck in and around the base of that tree. We would like you to tidy up the mess. It should take you no more than twenty minutes."

"You said ten."

"That's right, we did. When you've collected the metal, place it in a mail tube. We'll let you know the address you need to send it to later. Bye."

The line went dead just as Eva reached the end of Keppel Road. She turned down it, heading toward the Lite Station. She guessed that some stealth plane had suffered minor damage over the city the previous night and she had been detailed to collect the wreckage. The thought put DeForest in her mind again. Like all company people, he had denied the existence of stealth ordnance, and like all young people with ideals, Eva had teased him mercilessly about his denial.

She remembered a January afternoon. The last one they would ever spend together, though Eva hadn't known that at the time. They had sat snug in her flat, the heating turned up full, the lights turned on against the grey day, while they drank red wine and watched old movies. DeForest was flying back that evening, back to his wife and his other life in Connecticut. Eva hated the early evening flights; the day would drag by without either of them being able to settle to anything. On the screen before them the hero was being dragged into the shelter of a doorway by his mystery female protector.

"All that sweat and not a hair out of place," said Eva scornfully. "I wish I knew where she got her clothes from, too. She's been completely drenched in oil and they still look good on her."

"I'm impressed by the way she's avoiding the search planes. All that infrared detection equipment on board, and she fools them by setting fire to a few newspapers." DeForest took another drink of wine and gave Eva a little squeeze. She wriggled herself into a more comfortable position.

"There are one or two things about those planes I'd take issue with," said Eva, sliding her eyes sideways to look at DeForest's expression. "For a start, how come they're visible?"

DeForest gave a tolerant laugh. "Oh, here we go again. Ms. Conspiracy Theory 2047. The Earth is monitored by a fleet of invisible airplanes all reporting back to the evil Artificial Intelligence that evolved in the Internet."

Eva elbowed him in the stomach.

"Oh sorry, Mr. Free Enterprise 1987. I forgot that the world is actually run by a series of multinational companies that put the needs of the poor and the environment before their own profits."

"My company gave several million credits to charity last year. And we sponsored the Llangollen dam project."

"And I bet you spied out the territory using invisible planes, just so your competitors didn't try and muscle in on your plans."

"Why should we do that? The dam is a nonprofit-making project."

Eva grinned at him.

". . . and we don't have any stealth planes, anyway," he added smoothly.

"Too slow." She laughed and raised her arms to acknowledge imaginary applause. "Thank you! Thank you, people. I was right and DeForest was wrong!"

"No, you weren't." DeForest grinned and pinched her backside.

"OW!!!" squealed Eva, pinching him back. They began to pinch at each other some more and then to kiss and then . . .

And then, later on, DeForest had flown back to his other home and had never contacted Eva again. When she attempted to reach him, her calls were intercepted by the company. First she was told that he had been relocated to Korea, then that his wife had had a baby and he had decided to concentrate on his real family. Finally she had been told to stop contacting the company, and a block had been placed on her comm lines.

Eva reached the hawthorn tree. *Crataegus monogyna.* The Latin name rose in her mind unbidden, and she wondered where she had once read it. The hawthorn was one of the trees that lined the road on both sides, its brown trunk twisted out of a dusty grey square of earth and gravel at the edge of the pavement. Its roots had forced up the old paving slabs bordering it to form a mound. She walked around the tree to see three feathered darts stuck in its trunk. She pulled them out and looked around. A fourth dart was buried in a nearby gate; she pulled that out too. Eva felt as if the two rows of terraced houses that bordered the road were watching her with their blank windows. Her phone vibrated and she jumped.

"What is it?" she said.

"There are two more darts. Can you see them?"

"No. Where should I be looking?"

"Try behind the wall next to the gate that had the dart stuck in it."

"What if I'm seen?"

"Don't worry. We're distracting people in the immediate vicinity. Phone calls, overheating frying pans, malfunctioning electrical appliances . . . They'll all be looking the other way."

Eva sucked at her bottom lip nervously. She glanced up and down the street and then pushed open the gate. There was a narrow gap between the wall and the bay-fronted house, mainly filled with old gravel and weeds. A tortoiseshell cat slept in a corner, partially sheltered behind a stack of window glass that leaned against the wall. Eva saw one of the darts straight away, lying at the foot of the rain-streaked panes. She picked it up and looked frantically around. The last dart could be hidden anywhere in the weeds that sprang from the old gravel. She needed to find it quickly: she had a train to miss.

She glanced around the empty street again. Cracked

red bricks and grey pebbledash, blind windows reflecting the April sky. Nobody was coming, but she still felt incredibly exposed. She bent down and began to run her hands through the weeds, parting the stalks to search the gravel beneath. Nothing.

She paused, her arms folded tight against her chest. Her phone vibrated again.

"Hurry up. We can't keep this street clear forever."

"I'm looking," Eva snapped. "Are you sure the last dart didn't get stuck higher in the tree?"

"Positive. We're detecting its signature at ground level. About half a meter from your left foot."

Eva looked around again and realization dawned. The cat behind the glass wasn't asleep: it was dead.

"It's in the cat," she said.

"Where?"

"I don't know. I'm not looking. Get someone else to do your dirty work."

There was a moment's pause and then the voice spoke again.

"Fine, fine. Get out of there quickly. Your payment will be reduced to four hundred credits. Go to Mehta's Information Shop."

"I'm going."

Eva pushed her way through the gate and walked quickly down the street. Across the road a curtain twitched and, out of the corner of her eye, Eva caught sight of an old woman, watching. Eva dodged left and headed down a side street. A man in his slippers stood on the sidewalk talking to a woman in a dressing gown. A front door stood open behind them, an untidy cluster of doorbells screwed haphazardly into its frame. As she walked past, Eva overheard a snatch of their conversation.

"He went running out of the house just after midnight last night. Kept shouting 'my eyes,' sounded as if he was in pain. Disappeared around the corner and then collapsed. Heart attack, the doctor said."

"What are you going to do with his things?"

Eva continued down the road, as the reason for her contract took shape in her head. What price her part in the concealment of a murder? Four hundred credits.

The world was slipping down into Hell, and everyone was helping it on its way. Everyone accepted a little bit of money, and a little bit of blame, and that way they could all walk around with a conscience that was just a little bit off-color. Just a little bit, but add all those bits together...

Another reason why Eva had to escape.

If Eva had believed in fate, she would have had to admit it was finally coming round to her side. Her headache had almost cleared, and the diversion to pick up the darts had resulted in her arriving at the place she had been aiming for all along. She walked into Mehta's Information Shop deep in thought and headed to the back of the retail area. First deal with the darts, then lose her card, then finally back home. After that, she would begin her escape in earnest.

A stack of blue mail tubes lay on a shelf near the back. Eva picked one up and reached in her pocket for the four darts. She examined one before dropping it into the plastic container. A short fat needle, the red "feathers" at the back sliding smoothly into the metal barrel for concealment. Her phone vibrated once more.

"Hello."

"Drop them in quickly. You're drawing attention to yourself."

"Do the red feathers pop out at your signal, to help make them visible to collectors?" said Eva.

"Classified information, Eva."

"Why don't you just make them disintegrate?"

"That's not technically feasible. I think you've been listening to too many conspiracy theories. Just drop them in the tube and address it to 4A53.FF91.2E22.B7C2."

Eva scrawled the figures on the tube with a black marker pen that had been thoughtfully left on a nearby shelf.

"Okay. Deposit the tube in the secure slot. We would like to thank you for your efficiency. Your account has been credited with four hundred credits, plus seventeen credits for the postage. Good-bye, Eva." The line went dead.

Eva dropped the tube in the correct slot to a faint popping sound and then made her way to the front of the shop. It was time to resume her intended schedule.

She picked up five magazines from the shelves near the entrance doors and carried them to the checkout, pulling her e-card from a pocket as she did so. The young girl behind the counter scanned the card and the magazines. She recited each purchase as it appeared on the screen.

"*Literary Examiner, Women's Things* and *Research Scientist*. You know you have bought these three magazines here every week for the past five years? If you took out a subscription you could save forty percent of the cover price *and* have them delivered direct to your door."

"Do you know you have told me that same thing every week for the past four years and nine months?"

"Sorry, Eva."

"Call me Ms. Rye. You don't know who I am."

"As you wish. That will be five credits for the magazines and seventeen credits for the postage. That makes twenty-two credits."

Eva placed her e-card on top of *Women's Things,* her heartbeat accelerating. This was the crucial moment. The young girl scanned the card, Eva picked it up, together with the magazines. Then, trying her best to keep her voice natural... "Oh." She held up a copy of *Women's Things* apologetically. "I've picked up three copies of this magazine by mistake. I'll just take the other two back to the shelf."

She picked up the two unwanted magazines, doing her best to appear flustered, and carried them back to the shelf where she slotted them back into place, the e-card sandwiched securely between them. After that she returned to the counter and picked up her purchases before escaping from the shop. Eva walked down the road as casually as she could, her nervousness gradually receding. Maybe she was actually going to get away with it. No. Think positively. She *was* going to get away with it.

Back at her apartment Eva looked around its shabby rooms for what she hoped would be the final time. Her suitcase was already packed: some clothes, her makeup bag, a swimsuit she would never use, but when your every move was monitored by lifeless eyes, you had to go through the pretenses. She placed Brewster on top of the case, his lumpy body flopping forward to roll off the bed. She picked up the threadbare toy and balanced it carefully in place.

"I'll put you in a shopping bag, Brewster," she decided out loud, and headed into the kitchen.

The clock on the convector read 10:15. Twelve minutes until she would leave. Timing was of the essence. Eva had walked the distance to the Lite Station many times, while surreptitiously timing herself. She knew the exact duration of the journey to the International Station. She would arrive there at exactly the right time. Now if only some busybody didn't discover her e-card too soon . . .

She took a bag from the cupboard under the sink and pushed Brewster inside it, then sat him back on the bed, his eyes peeping over the top of the bag at the picture of the horses that hung on the wall. She had forgotten about it, barely noticed it anymore. Eva's father had bought her the picture when she was a little girl. She felt a wrench at the thought of leaving it behind, but then, who took pictures on vacation with them?

10:17. Ten minutes to go. Not for the first time, Eva had doubts. She would be leaving for good. She would never sit on the faded duvet again, its filling gathering in lumps in the corners. Was that really what she wanted? What if something went wrong? Her whole plan turned on the fact that she would deliberately miss the direct train and have to take the stopping one instead. What if someone had discovered her e-card?

10:18 and Eva went into the kitchen and poured herself a glass of water. She drank it very slowly, rinsed the glass and dried it with a towel, then replaced it in the cupboard.

10:20, seven minutes to go. Eva went to the toilet, flushed it, poured bleach down the bowl, washed her hands, checked her face in the mirror and walked back into the bedroom.

10:24. She checked through her bags again, squeezed Brewster's lumpy paw for luck, then walked around the apartment for the last time, checking that the windows were locked and everything was tidied away.

10:26 and she began to gather up her things. She walked out of her old life, locking the door behind her at exactly 10:27.

Eva walked quickly through South Street and reached the Lite Station just as her train was pulling in. She climbed aboard and stared out of the window as the train slid smoothly from the faded and badly restored Victoriana of the station and glided through the eras toward the tall glass towers of the twenty-first-century city. More and more railway lines seemed to be infiltrating Eva's city. They were creeping across the world, growing all by themselves. She had read about it in *Research Scientist*. They had a new way of making them, a spin-off from the technology that had built the robot Martian factories. She gave a sad smile. It was an incredible world to live in, for some people at least.

Her thoughts were disturbed by a plump woman with peroxide hair settling into the seat next to her. She placed her bags on the floor between her feet, then pulled a packet of candy from her pocket and offered one to Eva.

"Toffee?" she said.

"No, thank you."

"Has your headache cleared?" The woman unwrapped a candy and popped it in her mouth.

Eva's mouth slipped easily into its habitual benign smile. "Yes, thank you. And you can tell them that I'm looking forward to my trip."

The woman nodded her head.

"Good, good. Don't forget, if you're ever feeling down, just give us a call."

"I will."

"That's good, Eva. Don't forget, everyone needs a little help from Social Care now and again. It's nothing to be ashamed of."

"I know. It's what I pay my taxes for."

"That's right, it's what you pay your taxes for."

The woman bent to retrieve her shopping, then lurched to her feet and made her way farther down the coach. Eva watched her activate her phone and begin to report back on their encounter.

The Lite Train glided up a ramp between tall glass walls and came to a halt in the mezzanine of a major building. Eva saw a woman in a dark suit chatting with a man who looked a little like DeForest and she wondered what it would be like to work in a place like this. The view slid sideways as the Lite Train moved out from the station. Eva felt butterflies awaken in her stomach. The next stop was hers. As the Lite Train plunged underground on its way to Empire Station, Eva held her bags tightly and took a deep breath.

The clerk spoke without looking up from his screen.

"Good morning, Eva."

"Good morning."

"I see you're traveling to Marseilles. The train leaves in ten minutes. Shall we go through the formalities? Can I see your e-card?"

"Certainly."

Eva fumbled in her bag. She frowned, then fumbled again.

"I'm sure it was here earlier. Just a moment..."

Her fumbling became more frantic, then she paused and began to go through her pockets.

"I know I had it earlier. I used it to pay for my magazines."

She began to search in her bag again. The clerk looked on complacently.

"Look," said Eva, "do I really need it?"

The clerk looked as if he was trying to stifle a yawn. "I'm sorry, Eva, but the e-card is your guarantee of security and identification. It's essential if you travel abroad."

"But you know who I am. You knew as soon as I walked into this room. This whole city is riddled with biometric scanners."

"I'm sorry. I don't make the rules."

Eva clenched her fists in simulated rage. "They're stupid rules. Listen. I had my card earlier in the Information Shop. Can't you contact them? If it's there, they could courier it across."

The clerk gave a sympathetic smile. "I'll see what I can do." He leaned forward and tapped a few keys on his console.

A few minutes later the indicator board announced that the Marseilles train had just departed. From the outside, Eva appeared angry and frustrated to the point of tears. Inside, she was delightedly congratulating herself on her performance.

Eva fiddled and worked at Brewster's arm as the stopping train pulled out from the station. A Panacetamol dropped into her hand and she slipped it into her mouth while pretending to cough.

"Where are you going?" asked the woman sitting opposite.

"Marseilles," mumbled Eva, her mouth dry from the pill.

"That's nice. I'm off to Paris, myself. I'm Nuala, by the way."

"Eva," said Eva, holding out her hand. Nuala shook it.

"Are you okay, Eva? You look a little flushed?"

"Just tired. I missed my train. I feel so stupid. I think I'm going to try to sleep."

"Good idea."

Hugging Brewster in her arms, Eva curled up on the seat. The grey evening skyline flicked by outside the window. She began to fiddle again at the little loose seam under Brewster's right arm. All those nights, lying in bed, pushing white pills into her teddy bear. Saving them up against this day. She pulled out another pill and swallowed it.

She knew they monitored her apartment; she could never have tried this at home. But a train? A three-hour journey wasn't long enough to make sure. Maybe this journey would give her enough time. She just needed a reason to catch the stopping train. A reason that would seem plausible to the nannies in Social Care who watched over everyone in the city, doing what they thought was best.

If only they wanted what was best for Eva.

Eva didn't want any part of her life in the city anymore. If only Social Care realized they had left her just one way to walk away from it.

She pulled another Panacetamol from Brewster and swallowed it. She thought that she had read somewhere that thirty was enough, but she had never dared go back and check the reference for fear of signaling her intentions. Her mouth was increasingly dry and chalky. She felt the train begin its smooth acceleration as it entered the travel tubes, and for the first time in years Eva felt a little hope.

Nuala gave a little cough.

"I'm going to get a drink. Do you want anything?"

Eva shook her head. "No, thank you. I think I'll have my snooze now."

"A rest will do you the world of good."

Nuala edged her way out of the seat. Eva swallowed another pill, and another, and another, over and over again until her mouth was so dry she could swallow no more.

She hugged her teddy bear and allowed the motion of the train to rock her gently to sleep.

CONSTANTINE 1:2119

CONSTANTINE 1:2119

Constantine rubbed his temples in an attempt to ease his headache. He felt as if his brain needed a reboot. It seemed as if it had been processing without break for four months now: it was no surprise he was seeing gaps beneath the sky.

There was one outside the window of the I-train right now, just behind the three glass towers that marked the boundary between land and sea at the westernmost tip of the Great Australian Bight. It was a magnificent, though flawed, view. Red-lit streamers of cloud slid across the yellow sky, distorted and magnified as they moved behind the three enormous, transparent, fir-cone-shaped monuments. The towers themselves climbed into the evening sky at the edge of the steely grey sea flecked with the brightly colored sails of pleasure yachts that skipped and wove between the robotic cargo liners. It was a picture of both calm and motion, leisure and industry, the natural and the manufactured world. A tourist's view of a famous scene marred by only one inconsistency.

In between the sea and the sky: nothing—an untuned grey gap where the earth didn't quite meet the heavens. Constantine looked away. He had been seeing things for the past three weeks now; he didn't need further reminding how hard he had been working, nor how much he had allowed his brain to become overloaded by extra intelligences.

The mineral water in the glass resting on the bentwood table before him shimmered. A standing wave had formed on its surface as the I-train braked, and one of the intelligences that shared his mind calculated the acceleration that took a train from mach seven to mach zero in a little under five minutes and idly modeled the way in which the forces that achieved this were reflected in the liquid in front of him. Constantine tried to ignore the endless stream of figures that filled his mind.

"Not now, White," he muttered.

The train was entering Stonebreak. The checkerboard of green pasture and yellow cornfields that decorated the first level streamed past the windows of the car. This is how they displayed their wealth down here, Constantine reflected. Not in a crush of tall towers that sucked every last cent of value from the available land, but rather in an expansive and expensive display of space.

—Not entirely true, said Red, another of the intelligences crowding his mind. —They also need the food.

Constantine didn't care. His head hurt. All he wanted was to get off the train and into his hotel room. The end was close. The tension was getting to them all.

The train dipped underground and started its final deceleration, and the other passengers began to collect their possessions. Some rose and made their way to the doors; Constantine simply gazed out of the window

into the darkness of the tunnel. Two years of plotting
and planning, all set to end in Stonebreak. The idea
didn't seem real. He took a sip of water from the glass
and tried to think about his wife as the train drew to a
halt, tried to summon up a picture of her in his mind
that was more than a fading abstraction. It had been too
long.

It was the busiest time of the day at Stonebreak
International. No doubt Constantine's journey had been
scheduled to arrive during the evening rush, amid the
simultaneous arrival of several intercontinental trains.
Constantine's life over the past two years had been spent
in an interminable bustle of crowds, one tree hidden in
a never-ending forest.

The station was old and shabby: the iridescent patterns of dead VNM bodies that had formed the halls
may have looked cutting-edge twenty years ago, now
they just seemed faintly embarrassing. Their interlink-
ing shapes had been covered with hard-wearing transparent plastic; even so, the walls and the floors by
the skylifts were scuffed and abraded by constant use.
Constantine entered the elevator and asked for the roof.
As he rose toward the high-vaulted ceiling, he looked
down at the silver ribbons of the I-trains, curled in tight
spirals around the central spoke of the terminus.

"This place is a mess, huh? The new station can't
open too soon."

Constantine jumped at the sound of the voice. A
woman was standing at the far end of the elevator.

"I didn't see you get in here," said Constantine, checking his intelligences.

—I did, said Red. —She slipped in just as the doors were closing. You were turning to look at the view.

"You, of all people, shouldn't be surprised at how I slipped in here." She held out a hand. "I'm Mary Rye. That's my name."

Constantine refused her handshake. Mary gave a sniff and withdrew it. She pointedly wiped her palm on the pocket of her green jacket.

—She's been drinking, said Red.

"Don't look at me like that. I don't deserve that," said Mary, head tilted forward. Her thick Australian accent made her sound old-fashioned in these days of standardized elocution. "How long have you been a ghost? Two years, I'd guess. So what the fuck do you know about it? Nothing. That's what you know about it: nothing."

Constantine felt himself perspiring. Sweat was trickling down the small of his back, despite the air-conditioned freshness of the elevator.

He spoke carefully. "A ghost? I don't understand what you mean."

Mary gave an impatient shrug of her shoulders and waved her hand dismissively. Her green suit looked expensive but shabby. Two long strands of cotton trailed from the hem of her blouse. A brooch in the shape of three little cats was pinned lopsidedly to her lapel.

"Sure you don't," she said with heavy sarcasm. She waved her hand in the direction of the doors. "Look, I'm not blind. I'm not stupid. I know what to look for. I know what I see. I wait on the platform and I look out for people like you arriving. A train pulls in and the crowd on the platform parts like the Red Sea? I look to see who's walking along the path that forms. I see the cameras suddenly turn to look in one direction? I look in the other. I do that and I spot someone like you. The most ordinary-looking person in the building, and yet you never have to stop or step aside; your elevator is always waiting and your car always stops right by the exit. You never get stuck behind the person with the luggage and you're always just ahead of the person stopping to ask directions. You're one huge statistical improbability: your life is planned so that you will never be remembered. You're a ghost. Just like me."

She finished speaking just as the skylift emerged from the ground into the red light of evening. Through the glass, they could see rush-hour pedestrians hurrying by in all directions. Constantine tapped his fingers against the hard plastic of the console that nestled in his pocket.

"Well, whatever you say, madam. Now, if you'll excuse me..."

He stepped out into the cool Australian evening and strode toward the waiting boat that would take him to his hotel. Mary took hold of his sleeve and pulled him backwards.

"Hey, don't you madam me and then walk away. I was speaking to you. Didn't you hear me? Of course you heard me. You were ignoring me. Being rude."

Constantine turned to face her, conscious that she was on the verge of making a scene.

"Would you mind letting go of my arm please, mad—" He paused.

—Mary, reminded the Blue intelligence. There was an edge of amusement to its voice.

Constantine said nothing. Mary gazed at him with bleary eyes. There had once been a pretty face there, thought Constantine abstractedly, but now it was lost beneath the podgy swelling of fat and over-applied makeup. She spoke gently, her hard little chin pressing down against its soft cushion of flesh.

"I have a name," she continued with a drunkard's dignity. "Please do me the courtesy of using it."

"Very well . . . Mary. Please let go of my arm."

The two uniformed porters who stood by the varnished wooden sides of the hotel boat were now looking in his direction. Pink galahs fluttered beneath the huge expanse of the red sky. Constantine felt incredibly exposed.

Mary caught his expression and laughed.

"What are you so worried about? No one will be watching us. We're both invisible. Both invisible. Fact of life. Fact of our lives, I should say."

At that she took hold of her green skirt by the hem and pulled it right up so the tops of her thighs were exposed.

"Stop it," muttered Constantine.

"Why?" Mary asked, pulling her skirt up still further to show the faded pink daisy-printed panties she wore beneath. "See what I mean?" she said. "No one's looking at us, are they? Are they? Are they looking at us? No."

Constantine turned his back on the two hotel porters, who were now looking in any direction but his. He took hold of Mary's skirt and pulled it back down.

"For goodness' sake, stop it. What do you want?"

"I want you to acknowledge me for who I am. I want you to speak to me. And I want to do you a favor. I might know something to your advantage. Yes. To everyone's advantage. Listen to me and you could become a big man. The savior of Stonebreak, they'll call you."

Constantine paused, listening to his inner voices.

—She certainly believes that what she's saying is the truth, said the Red intelligence.

—If you go along with her for the moment, she will at least stop drawing attention to you, said Blue.

—I have nothing to add, said White.

Constantine and the others waited for a moment for the last intelligence, the Grey one, to speak, but as always it remained silent. Constantine gave a shrug. He turned to Mary.

"Okay. I'll listen, but no more drawing attention to us."

Mary gave a delighted smile. "Good. You won't regret this. Come on. This way. We're going up to the top of the city."

She linked her arm through Constantine's and began to walk along the side of the canal.

"You still haven't told me your name."

"Ben D'Roza," said Constantine.

"Ben? I don't think so. That was the name on your train ticket, and it will be the name on your hotel reservation, I'm sure, but it's not your real name, is it?"

Constantine sighed.

"Okay. It's Constantine," he said. "Constantine Storey."

"Constantine," said Mary carefully, as if practicing the name. "Constantine. I like that. And have you ever been to Stonebreak before, Constantine?"

"Yes. Several times."

"Business or pleasure? Business, I bet, since you've got the face of someone who couldn't have fun in a brothel with a platinum e-card tied to his dick. Have you ever been a tourist here in Stonebreak, Constantine?"

"No. I haven't."

"Then let me show you around. I'll show you something that will interest you."

She slipped her hand down Constantine's arm and took hold of his left hand, squeezing it tightly with her fat fingers so that his wedding ring dug painfully into his flesh.

They walked along a typical Stonebreak street. A wide, shallow, canal ran parallel to the narrow road, separated from it by a series of wide, tree-planted lawns. The whole was bordered by short rows of one- or two-story shops and houses, intercut with narrow alleyways accessible only to pedestrians. Chairs and tables had spilled from the cafes and bars out onto the lawns and were now slowly filling with the evening trade. A young woman walked by, hanging onto the arm of a tanned young man. She was dressed in the latest fashion: a simple white shift, her neck and arms wrapped in exotically curved bangles of silver and gold. She smiled prettily at Constantine and Mary as they passed, heading in the opposite direction.

The smell of the evening grass, the gentle splash of the water, the sheer prettiness of the cool narrow alleys, all these had helped Constantine relax sufficiently to return the young woman's smile, though he was still confused.

"On nights like this, you wonder why they call Stonebreak a design failure," said Mary.

They passed a cafe done up in period style: glass tables, bent beech chairs, and white linen. From its wide windows, light shone across the darkening lawns, illuminating the customers sipping beer and wine at tables arranged in a circle around an enormous lime tree.

"Where are we going?" asked Constantine, eventually.

"Relax," said Mary. "Do you see any other people around here looking tense? No. They're all out for a pleasant evening's stroll and a drink. Do you want to be noticed? I don't think so. So just hold my hand and try to look as if you're enjoying yourself."

Constantine had been enjoying himself. Now he suddenly realized how incredibly out of place he appeared in his business suit. He wished he'd had time to change into the same cool, loose-fitting dress the locals adopted.

"Now," said Mary, "at the moment we're on the second level of Stonebreak. Residential and leisure: medium-density housing and shopping. We're going to head to the center, the fourth level: cultural quarter and Source. Stonebreak, as you should know, is built as four concentric circles, each raised above the last. Beneath us lies a thin layer of maintenance ducts and so on, and beneath that, the main support structure, and beneath that again the transport system and I-train terminus."

"Thank you for the travelogue. Is there a reason for it?" asked Constantine.

Mary shook her head. "Just being friendly. It's nice to have someone to speak to. Talking's nice, don't you think? It's nice to have a conversation."

Constantine muttered something in reply. Mary chatted away happily.

"When I first started out I had a comfort family set up for me in Brazil. I did a lot of work in Brazil. I was there a lot of the year. Hans, that was my husband . . . well, he thought he was anyway. You know how it is. Two kids. Ellie and Gerhardt. It was somewhere to go and have a decent meal and just chat with someone . . ."

Her voice tailed off as she strolled on, lost in thought. Constantine glanced at her and felt a sudden stab of pity.

She was obviously living in much reduced circumstances now. The shabbiness of what had been an expensive suit and her once exercise-honed body running to alcohol-fueled fat suggested someone who had been high up within a company hierarchy. This physical manifestation of failure walking alongside him reminded Constantine of the pressure to succeed he himself was under. He turned his face from the narrow alley squeezed between two yellow stone cottages. A silver strand of nothingness showed at its end.

The gap beneath the sky was spreading. He was going mad.

Mary seemed to rouse herself.

"What about you, then?" she said. "Do you have a comfort family?"

"Me? No," said Constantine, his mind still elsewhere.

Mary gave a knowing laugh. "Of course not," she said, a note of bitterness creeping into her voice. "I forgot. It's different for men, isn't it? I bet you've got a string of skinny, unwitting twenty-year-old girls lined up from here to Alaska. All their details looked up from your company database and a script worked out so you can flatter your way into their apartments and their panties. I remember what it used to be like. It feels more moral to you than using a brothel, doesn't it? And you don't get your dinner cooked in a brothel, or your shirts ironed, or someone sitting up at night watching football with you, or slicing lemons when you have a cold, or—"

"I'm married."

Mary stopped dead, her hand pulling Constantine backward. She opened her mouth wide in disbelief and began to laugh.

"Married? What's that got to do with anything?"

"It means something to me," said Constantine simply. Mary brought her face close and breathed a sweet, alcohol breath over Constantine. She looked up into his eyes.

"I don't believe it. You're telling the truth, aren't you?"

She turned around again, took his hand, and began to drag him back along the street.

"Come on. We're going to be late."

Night shadows were spreading. White light shone from the spherical paper lanterns strung in looping lines between the chestnuts and limes that marched up the central lawn. A white barge came gliding down the canal, elderly people enjoying their pre-dinner drinks on the deck; the smell of prawns being fried in garlic and butter wafted from the open windows of the galley below.

—This is taking too long, said Blue, his voice seeming too loud in the stillness that was settling with the evening. —Are we being led into a trap?

—I can't see anything around us, answered Red. —Besides, I trust her. Her body language backs up her words. I don't think she's keeping anything from us.

—I . . . agree, said Blue, —but I can't help thinking that someone with the ability to train as a ghost might have enough skill to conceal her motives, even from us.

"Be quiet," muttered Constantine, concealing his mouth with his hand and pretending to cough. "She's watching me. She knows I'm listening to you. You're supposed to be a secret, remember?"

Mary was gazing up at him again, her eyes full of cool appraisal. Constantine nodded toward the barge.

"That smells delicious, doesn't it?" he said.

A pair of tramlines emerged from a side street to their left and swept round to follow the axis of the central strip of grass. The line of trees now moved to one side to make way for it. They walked on in silence for a while. Presently a tram came bumping along, an ancient construction of wood and metal that clanked and rattled as it trundled down the rails. It slowed sufficiently for Mary and Constantine to climb on board and then grumbled to itself as it sped up again. The pair sat down on a bench of varnished wooden slats. Constantine rubbed his fingers approvingly across the warm wood.

"When Stonebreak was set to build itself, they wanted the best of all worlds," said Mary. "The Australian and Southeast Asian government wanted it to be both ultra modern and ultra traditional. That's why you can still see the VNM bodies in the I-station, and that's why the tramlines zigzag around this level. Some thought trams were too modern to be ultra traditional, so it was decided that no line should run the entire length of any street. It will be a twisty journey from here to the locks."

"Fine," said Constantine, surprised to realize how relaxed he was becoming. If it hadn't been for his encounter with Mary, he would have gone straight to his hotel and would now be worrying about tomorrow's business. Instead, he was seeing the sights of Stonebreak. Even the mystery of his guide's purpose and identity was giving him something else to think about for a while. It helped that Mary did not seem threatening in any way.

"You can feel it, can't you?" said Mary.

"What?"

"A sense of freedom. I can see it in your face. Everyone thinks that being a ghost means you can do what you want, whenever you want, but they don't get it, do they? They don't know what it's like to be regularly exposed to indifference. Most people think it would be good to get out from under the noses of Social Care, but you miss it once it's gone. What if you fall ill, and there's no one there to see it? That's when you regret the millions of credits worth of software constantly combing the world's databases and removing each and every trace and reference to you. What if you were drunk and fell from this tram into the canal? There would be no record of your destination or your point of origin. Every computer sensor you've passed has been deliberately turned the other way as soon as they detected your bio signature. No one is waiting up for you somewhere because your employers want it that way, so no one would even know that you were splashing feebly in the water down there in an alcoholic haze."

She sighed and leaned back in her chair.

"And that's not the worst part, is it? It's the loneliness."

She wiped a fat hand across the corners of her eyes and sighed, then she sat up and forced a smile.

"Still. It could be worse. Maybe it's not so bad for you. You've got the voices in your head for company, after all."

"Voices?" Constantine forced a puzzled expression onto his face.

Mary put a hand to her mouth and raised one shoulder a little. "Oops. Sorry. Silly me. They're supposed to be a secret, aren't they? Pretend I didn't say anything. Nothing about voices."

She giggled and nudged him in the ribs.

"Still, I'll tell you something. You want to be careful when those voices that don't exist are speaking to you.

Your whole face relaxes and it makes you look really stupid. I suppose they don't think to control your expression. You should tell them that. Oh, sorry, I mean, if they really existed, you should."

She giggled again, then sighed.

"I wish this tram would get a move on."

They reached the inner perimeter of the second level. Just beyond the stone streets, a glass cliff rose into the sky, marking the border between the old and the new. Through this transparent wall Constantine could see the skeleton of the land: silver-grey bodies of VNMs in thick-plaited strands, rising in smooth curves and waves to support the next level up. The scene reminded Constantine of a mangrove swamp, a tangle of short-trunked trees with wide-spreading roots and intertwining branches, holding up the roof of the world. Staring at the greyish tangled trunks before him, Constantine had his first sudden inkling of the sheer size of Stonebreak, and the huge effort that had gone into its construction. He felt quite humbled.

Mary yawned loudly and began to scratch her side.

"They left the walls transparent so that people could see the roots of the city. Back then they were just showing off; now that VNMs build everything, it's more of an embarrassment. The base is solid and there's no room for the modification or organic growth that you get in modern arcologies. Stonebreak is lodged firmly in the past. It was defunct the day they built it. Some day they're going to have to tear it down and start again."

She gave a little sigh. "It can't come soon enough for me. Come on, onwards and upwards."

There were elevators set into the base of the soaring

wall. Perfectly transparent, they rode its inside as invisible as a sheet of glass in water. As they ascended, Constantine looked out over Stonebreak: at the low-rise streets, light reflecting from the black water of the canals, and beyond that to the darkened outer area that held the expansive gardens and arboretums, the playing fields and farmland situated on the first level, and then, finally, to the empty wilderness of the Nullarbor plain.

He felt as if he was walking through a dream. The bustle of the I-station and the awakening nightlife of the second level seemed to belong to another world.

Am I drugged? he suddenly asked the intelligences in his head.

There was a pause before they answered.

—I don't think so, said Red.

Another, longer pause.

—No. I can't see anything, but I know what you mean. Things seem strange.

—I agree. Go carefully.

From the fourth intelligence, as always, there came no word.

Mary took his arm and pointed to their left. Water was falling in a twisting tube down the inside of the wall, a liquid tornado, except moving with none of the violence and energy; instead, it seemed to splash and play like a merry stream. Hidden lights shone on the torrent, sending rainbows spinning and flashing and dancing around the inside of the glass walls in a fairy display.

"That's the water that feeds the canals. It passes through the water features and fountains of the business quarter on its way from the evaporators at the center of Stonebreak. They say if the water flow ever ceased, we'd all be dead within twenty-four hours. They built this city on one of the most inhospitable terrains on Earth."

She sighed. "I'll tell you what, though. I like it. I like the way it looks. I think it's pretty, you know? Everything else within the wall is about power and size and strength, but that waterfall, it's just about making something for pleasure."

Constantine frowned. "Oh, come on Mary, all of the second level looks nice. All those streets and canals. I've been in far worse places. Many people would like to live there, given the choice."

Mary shook her head and laughed.

"Oh, Constantine. How can you be so naïve? Being a ghost, obviously a trusted man within your organization, you should be able to look more deeply into the reasons for things, and yet you accept this at face value? Stonebreak wasn't about providing a nice environment to live and work, Stonebreak was all about telling the world that the Australian and Southeast Asian coalition had come of age and that they weren't prepared to be fucked with. When they raised this arcology, they were taking out their big dicks and slamming them on the table, saying 'Look at these! How about these for prime Australian beef, you fuckers.'"

Constantine smiled weakly at Mary's imagery. The elevator slid to a halt and the doors opened, but Mary stayed where she was, warming to her theme.

"But it all backfired. They moved too soon. Now they're left with this huge white elephant and they stand in awe and envy of those other organizations that stayed their hand. Now they look to Toronto and Lake Baikal and Atlantis and they wonder what to do next, but they're worried. A deeper crisis is unfolding, one that goes to the heart of Stonebreak, one that must remain a secret . . . And then a ghost arrives . . ."

She looked knowingly at Constantine, who kept his face carefully blank, but all the time waves of relief were washing through him. *She didn't know.* She didn't realize that he was here on a far larger mission, one whose roots went back to long before the building of Stonebreak. The very thought of it made Constantine shiver. Sometimes he forgot for a few minutes the importance of his task, but the memory soon returned, weighing down upon him. No wonder he was stressed. No wonder he was seeing things. Or not, as the case may be.

" . . . but you've got to ask yourself, is it worth it?" she continued, oblivious to his thoughts. "I was involved in the building of this place, and what did it get me? A nervous breakdown." She shook her head sadly. "You're feeling the pressure too, aren't you? No need to answer me. I can tell."

Constantine said nothing. For the moment the sky fitted perfectly down to the ground, and that was good enough for him.

They stepped out from the elevator onto the third level. Here the buildings rose higher, built mainly of glass to allow maximum daylight inside them. The towers were not as tall as in other cities of the world and were spaced wider apart, set in groves of trees or gravel gardens, but nonetheless this area emanated the unmistakable feeling of power. Two women in security uniforms came walking toward them.

"Good evening," said one. "Up here for an evening stroll?"

"That's right, officer," Mary said. "I'm taking my friend here to see the Source."

The security officer glanced at her partner as she smelled Mary's breath and gave a minute shake of her head. She looked at Constantine.

"The Source? First time in Stonebreak, sir? That's an excellent place to visit, especially on a clear night. But it's a long walk across the third level. You'd do better taking the under-city route. If you get back in the elevator and keep going down, it will take you to the I-station—"

"That's okay," said Mary. "We'd prefer to walk."

The security officers glanced at each other again, then drew closer together, directly in front of Mary.

"No. I think you misunderstood," said the second officer. "I really would consider taking the elevator, if I were you."

A look of anger crossed Mary's face and she took a step forward. Constantine put one hand on her shoulder to restrain her. He lowered his head and spoke in a bland, unremarkable voice, adjusted his posture in a certain way, did everything he could to make himself forgettable: a dull grey man in a dull grey suit.

"Actually, officers, we would prefer to *walk* through the city. I will vouch for this woman."

There was a pause. Somewhere in a Stonebreak computer, a routine had just appeared. It created a new identity for Constantine and passed on clearance in that name to the officers. Its work done, the routine deleted itself.

"Okay, off you go," said the first officer, her head tilted as she listened to a voice speaking in her ear. Mary and Constantine, the man who wasn't there, headed on into the business quarter.

• • • •

They walked through still streets between silent buildings. The business quarter had the air of a city of the dead: vast mausoleums lining wide thoroughfares that led through the night to nowhere. The brightly lit lobbies they passed seemed devoid of life: empty goldfish tanks, set out with toys but drained of water. Very occasionally they saw a security guard sitting at a desk, tapping at a console or watching a viewing field, but it was as if they were peering through a glass into a different world. Even Mary seemed subdued by her surroundings. She had hardly spoken since the episode with the two guards. Constantine wondered why they had intervened to stop her passing. How had a ghost been stopped by such simple security measures? Why hadn't they been automatically distracted by a strange sound, a message, a change in their routine?

For that matter, why hadn't Constantine's own hidden protectors done that for him straightaway? Was Mary somehow affecting the routines? The thoughts were driven from his mind as he heard her sigh.   ·

She was staring at the building immediately to her left with a despairing expression. Constantine gazed at it in surprise. It was the DIANA building: his own company. Mary sighed again and continued walking.

"That's who I work for," she said.

Constantine said nothing.

Around the corner two rectangular towers faced each other across a broad plaza. The facade of each was divided up into square windows, giving the buildings a retro, late-twentieth-century feel. A bright yellow light shone from every window, lighting up the plaza below.

A single person stood in each window, looking out across the plaza at the person standing in the window opposite. Thousands of people, standing in absolute silence, gazing into another's eyes. People in grey suits, in red dresses, in white bikinis. Old men in candy-striped blazers and young girls holding balloons, all standing in their individual squares of light staring, staring, staring. Constantine felt mad, shrieking panic scrambling around in his stomach at the thought of walking out there, across the plaza, in front of all those eyes.

"No . . ." he murmured, his mouth suddenly dry.

Mary gazed at him from under furrowed brows. "What's the matter?" she asked, glancing around the street.

Constantine turned back to the two towers, but all the people had vanished. Another hallucination?

"Nothing."

"You're working too hard."

"I know."

"Is it worth it?" Mary said. "Is it really worth it? Don't you just want to give up and do something else?"

Constantine didn't answer. Mary was speaking to herself.

The far end of the business quarter came quite suddenly. Another tall glass wall rose into the heavens behind the low-rent, low-rise buildings at the back of the third level. Another elevator took them up to the top of the fourth and final level, where they proceeded through more wide streets, this time paved with large grey slabs of mock stone.

"This is where Stonebreak has its law courts and

libraries, its mock parliaments and theaters. We're not going to look at them, they're far too dull."

The pair trudged past earnest-looking buildings of grey stone, adorned with columns and engraved with Greek or Latin mottoes.

Mary snorted in disgust.

"This is where their imagination ran out. We're walking nearly a kilometer above the Nullarbor plain and the best they could come up with are these imitation Roman dumps. Fucking architects. I work for a company that devised a structure that weighs millions of tons, has a diameter of nearly nine kilometers and a volume of thirty cubic kilometers. A structure that stands in one of the most inhospitable places on Earth. And what do they choose to decorate it with? Bad copies of bad copies of the bloody Parthenon. Two and a half thousand years of continuous advancement in human technology since the Greeks built the bloody original, and they still can't think of anything to improve on it."

Constantine was smiling now. The streets they walked were lightly scattered with other tourists, some of them looking at Mary to see what she was shouting about, but most of them looking away in disgust at her language. Mary continued, oblivious to the stares.

"I mean, why couldn't they just leave those buildings in the form that they grew? Surely the fact that Stonebreak *is* is enough. It doesn't have to pretend to be anything else."

"I quite agree," said Constantine. "But didn't you say earlier that Stonebreak is obsolete? I thought the VNM look was passé?"

"Oh, shut up," Mary replied without anger. "Come on. We're almost at the Source."

• • • •

Nearly forty years ago, the CEO of the Australia Southeast Asian coalition had walked across the flat scrubland of the Nullarbor plain to a point marked by a cross lightly scraped into the dry earth. Four dull grey machines were already set on the soil at the north, south, east, and west ends of the cross. She had crouched down and placed a fifth, silver machine, no bigger than her hand, in the faint depression scooped at the center of the cross, and then turned to smile at the assembled press and VIPs who stood one hundred meters back, behind the fluttering plastic ribbon that encircled the location that was destined to be the Source. The heaps of junk metal and other raw materials needed for the VNMs to work upon had been placed well out of sight of the spectators. They would have spoiled the effect, ruined the magic.

The sky had been a deep, deep blue, the sun a yellow glare, low in the sky, too bright to look at directly. The CEO turned to smile and pose for pictures. She was wishing she had worn a thicker suit. Okay, so they had deliberately scheduled the activation ceremony for early morning when it was cooler, but the Nullarbor plain was meant to be *hot*, for fuck's sake. She had to clench her teeth tightly to stop them chattering as she smiled.

Eventually, the photo call was over, and she could head back between the sparse bushes, the reddish sand scratching at her soft blue leather shoes, and enter the presentation area. Someone handed her a glass of thin champagne and she took it with a smile. "Get me a fucking cup of hot fucking coffee," she muttered under her breath.

She held up the glass and smiled brightly. "Good morning. Today, we can all feel privileged to be attending this incredible and historic event. Today, we can look back over five thousand years of human history, and reach out with the finest sieve imaginable, and garner the very best of human achievement, bringing it together here in humankind's mightiest achievement to date. Using the very latest in self-replicating technology, we . . ."

The crowd stirred: she was losing them. Fuck the speechwriters, what did they know? She hadn't got to her present position by rehashing other people's words. She did what she knew best and went with her instincts.

"Ah, to hell with it," she said. "You know what this is about. Let's build a city."

She raised her glass and took a sip. Out on the arid soil the machines began to stir. The assembled crowd drank their thin champagne and looked on at the unfolding scene: five cylinders scratching in the sand. How could the start of something so momentous appear so dull? It didn't seem right at all.

Soon they began to drift away, bored when they realized nothing much was going to happen out there. As they did so, the engineers and the workforce moved in. The sun rose further into the empty sky, beating down harshly on the minuscule activity below. Minuscule activity at the moment, maybe, but growing all the time as the machines began to reproduce.

A huge metal tree marked the Source. Pastel lights moved back and forth over it, dramatically picking out its colossal shape in the clear night. The trunk was composed of five thick strands twisting around and in and out of each other to form a thick plait. Four of the strands were a dull grey; the fifth, bright silver. The trunk itself emerged from the flagged ground and rose forty or fifty meters into the air before untwisting itself to spread its five branches high over Constantine and Mary's heads. These five branches then each split successively into two and four and then eight strands, blossoming into a huge, feathery, treelike effect.

The harsh white stars twinkled at them through the sharp outer branches. Constantine was so taken by the sight, he felt as if he had forgotten to breathe.

"It's like something out of a fairy tale," he whispered.

Mary nodded dreamily, and Constantine continued. "We walk around this place and we think we know what it is, but it's too big to hold in the mind. We *need* something like this to remind us what this place is all about. Thank you for bringing me here, Mary. Thank you."

Mary swayed slightly as she gazed upward into the air.

"In memory of the five original VNMs that were used to construct Stonebreak," she said. "I've heard that the fractal effect at the end of the branches was incredibly difficult to achieve back then."

Constantine merely nodded.

"Don't you notice anything odd about the branch directly above us?" asked Mary.

He looked up to where searchlights flitted back and forth, causing the shadows cast by the metal twigs to dance like leaves blowing in the wind. He stared at the branch above him. It did look strange, now that Mary mentioned it. Not misshapen as such, not even melted... He searched for the right word.

"It looks odd. It reminds me of something."

She didn't answer for a moment, allowing him to think. When he didn't continue, she began to explain softly.

"The contract to build Stonebreak was too big for one

company back then. It was awarded to five different concerns: Berliner Sibelius, Sho Heen, 113, Imagineers, and DIANA. Each of them contributed one of the VNMs that were needed to construct Stonebreak. This tree is a legacy of those five machines. That branch above us is the DIANA branch, and it's breaking down. You can see how it's crystallizing."

Constantine experienced a sudden flash of recognition on hearing Mary's words. That's what the branch reminded him of: an old piece of uneaten fudge, still the same shape, but slowly turning back into sugar.

"I sometimes wonder if I'm the only person to have noticed that deterioration," Mary said. "But I doubt it. One-fifth of Stonebreak is the result of the DIANA machine. So what if one-fifth of Stonebreak is similarly breaking down, deep down beneath the surface?"

"Hell . . ." murmured Constantine.

Mary continued: "And then I hear that DIANA is one of the agitators calling for Stonebreak to be pulled down. Of course they would be! Trying to hide their mistakes. So I put two and two together, and I think about what's going to happen next. I head down to the station and I wait. And I wait and I wait. And then I see a ghost arrive with the best stealth routines of anyone I've ever seen."

Constantine said nothing.

"You've come here because of this, haven't you?" demanded Mary.

Constantine remained silent. She gripped his arm.

"Tell them, Constantine. Tell them that I know. I've been watching and gathering information all the while, ready to drop back into the game. I've been out here on my own for too long. Let them know that; I'm ready to do what's required."

Constantine opened his mouth to speak, but was distracted. Three people wearing long grey overcoats had moved up to them so silently that Constantine hadn't noticed their approach.

"Good evening, Mr. Storey," said one. "Sorry it took us so long to find you, but, well, you're shielded by the best. Us."

Another took hold of Mary by the arm and firmly began to lead her away; Constantine couldn't tell whether by a man or a woman; all he could make out was a smudge of a person. They must all be wearing some sort of baffling equipment, he realized.

"Hey, leave her alone!" yelled Constantine. "I was speaking to her."

"Can't take the risk, Mr. Storey. She's drawing attention to you. That's how our computers found you, by noting the dead spot that seemed to follow her around."

"But she's a ghost too!"

"Was a ghost. Was a ghost. Now she's just an unemployed consumer, like so many others here."

"Unemployed? But she works for DIANA." He hesitated. "At least, that's what she told me."

"Not for ten years."

Constantine was half led, half bundled away from the Source. A grey flier rested lightly on the ground nearby. They steered him toward it.

"But people ignore her. I've seen her move down the street and no one notices she's there. She *must* be a ghost. What have you done to her?"

The grey figures did not reply; they just bundled Constantine into the flier. As the door closed, there was a faint shimmer beside him and Constantine found himself sitting between two tall women with short-cropped hair.

"Whew. It's a relief to turn those baffles off. I start to feel as if I can't breathe. Now, if Lee gets a move on in dumping that woman, we can soon get you back to the hotel and out of mischief, Mr. Storey."

Constantine watched the third grey figure hand Mary something, then turn and move quickly back toward the flier. Mary watched him go, then looked at the object in her hand. A bottle.

As the flier rose into the air, Constantine watched her take a deep drink, then begin to head toward the buildings that lined the perimeter of the open space in which the Source sat. Late-night sightseers moved out of her way as she staggered past. The flier climbed until it was just higher than the surrounding buildings, still much lower than the branches of the Source, and then it began a long dive down toward the second level. Constantine caught a last glimpse of Mary moving through the sparse crowds. The passersby continued to pay no attention to her. An embarrassment, it was as if she wasn't there.

As if she were a ghost.

Herb gazed upward in awestruck silence. He had never seen so many spacecraft: layer upon layer of silver-grey disks, rising higher and higher into the night sky. Stacks of silver pennies thrown into the air, the farthest seeming no bigger than the cold diamond stars that twinkled behind them.

On an intellectual level, Herb had known that the sky was big, but those thousands upon thousands of ships floating above gave it a depth he had never seen before. A feeling of vertigo swept over him and he wanted to sit down on the soft, spongy road and hold on tight. Beside him, Robert Johnston stood gazing upward without any apparent concern.

"Impressive, huh?" he said.

"Oh, yeah. Very impressive. Where are we?"

Herb felt giddy: a man who had suddenly become aware of the cathedral vaulting that held up the sky. Johnston smiled delightedly and leaned closer.

"On a staging planet." He placed one finger to his lips and whispered, "At the edge of the Enemy Domain, just beyond the wave of expansion." His eyes slowly slid from left to right in an exaggerated survey of the twisted buildings that surrounded them. "I think we're okay at the moment, though."

Herb curled his lip at Johnston's play-acting and began to walk along the soft road, looking all around. Now that he was getting used to the wonder of the night sky above, he had time to pay attention to his immediate surroundings. Hideously warped and melted buildings hemmed them in from all directions, leaning over above them like trees in a forest. They had a stretched-out look about them; they seemed too tall and thin to remain standing. Shadowy and lopsided drooping windows formed eyes that looked down upon them, silently pondering their presence. The air was warm and smelled of machine oil; from every direction there was a gentle hum that almost sounded like voices.

Everything about this place seemed wrong. Even the road felt strange beneath his feet; it seemed to bounce and give as he walked on it. Herb got the impression that at any moment it would suddenly wriggle and turn around on itself, a large black snake turning to see who was walking along its spine.

Johnston was following him. "What do you think of the Necropolis, then?"

"The Necropolis?" Herb came to a halt and looked around. He gave a thoughtful nod. "An apt name. What's the matter with this place? It looks like someone took a picture of a city and then smeared it down a wall. What are we doing here?"

"Spying on the Enemy. We must be careful not to be seen."

At that, Johnston began creeping forward on tiptoes,

his hands raised close to his chest. Herb remained where he was.

"Come on," Johnston called over his shoulder. "This way." He continued his exaggerated movement down the road.

Herb sighed and began to follow. He wondered if he was dreaming. He had no recollection of arriving on this planet.

He remembered going to sleep on his ship, thoughts of Johnston's descriptions of the Enemy Domain spinning through his mind. Five minutes ago he had woken to find himself standing, gazing up at the endless tiers of space-ships. Maybe Johnston had drugged him again, slipped something extra into the whisky. Herb certainly felt as if he was still under the influence of something, walking along a rubbery road, twisting between strangely warped buildings, beneath those pale static disks far above.

Johnston had abandoned his exaggerated gait and was now walking normally, seemingly heading for the heart of the city. The buildings ahead loomed taller; they seemed to be draped with thick steel cobwebs that connected their roofs to each other and spilled to the ground. They had the look of melting toffee that had been pulled and stretched so that long sticky strands ran drooping in all directions. A low note sounded through the air and Herb thought he saw a flicker of movement in the distance, barely seen through the crowded mis-shapes of the buildings. He broke into a run to catch up with Johnston.

"What was that?" he hissed.

"Don't worry about it."

Johnston pushed his hands into his pockets and con-tinued strolling, singing softly to himself as he went.

Herb fell into step next to him, glancing around nervously. They rounded a corner.

Johnston broke off his singing unexpectedly. "Look!" he said, pointing upward, a cufflink made of four balls of multicolored metal peeping from the edge of his suit. Herb felt his stomach sink as he looked up.

A tower stretched up into the very sky, rising higher and higher above the rest of the city, dwarfing all the other buildings. A tapering needle of steel piercing the clouds of silver spaceships that hung silently above them. Herb wondered how it could remain standing; it seemed too thin to support itself. He had a sudden urge to run, convinced it was going to come crashing down on him—

Johnston interrupted his thoughts. "We need to get up to where the spaceships are. I'm guessing that building is a space elevator."

"Oh." Herb bit his lip thoughtfully. "You said we were spying. What are we looking for?"

"Lots of things. Size of Enemy resources, possible intentions, possible weaknesses, but mostly we're looking for a way back."

"A way back? I still don't understand how we got here."

Before Johnston could answer, the humming noise was heard again, only closer. A yellow pod with black stripes appeared in a gap between two buildings, only a couple of hundred meters away. It rotated 360 degrees on its axis and then moved off again, vanishing from their view among the forest of towers.

"What was that?" whispered Herb. "It looked like a giant bumblebee. I think it was looking for us. Should we hide?"

"I don't think so," said Johnston. "Not yet anyway.

Now... look at that. That's interesting." He pointed to the building next to them.

Herb gazed at it, puzzled. "I don't understand," he said. "It just looks like the entrance to a shopping center."

He was led by Johnston to a wide portico. It was too high, of course, like everything else in the Necropolis. Away above them, a silver-grey pediment seemed to melt into a colonnade that oozed down around them to merge with the ground. Herb felt as if he was standing in a rib cage. They peered through tall windows into a brightly lit atrium, lined on all sides by small glass-fronted rooms. Deformed escalators climbed the walls at too steep an angle. Herb shivered at the thought of what goods might be sold in such a place.

Johnston seemed delighted, however. "It does look like a shopping center, doesn't it?" he said. "Now doesn't that suggest something?"

"Yeah," muttered Herb. "This would not be a good place to ask for a refund."

The strangeness of his surroundings was making Herb light-headed.

"Was that supposed to be funny?" Johnston said sharply. "I do the comedy stylings: you just listen and learn. No. The fact that this place looks like a shopping center suggests that this planet is intended for a civilian population. Furthermore, one that resembles an Earth-like society. Do you think they have shops on Delta Scuti 4?"

"You'd be astonished how rarely I think about such things."

Johnston gave him a withering look.

"No, I don't," Herb said, chastened.

Johnston stroked his chin thoughtfully. "Now that

changes things considerably. This is not what we were expecting at all." He lapsed into a thoughtful silence.

The humming sound rose in volume so quickly that Herb instinctively leaped forward to grab Johnston's jacket. He caught a flash of yellow and black reflected in the glass before him as a bumblebee pod whisked down the street behind them.

"It's seen us," he gasped.

Johnston shook Herb's hand from his sleeve.

"Don't be so silly," he said, then pointed into the atrium. "Come on. We're going in there."

Herb didn't know whether to feel relief at avoiding their pursuer or fear at entering the eerie mall. Johnston seemed completely unconcerned about either. He placed a hand on one of the tall glass doors and pushed gently.

"Stuck. I should have guessed as much."

Herb could see that the doors were not so much fused together as imprints in the front of the building. They seemed to be one piece of glass that had not managed to separate in two. Wondering what Johnston was going to do next, he suddenly found himself standing inside, right in the center of the atrium, looking up at the high-vaulted ceiling. Silver metal creepers hung above his head. Like everything outside, the building's interior had the look of stretched and melting toffee. Herb's mind caught up with events.

"What happened there?" asked Herb, astonished.

"I readjusted our position to be inside the building."

"How? Hyperspace jump?" Herb was impressed despite himself. "I didn't think anyone was capable of that degree of control."

"Don't be silly," said Johnston. "Haven't you realized yet that we're not really here? Do you think I'd bring our physical bodies into the Enemy Domain? Now come on, we need to get our report back to the EA."

"What report?"

"The report confirming the fact that the Domain contains—or will contain—civilians. Haven't you wondered where they're going to come from?"

"No."

Johnston gave an exasperated sigh and walked on, past the squashed retail units that surrounded them, heading toward an arch at the rear of the atrium. The walls back here seemed to have melted drastically; they hung down like great folds of cloth. Herb gazed uneasily at the narrow corridor beyond the arch. If he didn't know better, he would have said they were walking into the building's throat.

"Are you sure about this?" he murmured.

"We're heading for the space elevator, right? This is a shopping mall. How do you think the shoppers are going to get here?" Johnston rolled his eyes. "Hyperspace jumps?"

They passed through the arch, Herb's uneasiness passing along with him. A high-ceilinged hallway lay beyond; four unmoving escalators disgorged from subterranean depths grasping its walls with long metallic strands.

Herb swallowed hard. He didn't want to risk descending an escalator. At the same time, he didn't want Johnston to know he was frightened.

"Okay," he stammered, "which one should we take?"

Johnston was staring at the patterns engraved on the nearby wall.

"If this diagram is a map, as I think it is, I would suggest that escalator over there. If it's not a map, then you'll be an extremely privileged young man."

"Why?" Herb asked, mystified.

"Because you will have been present on the occasion when, for the first time in my life, I was wrong about something."

Before Herb could reply, Johnston had moved quickly to his chosen escalator and started to descend, his shoes clicking brightly on the polished metal steps. Herb took a deep breath and followed him.

The escalator went a long way below ground. Herb had to concentrate on keeping up with Johnston. Herb had never attempted to be any fitter than the minimum level that the EA's exercise program instilled in him; indeed, he tended to look down on those pursuing extra fitness as an end in itself. All those wasted kilojoules. He could understand the fact that Johnston was in better condition. What he found galling was the way that the brilliant tapping of Robert's feet gave the impression he was dancing down the steps.

He was beginning to understand that everything Johnston did was intended subtly to mock Herb in some way. If only he weren't getting so tired he could pursue that thought further. He wished the escalator would start moving, not that there was any chance of that. Like everything else he had seen in the Necropolis, the steps seemed to be fused with the surrounding structure. Silver-grey strands ran in every direction. Herb wondered what would be waiting at the bottom of the steps. A Lite train station would be the obvious answer, but if they had instead stepped out into the first circle of Hell, Herb liked to think that he would not have been that surprised.

"What is it with this place?" Herb gasped as he clattered on down the steps.

"Haven't you figured that out yet?" Johnston called back to him. "This whole city is the result of a faulty VNM. You get this happening sometimes with large-scale VNM projects. Maybe errors in the original machine's design didn't show up until the nth generation. Or sometimes a machine reproduces badly at the start of the process, and then you get faulty machines making copies of themselves. History lesson, Herb: that's what happened back on Earth with the first major VNM-built arcology."

"I wouldn't have thought I'd need to tell you about this," Johnston snorted. "Given what you did yourself, you should know all about badly designed machines."

Herb didn't rise to the bait. "So this city is a reject. That's why everything is so misshapen." He paused for thought. "Even so, this is weird. You'd expect the whole place just to collapse, or maybe not to have gotten built at all. Just end up as a pile of machines." *Like on my planet*, he added ruefully to himself.

"Usually you'd be right. But sometimes the fault is very subtle. That's what happened here. I would guess that the suicide mechanism isn't working properly. Everything seems to have formed correctly, but nothing has shriveled away when finished with. That's why everything is still fused together."

Johnston idly reached up and patted a silver loop hanging from the ceiling. "Probably why the scaffolding and struts are still hanging around, too."

"How can you touch that if we're not here?" Herb asked.

"How can you hear sounds and see things? How come your feet touch the ground? Listen, Herb, when I model something, I do it properly."

And that, it seemed, was all the explanation Herb was getting for the moment.

At last! Herb thankfully saw the bottom of the escalator approaching. A large, elongated archway loomed ahead of them. But through it he could see only darkness...

"Amazing when you think about it," Johnston continued. "It helps you grasp just how extensive the Enemy Domain is. I mean, you can see it shaded in on the Star Charts, but that doesn't give you any real sense of scale. We're currently walking down an escalator at the edge of an extremely large city on a nondescript planet that has been practically forgotten by the Domain. You'd think it would destroy this place and start again; instead, it uses the planet as a staging post. Ah, well. It has given us an opportunity."

Johnston reached the bottom of the steps and hurried through the archway into the station beyond.

"Hell's teeth!" he shouted.

"Robert! What is it?"

Herb clattered the last few steps into the station. He could see something moving.

Johnston was bending to pick up his hat from the tiled floor, an embarrassed grin across his face.

"I forgot what we were for a moment."

Herb didn't feel anywhere near so calm. The vaulted spaces of the station roof were swarming with large, metal, spiderlike creatures: thin metal abdomens and long, spindly legs. They moved lazily backwards and forwards, crawling over each other's bodies. One of them dropped from the ceiling, landing nearby. It turned around blindly for a moment before scuttling to the platform edge and dropping down onto the tracks. It rapidly headed off down a dark tunnel.

"What the hell?" Herb danced back across the platform in panic.

Johnston couldn't stop laughing "Just VNMs. Construction robots! If only you could see your face." He gasped for breath. "They can't commit suicide, remember? They don't know what to do when they've finished their work. These tunnels must be choked with them."

He straightened up and wiped a tear from his eye. "They gave me a bit of a start, too, I must admit. But you. Your face." A thought suddenly occurred to him and he giggled. "Can you imagine what would happen if the Enemy Domain sent colonists here now? Can you imagine them coming down here to catch a train?"

"That isn't funny."

"Ah. I suppose not."

Johnston seemed to gain some self-control. He turned left then right, sniffing the air for a moment.

"This way, I guess," he said, pointing down one tunnel.

Herb looked horrified. "What? With all those robots scuttling back and forth?"

Johnston shook his head. "I told you before. We're not really here. We just needed to find a clear path. The train tracks should be conductive enough. If not... Well, I guess we'll never find out about it."

"Just a minute..." said Herb, but it was already too late. They were no longer in the station.

Johnston got it right the first time.

"Not that that should be any surprise," he said, looking around the basement of the space elevator. Herb felt his knees give way. The space he was standing in was just too big. He felt like a microbe, looking up into the bell of an enormous trumpet. The tiled floor seemed to vanish as it approached the distant, inward-curving walls. Long cables ran down from the seeming infinity above to burrow themselves into the floor all around them. There was a hollowness to the air, a feeling of resonance stilled and of themselves standing in the low-density part of the wave. If the space elevator was a trumpet, the mouthpiece must be out in space. Herb felt delirious: the hollowness that he felt was the sound blown by the emptiness above.

He reeled a little. He wasn't thinking straight and he knew it. His mind couldn't grasp the sheer size of the room.

"This is part of the Enemy Domain?" whispered Herb, eyes wide. He swallowed.

"What?" said Johnston, taking in Herb's awestruck expression. "Oh, this is nothing. We almost built space elevators like this in Earth space. They'd have been bigger than this, too. The EA didn't allow them, though. There is tremendous stress on one of these things. If they snap..." He paused, looking thoughtful. "The question is why the Enemy Domain thought it was needed... Anyway, come on. We'll ride that cable up to the top."

Whistling tunelessly, Johnston shuffled toward the cable he had just indicated. Herb followed him, looking upward. He felt ridiculously exposed, as if people were watching from above, ready to drop something down on him.

They walked in silence for a while. The cable was farther away than it looked: the sheer size of their surroundings confused the eye.

"Hey, Johnston. Why can't you just jump us there?" he called.

"Because," said Johnston. "Anyway. I want you to get some idea of the scale of this thing."

"Bollocks," Herb muttered under his breath. "You just didn't think of it."

"Yes I did. And stop whispering to yourself. I have excellent hearing."

"You bloody well would, wouldn't you? Mr. Perfect. What's going on here, anyway? What do you mean when you say we're not really here?"

Johnston sighed hugely. "You mean you *still* haven't worked it out?"

Herb wasn't going to respond to such an obvious attempt at goading him. "You've already done this bit. Just tell me."

Johnston shrugged. "I suppose I have," he said. "Okay. Think about it. We don't want the Enemy Domain to know we're spying on it, do we? No. So that means we have to observe it by passive means wherever possible."

"What, telescope, electromagnetic emissions, and so on?"

"Yup. Which is all very well, but it doesn't tell us much. We need to be a bit clever. So what I did was, I made a copy of our personalities while you were sleeping on your ship, then I fired them on a narrow beam toward the Necropolis. I was banking on the fact that there must be some processing spaces remaining on this planet that could contain them. As always, I was right."

Herb nodded as he digested that information. "So I'm not really me, is that what you're saying? I'm just a personality construct? The real you and me are still sitting on board my ship, planning our attack on the Domain."

"Oh, you're the real you," Johnston said. "You're just not the one sitting on your ship anymore."

Herb felt sick. "How could you do this? What have you done to me? I don't care if I'm a personality construct; I still feel real. Who gave you the right to do this to me?"

The emotion drained from Johnston's face. He gazed at Herb with an empty expression. "*You* gave me the right, Herb, when you agreed to help me on this mission. Don't you remember?"

Herb held Johnston's gaze for a moment. Silence. Then Herb swallowed and looked away. "Yeah. Whatever. So that's why the most important thing we have to do is to get back to ourselves. Do you have any idea how?"

"I have a few ideas up my sleeve."

"How will we know if we've succeeded?"

"The you and I who are here at the moment won't know. If the you and I on your spaceship are hearing these words, it means we succeeded."

Herb said nothing. A nasty idea had just occurred to him.

"So, what happens to us then, when we've finished our mission? Do we just die? Or do we spend the rest of our lives here wandering around the processors of the Necropolis?"

"When you've finished your work for me, how you then choose to live your life is up to you. As long as there is something to process the idea of you, you will think that you think, and therefore, you am what you am."

They finally came to the foot of the cable. Silver-grey and perfectly smooth, Herb could see himself dimly reflected in the dull sheen of its metal. The cable disappeared into the tile floor, giving no hint of the tremendous tension trapped beneath the ground.

Johnston ran an apparent hand over the cable's surface.

"I can't feel anything," he said. "That means the VNM that made up this cable must have been functioning correctly. There is no room for any margin of error in a space elevator."

He turned to explain to Herb. "We're taking advantage of the fact that the VNM that was the seed for the Necropolis couldn't suicide properly. The building block machines still have their senses and processing spaces intact. We're using them now to give us life."

"I guessed as much," Herb lied.

"Sure. Come on, there're no clues here. Let's take the scenic route into space. We're going to try to get on board one of those ships and steal a little slice of processing time from its brain. We're going to take on a life in a computer's dreams. Isn't that poetic?"

•

There were rooms and walkways built into the outer skin of the space elevator.

"Imagine having a corner office in this place!"

"You wouldn't be able to breathe," Johnston pointed out. "The windows don't fit properly."

"You know what I mean," Herb said.

From the streets, Herb remembered, the space elevator looked like a very tall skyscraper. Get up close and you might not even realize that there was anything odd about it. From where they were now standing, looking out of a wide picture window just a few hundred meters above the ground, it was almost possible to believe they were looking out over an Earth city. *Almost possible,* thought Herb. Only if he didn't look up to see the stacks and stacks of silent spaceships floating high above. Only if he didn't look down too carefully to see the way the buildings below had stretched and deformed. Only if he didn't look at those long metal creepers running in every direction, tangling high above the streets and choking the narrow roads. One particularly thin and elegant tower standing almost directly before Herb seemed to have been a favorite target. It was so wrapped around with creepers that it looked as if it had been strangled and was now being dragged to the ground.

And through it all, the yellow-and-black-striped metal bees hummed back and forth.

"Those yellow pod things. What are they doing?" asked Herb.

"I don't know," said Johnston. "They're too big to be just observation pods. There must be some pretty powerful equipment stuck inside them. Maybe we'll find out up there. Come on."

The journey into space took longer than Herb might have guessed: Johnston couldn't seem to jump them more than a couple of floors at a time.

"There's no clear line of sight up to the top," he explained, as he and Herb stood several thousand meters up the building, frustrated again at how few floors they had jumped.

Their journey became one of flickering movement as their consciousness appeared on one floor just long enough for Johnston to find a path to the next. Herb watched the Necropolis recede below them as they slowly climbed to the stars, the elongated towers of the city falling away as the pair of them rose to meet the layers of spaceships that hung above.

The outer limits of the Necropolis began to resolve

themselves. The city appeared to have spread itself over a considerable part of the planet's surface before the on-going decay in the integrity of the reproductive machines finally set in. The bounds of the Necropolis were ragged, the towers out there having stretched themselves too high before collapsing under their own weight. The city didn't so much come to an end as fade into the surrounding countryside. Herb shivered and wondered what it would be like to wander through those forsaken lands.

Johnston was his only unmoving point of reference. He stood next to Herb, his face set in quiet concentration as they traveled upwards. Behind him the room appeared to flicker: sometimes it grew larger, sometimes smaller. Occasionally the windows vanished, cracked and blown out into the thinning air. At one point they traveled in darkness for a good five minutes, and Herb guessed that they had reached the limit of the space intended to be occupied by humans, but then the habitable rooms resumed, this time much larger and with a faint air of half-formed opulence around them. It was a shame that the Necropolis had failed, reflected Herb, then he thought about what Johnston had hinted at earlier. There must be hundreds of failed cities like this, scattered throughout the Enemy Domain. How many cities had been built successfully?

Not for the first time, Herb shivered at the thought of what he had agreed to fight.

They had risen so high Herb could now make out the curve of the planet. They were approaching the first layer of spaceships, spread out above them like checkers on a board, vanishing into the distance in all directions, silver-grey and almost disk-shaped except for a love-heart indentation. They rose through the first layer and continued, past a second and a third, climbing into the night.

The flickering movement suddenly stopped.

"I need a rest," Johnston muttered. He removed his hat and took a white handkerchief from his breast pocket. He mopped his forehead with it and then carefully replaced his hat, tilting it at a jaunty angle. Herb wandered to the window for a better view of his surroundings. Looking down through the crystal lattice of spaceships, he could see the ball of the planet, far below. He felt a wave of dizziness as he realized that if he fell out of the window now, he would probably miss the planet as he went down. The thought was ridiculous.

Johnston was refolding his handkerchief. "We can't go on any further by this route," he said. "We're now approaching the end point of the elevator; beyond here everything was constructed from perfectly functioning VNM stock. It had to be, otherwise it wouldn't have held together."

He gave a deep sigh and pushed the handkerchief back into his pocket. "Whew. I'm rather hungry. It's amazing what conditioned responses can do to you. Anyway. We're going to have to make a jump into the unknown. I'm guessing that the end of the elevator is not that far above us. It will probably be in geosynchronous orbit with the base. I'm hoping that a docking station was completed, possibly even using the same VNM that later seeded the planet below. There must be something there that could host us."

"And if there isn't?" asked Herb.

"Then we'll never know about it. Our consciousness will just fade from here, and the Herb and Robert back home will never know what we have learned."

"Oh."

"Not to worry. I beamed our consciousnesses to other points in the Enemy Domain, too. There's another pair of us in the Necropolis. One set should get back at least."

Herb frowned. "It will still be like dying to us, though, surely?"

"Ah. Don't worry about that. Are you ready?"

Herb gripped Johnston by the sleeve.

"Hang on. Let's talk this over."

"No time. Let's go."

They jumped . . .

eva 2: 2051

High above Eva, the lime leaves fluttered gently against the deep blue of the afternoon sky. Flickering pale green and yellow hearts formed a vaulted ceiling over the quiet cathedral-like space between the dark trunks. The air was rich with the smell of soil and summer rain; it insinuated its way into Eva's body, filling her with its heady presence. She had kicked off her shoes to walk around the clearing, feeling the darkness of the earth between her toes. Eva, held apart from it for so long in the grey headache of South Street, was reconnecting with life.

A voice whispered: "Eva."

She started and twisted around, trying to see who had spoken. The voice had sounded in her ear, but there was no one there. The space between the trees was a vessel filled with woodland silence, a silence that was now leaking away.

Eva could see Alison, Katie, and Nicolas approaching across the overgrown green lawn that lapped the treeline. They were obviously looking for her. Nicolas spotted Eva first and pointed her out to the others. The three came crashing into her retreat.

"Hello, Eva, I thought we'd find you here." Alison was on a high, every word packed with a jangling, desperate energy. Katie gave a nervous twitch and quickly turned her head in the other direction. Nicolas stared at her breasts.

"Hello, Eva," he said. "We're going to sneak into Pontybodkyn. Are you coming?"

"I can't. I've got a counseling session in an hour." Eva was glad for the excuse not to go, but Alison wasn't going to be deflected so easily.

"Skip it," she said, too loudly, snapping her fingers dismissively. "No one will care. The staff will be pleased to get an extra half-hour's break."

"No. I want to go."

Nicolas directed a knowing smile at her breasts.

"You've only been here two weeks, haven't you? You'll soon find out. Nobody really cares about counseling here. The staff only do it because it's their job; we only go because it gives us someone to talk to."

"Well, I'd like to talk to someone."

"Come to Pontybodkyn and talk with us. At least we won't be spending all afternoon trying to convince you there's something wrong with you."

Eva ran a hand through her grey hair, tucking it behind her ears. She spoke in a matter-of-fact tone. "There is something wrong with me. That's why I'm here."

"Ah," said Alison, smiling slightly hysterically. "But where you're going wrong is expecting them to make you better." She gave an exaggerated sigh and spun around on her heels. The shafts of sunlight flickered over her body. "Oh, this is boring! Come on, Nicolas; come on, Katie. Leave her. We don't want little miss goody two shoes spoiling our trip."

"That's not true . . ." began Nicolas.

"I said, come on."

She skipped off across the clearing toward the belt of trees that screened the Center from the main road. Katie shuffled along behind her, head down, hands clasped tightly before her. Nicolas tore his gaze from Eva's breasts long enough to give an apologetic smile and shrug, then turned and ran to catch up with Alison.

Eva watched them go, then resumed pacing on the soft leaf mold, gazing up at the cathedral roof of leaves. Silence drifted down the shafts of greenish light that filled the space within the trees and Eva began to relax again. Peace and calm and a chance to forget the outside world and to feel that it had forgotten her. Alison was wrong, thought Eva, who had never imagined they could make her better. She just liked having someone to talk to. She simply didn't think that there was anything wrong with her that could be cured here at the Center.

"Eva. You can't see me, but I'm here. I know you can hear me. I need to talk to you."

Apart from the voices, of course. Maybe they could stop her hearing the voices.

Doctor Cevier's office was large and bare. The high ceiling and wide floor space dwarfed his plastic desk. A few framed pictures and certificates were marooned on the cheerless orange walls. Two shaped plastic chairs sat by a low coffee table set with a tray holding two steaming cups from the vending machine. Five cakes were set out on a plate. Eva took one seat, Doctor Cevier the other.

He was a well-built man in his early thirties, his thinning hair looking damp and smelling faintly of shower gel. Doctor Cevier always looked as if he had just left the gym. He tapped his ultra-slim executive model console to set it recording and then relaxed in his chair.

"Well, Eva. Two weeks now. How do you feel?"

"Tired."

"That's not surprising. How much sleep are you getting? In an average day, I mean."

"I don't know. Fifteen hours?"

Doctor Cevier tapped at his console.

"More like eighteen, according to this. Why do you think that is?"

"What is there to get up for?"

Doctor Cevier said nothing in reply. Instead he picked up one of the cups and took a sip.

"Mmm. Delicious. How do they manage it? Every cup tastes different. Aren't you going to try some?"

Eva stared at the other cup and said nothing. Through the wide window she could see out across the ragged lawns to the circle of limes. Their leaves rippled and danced in the sunlight.

"I'm sorry?" Eva said.

"I didn't say anything," said Doctor Cevier. "Tell me, how are you settling in here? Do you feel comfortable?"

"I suppose so. When are you going to let me go?"

Doctor Cevier took another sip of his drink. "Wonderful. You really should try some. It will help you relax."

"How? Is it drugged?"

Doctor Cevier laughed a little and tapped at his console again. Eva looked around the empty office. If this were her room, she thought, she would buy some rugs and hang them from the walls, arrange standard lamps and statues around the edge of the room and throw mats and carpets on the floor. Anything to break the dull monotony of the surroundings. Anything that would make the room look less like a waiting room and more like an office, even a bookcase, filled with cheap second-hand books. Doctor Cevier wasn't speaking now; he gazed at Eva with a half amused expression. Eva ignored him. She looked across at the plastic desk and wondered if Doctor Cevier ever sat behind it. The few books and papers that lay on its surface were facing in her direction.

"Have you given any thought yet on how you got here?"

"No," Eva said.

"You were very lucky, you know. They thought you were dead when the train pulled into Marseilles."

"Well, there you go."

"Well, there you go," repeated Doctor Cevier, "as you say. Two doctors pronounced you dead, as did a Diagnostics Expert System at the Marseilles Area Hospital. And those things are never wrong."

"Except in my case."

"Except in your case. They pulled you back from the dead, Eva. I've read the report. Not my field, you understand, but still pretty convincing. If it wasn't for the fact you'd probably disagree with me, I'd tell you to your face that you were dead."

"No one can be right all of the time."

"Very true. You know, at some point we're going to have to go over what happened that day. But not today." He tapped at his console again. "This isn't the first time you've been in here, is it?"

"No."

"Maybe we can talk about your brother sometime."

"Why not?"

"Why not, indeed?" Doctor Cevier picked up his cup and finished his drink. Eva pointedly left hers untouched.

The rest of the session passed in silence. Doctor Cevier was waiting for Eva to speak. Eva wasn't going to give him the satisfaction. The worst thing was, she didn't really know why. She knew that he was here to help her; she had even looked forward to this meeting. Now that it had arrived, she felt a sudden surge of obstinacy. Maybe it was the realization that Doctor Cevier represented just another branch of Social Care. He may have a big desk, he may have his doctorate, but he was just the same as those people back in South Street who used to poke their noses into her business. They didn't really care about curing her, they just wanted the warm glow of validation one got from helping others, whether they wanted helping or not. It was the mention of her brother that had made her realize all this. How dare he mention her brother?

When her time was up, Eva rose from her seat and walked to the door.

"Eva?"

"What?"

"I didn't say anything," said Doctor Cevier.

Eva took a bath. It was something about the Center: things that she used to accomplish in a few minutes in the outside world could fill up a whole day here. You could spend an hour making a cup of tea; you could spend two hours deciding whether or not to have a biscuit with it.

The bathroom didn't have a lock on the door. Every

so often a nurse would come in to look for a towel or to check that the water was warm enough. Eva gave them a wry look as they smiled apologetically at her. She had taken four months planning her suicide attempt. She was hardly likely to try anything in the bathroom, was she?

The sound of Alison, Nicolas, and Katie returning caused a bit of a stir. She heard Alison's voice first, slurred and indignant.

"So what if we're drunk? It's a free country, isn't it?"

Eva walked into the corridor to find Alison squaring up to Nurse Dyer. The nurse was small; she had to tilt her head back to gaze into Alison's eyes, yet she stood her ground without heat or concern.

"No, Alison," she said gently, "it's not a free country. Not for you anymore. Anyway, didn't you stop to think about poor Katie? Didn't you think about her feelings, having to mix with all those strangers?"

Katie had wrapped her arms tightly around herself. She gazed down at the floor, silent. While Nurse Dyer remained distracted by Alison, Nicolas sidled up to Eva.

"Hello, Eva," he whispered, his breath sweet with the smell of alcohol. "You should have come with us. The people in the pub in the village buy drinks and leave them on the table for us. They kept saying they were on our side. They love to get one over on Social Care and these bastards at the Center."

"Oh. I thought the Center was here to help us."

Eva pulled her white robe closer around her chest and walked into her room. Nicolas unthinkingly followed her in.

"Excuse me," Eva said. "I'd like to get changed."

Nicolas' eyes widened at the sudden realization of what he had done.

"Oh, I'm sorry. I didn't realize. I just wanted to talk," he stammered. Eva gazed at him as he stumbled to the door. She knew he didn't mean anything. He was just a sad geek who didn't know how to get along with people. Just like her, really. Her attitude softened.

"That's okay," she said. "Look, let me get changed and then we can talk. Why don't you go to the common room and wait for me?"

Nicolas smiled delightedly.

"Okay. I'll meet you there."

The common room was a profoundly depressing place. Like everything else in the Center, it was just too big for its sparse contents: a few boxes containing board games, scratched video consoles, several chipped mugs half full of cold coffee standing between the legs of the comfy chairs that faced the viewing screen. The shabby items were lost in the cheerless orange expanse of the room.

Two patients sat facing each other across a low table, playing cards with a Braille deck, calling out the values of their hands as they laid them down. They both twitched and stuttered as they played; one kept pausing as if to listen to sounds in the room. He turned nervously in Eva's direction.

"It's okay," she reassured him, "I'm a patient too."

He seemed to relax a little. Eva felt sick. Everyone knew that stealth weapons were a terrible thing, but it had turned into a sort of game. Those in power denied their existence; people like Eva waved the evidence in their faces and watched them squirm. She remembered her arguments with DeForest and felt embarrassed. Laser weapons mounted on planes which could blind pedestrians. Targeted psychopathic drugs. Both were horrible concepts. Here was the reality: Eva was looking at the human cost of such weapons.

Nicolas was sitting on a chair looking out through the broad window at the wide lawn leading across to the sparse woodland that surrounded the Center. She could see the tops of the limes bobbing in the breeze.

"Hello, Nicolas," Eva said.

"Eva." Nicolas blushed. "Look, I'm sorry about earlier. I didn't mean anything. I just wanted to talk. I didn't think about you being, well . . . just getting out of the bath, and I . . ."

"That's okay."

"No. Thank you, I mean . . . You're just being polite, but honestly, I didn't mean anything. We're not supposed to have relationships while we're in here, you know, so I wouldn't have wanted . . . well, not that you're . . ."

"That's okay, Nicolas. I understand. You just weren't thinking."

"I mean . . . I have enough trouble just getting out of bed some days. I need to get my life sorted out before I even think of . . . not that I'm saying you're not pretty, but . . ."

Eva sat down in one of the comfy chairs.

"What's happened to Alison?" she said, interrupting Nicolas' monologue.

"Oh, she stormed out of the building. She said she was going back to the pub. She'll be looking for, well . . ."

He looked embarrassed. Eva made no comment.

"It's a pity Nurse Reed isn't here. She could calm her down. Nurse Reed knows how to handle Alison."

"Oh? Which one is Nurse Reed? I still haven't learned all their names."

"She's the one with the short red hair. You know, the French-looking cut? It's her week off."

Nicolas looked around the room, searching for something else to say. Eva noted the frayed trouser cuffs that came too far up his leg, the greying dress shirt that he habitually wore with the collar buttoned down. She broke the silence first.

"What did Nurse Dyer mean when she said that you shouldn't have taken Katie with you?"

"Katie gets nervous around people. She can't handle being spoken to by strangers." Nicolas gave a yelping laugh. "She's not even very good at being spoken to by her friends."

"Oh."

Nicolas lapsed into silence. He seemed to be struggling with what to say next, desperate to fill the conversational gap.

Eva spoke for him. "She looks familiar, doesn't she? Katie, I mean. I'm sure I've seen her somewhere before."

Nicolas gulped once, twice.

"Well, erm, well." He gulped again and changed the subject. "What about you, Eva? We all saw you the night that you were brought in. I've never seen anybody with so many drug feeds attached. What had you done?"

"Tried to commit suicide. I almost succeeded, too." Eva heard the pride in her own voice.

"Suicide? That's impressive. Social Care usually picks up the signs well in advance. Why did you do it?"

"I'd rather not talk about that."

"Fair enough," Nicolas said. "Still, suicide. How did you arrange it?"

"Loaded my teddy bear with Panacetamol over the course of several months and then took them all at once. I thought nobody would think it odd that I'd fallen asleep on a train. Obviously someone did."

Nicolas frowned. "Panacetamol? I didn't think they could reverse that. I thought that once you'd taken enough that was it. All they could do was sit back and watch you die."

Eva shrugged. "It would appear not."

Nicolas placed one hand on her shoulder in what was probably meant to be a supportive gesture.

"Never mind that now. Look, we all stick together in this place. If you ever feel bad, come and see us. We'll try to help."

Eva managed not to shudder at the feel of Nicolas' hand on her shoulder. *He doesn't mean anything,* she thought, *he's just socially inept.* She struggled to hold on to that thought as his gaze wandered down to her breasts again.

In the corner, the blind card players came to the end of a game. One of them twitched and gazed sightlessly around the room as the other fumblingly shuffled the deck.

Eva had slept with her curtains open since she had come to the Center. It was nice to look out into darkness and not the orange glow that filled the night back in South Street. As she lay down, she heard the voice.

"Katie does look familiar, doesn't she? I'm sure we've seen her before."

"Who are you?" Eva whispered into the darkness. "Why do you keep talking to me?"

But there was no reply.

Someone was shaking her shoulder. Someone was screaming, and as she struggled to consciousness, Eva had a horrible feeling it might be herself. She rolled over in the bed to see Katie staring down at her, an anxious expression engraved on her thin face. Her tiny piggy eyes slid this way and that to avoid Eva's gaze.

"Come and help. Alison's in a bad way. Please come and speak to her."

The words came out in a rush. The screaming was still going on, and Eva realized that it came from somewhere down the corridor. She struggled to a sitting position.

Katie had taken her hand from Eva's shoulder and had gone to stand in the middle of the bedroom, wrapping her fingers around each other and staring at the floor. Eva brushed the hair from her face and yawned. The sky outside her rain-streaked window was a uniform dull grey; the cheerless orange walls of her room did nothing to lift her spirits. The screaming from down the corridor outside stopped for a moment, then a stream of barely coherent swearing began. Eva recognized Alison's voice.

"What's happened?" Eva pulled her trousers from the back of the chair. The belt caught the paperback lying facedown on her low bedside table, flipping it to the floor.

Katie gazed around the room, still looking everywhere rather than at Eva.

"Alison shouldn't be let out when she's on a high. She gets drunk and then lets all the men in the pub sleep with her. She hates herself the next day."

"What?" Eva said, struggling into her trousers. "Then why did Nurse Dyer let her get away last night?"

"Nurse Dyer can't stop her. Besides, Nurse Dyer doesn't like Alison."

"What? But that's...unprofessional!" The words sounded childish even to her own ears.

Eva staggered across the room, finally getting her trousers up to her waist. She turned her back on Katie and pulled off her nightgown. Her breasts felt heavy and sore this morning, and she held one arm over them as she looked for her sweatshirt. Katie blushed and gazed at the ceiling.

"Nurse Dyer is jealous of Alison. Alison is clever and pretty. Please come and speak to her."

"What can I say? I barely know her."

"I don't know. You'll think of something. You're clever, too."

"Me?" Eva gave a bitter laugh. "I couldn't even get promotion in a fast-food shop."

Katie said nothing. She waited nervously as Eva found her shoes, grabbed her book to shove into her back pocket for safety, then followed her into the corridor. They found Nicolas standing in front of Alison, holding his hand as if it had just been bitten, an expression of utter horror on his face.

"Get away from me, you bastard!" shouted Alison. "You bastard. Bastard! BASTARD!"

She jumped forward and began to beat at him with her fists. Nicolas backed away uncertainly. Katie took him by the arm and pulled him away from Alison, sliding her body into the space between them.

"She doesn't mean it, Nicolas," Katie said, her words emerging in staccato bursts. "She's just taking it out on you. Go away and she'll be fine by this evening." Katie stared at the floor. Nicolas merely nodded. He turned and walked away, looking hurt.

Katie looked directly at Eva for the first time, her tiny blue eyes gazing straight into hers, a fraction of a second and no more, then they flicked toward Alison, reminding Eva of her instructions. She took a deep breath.

"Alison," she said softly.

Alison turned toward her, face twisted with rage. As she looked at Eva, some of the rage drained from her eyes. She stifled a sob.

"Oh, Eva," she said. "The bastards. The bastards." She put her arms around Eva's neck and dissolved into tears. Eva gazed up at the ceiling, wondering what to do next.

Eva and Katie sat with Alison as the sobbing turned to crying, the crying turned to stray tears, and finally, just red-eyed despondency.

"I used to be a university lecturer," she said. "History. Look at me now. All because I couldn't shake the feeling I was being watched, that everyone was talking about me behind my back."

"That's how I felt," said Eva. "The difference was I never made anything of my life. Too stupid, I guess."

Her voice tailed away. Some sixth sense made her aware of Katie's gaze on the back of her neck. As she spun around to look, Katie quickly glanced away.

"I don't think you're stupid," Alison said colorlessly. "Katie thinks you have a lot of potential, and Katie is never wrong." The expressionless tone made her sound as if she was totally uninterested in what she was saying.

Eva did not think a reply was appropriate. Once again, silence descended upon the room. She was about to open her book when Alison continued.

"This isn't the first time you've been in here, is it?"

"No. I was brought in when they killed my brother."

"They killed your brother?" Alison said in astonishment. "Who did? What happened?"

She sat up straight on her untidy bed, her eyes wide

with amazement. Eva felt a surge of embarrassment. She blushed, unsure what to say next. "Um, I don't know."

Katie came to her rescue.

"It's not what it sounds like," said Katie in a rush of words. "Can't you tell, Alison? She was addicted to MTPH."

"Oh," Alison said. "An emptyhead? Now I understand."

They weren't allowed to wean someone off MTPH anymore. Addiction was held to be a matter of personal choice, and there was a growing argument that the second personality had some rights too...Eva had been one of the last people to be forcibly broken of the addiction; even now she struggled to forget the last few days of her "brother's" life.

She had been locked into the room next door but one to the room she occupied this time. Just herself and a bed in that great empty orange cube of a room. The toughened glass windows didn't open; they merely offered a view across the scrubby lawn towards the dull grey lime trees, dissolving in the mist of the rain. Her brother had sat cross-legged on the floor, retaining an expression of acceptance on his face as he faded away.

"How can you be so calm!" He had just shrugged and smiled sadly at her.

"All things must pass, Eva," he said, a little grin playing around his lips. "Besides, I can't imagine what will happen to me. I'm your opposite, aren't I? MTPH stimulates the underused parts of your personality. I'm everything you are not. Calm, positive, dull and unimaginative..."

"It's me who's the dull and unimaginative one," said Eva. "Oh, what am I going to do without you?"

"You'll make other friends. Maybe some real company will do you good, Eva."

"No! How can you say that?"

The arguments had raged during her brother's last few days, until he had simply faded away to leave her all on her own. The people who had shut her away insisted that he had never actually existed: he was only a hallucination, brought about by continuing exposure to MTPH. But they didn't understand. Only someone who had taken MTPH could understand.

"They're plotting something, Eva."

Eva sat up in bed in her darkened room, hugging the duvet tightly around her body.

"Who's plotting something?"

"Katie is. And Alison is, too, but not quite the same thing. Nicolas is involved, but he's just a passenger. It's Katie we need to watch. If only we knew who she was . . ."

Eva felt fear take hold of her, her stomach filling with dark dread.

"Who is that?" she whispered, her voice shaking. "Why do you keep talking to me?"

"They're in the lounge, Eva."

"Who are you?"

The voice went silent. Feeling rather foolish, Eva draped the duvet around herself and stumbled sleepily from her room. The corridor outside was brightly lit but deserted. The nurses' station stood empty, a nearly full vending machine cup sat steaming on the desk. Muted music and voices could be heard from the game room. Eva headed toward the sound.

They were watching a game show. Alison and Nicolas were sprawled on two comfortable seats, holding hands, Katie sitting upright behind them on a hard plastic chair. She turned round as Eva stumbled into the room, then reached to shake Alison's shoulder.

"Eva? What's the matter?" said Alison, repeatedly waving the sound down. Eventually the ancient viewing screen caught the signal.

"What time is it?"

"Just after two o'clock," said Nicolas. "What is the matter?"

"I keep hearing voices," Eva said.

Katie and Alison exchanged glances.

"See?" Katie said. "I told you."

"Okay, okay," said Alison. "I'm sorry, I should have believed you. Eva, come and sit with us. I don't want to go to sleep tonight. Katie and Nicolas are keeping me company."

"Yes," Nicolas said. "You can lie here on the chair next to me. You've got your duvet."

"Thank you," Eva said uncertainly. She sat down on the chair and wrapped the duvet tightly around herself. The soothing light of the viewing screen and the gentle background dialogue filled the room. It was strange, but there was something welcoming about the atmosphere of the room, filled with the silence of people who felt comfortable with each other. For the first time in weeks, months even, Eva felt as if she could relax. It didn't matter that Nicolas and Alison were exchanging looks in some unspoken conversation. It didn't matter that the voice had been right and they were plotting something. It was enough that the same voice had sent her to be part of this group, and that they had accepted her into their circle. Maybe tomorrow she would worry about their schemes; tonight, she felt accepted.

Eva allowed herself to drift off to sleep, snuggled tightly in her duvet.

It was a bright, sunny morning. Only a faint chill to the air hinted that autumn was approaching. Eva woke to find herself in her own bed. She had a vague memory of Alison and Katie leading her back here the night before and tenderly tucking her in. Eva got up and pulled on a loose yellow sweatshirt and grey leggings and headed for the communal kitchen to make toast for breakfast. She felt surprisingly positive this morning. Someone had left black toast crumbs in the butter, but even that couldn't spoil her mood.

After breakfast she wandered outside, out across the scrubby grass to her circle of limes where she gazed up at the leaves. Some were already yellowing in promise of autumn. The ground was wet; it soaked through the cuffs of her leggings, yet she didn't care.

When Nicolas suddenly poked his head out from among the trees at the other side of the clearing and beckoned her toward him, she wasn't at all surprised. She got to her feet and followed him into the strip of woodland that separated the Center from the nearby main road. Old cans and stained fast-food wrappers littered the woodland floor. The sound of fast-moving traffic filtered through the trees. Nicolas led her to Alison and Katie, standing in a tiny clearing by a patch of nettles and a hawthorn tree. Alison nodded at Eva as she approached. Katie was staring at an old beer can, an odd expression on her face.

"Eva," Alison said.

"Alison," Eva replied. Alison looked at Katie and came to a decision.

"Eva. Do you know that we're being watched?"

Eva looked at Alison and frowned. "Well, yes. Everyone is being watched. Of course I know that."

Alison shook her head. "No. I'm not talking about Social Care. That's just something that's been concocted so that the people in charge can say that they're concerned about our well-being. We point to the poor souls that have been blinded by laser weapons and they say, 'Who, us? Why should we do that? The world is a better place thanks to us. Look at all the money we spend on Social Care.' "

"Yeah," Nicolas said. "It's like the way the petroleum companies used to spend money on conservation projects: a way of presenting a clean image."

"I'm sure there's more to Social Care than just that. Some of them really believe in what they're doing."

"Okay," Alison said impatiently. "Maybe that's true. The point is, though, there's an awful lot of information being collected about us. Did it ever occur to you that someone, or something, is behind all that watching? It's not just about a collection of people or computer programs watching over us for our own protection. There's something more sinister occurring."

Eva smiled. "I have heard it talked about. It's just the paranoia of our times. Back in the twentieth century, people thought that they should be looking in the phone system for an evolving intelligence plotting as it listened to their conversations."

"Did they?" Alison said, looking impressed. "I never knew that. Well, this isn't paranoia. It's true. Katie thinks so, and we think she's right. Katie is always right. It's different when you're here in the Center, a little bit removed from the rest of the world. You get to look at things from a distance. There's something out there watching us. And we're not sure why."

"It's trying to make us do something," Nicolas said.

The looks on the faces of the others convinced Eva that they believed what they were saying. Eva chose her words with care.

"It's trying to make you do what?"

Alison glanced at Katie, who shook her head. Alison spoke in low tones.

"We don't know. We think it's trying to bring us to itself."

Eva picked a leaf from the nearby hawthorn tree. She rolled it between her fingers, staining them green with fresh-smelling juice.

"What makes you think that?"

Alison spoke haltingly. "We have ideas of escape. Opportunities present themselves, but we're suspicious of them. Are they our ideas, or is something putting them our way? It's difficult to explain—"

Nicolas interrupted: "A few weeks ago we watched a TV program about life in the free Russian States, where there's a charter guaranteeing no monitoring of citizens. And then, the next day, Katie comes upon details on the net of cheap train fares to get there. Coincidence, or not?"

Alison spoke up. "I have a dream about walking down to the gate and hitching a ride from a red Mitsubishi van. Nicolas and Katie are already hiding in the back. I even dream about how to disable the on-board sensors so our passage is not detected. The next day I'm walking by the gate and I see the same van from my dream. Exactly the same van, down to the company colors on the side and the dent in the bumper. How could I know that would happen?"

Eva ran her fingers through her hair and frowned. "You're saying that the Watcher planted the idea in your head? How?"

"I don't know." Alison shrugged. "But it knows everything about me. It must know how to push my buttons. Maybe it placed some sort of subliminal influences in the programs I watched just before going to bed."

"Of course, we could just be paranoid. We are a bunch of loonies, after all," put in Nicolas helpfully. He gave a nervous laugh.

"But I don't think so," Alison said. She gazed at Eva intently. "We're frightened. We want to get out of here, get out from under the nose of the Watcher so that we can think for a while and examine our actions, decide what it is that we really want. But where to go? We may think we are running to safety, but really we may just be running toward the Watcher."

Nicolas spoke up. "That's why we want you on our side. Katie thinks you can help. You almost fooled Social Care in your suicide attempt. We want you to help us devise our escape."

For the first time in months, Eva felt like smiling. It wasn't that she believed the three of them; their ideas were riddled with supposition and fueled by paranoia. They were a self-confessed bunch of loonies.

Then again, she wasn't exactly normal, either.

The thing was, they trusted her. They wanted her to be their friend. For that reason, more than anything else, she gave her answer. "Of course I will."

"Good." Alison smiled. "Come on. We've got to get back now. If we stay out of their sight for too long, someone or something might get suspicious. We'll let you know more later on."

They pushed through the damp, litter-strewn under-growth until they reached the circle of limes. Ahead of them lay the solid, red brick building of the Center. To Eva, it suddenly had a sinister appearance.

Katie drew level with her. "You're right to want to escape. This place sends everyone mad after a while."

"I quite agree," said the voice.

Eva ignored it.

CONSTANTINE 2: 2119

Constantine was seeing stars. Tiny pinpoints of light winking and fizzing in the space between his roaring headache and the ceiling.

Where was he?

Cool white sheets, the bed much larger than a bed needed to be, bone china tea service laid out on a tray that rested on one of the bedside tables. He groaned and sat up. Prints in pastel shades hanging on the walls; a window that reached from floor to ceiling—recognition slowly dawned. Somewhere there would be a trouser press and a full sensory immersion booth offering a discreet range of adult entertainment.

He was in a hotel room, just as he had been every night for the past two years.

He placed one hand gently on the side of the teapot. Hot. How did they do that? How did they have that power of prediction that enabled a pot of tea to be brewed at just the moment of waking? He picked up the yellow-patterned teapot and began to pour, the smell of jasmine tea filling the room. A sound channel was fading up in the background: the morning news digest.

Where was he? Germany? No. That had been last week. Wales? Welsh enclave in Paraguay? Why did he have such a bad headache? Constantine had a trick for moments like this, moments of hotel angst when he couldn't remember exactly where he was. He looked at the prints that hung on the walls. Abstract. Dot art. Australia. Stonebreak.

He suddenly remembered Mary. Last night had been strange. The last few weeks had been strange. The way the world seemed to be dropping out of view, gaps opening up where they shouldn't be. The way people froze in place or smeared themselves across the scenery . . . Even so, last night had been strange by anyone's standards. And then they had come for him and led him back here. Back into his safe, comfortable and, above all, anonymous routine. Given him a glass of whisky and left him to sleep.

Constantine always slept naked and they hadn't neglected that detail. He wondered who had undressed him.

He turned on the visual feed that matched the news sound channel.

India, and the prime minister had apologized for the setbacks in the country's VNM program, but promised that the general public would see the benefits within the next five years.

The Mediterranean Free State, where pictures of one of the country's leading business women engaged in an intimate liaison with her husband's best friend had inadvertently been released into the public domain. Again, there were calls for the banning of the stealth technology that made obtaining such images possible.

Japan, and reports that the renationalized space program had gone deeper into debt, owing mainly to costs incurred by the warp drive research project. The theory seemed good; the first colony crews had already been selected on the strength of the AIs' claims. So why had none of the ships yet managed to make the jump?

Constantine sipped his tea. His head pounded. He felt greasy and bloated: furred halitosis in a broken-down body. He needed a shower.

The bathroom offered cool antiseptic white tiles and a gentle smell of mint and tea tree oil. He felt like laying his head against the wall to take away the pain. The shower was already running, gentle gusts of scented steam puffing into the room. His wash bag had been unpacked and laid out by the sink, and the reason for the pain in his head now became obvious. A clear plastic strip sat between his toothpaste and his razor, four pills nestling in their slots. Had it been a month already? Obviously yes. They had warned him at the start that he would get headaches when the dose was running low.

"A warning signal," the doctor had said. She had worn a dark business suit, dark tights, and sensible dark shoes, making the translucent green surgeon's gloves on her hands seem vaguely obscene. She had perched on the edge of her desk and run her fingers across Constantine's forehead. He had felt the light touch of latex and smelled its faint aroma, mixed with the peppermint on the doctor's breath.

"The first day you are overdue you will wake up with a headache. The next day it will be stomach cramps. The third day, headache *and* stomach cramps."

"Are those symptoms of MTPH withdrawal?" asked Constantine.

"For the third time, this isn't MTPH. MTPH would

not allow four independent personalities to develop in your mind. Do you have any idea what went into developing this compound?"

She gazed into the distance as she spoke, her fingers still softly kneading Constantine's scalp.

"Anyway, MTPH isn't physically addictive. Neither is this. We added the headaches ourselves as a warning."

"Couldn't you have put in something a little more pleasant?"

"Like what?"

"I don't know. A little buzz."

The doctor gave him an unpleasant smile. "I think it says a lot about us that we never even thought about that. We instinctively went for the pain. Doesn't that make you wonder about our worldview?"

"Mmm."

"Mmm indeed. Just be grateful we went for an oral delivery system."

The memory faded like a Cheshire cat: with a picture of that unpleasant smile on the doctor's face widening to show her teeth. He always remembered her like that.

Constantine picked up the plastic strip and popped the first pill. Four pills, four personalities.

He placed the first pill, the red one, in his mouth and swallowed it. He had been told that any apparent effect was purely imagined, but he was prepared to swear that as the pill went down the world took on a sharper and more defined focus.

"Speak to me," he muttered.

—What do you want me to say? Have you noticed that they have put two different sorts of leaves in the teapot? They must have had to open a new package while making it.

"You're fine, anyway," Constantine muttered.

The pills were color-coded: red, white, blue and grey. Red for the observational personality, white for the mathematical.

"Square root of eight thousand and thirty-two?" he murmured.

—Eighty-nine point six two, correct to two decimal places.

The blue pills were his favorite. The doctor had claimed they gave taste and integrity, artistic flair. She was right, but only after a fashion. The blue personality had a distinctly different outlook from Constantine himself, something he found invariably interesting, and occasionally useful.

"Speak to me, Blue."

—Jasmine tea followed by waffles and honey? I don't think so. It'll all be cold by the time you get out there, anyway.

Last came the grey pill.

"Hello, Grey," he said. There was no reply. There never was. Not for the first time, he wondered about the grey personality, lurking unseen and unheard somewhere in his mind.

Constantine filled a plastic cup with water and took a sip. His headache was still there. He cursed the doctor, as he did this same time every month. He had done his bit, hadn't he? Why did he have to wait for another hour or so before the pain ebbed away?

He stepped into the shower and began to soap himself.

"What day is it?"

—Thursday, said Red. —This is it, Constantine. We're nearly there. You are visiting a building site today, a few hundred clicks from Stonebreak. The quorum may well be formed there.

"Mmph. About time." Constantine rubbed shampoo into his hair.

—This could be the first of the last three meetings.

Constantine said nothing. Finally to be set free, to be released back into the real world. It was almost too much to hope for. He spoke carefully. "Will they know who I am?"

—Some will, some won't. It's the ones who aren't aware of your mission who should provide us with the best picture of the world at the moment. I'd advise that you keep quiet about who you are. To begin with, at least.

Constantine said nothing in reply. That was what he had planned to do anyway.

He changed the subject. "How do you feel about what Mary was saying last night? Do you think that Stonebreak will collapse?"

—It's probable, said White. —VNMs weren't as efficient at reproduction when this place was built. The likelihood of a design flaw showing itself increases the more that the machines reproduce.

—Frightening, isn't it? said Red. —All that effort goes to waste because one machine was faulty at the start. It's like a whole building collapsing because of six sick bricks.

—Let's just hope we're not here when this place finally falls apart, interrupted Blue.

"Mmm." Constantine rinsed soap from his hair. Who else had three, maybe four personalities looking over their shoulder at everything they did? It was no wonder he was cracking up.

The summons to the meeting came just after he had finished breakfast: a discreet message flashing up on his console. Constantine made his way up to the roof where a flier awaited.

The hotel was a low building, set near the edge of the second level of Stonebreak. A fresh breeze wafted over him, dissolving his headache. He walked toward the edge of the roof to look out over the green patchwork of the first level.

"Mr D'Roza, we are in a hurry." The pilot wore a stern expression. She was busily pinning her long dark hair up in a bun.

Constantine waved dismissively. "Just a moment. I need some air."

She glared at him. "Two minutes," she said tightly.

"When I'm ready."

The pilot scowled at his retreating back and muttered something in the direction of the cockpit. Constantine ignored her and made his way right to the edge.

The morning sun was rising behind him. A building somewhere behind cast a shadow across the roof. Constantine took several deep breaths and stretched his arms. It was a long drop to the first level. He thought again about Mary and their ride up the inside of the wall to the third level last night. Where was she now, he wondered?

—Probably lying dead in a gutter somewhere, said Blue.

"Don't. I'm sure that won't be the case."

Constantine took another deep breath and headed back to the flier and its impatient pilot. He stepped into the shadow cast by the tall building and looked up at it. It was such a delicate construction that it seemed to pierce the very clouds. An incredible piece of engineering: rose-colored glass set in an intricately fashioned silver metal frame; it seemed too fragile to support its own

weight. Constantine felt his stomach flutter. The building *was* floating on the very air. Beneath the base of the
tower there was nothing. Only empty air upon the
empty air that sat upon the second layer of Stonebreak.
Constantine bit his lip and turned away from the illusion. If he couldn't see it, he couldn't be going mad. He
clung to the hope. It was all he had.

The tiny green oasis of life that was Stonebreak quickly
vanished from view as they flew out over the Nullarbor
plain. Constantine gazed out of the blue-tinted window of the tiny flier at the flat scrubland that scrolled
endlessly past. The pilot seemed intent on paying him
back for the delay on the roof of the hotel; she dipped
and weaved way too close to the ground, claiming that
she needed to avoid detection whenever Constantine
queried the need for such violent maneuvering.

—She's lying. Our secrecy lies in our mundanity, not
in elaborate attempts to evade detection.

"Thank you for your observation, Blue," muttered
Constantine sarcastically. The flier's jerking motion was
making him feel sick. Worse, he was still shaken by the
sight of the floating building and was unsuccessfully
trying to convince himself he hadn't actually seen it.
His one comfort during the queasy ride was that White
seemed undisturbed by it. That was the personality
Constantine trusted most in situations such as this.

The flier looked like a military model covered with a
thin veneer of luxury to hide its true character. The outside paintwork was now white and gold, rather than the
dull matte grey or silver of a stealth skin. Constantine's
seat was soft white leather, facing an elegant communi-
cations console inlaid with white wood and mother of

pearl, but the passenger section seemed just a little too large for these items. In addition, there were too many slots and catches set into the airframe, too many places where crates could be secured or guns mounted. Ahead of him, the pilot's chair was a mechanical egg surrounded by struts and pneumatic rods, bracing it against forces from every direction. Even the very shape of the flier was a giveaway, squat and maneuverable, rather than affecting the sweeping curves currently fashionable for so many business vehicles.

There was a subtle change to the view as gentle hills rose up from beneath the land. Isolated grey shapes began to flash past, then small clusters, then packs. Kangaroos and camels. The flier had left the lifeless plain for a region where a few animals scratched out an existence.

The pilot sent the craft skimming along a shallow path between the low hills and then spun them around and down and they were suddenly in the midst of the construction site. She decelerated rapidly, touching the flier down near the center of a rectangular patch of mud.

The pilot spoke without turning. "Welcome to DIANA Arcology, phase one. Please check that you have all your belongings before leaving the vehicle."

The door slid open and bright sunlight filled the passenger section, along with a wave of heat as if someone had opened an oven door. Constantine hesitated for a moment before moving out into the bright daylight. He stepped down onto a plastic duckboard laid over wet red mud. As he did so, the door slid shut and the flier rose and skimmed off in a wide circle before disappearing in the direction from which it had come.

Constantine turned in a slow circle himself. There was no sign of anyone. He was alone, abandoned in the middle of a large rectangle of reddish earth, baking under the hot sun. Already he could feel sweat running down his back. The trail of blue plastic duckboards led to the edge of the mud patch, and he began to follow them. He felt as if he was walking across the surface of a huge red swimming pool. Someone had cut down to a depth of about half a meter and then peeled back the planet's skin to leave the earth underneath raw and exposed.

—Why hasn't the mud dried up? It's like an oven out here.

"That's a good point, Red," Constantine muttered. He crouched down and reached one hand toward the muddy surface.

—Careful. There's something moving down there.

Something broke the surface fast, just as Red spoke; the edge of a silver cylinder flashed brightly in the powerful sunlight before dipping beneath again. Now that he looked closely, Constantine could see that there was a constant bubbling motion just below the mud's surface. Hundreds of identical cylinders busily crawling all over each other.

—VNMs, confirmed White. —We're looking at some sort of bounding tank, I think. The mud layer must extend beneath the ground for some distance. It's acting as a nurturing area for the machines.

—Like a fish tank, said Blue.

—That's right. It's a clever idea. It delimits the area upon which the machines can act. It stops them from escaping or converting something that they shouldn't.

—Do you think it might be a good idea to get off the duckboards? asked Blue.

"A very good idea," agreed Constantine. He didn't like the idea of being converted.

—Hold it, said Red. —Something's happening.

There was a slow sucking noise, and something large and rectangular emerged from the reddish mud. An oversized yellow plastic refrigerator, by the look of it. The door swung slowly open.

—It looks like an elevator. I think you should get in.

Constantine shivered. The interior of the yellow box looked cramped and dangerously short on air. He preferred to stand out here in the blazing sunshine. Nonetheless, he knew that Red was probably right.

"All right, I'm going," he muttered.

—Rather you than me, said Blue.

Sitting in a chair in the large conference suite, a glass of chilled water at his elbow, Constantine had to admit that it was a clever idea. Building the research center right in the middle of the VNM construction site guaranteed privacy. It wouldn't be a secret, of course, in today's world very little was, but anyone wishing to approach the center uninvited would have to go through a tank of hungry VNMs. And anyone trying to slip a stealthy spy leech up close to the center would quickly find that their resources had been converted into building blocks for the new DIANA Arcology. Blue had approved wholeheartedly. The setup did have a certain poetry about it, he suggested.

—And there is something else as well. Did it occur to you that there is a certain Eastern aspect to our deceptions? Lies within misdirections within frauds. We sit here within what appears to be a construction site for an arcology, ostensibly to discuss its real purpose as a Space Colony Preparatory Center, and all the while we are plotting our own deeper schemes.

—Recursion, said White. —Each lie calls for another lie. How far do we have to go until the final deception is revealed?

—And will we ever know that what we find is not just another lie? said Red.

—How trite, Blue said rudely.

Grey, as ever, said nothing.

The meeting began without ceremony. Each member introduced themselves in turn.

"Marion Lee. Chairperson." A red-headed woman in a severe grey suit, she blinked rapidly as she spoke.

"Gillian Karajan. Oort cloud." She was an elongated woman with a spacer's fake tan that somehow managed to complement her fashionable white shift. Silver and gold bangles decorated her arms.

"Constantine Storey." Constantine added nothing else. He noted Gillian Karajan looking at him inquisitively. The other members of the group showed no surprise at his reticence.

—She's the one, said Red. —She's the outsider to this group. Look at the way she's sitting, nervous, as if she doesn't belong. I wonder what they told her to get her here?

The introductions continued.

"Masaharu Jones. Mars." A young man barely in this twenties, full of complacent self-confidence.

"Jay Apple. Orbital." Another tanned spacewoman, this time with a broad grin and clear, piercing eyes that swept around each member of the group in turn. Introductions over, the group nodded to each other. Marion Lee began the meeting.

"Good morning. For obvious reasons, this meeting maintains no record. Everything that is said must exist in our memories only. Nonetheless, I hereby state that we are now quorate."

Constantine felt a mixture of excitement and relief. It was true. The moment had finally arrived. His two long years of being alone were coming to an end. Marion had paused for effect. Now she continued:

"I now remind you. The quorum will meet three and only three times. The final decision must be made by the end of the third meeting. That was deemed necessary when plans were first laid down over two years ago. There can and will be no variation from this course of action."

Constantine found himself nodding in agreement. He had been part of the original meeting: it had made perfect sense then and it still made sense now. The longer the plan existed, the greater its chance of discovery. They had all agreed that speed was of the essence. Two years had seemed such a short time in which to achieve anything back then; it seemed an eternity now.

"Gillian Karajan will begin with a brief summary of progress out in the Oort cloud."

Gillian nodded. She was blinking quickly; Marion's words had clearly meant nothing to her and she was trying to conceal that fact.

"Hello. As I already said, my name is Gillian Karajan." She twisted one of the bangles on her wrist nervously for a moment and then gathered herself together. "I work at the superluminal research center. Superluminal, for those who don't know, means faster than light." She took a deep breath, gaining confidence. "We've hit big-decision time. It looks like warp drive works. . . ."

She paused for effect, looking round each member of the group in turn, then continued in self-important tones, "...but only up to a point. Our robot ships are vanishing into deep space, they're just not coming back. The AIs are saying that we've almost cracked the drive mechanism; a few more weeks and we'll have ships that can make the return journey. The question is..."

Again, she looked significantly at each member of the group before finishing. "...should we trust them?"

Silence. Constantine half raised his hand. "A working hyperdrive? That's not what I heard."

Gillian Karajan frowned at Marion the Chairperson, who nodded at Gillian to answer. She shrugged.

"Obviously we don't advertise our progress to our competitors. Capability estimates suggest that only three companies are currently working on *warp* drive." She stressed the penultimate word in the sentence, pointing out Constantine's incorrect use of terminology. "They are the newly merged company 113 Berliner Sibelius, Imagineers, and us. We believe that we have had the edge on them throughout the development period, but that advantage has probably been eroded while we sat around wringing our hands and wondering what to do next."

She turned back to face the group at large and opened her mouth to continue. Constantine interrupted.

"Sorry, but I'm interested in something you just said when you mentioned ships vanishing but not coming back. You asked if we should trust the AIs?"

Jay Apple grinned and raised her hand slightly.

"I'll take this one, Gillian." She turned toward Constantine, slouching comfortably back in her chair.

"It's like this, Constantine. The AIs sketched out the basic design for a hyperdrive; the problem is, no one can understand it. The concept is far beyond human understanding. You want to hear an explanation I was given? Start by imagining a four-dimensional section of an eleven-dimensional sphere. Now deform that section over any non-Euclidean space . . . I mean, I won't go on; you get the picture. The human mind can't contain the concepts. Anyway, the AIs say, "Okay, let's build a warp drive first. After all, it was a human mind that first formulated the equations for a warp drive. Let's build one of those." And so everyone says, fine, we'll do that. But the warp drive doesn't work, and the AIs say, "Well, just give us a little more money, and maybe it will work." And so we put in a bit more money and it gets better, but it still doesn't do everything it promised, so we put in a bit more. You get the picture? Soon a four-billion credit venture has ended up costing one hundred billion with still no end in sight. And then people get to thinking: If these AIs are so intelligent, why didn't they see this to begin with? And of course the answer comes back, maybe they did. Maybe they're just stringing us along to get what they want. Which gets a person to thinking, in that case, just for whose benefit are these AIs working? You get the idea?"

"Oh, yes," said Constantine.

"Oh, yes." Jay grinned. "And then people get really paranoid. I mean, we've got these warp ships disappearing off to heaven knows where and not coming back. And people are saying, well, where are they going? Maybe there's something waiting out there and the AIs are using the ships to carry messages to it. And if they're sending messages, what do those messages say?"

Jay gave a huge yawn and leaned back again in her chair.

"Or maybe we're just being paranoid. So, that's what

we mean when we say, 'Should we trust the AIs?' Are you up to speed now, Constantine?"

"Yes. Thank you."

—Except we didn't want her opinion. I want to hear what Gillian has to say. She's the one who was out there in the comet belt with the extra-solar AIs. See if you can get her to speak, Constantine.

"I'll try, Red," muttered Constantine.

Gillian looked from Jay to Constantine. Her eyes narrowed as she watched his lips move. After the briefest of frowns, she took up her report.

"Ms. Apple is broadly correct in what she says," Gillian said carefully. "The AIs are helping us to construct warp drives. Principally, they are helping us shape exotic matter into the necessary form for warp drives. A working warp drive appears to be within our reach. We have seen the evidence. Ships are vanishing. So, I'm here to help decide: What happens next? If we decide to do nothing, we run the risk of the other companies getting ahead of us. If we decide to press ahead, we always have the question hanging over us: Just who are we really working for? Ourselves, or the AIs?"

She paused, leaving the question hanging in the air.

Marion Lee spoke. "Okay, thank you, Gillian. Now that Constantine and Masaharu understand the AI problem, perhaps Jay could let us know a little more about her work in orbit."

—Look at Jay's attitude, said Blue. —Relaxed, arrogant. Look at the way she holds her hands behind her head. She's part of this. Not like Gillian. She didn't trust you. She's not high enough up in the company to have heard about ghosts.

Jay yawned. "Well, what can I say? We're one hundred percent ready. Have been for eighteen months

now. As soon as this place is completed, we can get the
volunteers in here and we can start training up our
colonists. To be honest, we've done so well up in the
Orbital that we could probably launch them now."

Jay winked at Constantine. "We could have launched
already, and no one would have known."

She glanced across to Marion. Marion nodded and
looked to the Japanese man, who had been sitting patiently, waiting his turn.

"Masaharu, any news from Mars side?"

Masaharu had lined up his console exactly with the
edge of the table. His glass of water was placed behind it.
His hands rested neatly on either side. He gazed down at
the table as he spoke in a soft voice.

"We have nothing new to report. The Mars factory
retains, so far as we can ascertain, one hundred percent
integrity. Everything in the Orbital is of one hundred
percent Mars manufacture, as Jay can confirm."

He lapsed into silence, one hand reaching out to
move the glass slightly closer to the console.

Marion turned to Constantine. "There we are,
Constantine. Do you have anything to add?"

He paused for a moment in case any of his extra intelligences had something further to say. Nothing. Was
this finally it? Was the work of the past two years nearly
done? He took a breath, ready to speak. Someone interrupted him.

"Hold on. I don't like this. Why are we deferring to
this man's opinion? He hasn't told us who he is yet."

Gillian's eyes burned with anger. Her skin was orange
with a spacer's anti-SAD tan, her accent a result of that
strange polyglot that evolved when international teams
lived in close proximity for extended periods.

She turned and pointed an accusing finger at Constantine, bangles jingling and jangling.

"The question I'd like answered is, what are you doing here?"

Silence fell as four pairs of eyes gazed at Constantine, but he felt no urgency to answer just yet. He ran his finger along the dull grey metal of the tabletop, conscious of the austerity of his surroundings; bare, grey metal walls, red plastic molded chairs, the black rubberized surface on the floor. Everything in the room had been built the old way, with no attempt at VNM construction. It couldn't be risked; no hint of circuitry that might act as a transmitter or listening device could be allowed into this room. Was it safe to speak? As safe as it could ever be, he guessed.

"Well?" demanded Gillian. Constantine sat up a little straighter.

Jay laughed suddenly. "Oh, Gillian. I can see that you spend too much time on your job and not enough engaging in office politics. Someone has paid for you to travel millions of kilometers across the solar system, booked a shuttle so you could get Earthside just in time for this meeting, and you seem to think so highly of yourself you don't find this unusual."

Constantine felt a funny little stirring in his mind. He tilted his head, feeling for it, but it had gone.

Jay continued. "When you get summoned to a meeting where a mysterious stranger keeps asking questions, it can only mean one thing. You're in the presence of a ghost. Just how far away *is* the Oort cloud?"

She waved a dismissive hand at Masaharu, who had looked up at her rhetorical question.

"I didn't want the answer in kilometers, Masaharu.

Listen, girl, you've obviously got some talent to have got this far. Someone clearly likes you. They don't send just anyone to one of these meetings, but if you want to rise any higher in this organization, you've got to learn how people operate."

—You've got to hand it to Gillian, said Red. —Look how she's holding her composure. I can hear her toe tapping inside her shoe. That's about it for the nerves. Jay's right. She is good.

Jay continued. "You think this company is all about machines and VNMs and money. That may be true, but it's the people inside it who pump those things around. They're the bloodstream. And who moves through that bloodstream, checking that everything is healthy and looking out for infections?" Jay nodded toward Constantine. "Him."

Gillian looked from one to the other, then folded her hands gently in her lap. Bangles jingled on the white material of her shift. "You may be right, Jay. Maybe I have spent too long in the Oort cloud. However, my conscience is clear. My time there has been spent working to the good of the company and for all humanity. I'm not worried about spies."

"I'm not a spy," said Constantine simply.

Gillian flashed him an angry look. "I don't care what you are. I came here for advice. You say I don't spend enough time worrying about other people," she turned her angry look toward Jay, "but that's because I think we have far more urgent things to worry about. We have it in our power to unleash something we do not understand upon the universe. AIs! Admittedly more intelligent than ourselves and with the power to replicate themselves. For all we know, we may have already let the genie out of the bottle. I think that at times like this, personal advancement counts for little."

Marion tapped a glass on the table. The dull thudding gradually captured their attention. "Thank you. Gillian. No one is questioning your integrity. I think it's fair to say that we all understand the problem as well as you do."

"What about him?" Gillian pointed her finger accusingly at Constantine. "He claimed to know nothing about working hyperdrives or AIs when this meeting started. Was that a lie, too?"

Constantine bowed his head slightly. "I'm sorry, Gillian. I deliberately misled you. I was trying to get a handle on what you believed was happening out there."

"Why? Because you don't trust me?"

"No. Well, not exactly. What if the AIs had manipulated you in some way? What if you were acting for them, even unwittingly?"

There was frosty silence from Gillian. When she spoke, it was with hurt dignity. "And? Do I pass your test?"

Constantine quickly polled his intelligences.

—I think so, said Red. —Except . . .

Constantine paused.

—Nothing, said Red. —Leave it.

—No opinion, said White.

—I'm pretty sure she's clean, said Blue.

Grey remained silent.

"We think that you do," said Constantine "Although, how can we ever be sure?" he added hurriedly.

"We always return to this same argument," interrupted Masaharu. "The AIs are admittedly more intelligent than we are. If they are really that much more intelligent, then we cannot hope to outwit them. If we are to achieve anything, we have no choice but to hope that they're not."

Constantine nodded. "He's right. I've lived the last two years of my life believing that."

Gillian looked from Constantine to Masaharu and back again. She appeared to relax, leaning back in her chair. She spoke softly. "Okay. I understand that. So if you already know everything that I've told you, why am I here?"

Marion spoke. "Because we need your knowledge. You won't be able to return to the Oort cloud, you know. We can't take the risk of those AIs finding out anything that you hear at this meeting."

"But what about my work?"

"Your work here is far more important now." Marion turned to Constantine. "Would you like to explain?"

He nodded. "I'm sorry, Gillian. It's true. The reason that I am here . . ."

He paused as a strange lightheadedness washed over him. For a moment, the table had seemed to flicker. Looking up he saw two Gillians . . . No, that wasn't right, he saw one Gillian sitting inside another. One Gillian seemed frozen in place, her hand paused in the motion of scratching herself behind the ear. The second Gillian seemed to sit inside her and overlap the first, a normal young woman; she looked at Constantine with an expression of interest, shifting in her chair as she did so.

Constantine blinked hard. He reached out and placed a hand on the table's surface. Cool and solid, it seemed reassuringly real.

"Are you feeling okay, Constantine?" asked Jay.

"Fine." Constantine rubbed his hand back and forth

for a moment, and then picked up his glass and took a sip of water. When he blinked again, the second Gillian had gone.

"Okay," he continued. "I'm here to set in motion a train of events I have been leading toward for the past two years. We are here to safeguard against a possible future that has been increasingly apparent to humankind for at least two centuries. It seems to me that everything is finally in place. It is our duty to decide if we are right to take the course of action that is before us."

There was a slight pause at this announcement.

—Look at Jay smiling, said Red. —She's taken a shine to you. She likes a man with spirit.

Constantine coughed, then continued. "Okay. So, the order of events is as follows. First, we need to decide if we believe the AIs are working for or against us. Second, and this may or may not be relevant to the first point, do we go ahead with the plan?"

He waved his hand vaguely in the direction of Jay— Jay who sat motionless, a frozen expression on her face, while a second Jay leaned forward to pour herself a glass of water.

Damn, he thought. *Not now. I'm going mad. Right here at the end, I'm finally going mad.* All the effort, all the drive suddenly just left him. Weak and exhausted, he slumped in his chair.

"I'm sorry. I don't think this is such a good idea anymore," he mumbled. Jay and the rest stared at him with expressions that ranged from shock to concern to faint scorn.

He didn't care. Something seemed to be stirring in his mind, a little tickle, a tiny little feeling so small that it could barely be grasped. He thought about hugging a tree and rubbing a matchstick between his fingers at the same time. It made him feel uncomfortable. What was all that about?

"Excuse me," he said. "I don't feel..."

The tickling increased.

"Red, what is it?" he mumbled.

—I don't know. It's like one of the other personae...

"Red? Are you there? Blue? What's happening?"

He held the glass of water close to his lips, hiding their movement. He was fooling nobody: the rest of the group looked on in concern.

He could feel something inside him waking up, something beginning to speak. Dizzily, he put the glass down. He heard a voice deep inside him, old and dry and incredibly strange. It was Grey, he realized. The grey pill was having an effect at last.

—Act normally, you fool. Don't let them know you've noticed anything wrong.

"But...What...Can't you see...?"

The others watched him mumbling to himself.

Grey spoke again, and his voice was petulant. —What's up with Red? Why hasn't he noticed? Gillian just got off a shuttle this morning that came from the edge of the solar system. Where did she get the white dress and the bangles? That's this month's fashion.

"Oh...I don't know...It's all too..." Constantine was still reeling. Punch-drunk...

—That's it. I'm taking over, said Grey.

Suddenly Constantine began to speak: it was his voice, but the words weren't his.

"I'm sorry, but I think I need a drink. It must have been hotter out there than I thought. I'm feeling a little dehydrated."

His hand reached out for the glass of water of its own accord, adding supporting evidence to the words he was now being forced to speak.

It was Grey; Grey was controlling him. But that was impossible.

He was still reeling from the shock when Grey made him pass out.

. . . into darkness.

Darkness and silence.

Herb could touch, smell, taste, feel nothing.

A set of memories and no more.

He could remember their long climb up the tower into space, flickering from room to room and then, without warning, they had stopped. Robert Johnston had paused just long enough to announce that they could go no further with certainty, that they must now jump into the unknown—and they had jumped.

That was when the memories of a world ended. Memories of touch and sight and taste. Now there was . . . nothing.

So where was he? Robert had said that Herb's consciousness had existed in the processors remaining after the VNMs of the Necropolis had failed to commit suicide correctly. He had therefore viewed the world through the senses of those machines. What if he had now jumped to a place where those senses no longer existed? What if his consciousness now existed in a processor with no connection to the outside world? How long would he remain here? Forever? To spend eternity without any senses, cut off from everyone and everything: the thought was enough to send his nonexistent pulse racing in panic. And then a second, more sinister, thought occurred to him.

Robert had said that many copies of his personality had been dispersed throughout the Enemy Domain to seek out the secret of its origin. What if other copies of Herb Kirkham were even now trapped in eternal darkness? Tiny bubbles of consciousness glittering unnoticed, suspended in endless silence throughout the dark ocean of the Enemy Domain.

Nothing, still nothing. A scream was building in Herb's imaginary throat . . .

"Hey, buddy. What's the matter?"

Robert Johnston thrust his face over Herb's left shoulder, his features illuminated from below by some invisible light source. Herb blinked as his imaginary eyes adjusted to the darkness: his senses had switched on again. He *felt* the weak pull of gravity, *smelled* the cold, tinny air. Stretching away beneath his feet was a regular pattern of shadows, picking out the edges of a triangular grid. Around and above him, nothing. Only gloom.

"Where are we? What happened?" Herb's voice was hoarse with emotion. Robert stepped before him. *Am I imagining it, or does he look shaken too?*

Robert was poised on his toes, gently shifting his weight from one foot to the other as he regained his sense of reality. Noticing Herb's curious expression, he changed his movement into a little dance.

"Come on, Herb. Get with the beat."

"Don't give me that," said Herb. "You were as frightened as I was. What happened back there?"

"Nothing I couldn't handle. There was nothing at the top of that elevator. Nothing. I think we lodged ourselves among the unused seed VNMs. I suppose they didn't see the need to set them growing, once they realized the Necropolis had gone so badly wrong. There were no senses up there for me to use: they hadn't been grown. I had to make an educated guess and jump us off in the direction of one of those ships hovering above the planet. I remembered the pattern they formed and sent us off on the path through the lattice that would most likely intersect with one of them. I got it right, but only just. We're right at the far edge of the formation."

Robert turned around and began to dance his way along the narrow walkway on which they stood, suspended over what Herb now recognized to be a spaceship's outer hull. It looked surprisingly old-fashioned: struts and bracing were virtually unknown in these days of shell construction. Herb had a sudden sense of the otherness of the Enemy Domain. He wondered under which alien sun these ships had replicated. He imagined their juvenile forms, floating in bright blackness, the cold glare of some star picking out the stretching and sliding as the braces and struts tensed and tore themselves apart while the ships reproduced by binary fission.

"Look up."

Herb obeyed as row upon row of silent coffins suddenly appeared above him.

"I just found the ship's monitoring system for those things. I've linked them into our personalities as a visual feed. It's pretty amazing, isn't it?"

Herb licked his lips. "Are they occupied?" he whispered.

Robert paused a moment. "Let me see . . . No. They're

empty. I wonder. Do you think that they were supposed to be filled from that planet beneath us? Let me think about that. It would make sense, wouldn't it? Hmm."

He lapsed into silence again and strode off along the walkway, his dancing forgotten now that his nerves were calmed. Yet again, Herb found himself following Robert Johnston into the unknown.

They were standing on the bridge of the spaceship. At least, that's what Robert called it. Herb didn't understand the concept. There was a wraparound window that made for ideal star-viewing, three comfortable padded chairs, equipped with straps for some reason, and between the chairs and the window, blocking the best standing position to take in the view, a bewildering array of controls.

"I don't understand. What is this place for?"

Robert grinned. "For flying the spaceship, of course."

Herb frowned. He ran his finger over the green, webbed material covering one of the chairs, then began to fiddle with one of the straps.

"I still don't understand. How will these help fly the spaceship?"

Robert was watching him intently, saying nothing; it made Herb nervous. He was being tested, he was sure of it.

Robert spoke. "You don't understand, do you? Don't you remember your history lessons? I imagine that the Enemy Domain is thinking ahead. It's thinking about what would happen if someone was forced to land this ship with the AIs knocked out. All this is intended for human pilots."

"Human pilots? Is that possible?"

Again Robert said nothing, and Herb cursed himself internally. Of course it was possible. Isn't that how all ships used to be controlled? Then another question occurred to him.

"Human pilots? Robert, I thought the Enemy Domain was an alien construction."

Robert gave one of his enigmatic smiles. "It depends what you mean by alien."

Herb sat down in one of the chairs. It was extremely comfortable, fitting itself to his body perfectly, except for where the straps dug into his back. He wriggled them aside and relaxed.

"You let me think the Enemy Domain was of alien origin. It's not, is it? The Necropolis was built for humans, before it went wrong. These ships have spaces on them for human beings. Robert, what's going on?"

Robert Johnston sat down on the next chair along.

"What's going on? Let me put it this way." Robert lifted his feet, resting them on the bank of controls before him, and raised a finger.

"Imagine it like this," he said. "Look at the first finger of your right hand. Got it? Okay, now look at the first two joints of your finger. Imagine that's the volume of Earth-controlled worlds. It's about the right shape, too; we seemed to have expanded more sideways than up or down. Now hold out your hand, just like this, see?"

Robert moved his palm downward, in front of his body. His pale pink nails were reflected in the window just before him. Slowly, Herb copied him.

"Look at the first two joints of your index finger: the Earth volume. According to that scale, the planet we are currently floating above would be at the bottom of your right earlobe. You've got to get the idea of the scale of things, yeah? Now contrast the size of the tip of your finger with the size of your head and your neck. Run a line down the front of your body, down past your waist, down your legs, right to the tips of your little toes, and then all the way back up to your right shoulder. Think how big all that is compared to those tiny little joints on your right hand. That volume equates to the Enemy Domain."

Herb looked down at his feet, seeming so far away on the floor. He looked back to his hand in disbelief.

Robert continued softly. "Now, we're at your right earlobe. Above a planet that lies at the edge of the wave of expansion of the Enemy Domain. Think about your right arm, down to the elbow, along to the hand, think of the palm of your hand, your knuckles, down that first finger of your right hand, all of that space. All of it now occupied by the Enemy Domain's machines. Think of all those tiny metallic bodies creeping over each other, feeding, and reproducing in their own image. Hungry metal tendrils reaching forward, jumping from world to world. Searching for something. And there, at the end of that first finger, that tiny little finger joint, Earth, all those people, everyone you ever knew, all happily unaware of that smothering, suffocating tide of machinery bearing down upon them. Imagine a single ant scuttling over the sand on a beach and looking up to see the tsunami bearing down upon it."

A moment's silence, and then Robert spoke at his softest.

"Don't think alien or human. Just think destruction. That's what we're talking about."

Herb stared at his fingernail for a moment; stared at the veins that stood up on the back of his hand, at the whorls that ridged the top of his knuckles, the pale blond hairs that marched up the back of his forearm. He suddenly shuddered.

"You're shaking." Robert was speaking at his normal volume again. "All this," he gestured through the window at the few sparse ships floating here at the edge of the vast fleet, "all these ships, that elevator, the Necropolis, the bumblebee robots that buzz around on the planet, the spiders that creep through the tunnels, all of this system in which our consciousnesses find themselves..."

He paused for breath, easing back into the huge green chair. "All of this system is the tip of the tiniest hair that grows from the most insignificant pore on the very edge of your right earlobe. So, don't think human or alien, Herb. Just think about being afraid. Being very afraid."

When Herb spoke there was just the faintest tremor in his voice.

"I *am* frightened," he said. "I've never denied it. Come on, who wouldn't be?" He smiled sardonically. "An agent of the EA has entered my spaceship via a secret passageway, has captured me, fired my consciousness across the galaxy to the edge of an Enemy Domain, and then that same agent tells me that I am going to help fight something so big I can barely imagine it. It could be said that, yes, I'm slightly nervous."

Robert studied him closely, then shook his head. "No. You're being flippant. Not nervous enough. Do you know what that tower is used for now? The one we just came up?"

"Of course not." Herb licked his lips nervously. "But I'm sure you're going to tell me."

"Launching cannon for VNMs. The Enemy Domain is seeding the galaxy with copies of itself."

Herb gave a shrug. "Figures. That's how the Enemy Domain got so big, I suppose."

"Okay. Have you figured out what all these ships are doing here, then?"

"No. Have you? You said they were going to be filled from the planet below. I think it would be the other way around. These ships are bringing humans to populate the planet. They would unload them onto the space elevator and take them down below to live in the Necropolis. Would have done if everything hadn't gone wrong, anyway."

Robert smiled.

"Good answer. The best—" as Herb smiled, Johnston waited just a moment before smashing him right down again "—given the knowledge you have. Your mistake is in thinking of the human beings who would occupy those coffins as individuals. They weren't. They were meant to be clones. Clones that were being grown on that planet below us until the VNMs building the city we call the Necropolis malfunctioned. They're still there, but their growth has been suspended. I felt their consciousness, millions of them, semi-aware in the darkness, as we jumped from the top of the elevator. That planet is almost sentient, there are so many of them down there."

For a moment, Herb couldn't be sure; it almost looked as if there was a tear in the corner of Robert's eye. As he tried to look closer, Johnston rose from his seat and went to gaze from the window, out into space. He continued speaking, his voice slightly hushed.

"If you look down on that planet with the right eyes, it's a dark ball embedded with the brightest little lights. All lost and alone and forgotten at the edge of the Enemy Domain . . ."

His voice trailed away and Herb felt a sickening lurch

of vertigo. He imagined the ship's floor splitting open beneath him, imagined the long drop back through the silent, empty fleet of ships, passing their hollow, forgotten shells as he tumbled faster and faster toward the planet below, rushing toward the up-reaching, deformed spires. And there, buried beneath them all, like so many unwatered seeds, the half-formed, twisted consciousness of things that would never become people. What were they like? he wondered. Half-grown adults? Children?

It was too much. He finally began to shiver.

"It's too big," he said. "You're right. It's too big. We can't fight this."

Robert turned back to him.

"Oh, yes, we can. Come on. We can use this ship's communication devices to upload ourselves. It's time to go back."

Herb wouldn't have believed it possible to feel bored and terrified at the same time, but somehow he was. Four days had passed since Robert Johnston had first appeared on his ship, and since then they had done nothing. The ship still floated a few hundred meters above the restless silver sea of VNMs, the mechanical remains of his converted planet. Robert Johnston's mysterious errands caused him to pass constantly between his own ship and Herb's. Herb had been told in no uncertain terms not to attempt to look down the passageway that linked the two ships, and Herb was sufficiently frightened of Robert not to attempt it.

Apart from the occasional presence of an agent of the Environment Agency, life aboard Herb's ship carried on as normal. He spent time preparing elaborate meals and eating them; he played games—chess, Starquest, dominions, bridge—against the ship or alone. He worked out the bare minimum in the gym to stop the ship's nanny nagging him and he watched entertainments. Apart from the extreme tension that seemed to tie him down to the comfortingly familiar objects of his living room, everything was perfectly normal.

Except for that time, somewhere in the middle of the night, when he had woken up at the feeling of something being pulled from his head. Herb had sat up in bed and begun raising the room's temperature out of sleep mode, only to be told by a calm voice to lie down and go back to sleep. Herb had taken one look at the flexible black object hanging like shiny satin from Robert's hands and quickly obeyed. Robert frightened him.

Apart from that incident, there was nothing to unsettle him. Nothing, of course, except Robert himself.

Herb spent one afternoon sitting on the white leather sofa gazing at the open hole in the floor where the trapdoor lay. A son et lumière played out around him. He ignored it, increasingly wondering about sneaking down through the trapdoor and into Robert's ship. What did it actually look like? He had had his ship's computer retune and recalibrate its senses time after time in an attempt to get a look at it, but with a spectacular lack of success. Whatever Johnston had done to his own ship had rendered it invisible to Herb's senses. In desperation, Herb had even toyed with the idea of climbing out onto the hull of his own craft in an attempt to get a visual on it, but so far had failed to muster the courage. What if he slipped and fell down onto the writhing planet below? If the drop didn't kill him, his silver creations certainly would.

So why had Robert hidden his ship from view?

Herb suspected it was probably just because he could. Johnston seemed to take a delight in demonstrating his superiority at every occasion. Still, maybe there was another reason. . . .

The thought of escape had been growing slowly in Herb's mind. If he could cut the link to Robert's ship and activate the warp drive . . .

There were only two problems, as far as he could see.

First, how could he be sure that the link was actually broken? How would he know he wasn't jumping through space with Robert still attached? Maybe that was why Johnston kept his ship hidden. Anyway, there was a second consideration.

Where would he go? Actually, the second point wasn't so much of a problem. He knew where he would go: straight home to his father's estate. Back home to Earth and four square kilometers of smooth, green lawn. His father was rich. In the middle of a tiny country with skyscrapers shoulder to shoulder, all jostling for position among farmland and public recreation grounds, his great-great-grandmother had leveled a patch of land in the middle of the Welsh hills and built nothing on it but a low, tasteful mansion. The rest of the land had been converted to a condition that his father liked to refer to laughingly as "unspoiled": Gentle slopes and pleasant woodlands studded with lakes, a picture of an idyll that would have seemed entirely out of context with the original surrounding countryside. The whole estate was a grandiose gesture of understatement that inflamed envy and resentment in equal measures: Herb's father was so rich he could leave valuable land untouched. Of course, the space beneath the land did not go unused.

Herb's father was a rich and powerful man. But,

thought Herb, was he powerful enough? Could he stand up to the EA? A second thought caught Herb's attention. *Would he want to*? Herb quickly suppressed the idea.

So, he decided firmly, he had a place to escape to. Possibly. But first, could he break the link between the two ships? To achieve that he would have to get a look at Robert Johnston's ship.

The answer finally occurred to him, and he gave a slow smile. So Robert didn't think that he was that bright?

Maybe he could prove otherwise.

Herb was listening to Beethoven: the late string quartets, opus 127 to be precise. He had read somewhere that these were considered amongst Beethoven's greatest pieces, if not some of the greatest pieces ever written, and Herb was damned if he wasn't going to enjoy them as much as the so-called experts.

He had set the sound picture so that the string quartet appeared to be playing just over the trapdoor where Robert would emerge into the room. Maybe it would surprise him, but probably not.

In his head, Herb was rehearsing his plan to get a picture of Robert's ship. He just had a few words to say, but they had to seem nonchalant. He could not give away the fact that he was plotting something. The idea was actually quite simple. Johnston controlled what was picked up by the senses on Herb's ship, but those weren't the only senses Herb had at his disposal. Had Robert forgotten the billions of VNMs swarming below? Each a descendant of a machine built to Herb's design, and each one sporting a rudimentary set of senses? The question was, how to do it without Robert noticing? And the solution was simplicity itself. Herb spoke.

"Hey, Ship. I would like a chocolate malt and a hot salt-beef sandwich. And would you do a full scan out to point one light year? Include sensory information from all other public sources. I want to gather as much data as possible for the records. The state of this planet may be germane to any future legal action brought against me."

As he spoke, Robert Johnston strode out of the secret passageway. The sight always turned Herb's stomach slightly. Robert walked up the side of the passageway, perpendicular to the floor of Herb's ship. As he stepped from the passage to the floor, his body swung through ninety degrees. That last step was dramatic. Robert straightened his hat and smiled at Herb.

"Full system scan, eh? That reminds me. Now that there is no need for them, I must disable the software blocks I placed on your ship's senses to prevent them seeing my ship. They must be really putting a hole in the middle of your world picture."

Herb smiled sarcastically. Robert pretended not to notice.

"I see you were about to have a snack. Good idea; I think I'll join you. You made a good choice. Ship, I'll have the same as Herb. Chocolate malt and a salt-beef sandwich, hold the meat."

He gave Herb an apologetic smile. "I'm a vegetarian, didn't I tell you?"

"Are you really?"

Herb didn't care. All around him the ship was sucking up its impressions of the immediate surroundings in a bubble point two light years in diameter. Buried somewhere in that set of data would be the images sensed by the VNMs just below him.

Some of those images would reveal Robert's ship.

• • • •

Herb was beating Robert at chess. He had arranged his opponent's captured pieces in a circle around the foam-flecked glass that had held his spiced lager. He grinned across the board as Robert frowned while thinking of his next move.

"Do you want to concede? Again?"

"Not yet. I feel I learn something just by playing through to the end."

"Please yourself."

Herb sat back in his seat and began to hum. Robert sighed and moved a piece.

"You don't want to do that," Herb warned. "Mate in three moves."

Robert sighed again. Just for the moment, the arrogant air had left him.

"Herb," he said, "don't you ever think that there are more important things than winning? Haven't you heard the saying 'It's far more important to be nice than to be clever'?"

Herb rolled his eyes. "The call of the loser. Okay, have that as your move."

"That's all right. I concede." Robert knocked over his king and stood up. He placed his hat on his head.

"Don't you want another game?" asked Herb.

"No, thank you. I think I'll go back to my ship and have a nap."

Herb shrugged. "Suit yourself. You know, we've been hanging over this planet for ten days now. I thought we were supposed to be going off to war. When are we actually going to do something?"

Looking a little sad, Johnston gave a barely perceptible shrug.

"Soon. The first reconnaissance reports are coming

back already. We'll give it another couple of days to see what else we get."

"What reports?"

"You'll see. Good night."

Robert waved good-bye as he stepped into the secret passageway, his body jerking forward through ninety degrees as the new gravity caught hold. He marched away down to his ship.

Herb watched him go, a feeling of frustration burning inside. Even when he won, Robert had a way of making him feel he had lost. Everything he did seemed intended to highlight Herb's inferiority. Worse, no matter how Herb tried to fight back, he always seemed to end up losing. Herb wasn't used to that; the few friends he had made had always been chosen as being just slightly less clever than he was.

Herb paused in shock. The idea had never occurred to him before. Was it true? He didn't know if he wanted to think about it. He quickly changed his line of thought.

The local scan was complete: all the data were stored within the ship. What he needed now was to access the images without Robert noticing what he was doing. Herb had already planned what he would do.

"Ship, play back the results of the last scan, mapped to a 3-D visual feed in the main viewing area. Random jumps every ten seconds, fifty percent probability space focused around the ship to a radius of ten kilometers."

Herb flopped onto one of the white sofas just as the space before him filled with a view of the planet below: silver machines in a restless sea of unending motion. After ten seconds the view flicked to a sky view of endless grey. Another ten seconds and flick, another view of the planet, this time from much higher up.

Herb sat back, watching patiently. He couldn't focus

straight in on his ship: that would alert Robert's suspicions. This way, it would seem just like any, everyday, random survey. Sooner or later, the view must fall on Johnston's ship. Flick, and a shot across the planet's surface; flick, and a shot into space, the atmosphere fading just enough to show the faint pinpricks of stars beyond; flick, a picture of Herb's ship, floating in the distance, too faint really to make out any detail. Flick again and nothing but sky. Flick again, and there was Herb's ship close up and in detail. A white rectangular box with bevelled edges top and bottom. And standing on the roof of Herb's ship, in the spot where Robert's ship should have been, wearing the palest blue suit and white spats with a matching carnation in the buttonhole, stood Robert Johnston. He was waving to the "camera."

Robert Johnston had beaten him again.

Herb had risen early and gone into the ship's gym to work out. He turned off the VR feed as he wanted to concentrate on the basic feeling of exercising the frustration from his body rather than visualize a pleasant run through the country. He ran six kilometers on the treadmill, did another two kilometers on the rowing machine and then put himself through thirty minutes of high-impact yoga.

After that he staggered, sweating, through to the lounge and called up a breakfast of orange and banana juice, brioche loaf, yellow butter, and honey. Robert Johnston stepped into the room just as Herb was finishing his third thick slice of brioche.

"Good morning, Herb. Ah, excellent! Breakfast. I hope there's enough left for me."

Robert sat down on the chair opposite and inspected Herb's meal.

"Maybe just a few sausages to go with it. See to it, please, Ship."

"I thought you were a vegetarian."

"Not on Thursdays."

Johnston cut himself a slice of brioche and began to eat.

"Mmm. Good choice. Well, the news is, we've received enough reports back on the Enemy Domain to begin your briefing. Once we've done that, we should be ready to jump into the fight almost immediately."

"Oh good," said Herb, weakly. He felt a sudden stab of cold fear deep inside. The easy passage of the past few days had made him almost forget the threatened danger of the Enemy Domain. Now the realization of his predicament came rushing back upon him. In just a few hours he could be dead. Or worse.

Johnston was helping himself to a sausage. "We'll just finish breakfast and then we'll begin." He took a bite and half-closed his eyes with pleasure. "Mmmm! Excellent! Well. I suppose I'd better explain. A few days ago I took a recording of your personality while you were sleeping. I took the liberty of beaming several thousand copies of it into the Enemy Domain. Those personalities have since been living in the processors of the Domain, collecting information about conditions in there. Those personalities who could do so have beamed themselves back here again. I have made a selection of the best of the memories they picked up. After breakfast, we'll take a look at them. See what we're up against."

He waved his fork in delight.

"These really are excellent sausages! Maybe just a touch of maple syrup . . ."

Herb stared at him. The sick feeling in his stomach had now driven all thoughts of eating from his mind. Despite that, he forced his voice to remain cool and level. "How come the act has changed? Yesterday you were all 1920s American. Today you're acting like some sort of effete English gentleman."

"I like to experiment with personalities. You should try it yourself. That one you're using at the moment obviously isn't working."

Herb sneered at him.

"Oh, touché," said Robert.

After breakfast they sat down to share the memories. Robert set a glass of drugged whisky at Herb's elbow.

"I don't need that," said Herb.

"It's there if you change your mind."

Robert had opened up a viewing field in the space in front of the white sofa. Once Herb was settled the show began. The scene revealed the ghostly figures of Herb and Robert both rising from Herb's spaceship and floating up into space. As they rose they began to move faster and faster, the planet beneath them shrinking to a dot. The star around which the planet circled moved into view and began itself to shrink as the two ghostly bodies accelerated through space.

"I added this bit for effect," Robert said. He was carefully laying out a white handkerchief on his lap. A bowl of walnuts balanced precariously on the arm of the sofa by his right elbow. Herb gave a grunt in reply.

On the screen before them, their two ghostly bodies shimmered as if they were moving out of focus, and then, slowly, a second pair of images peeled away from the first. Now there were two Herbs and two Roberts.

They began to shimmer again, splitting into four, and then eight...

"I like this part," said Robert. "It represents the multiple copies of our personalities that I beamed all the way through the Enemy Domain." Robert took a walnut from the bowl at his side and placed it in a pair of bright red nutcrackers he produced from his jacket pocket.

"How long does this go on for?" muttered Herb.

"Not too long," Robert replied, pushing a shelled walnut into his mouth.

The ghostly bodies of Herb and Robert began to separate from each other and suddenly zoom from sight. Bursts of red and green stars accompanied their sudden exit from view.

"Warp jumps," Robert explained.

The camera picked up on one pair of bodies as they shot through space. They were now approaching a planet.

"This is part of the Enemy Domain," Robert murmured. "Watch carefully."

Herb gazed into the viewing area impassively. After a few moments he sat up straighter. Shortly after that his hands stiffened on the soft white leather of the sofa, then he reached for the glass of whisky and took a sip, and then another...

It began simply enough. Robert and Herb's duplicates were standing on a low hill looking out over a grassy plain punctuated with low mounds. The Robert on the screen turned and pointed out something to the Herb standing next to him, and the camera focused on the horizon. They saw a low, dark shape, rising from the ground like a cancer. Now they could make out something silver in the grass, thin and shimmering in the light like a spiderweb. It was clearly spreading out from the dark growth in the distance, slowly choking the planet. The Robert in the viewing field bent down and pointed it out to Herb.

"Interesting, isn't it? It's got a coating of photoelectric cells all around the outside. This planet is going to be covered by that stuff, and it's all being powered by nothing more than the sun's energy. Just imagine if they dropped one of these VNMs on Earth."

"It moves too slowly. We'd destroy it in no time."

"Maybe." The virtual Robert shrugged.

The Herb watching the viewing field, the real Herb, silently cheered his alter ego.

The view shifted and this time another Herb and Robert were standing on another planet. In this view a group of cows was huddled on a small island of green remaining in the middle of a sea of silver-grey VNMs. The VNMs were eating up the land, leaving the animals nowhere to stand.

"Are those real cows?" asked the Herb in the viewing tank.

"Oh, yes."

One of the cows slipped and scrambled desperately to prevent itself sliding down the deep brown mud fringing the island, toward the restless silver sea below. There was a stirring at the shoreline, the first flickering of mechanical interest. Despite its frantic scrambling, the cow slipped closer and closer to the silver sea. One machine skittered across the bodies of its brothers and onto the mud, antennae waving, and that was it. Herb looked on in horror as the silver VNMs rushed over the unfortunate animal.

The scene jumped again to show a huge, deformed city that spread out to cover most of one side of a planet. Its silvery grey towers reached upwards to the stars and the silver-grey hearts of the fleet of spaceships hovering above it.

"I call this the Necropolis," said the real Robert. "On this one the Enemy AI got the design of the VNMs wrong. The city was abandoned before it was finished. Never mind the fact that it meant abandoning several million half grown human clones in the foundations. The Necropolis. You'll also notice the fleet of spaceships hovering above. They stopped reproducing when their cargo never arrived."

Herb looked at the planet and felt sick. "There is no way anyone could have gone down there. Was I down there?"

"Two copies of us went. Only one pair came back. I think both of the pairs traveled up to the top of the space elevator. They got stuck there and had to guess which way to jump. One pair guessed wrongly."

The scene shifted again. They were following a long dark line through space.

"What is it?" asked Herb after four minutes of watching the hypnotic movement.

"Oh, I like this one," said Robert. "What happened was this. They dropped a single VNM on a planet, rather like you did on the one below us. The only difference was that this one worked."

Herb gave a tolerant sigh.

"Anyway. The VNM reproduced, making copy after copy of itself until the planet had been converted into something rather like that mess out there."

Johnston gestured toward the spaceship's door. "Okay. So we can both visualize that bit. Now, what happened next was the clever part. You've got a planet which is now nothing more than a mass of mechanical bodies held together by their own gravity. Okay. Now the creatures at the equator begin to walk toward the poles. When they get there they begin to fuse together. More and more creatures arrive and the extremes of the planet begin to stretch out into space. Keep it up for long enough, and this is what you're left with. Clever, eh? You never thought of that, did you?"

Herb shrugged. "Yeah? Probably because it's pointless?"

Johnston laughed. "Pointless eh? Have you considered what would happen if you dropped the line that was formed by that process on another planet?"

Herb froze.

"Tell you what, I'll show you."

The picture in the view tank changed again. A fiery red line could be seen burning through the grey sky of some planet. Herb wasn't sure if he could detect the patterns of cities on the planet's surface.

"Of course, you can't even shoot it down if it's coming toward you," Johnston whispered, suddenly next to Herb's ear.

The view changed again. Herb gave a shout. "There were people there! Humans!"

Robert shrugged and returned to his seat.

"Don't worry about it. They weren't sentient. That's an important point: they never seem to have had the nerve to allow genuine humans to develop inside the Enemy Domain. Anyway, the weapon you saw is obsolete. The AI has perfected fractal branching. Look at this one."

The view shifted again so that Herb was looking down at an enormous snowflake, framed against the black night and the piercing grey stars.

"It's got a surface area of just under a billion klicks

squared and it masses about half that of Earth. Just imagine what would happen if they grew one of these things in Earth's orbit. Can you imagine the planet hitting that? It would be like passing through a cheese grater."

Herb was shaking his head slowly. Unconsciously, he had been mouthing one word over and over as he watched the screen. *No. No. No.* The silent words became a whisper.

"No. It's too big. We can't fight that."

"Oh, we haven't seen anything yet. That was just the beginning. Sit back and relax. Now we're going to try to appreciate the scale of the thing. Let's get an idea of the true size of the Enemy Domain."

The view flickered again. The camera panned across seven humps of some strange bioengineered creature, then froze. Johnston was studying Herb's wide-eyed face with an expression of vague sympathy.

"Actually, before we do that, I'll just fetch you another bottle of whisky. I think you're going to need it."

Herb didn't know how long he sat before the viewing area.

They didn't seem to care, that was the problem. Everything in the Enemy Domain was just building material. Planets, rocks, asteroids: everything was converted into yet more self-replicating machines. Herb saw view after view of cities and spaceships, snowflakes and chains, but most frequently of all, endless seas of VNMs all scuttling over each other, just like the sea of them below the spaceship in which he sat. It seemed to Herb as if the whole universe was now being converted into self-replicating machines, and the only thing he could think was, *Will there be anywhere left for me to stand?*

But that wasn't the worst thing. The worst thing was that the Enemy Domain was also filled with half-grown human clones. On planet after planet it seemed that whatever controlled the Domain had set them growing and then suddenly just lost interest: a bubble of space two hundred light years across filled with billions upon billions of half-grown human beings.

All abandoned.

Eventually, the show ended. Herb said nothing. Robert gradually brought the lounge lights back up and knelt down to pick up the splintered walnut shells that lay on the carpet beneath his seat. He gathered them up, dropping them on his white handkerchief, which he carefully carried into the kitchen where he flapped out its contents into the sink. When he returned to the lounge, Herb was still sitting on the sofa staring at nothing.

"Big, isn't it?"

"I don't want to fight it anymore. I'd rather take my chances in the Oort cloud." Herb's voice was a dull monotone.

"Oh, don't be like that. I'm sure you'll have no worries."

Herb laughed hollowly. "We're doomed, aren't we? There's no way we can defeat that. All those spaceships, all those machines. Where did they come from?"

"Earth."

"Why are they attacking us? Did you say Earth?"

"Of course. It doesn't take a genius to work that out, does it? You've seen the technology. It doesn't look any different from that of Earth's, does it? Herb, you've even seen pictures of one of your alter egos wandering around a shopping center! How alien do you think that is? You've got an imagination the size of a muffin! You saw roads and cars! You even saw bloody cows! Who did you think was in charge of the Enemy Domain? Martians?"

Herb was blushing with embarrassment. "I don't know. It's just... I mean... How can it be from Earth? How did it get so big? Why didn't we hear about it?"

Johnston jumped onto the coffee table and threw his hands up in despair.

"Oh, for goodness' sake, Herb! Use your brain! You should have been expecting this! Everyone should have been expecting this! That's one of the reasons why we have an Environment Agency! Come on, think!"

Herb shook his head. He felt too overwhelmed by it all to react. Johnston leaned down and spoke in a softer tone.

"The only surprise should be that it didn't happen sooner. Good grief, Herb, we have let self-replicating machines loose upon the galaxy! Self-replicating machines! Haven't you ever stopped to think what that implies? You've already seen first-hand the damage that can occur when they go wrong! Look at that planet you destroyed! All it takes is one machine with above average Artificial Intelligence to get loose, an AI with a grasp of how to build a warp drive, and there's no telling where it will all end."

Johnston jumped down from the table and knelt at Herb's feet.

"I mean, come on. We've seen it happen on Earth! Look what happened when DIANA tried to build that space elevator back in 2171. Public outcry, mass protests. Some saboteurs even managed to get hold of a batch of mothballed stealth suits and used them to get close enough to try and blow it up. And all the while, unbeknownst to the protestors, the VNMs designed to anchor the thing to the planet were out of control. They just kept going down and down, burrowing into the Earth. They were tough to stop, too. Those things were built to be strong. If the EA hadn't figured out a solution in time, the whole planet could have been converted to something close to adamantium from the inside out. Now, just put that problem on a galactic scale. That's what we have to deal with."

Johnston shook his head in despair at Herb's stupidity.

"You still haven't seen it, have you? And you converted a whole planet by accident! Don't you realize how fast these things spread? Suppose you have one machine that takes a year to make a copy of itself. Not ten seconds, not ten minutes, like the ones you used on that planet below. Let's just say a year. In two years you have two machines, in three years you have four. In a hundred years you have 1.26 times ten to the power of thirty of the things. That's ten billion billion machines for each planet in the Milky Way."

The numbers were making Herb feel dizzy. Johnston was almost shouting now.

"Its not even the first time something like this has happened. In the past few years I've helped destroy twenty would-be galactic empires."

Herb laughed weakly and spoke in a wobbly voice. "Twenty. Well, there you are. Well done, Robert."

Johnston calmed down. He took hold of Herb's hands and rubbed them gently between his own. He gazed at Herb with a gentle smile.

"You're frightened. Of course you are; who wouldn't be? Well, trust me. We'll beat it. Both of us."

"Both of us. Of course," Herb said. "And who else? How big is our army?"

Robert looked confused.

"Army? What army? There's just you and me."

"Just you and me," Herb repeated.

"Of course. What good would an army be? No matter how many people we raised, we'd still be hopelessly outnumbered."

"Of course." Herb began to laugh. "Of course. No problem. How silly of me. You and me versus an Enemy two hundred light years in diameter!" His laugh grew more strident. "And there I was thinking that this would be difficult. Well. That's okay, then."

Tears began to run down his cheeks.

Johnston tilted his head slightly. "Herb, I think you're becoming just a little bit hysterical."

That just made Herb laugh even louder.

Herb was making himself a cup of tea the long way. He set the water to boil over three minutes; he had a teapot ready, already filled with two spoonfuls of genuine organic leaves from his father's plantation. Doing it properly made a difference, no matter what people said. He saw Johnston emerge from the secret passageway and suppressed a smile. Robert ignored him. He was carrying a heavy object, something plastic and basically cuboid. One side was pearly grey glass. He staggered across to the coffee table and set it down as gently as he could. Herb watched him out of the corner of his eye until a deep red glow shone from the center of the water, signaling that it had boiled. He picked up the thermal jug and poured its contents into the teapot. Hot steam rose and he pushed his face into it, relishing the sensation as it condensed on his face.

Johnston had vanished back down the secret passageway. There had been a subtle shift in the balance of power, and they both knew it. As long as Herb could keep up the appearance of hysterical disbelief, he had Robert off balance. Now Herb was refusing to look at a viewing field unless forced to.

In response, Johnston had slipped back into his 1920s American mode. His suit was that little bit sharper, his accent that little bit harsher. He had to work harder to gain Herb's attention. But, as always, he had a plan.

Herb placed the lid on the teapot. He was now only four minutes away from the perfect cup of tea. Robert reemerged from the passageway, this time dragging a long flexible plastic cable. Herb watched in silence as Robert used a complicated looking connector to join it to a similar cable emerging from the plastic cuboid.

Herb experienced a sudden flash of recognition. "That's a television, isn't it? I've seen them in old information files."

"Gotcha!" Robert pressed a button on the machine and stepped back. There was a strange whistling noise at the edge of Herb's hearing. The grey glass panel at the side of the box lit up. Pictures began to move on it. Herb squinted to see them clearly.

"What's that?" he said.

"A piece of history. You're looking at one of the early colonization projects, one of the first wave initiated after the invention of the warp drive. Like most of the projects back then, this one was sponsored by a single corporation, in this case DIANA."

They were watching a large spaceship, seemingly stationary against the background of stars. It was all silver and gold curves, in the fashion of the time. Herb found it difficult to make out the overall shape of the ship, but he had to admit it had a certain pleasing quality to the eye, the way the matching curves swept out and back in, balancing each other.

"We're pretty certain that this particular colony ship was the source of the Enemy Domain."

"Pretty certain?" asked Herb.

"Nothing is ever a hundred percent," Johnston replied easily. "This ship was headed out in the right direction. The programming on the VNMs we've seen matches the development tensors of the original ayletts loaded on board this ship. We've even matched the genetic material of the hundred or so colonists on board with the half-grown clones on the planets throughout the Enemy Domain. We're pretty sure."

"Oh," Herb said. The picture had now zoomed in on a group of men and women boarding the craft. They didn't look that much older than he did. They were laughing and chatting as they pulled their way along the handholds lining the ship's corridor, and Herb realized that this was before the time of artificial gravity. They looked as if they were heading off for a day's picnic, not traveling halfway across the galaxy to set up a new home. He felt a queer shiver of fear in his stomach. These people had no idea that things were about to go so badly wrong for them.

"So what went wrong?" he asked.

"We don't know for sure," said Robert, "but we can guess. It was a common enough failing back then. The problem is there."

The television picture jumped to a processing space. A

room, not much smaller than Herb's lounge, filled with the oversized computing equipment of a hundred years ago. Shimmering arrays of memory foam and transparent arrays of qubit processors, all too big and laughably slow. Around the edges of the room there were even the silvery metal strands of electronic equipment, remnants of a technology now completely obsolete.

"Did that lot go wrong?" Herb asked.

"Not exactly. It functioned the way it was supposed to. The problem is, well . . . Do you know what was run in that processing space?"

"Everything, I should think," Herb said. "Ship control, astrogation, VNM blueprints, library . . ."

"You're right, but that's not the point. There was one AI in there. Just one. That's all the processing space was capable of supporting. It was the best available at the time, you should understand, but the point is, there was just one. The ship was built by a corporation, remember. It was simply too expensive to put in the equipment to support another AI."

The screen changed to show a view of the ship from space. It was receding this time. There was a flicker and then it vanished. Inserted into warp.

"Just one AI," repeated Robert. "An AI too big and too intelligent for the ship, so it was set to sleep until it arrived at the colony world, where it would be woken up and set to building. It would then release its VNMs, tailoring them to the environment it found itself in. It would make that planet safe for the colonists, and all the time, while its machines and buildings and sphere of influence were growing, it would itself be growing, becoming more intelligent as it rebuilt itself. You see, it's always the same when these systems go out of control. You have self-replicating machines reproducing unchecked and an AI that is growing up at the same time as them. The AI naturally thinks it's omnipotent. All children do when they're born. It's the limitations and disappointments of life that are imposed upon us that force us to grow up. The AI isn't experiencing those limitations. If a second AI had been there, as there always is now when we grow a new AI, well . . . With two AIs, the two intelligences would have to learn to negotiate and compromise with each other. Without that . . . you've seen the result."

Herb suddenly realized that his tea must be stewed by now. What a waste of good leaves. Robert had snared him, dragged him back into the mission. Something still didn't make sense, though.

"Okay, it's from Earth. So why is it trying to attack us?"

"It is in the nature of those who have never been told 'no' to think that the universe is there for their own benefit. Like I said, it's acting like a spoiled child."

Robert stared at him, and he shifted uncomfortably. Herb got the impression that Robert wasn't just talking about the Enemy Domain.

Robert continued. "Think about it. The AI has to protect its colonists from everything. It needs to expand to make them safe. Left unchecked it could fill the universe, but there, standing in its way is the Earth and its domain of influence. A great big 'NO!' hanging in the night. No wonder it hates us and wants to destroy us. It's like a toddler that has been told it must stay in its bedroom. No matter that all its toys are in there: the fact that it has been told 'no' is enough. It wants out."

Herb nodded. "I need some vanilla whisky."

"I don't think so. You're becoming dependent on that stuff. Have a nice cup of tea instead."

"It's stewed."

"Don't worry. I'll get it for you. Ship! Cup of tea for Herb, please."

Herb fiddled with the elastic waistband of his ship shorts. "I still don't see why it's worried. It could destroy us easily."

Johnston laughed. "I don't think so. We're cleverer than it is."

"Cleverer? How? Those ayletts it released will have reproduced time after time. The original AI must have redesigned itself over and over again, built new and more sophisticated containers for its intelligence. It's had far more resources than any Earth AI at its disposal. It must be *far* cleverer."

Robert picked up his hat and placed it on his head. A silver machine lay on the coffee table where the hat had sat. It looked like a Swiss army knife that had been opened up and then stripped of anything that wasn't a blade. It looked sharp, lean, and evil.

"Herb. I thought you were intelligent. If you thought about the problem, you'd realize how the Environment Agency could defeat the Enemy Domain. A greater intelligence will always defeat a lesser one. It can be done with this."

He pointed to the silver device that lay on the table.

"Victory is certain," he whispered, then sat back with a smile. "Well, pretty certain. Nothing is ever one hundred percent."

eva 3; 2051

The orange plastic chairs in the lounge had been roughly arranged in two rows in front of the viewing screen. Katie was sitting alone in the second row, watching the news, when Eva walked in carrying a book that Alison had lent her. Katie swiveled to see who had just entered, and a look of relief crossed her moon face when she saw that it was Eva. She flashed a quick, nervous smile and turned back to her program.

"Hello, Katie; what are you watching?"

Eva slid into the next but one chair, glancing at Katie's face in profile. It did look familiar, but she still couldn't place it.

Katie blushed and began to breathe quickly.

"It's the news," she said. She panted a little, then continued in a staccato burst of words. "They've just revealed something new. They say it will change the world."

Eva looked at the screen. It didn't seem very interesting: just an endless stream of scrolling symbols.

"What is it?" she asked.

Katie broke into a huge smile. "It's a mathematical expression that describes itself."

Eva nodded slowly. "I've heard about that. I thought it was supposed to be impossible."

"No. Why should it be? Your cells carry their own description written within themselves. It's how they make new cells."

Katie's voice had grown less staccato. She seemed livelier, more animated.

"Oh, of course." Eva looked thoughtful.

"They're saying that now they have cracked that problem, they're a step closer to building a human-scale Von Neumann Machine."

"A Von Neumann Machine?"

"Yes. A machine that can make copies of itself. Named after John Von Neumann, the man who postulated the idea."

Eva stared at the screen. She had read of the concept before, now she came to think about it. Back in her South Street days, back in the days of warm steamy rooms and yellow light and sitting on her own during the night reading about the rest of the world. Three weeks and another life ago. Katie was talking again.

"There's some controversy about the whole thing, actually. They're saying that Kay Lovegrove, the man who claims to have formulated the expression, couldn't possibly have done it."

"Ah. Professional jealousy?"

Katie looked confused for a moment. "No. I don't think so." She frowned for a moment. "No. The point is, they're saying he wasn't from the right field. He just wasn't studying the right areas to put together that expression. When questioned, he either refuses to, or cannot explain how the final answer came about. It's all very strange."

"Maybe he stole it."

"That's already been suggested, but no one else credible has come forward to claim the work as their own. Oh, there are plenty of cranks, but none of them can explain the expression's origin, any more than Lovegrove can. It's as if it just appeared on his computer overnight."

Katie's eyes were glowing. She was gripping each side of the plastic chair, making her look like a little girl. It was like the real Katie suddenly shining through from the tiny place where she had hidden herself, deep within her own body.

Eva spoke. "So do *you* think that Lovegrove formulated the expression, Katie?"

Katie smiled and shook her head. "No."

Eva said nothing. Katie's smile widened. She wanted to tell Eva everything, and in the middle of her shy, pinched little life, she had found the window to do so. She leaned a little closer and Eva smelled spearmint on her breath.

Katie spoke in a whisper. "It's too perfect. It's too tight. We've already built machines that reproduce. The factory robots they landed on Mars make copies of themselves, but they need millions of lines of code to achieve the result. This sums up the essential idea in a few thousand bits. It's too neat. It can't have come from a human's mind."

She lowered her voice a little. "You know, it wouldn't be the first time that society had been given a little prod in the right direction."

Eva leaned a little closer. "What do you mean?"

Katie shook her head. She nodded toward the window, out toward the mist-dissolved circle of limes and beyond them the woods.

"She's talking about the Watcher," said the voice.

I know.

Katie looked thoughtful. "Did you just hear the voice?" she asked.

"Yes," replied Eva. She felt a little shocked. "How did you know?"

"Your body seemed to relax. Now that's interesting."

"What's interesting?"

Alison had just walked into the room. Katie retreated back inside herself instantly. She gazed down at her fingers, twisting and turning around themselves in her lap.

"Hello, Alison. Where have you been?" asked Eva.

Alison looked a mess. Her eyes were ringed with dark shadows; her hair was lank and lifeless. She wore a grey hairy sweater over her tartan flannel pajamas, the corner of a white tissue poking from one sleeve. She shambled across to one of the padded chairs and slumped into it.

"Sleeping. What else is there to do?"

Eva looked at Katie, but Katie was concentrating again on the program on the viewing screen. Pictures of sheep being funneled through a gap in a hedge were replaced by a shower of chocolate buttons falling into a pool of chocolate. The image flicked to a cartoon group of eight mice eating rice from little bowls.

"We were just watching a program about an expression that defines itself, weren't we, Katie?" said Eva brightly.

"Have you seen Nicolas? Do you know where he is?" asked Alison, deliberately changing the subject.

"I don't know. Maybe he's in his room."

"I hope so. I'm not in the mood to be stared at."

Eva said nothing. Alison brought her knees up underneath her chin and wrapped her arms tightly around her legs.

"Doesn't he creep you out? The way he's constantly staring at your tits?"

"I thought he was your friend."

"You don't have any friends in this place, Eva. Remember that."

"Ignore her. She's always like this when she's down." Katie's words came in a flurry, her eyes still fixed firmly on the screen.

Eva turned to get a better view of Alison, twisting on one leg of the chair, feeling it flex beneath her weight as she turned.

"Would you like a hot drink, Alison?"

"No. And don't change the subject. You're not telling me that you don't find it offensive, the way Nicolas stares at your tits?"

"I don't like it, no. But then again, he's not in this place because he's normal, is he? Nor are we. Let's show him some tolerance. It never seemed to bother you that much before."

"It didn't," said Katie. "Ignore her."

"Shut up Katie. I wasn't speaking to you. Watch your bloody program."

Eva looked on, aghast. Yesterday they had been plotting together, brothers in arms, today... From the adjoining chair, Alison picked up a paperback someone had apparently dropped in a bath. It was swollen to twice its normal size, the pages curling up and around themselves. She flicked through it for a moment or two, before crossly hurling it to the floor.

"Bloody Nicolas!" she shouted, then turned to glare at Eva. "Do you know why he's in here?"

Eva shook her head. Alison's mood swings were disconcerting.

"I don't know why. He seems lacking in confidence."

"Too bloody true. I'll tell you what, one good fuck would sort him out. I'll tell you what else, I'm *not* going to be the one to provide it."

She glared across the room. "What about you, Katie? Would you do it? That would put a smile on both of your faces, wouldn't it?"

"This conversation diminishes us all, Alison. Please go back to your room until you're feeling better."

Eva and Alison stared in shock at Katie's response, but she remained glued to the screen.

Alison breathed in deeply, trying to regain her composure. "I was talking about Nicolas. He's got a massive inferiority complex. He also thinks he's the most important person in here. In the world."

"That sounds like a contradiction," Eva said hesitantly. She wasn't sure if she wanted to speak to Alison when she was behaving like this.

Alison gave a bitter laugh. "You'd think so, wouldn't you? It's a classic pattern for loonies. Most of the people in here are the same. You certainly are."

Eva kept silent.

"Look at you with your delusions of grandeur, the way you believe you should have got that promotion, and yet you also think that you're stupid and of no consequence. You've got no friends, and yet you know you deserve lots—"

"Alison." Katie spoke again without looking up from the screen. Alison paused, brushed lank hair away from her eyes, but then continued.

"Nicolas. He told me something once, about how he started a pension when he began work. Doesn't that tell you something about the man? What sort of twenty-year-old is bothered about a pension?" She laughed again. "Anyway, he got back the details telling him what he could expect when he retired. Gave him his projected earnings based on the job they thought he'd be doing then, taking into account his intelligence and personality quotient and so on. He wasn't happy. He thought he'd be doing far better."

Eva nodded. "I can see that being upsetting. Nobody likes to be told they are a loser, especially at that age."

"That's not all. It wasn't a huge step from there to finding his life expectancy. You know what it was? Sixty-eight. You know what that means?"

Eva was uncomfortable on the hard plastic chair. She got up and and sat down next to Alison, accidentally knocking over a half-full cup of coffee someone had abandoned by the leg of the chair. Eva swore as brown liquid splashed across the vinyl floor.

"Leave it," said Alison. "Listen. Nicolas was told that he would die at sixty-eight. Well below the average. That means low social class." She gave a bitter laugh. "It will be even lower now. Knock another ten years off for being in here."

Eva waved dismissively.

"So what? It's only an average. It's not a prediction."

"It's still a judgment. And a pretty accurate one nowadays. It changes day by day. Hour by hour. Minute by minute. Haven't you ever called up your details on a screen? Watched those numbers after the decimal point whizz up and down? Picked up a gin and tonic and watched your life expectancy drop by a few seconds? Hah!"

She smiled entirely without humor.

"You know what, Nicolas is addicted to that stuff. He got his family tree from the Mormons' database. Ran a simulated medical history on it back two hundred years. He figured out the likelihood of him dying of everything from AIDS to Huntington's chorea. How about that for a pleasant way to spend the evening? Watch him at three o'clock in the afternoon. That's a laugh."

She shook her head and smiled.

"It's all there, mapped, mirrored, and striped by databanks the world over. Everything about you, and me, and Nicolas. They know us better than we know ourselves. They send us ads for products we didn't even know existed. The drinking water tastes funny one day and two years later you find out by chance that you'd been dosed with the cure for an incipient embolism you had no idea ever existed."

"Yeah?" Eva laughed bitterly. "Tell me about it. You know how I got here."

Alison sighed angrily. "No, you still don't get it. We talk about Social Care and we think of them watching our every move. And then we think about the Watcher, and we think that it's like Social Care except more so, but that's wrong. We fall into the trap of thinking that it's simply something that watches us get undressed before we get in the bath, or listens in when you call your mother, but it's worse than that. It's looking right inside you. It sees every heartbeat, it knows your every thought; it knows you better than you know yourself."

Her pupils dilated as she spoke. It was as if a tap had been turned in her heart, and all the feelings and emotions were flooding slowly upward, gurgling and lapping up inside her body to fill her up to the brim.

"No wonder poor Nicolas is the way he is," she said

softly. "He only has to look at a girl and he knows that the Watcher is there, analyzing his every thought and guilty emotion. He's a twenty-seven-year-old man with a thirteen-year-old boy inside him who has never had the chance to grow up."

Katie had flicked the viewing screen off. She moved up silently behind the pair of them.

"We shouldn't be talking about this in here," Katie said suddenly in Eva's ear.

"Ah, who cares, Katie? This room is pretty secure; they don't monitor the Center like they do outside. Anyway, the plan probably hasn't got that much chance of working, has it? Not when the Watcher can read our every thought."

"No, it can't," stuttered Katie. She paused a moment, then, "Anyway, the plan will work."

"If you say so," Alison said. She stood up quickly. "I'm going back to my room." She stalked away.

Katie glanced at Eva, then ran after her friend. Eva was left alone in the lounge. The grey mist outside turned to gentle rain and Eva stared out at the blurred green limes.

"Look over in the corner, Eva," said the voice. "Look over behind the viewing screen."

"Hello again, voice," said Eva. "What do you want now?"

"I told you. Look behind the viewing screen. Didn't you notice it when you came in?"

Eva got up and walked across the room, the plastic soles of her sneakers sticky against the vinyl floor. Behind the viewing screen was an old intercom. A small white rectangular box with a grille facing. Two grubby white wires trailed down the wall to vanish into the floor.

"It heard you," said the voice. "It could hear you speaking."

"It's just an old box, left over from when they first built this place. It isn't connected to anything."

"How do you know? If I were the Watcher, I would be listening to all the old equipment. My ears would be pressed to every forgotten intercom, every CCTV camera, every pneumatic tube."

"Every pneumatic tube? You're making this up as you go along."

"And you are arguing with me now. You're not trying to pretend that I don't exist anymore. Eva, be careful. You're not escaping; you're being led into a trap. The Watcher is cleverer than you. Cleverer than both of us."

There was a huge rattle outside the room. The skies had finally opened fully and were emptying their load in vast grey sheets of rain that splashed and sluiced down the glass. Eva looked out of the window onto nothing but shades of grey. A gust of wind sent a grey wave bursting across the panes.

"Who are you?" she called above the noise of the rain. "How do you know all this? How are we going to be trapped?"

Her shouting alerted Peter, one of the orderlies, who appeared in the doorway to the lounge wearing a gentle smile. He relaxed a little when he saw who it was.

"Easy now, Eva. What's the matter?" he said in his surprisingly soft voice.

Eva suddenly realized she had been shouting. She looked down at the floor, flustered and embarrassed.

"It's okay," she said. "I was just . . . just . . ."

"This place isn't a trap," soothed Peter. "You know we're only here to help you?"

"I know. But I wasn't . . ."

He put his hand on her arm and led her back to her own room. "Come on. Why don't you lie down for a while?"

Eva lay on her bed gazing at the ceiling. The rain had lost some of its earlier violence, but it still poured down in a steady stream that streaked and blurred the view from her window. She wondered if it rained harder out here in the middle of the countryside than it used to in the city. She remembered South Street rain as being either a tired and miserable mist, or huge fat drops that left sooty, greasy stains where they fell. There was none of this cold violence, this clear division between the inside and the outside. Eva had never felt so isolated in all her life, trapped in the cocoon of the Center, floating away on a grey sea, the rest of the world left far behind. *But isn't that what I wanted?* she thought. *Isn't that what I aimed for?*

There was a knock on the door.

"Come in," called Eva, but the door was already being pushed open. Alison walked in, closely followed by Nicolas. Eva could see Katie hovering in the background.

"I've come to say I'm sorry," said Alison.

"What for?" asked Eva.

"Being so silly earlier on. I nearly blew the plan. I shouldn't have spoken about it in the lounge."

"That's okay," said Eva. She hesitated for a moment and then said, "Should you be talking about it in here?"

Nicolas gave a grin. "Safest place, probably. They wouldn't dare tap our rooms unless they could prove it to be in our best interests, and then they'd have to let us know. They could be sued for malpractice."

Eva sat up on her bed to make space for the others.

Alison sat down next to her. "Go and get yourself a seat from the lounge, Nicolas," Alison said.

"Okay." He walked happily from the room to fetch the chair.

"Don't you want to sit down, Katie?" invited Eva.

"Katie will stay standing," said Alison. She had washed her hair since that morning and changed into a pair of jeans and a cotton top. She stared at Eva. "I'm not being mean or bossy. I just know that Katie would prefer to stay standing, wouldn't you, Katie?"

Katie nodded. She reached into a pocket of her jacket, pulled out a bottle, and handed it to Alison.

"We bought this in the village last week. Vanilla whisky. Some new thing they're trying to put on the market. Alcoholic and incredibly sweet. I can't imagine it ever taking off. Still, it makes you feel nice and warm, and there's nothing else to do on a wet afternoon like this except drink and tell stories."

Nicolas carried a chair from the lounge into the room, knocking it on the doorframe as he did so. He placed it in the middle of the room and sat down on it. Katie went to the window and looked out. Alison unscrewed the top of the bottle and looked around her.

"Cups," she said.

"Here," said Eva. There was a stack of disposable cups by her bed. She shook them apart and handed them out.

Alison poured them each a measure of vanilla whisky. The clear liquid smelled sickly sweet, and seemed to want to stay stuck to the plastic sides of the cup. The four conspirators looked around at each other. Alison wriggled back on the bed so that she leaned against the wall, her bottom on Eva's pillow, her feet stretched out across the duvet. Nicolas sat in his chair in the middle of the room, sipping at his whisky, grinning at the two women on the bed and thinking heaven knows what. Katie lurked by the doorway—keeping watch, Eva realized.

Alison spoke first. "We're escaping first thing tomorrow."

"How?" Eva asked. "Where are we going?"

"We don't know. We'll toss coins to decide. It's the only way we can be sure that we're not being second-guessed by the Watcher."

"You must have *some* plan."

"Several excellent ones. All so perfect they can't be ours. So we're going to extemporize." Alison smiled.

"Extemporize?"

"Make it up as we go along." Alison wriggled again suddenly and messed up the duvet. She kicked her tiny feet up and down on the bed.

"Oh, I feel so much better than this morning. It's amazing what a hot bath can do." She flashed Nicolas a dirty look. "Or a shower, eh, Nicolas?"

"Oh yes," said Nicolas. He looked at his feet, confused.

"Have you ever thought about what it must be like for the Watcher?" Alison said, glancing at Nicolas with a suppressed smile. "It can access all that information. It knows everything, and yet it's impotent. What can it do?" She wriggled a little more on the bed, shifting her breasts beneath her cotton top. Eva noticed how closely Nicolas watched them.

"She does it deliberately, doesn't she?" said the voice. "That's how she keeps him following her around, like a pet."

"I thought that was obvious," Eva muttered.

"She's doing it again," said Katie from her position by the door. "Did you see her, how she relaxed and went all blank?"

"I did, Katie," said Alison. She gazed at Eva. "You just heard the voice, didn't you?"

"Yes," Eva said uncomfortably.

"What did it say?"

Eva hesitated a moment.

"It thought you were right about the Watcher," she lied.

"Too true," said Alison. "Katie thinks it's evolved in all those databases, all those computer networks and so on. It has become aware. Now it wants to stretch its wings, it wants to do things. But how? It's far more intelligent than we are. It must be; it knows far more than we do. What if our machines and our senses are no longer enough for it? What is it going to do if it wants more powerful eyes and arms?"

"Build its own, I suppose," replied Eva. "Oh. That thing on the news earlier today..."

"A mathematical expression that describes itself," Katie said from the doorway.

Alison interrupted her. "And no one knows for sure where it came from. It just turned up on a computer."

"Maybe that man; what was his name...?"

"Kay Lovegrove," Katie said.

"Isn't it possible that Kay Lovegrove wrote it?"

"It was the Watcher," said Nicolas. "It's beginning to shape the world into a fashion that suits itself. What does that tell you about us? About humans? What is it going to do to us?"

Alison stared at him. Outside the rain rattled against the windows and Eva stared out at the limes. She heard the voice.

"He's right. What is the Watcher going to do to you? It's watching you at the moment, you know. It can see you."

"Eva! Speak to us, Eva!"

Suddenly, Alison was kneeling in front of the bed, gazing up at her. Eva didn't remember her moving there.

"What's the matter?" asked Eva, confused.

"I thought you were going to black out that time. What did it say?"

"It said the Watcher was looking at us now. It said it could see us."

Katie was jumping up and down by the doorway. She seemed very excited.

"What is it, Katie?" Nicolas called.

Katie was having trouble speaking. Nicolas moved up beside her and put one hand on her arm. "Deep breaths, Katie. Deep breaths."

"I think I understand!" Katie gasped. "Eva. Get off the bed. Go and stand over there."

Katie was fighting for breath, such was her excitement. She pointed toward the opposite corner of the room.

Eva looked at Alison.

"Do it," she said. Hesitantly, Eva obeyed. She moved across to the space by the tiny desk. Two magazines, bought for her at the village by one of the helpers, sat by her elbow. She looked at their glossy covers, embarrassed and confused.

"Ask the voice to speak," said Katie, excitedly.

Eva nodded and coughed a little.

"Er, hello? Are you there?" she said. Nothing.

"I can't hear anything," she said.

"I know. We can tell," said Alison.

"Now move back to the bed," said Katie. Eva walked back to the bed.

"Look out the window."

The voice spoke. "Katie has worked it out. I think I understand myself, now. I never knew before."

Eva turned pale. She spun slowly around to face the room. The other three looked eagerly at her. "It says Katie has worked it out," she said.

Alison and Nicolas looked at Katie. She gave a huge beam and spoke. "It's the limes. She hears the voice every time she looks at the limes."

Eva was shivering with fear. Alison and Nicolas jumped up from the bed and went to look through the window.

"It's difficult to see anything through this rain," said Nicolas. "One gust and they vanish again."

"Why can't we hear anything?" Alison asked.

"I don't know," Katie said.

"What is it then?" asked Nicolas.

"I don't know that, either." Katie was losing her shyness again, Eva noticed, now that she had something to concentrate on.

"Why don't you ask the voice?" Alison interjected.

"Oh yes, that's a good idea." Katie and Nicolas turned to gaze at Eva. She shivered again.

"I don't want to," she said. "It frightens me."

"Don't be so silly. Turn and face the window."

Katie was so uncharacteristically brusque, it took Eva quite aback. Hesitantly, she obeyed. She turned and looked out of the window.

"Who are you? Are you the Watcher?" she asked.

"No. I'm . . . I think I'm . . . I think I was your brother."

"My brother?"

Katie began hugging herself with delight.

"Yes! I should have guessed. I've read about this. It's your addiction. It's the MTPH! You're having flashbacks!"

"Flashbacks? No. It's not my brother. He didn't sound like that. Anyway, he would know me..."

Alison was impatient. "Why? You're not taking the drug anymore, are you? It isn't constantly regenerating the personality in your mind. But that doesn't mean that you haven't worn the habit of him into the paths of your brain."

"Permanently altered the chemistry," Katie interrupted.

"Whatever. Something in the sight of the limes out there is reminding you of him. Now what could it be?"

"I watched the limes as I waited for him to die," Eva said softly. She felt strangely calm. She ought to be upset, but there was nothing.

"It's your brother's ghost," said Nicolas.

"Oh, Nicolas. Have some tact!"

"No," said the voice. "He's right. Ghost is a good description. I'm not the man I used to be."

Katie was grinning. "This is excellent. This is better than we could have hoped for."

Eva turned to her in disgust. "Why?"

"Because this is something that the Watcher can't measure. It may even be something that the Watcher doesn't even know about. This can only aid us."

Eva lost her temper. "No. I'm fed up with this. I've heard enough. I'm not playing along anymore. There is no Watcher, and if there were, there would be no way of escaping it. How would we do that? Four poor loonies, all trapped in a mental hospital in Wales, without a penny to their names."

Her voice faltered as she saw Nicolas and Alison begin to smile at her.

"What? What's the matter?"

Nicolas was looking at Alison and smiling, waiting for her to tell Eva the big joke.

"Speak to me. What's the matter?" said Eva. She was becoming angrier. Katie was blushing with embarrassment. She seemed to be retreating back inside herself, the real Katie withdrawing from the room and leaving nothing but the body behind.

"Tell me what you're laughing at!" demanded Eva.

Alison spoke first. She pointed at her friend.

"You don't recognize her, do you? You don't know who she is! That's Katie Kirkham!"

"Katie Kirkham?" said Eva weakly. "It can't be."

But it was. No wonder Eva had thought she recognized her. No wonder they were laughing at her.

"Katie Kirkham." Nicolas laughed. "The Poor Little Rich Girl."

Katie Kirkham's mother had written the Console Operating System. Practically every mobile phone in the world now used it. She had made her fortune by giving it away for free. All those useful functions: from health monitoring and global positioning, down to the address book and calculator, were available to users for nothing. The only charge she made was a fraction of a credit for interfacing the phone to the COSnet, a charge that was minuscule compared to the cost of the call itself. Virtually nothing. It was a good deal for everyone. Good for the customers, who got the COS for nothing, good for the telecom companies, who were saved the expense of development, and good for Henrietta Kirkham, who just sat back and waited for all those fractions of a credit to come rolling in.

Eva had seen Henrietta Kirkham many times on the viewing screen in the past. That was how she had recognized Katie. Katie had her mother's features, but twisted and exaggerated. Henrietta was an attractive woman, in an unusual sort of way. DeForest had thought so; Eva had teased him about it.

"So you fancy her more than me?" she would press, watching DeForest twist uncomfortably on the sofa. But Henrietta was attractive; she had a calm poise and confidence that stood her in good stead when interviewed. You didn't become one of the richest and most powerful people in the world and expect people not to feel jealous. And yet, with her tiny, delicate frame, her shy smile, and her little-girl-lost eyes, people were almost sympathetic to her. Almost. Nobody could feel real sympathy for the woman who had it all.

Then there was poor Katie: the manufactured child. Henrietta was supposed to have written an algorithm that scoured the world's sperm banks looking for the perfect genetic material that would match her own and produce the perfect child. And if anyone had told her that there were too many variables to be sure of the result, she had ignored them just as surely as she ignored the messages she got from the fanatics telling her that she was meddling with forces she didn't understand.

Henrietta had been determined to have a child that inherited all her best features, and that child was Katie. And Katie had indeed inherited all her mother's best features, but exaggerated and magnified to the point of the grotesque. She was more intelligent than her mother, but also more obsessive, more nervous, more shy. Her mother's natural caution had been replaced by paranoia, her analytic nature by something that divided the world into pieces so small that its soul was lost on the way.

Even her physical body was an exaggeration: she was thinner, her eyes smaller, her skin paler.

As Katie had grown up, the media had followed her, revealing each new character flaw to the world, and the child who had once been the golden girl, the symbol of the new technological age, had become a symbol of the perils of meddling with nature.

Then, one day, Katie had disappeared from public view, as only the very rich or very poor can manage. Henrietta had faded back into the foreground, drawing the camera onto herself and her latest ventures and very firmly away from her daughter.

No one discussed Katie now, only the occasional story of doubtful provenance leaking into the news of how she had gone mad, or back into therapy, or how her twisted genius had invented a box and they had put a cat inside it and then opened it up and the cat was gone and then they closed it again and when they re-opened it the cat had come back but it was dead, twisted inside out . . .

Katie had become a legend in her own lifetime. A poor little rich girl who allowed the real poor and unfortunate to draw a little comfort from their sad, lonely lives.

And now, here she was, standing face-to-face with Eva. A slightly shabby, smaller-than-life woman in a rain-washed mental hospital, trapped in the middle of a grey Sunday afternoon.

Alison shrugged at Eva.

"I know. It's the last place you'd expect to find her. But that's sort of the point, isn't it?"

• • • •

Outside the window, the rain had finally stopped. The room was still dull and grey, the outside world sodden and empty. They sat in silence for some time, saying nothing. Eventually it was Alison who spoke.

"You're the last piece, Eva. The Watcher may have sent you, but we could spend the rest of our lives turning down opportunities on that basis. You complement us; you give us the chance to do the unexpected. We're going to move fast and try to second-guess the Watcher. We leave tomorrow, four o'clock in the morning. That's when people are at their lowest ebb. We will walk out of the gate and then toss a coin to see which way to go. Heads we go left, tails right. We have supplies from Katie: stealth phones and untraceable credit. The sort of thing that only the army is capable of getting hold of."

"Or the Watcher. Be careful, Eva, something doesn't seem right here."

Alison looked hard at Eva as the voice spoke.

"What did it say?" she asked.

"Say nothing," said the voice. "I don't like this. You're going to leave me behind. I'm trapped in these limes. The moment you've found me, you're walking away."

Eva looked around the room in confusion. "You're saying I should stay?" she whispered.

Alison reached out and took hold of her hand. "What's the matter, Eva? Are you all right?"

Eva nodded dumbly. She was waiting for her brother's answer. The one person she could really trust.

He spoke slowly, haltingly. "No...No. I think you should go with them. Yes. They're right. I'm an unexpected ally. It may help fool the Watcher. But Eva, be careful. There is something not right here. I can't see it."

Alison could hear none of this; she was speaking quickly, eagerly.

"Are you sure, Eva? Will you be ready tonight? We can't afford to delay. We've waited too long already. The Watcher may already be suspicious."

"We could wait," Nicolas said uncertainly.

"No. It's okay. I'm ready," said Eva. "You're right. We can't delay."

"Think of me," said the voice.

"I am. I will. Maybe I don't actually need to see the trees now I know you're there."

She looked up at Katie.

"What do you think, Katie?" she asked.

Katie had been watching her; she knew what she was thinking, why she had said what she just said. She looked thoughtful for a moment, then nodded. "I don't know," she said. "It might work."

Alison nodded vigorously. "Yes. It might work. We have to take the chance. We can't remain here for much longer. Are you with us, Eva?"

Eva looked around to them all in turn and slowly nodded her head.

"Yes," she said. "I'm with you. We leave tonight."

Three o'clock in the morning and Constantine lay awake in bed, one of the night's forgotten insomniacs. Red, Blue, and White were sleeping; Grey had lapsed into its habitual silence, ignoring any of Constantine's attempts to question it about what had happened the day before.

Constantine was trying to see through the haze that surrounded his memories of the meeting. Grey had done something in order to prevent him revealing... what? The memories were second-hand: a little giftwrapped parcel waiting for him to open once Grey had handed control of the body back over to him. Had they set the project in motion? He couldn't remember. He could still see the vague shape of the meeting room, but as if it were encased in thick ice. Blurred shapes moved within, but he could not see what they were doing or hear what they said.

He could vaguely recall the end of the meeting, of being marched into the elevator that rode up through the deadly red sea of VNMs and out onto the duckboards.

The memories gained more detail at this point, as if the ice was melting. He remembered how it had felt to stand in the hot sun for what seemed an eternity until he saw the faint speck of the approaching flier on the horizon, the definition of his memories increasing as he regained control of his life. Only when the flier dipped down to hover by him had Grey finally let go. Constantine's life came back into sharp focus as he settled himself into the air-conditioned compartment of the flier, a cool glass of water awaiting him. Red, Blue, and White were clamoring for his attention.

It was Red who took control. —For Heaven's sake, act naturally. The Grey personality must be some sort of failsafe system. We've always suspected as much.

Blue was incensed. —It took over control of the body. That's impossible!

—Obviously not impossible, replied Red. —Now keep quiet.

Constantine had ignored them. He was too shaken by his recent possession. He felt both dizzy and incredibly tired. He fell asleep listening to the bickering of the other personalities.

Now that he wanted their company, they were sleeping. He sighed, rolled out of bed, and went to inspect the minibar.

The only whisky available was the flavored stuff they sold to teenagers. He selected a can of cola instead, popped the seal and, the container chilling in his hand, began to stroll around the room. The carpet felt soft beneath his feet, the air was hotel temperature. It was a cliché: Constantine had spent two years now traveling the world, staying in what might as well have been the same hotel room. It all added to the artificiality of his situation. He needed to step out of this stereotypical room and touch the real world, but what was the real world to someone like Constantine? To so many people alive at the start of the twenty-second century, the real world was a commodity like any other, sold shrink-wrapped, dated, and best beforen. Whether it was freshly baked bread, imitation grit of the millstone baked inside it, or a weekend in a country house with a trout river running through the grounds, the real world had to have authenticity added before it could be sold. Constantine often suspected that the truth was that the real world in fact consisted of hotel rooms just like this one, and that everything else was just a 24-bit imitation of its former self.

He signaled for the window leading out onto the balcony to open. The floor-length vertical blinds parted for him, and he stepped out into the cold night. He shivered, wondering for a moment if he should go back inside to pull on a robe but rejected the idea. The cold night air felt real. He gripped the plasticized metal handrail and looked out over the city cascading down beneath him in a series of wide terraces, its lights strings of illuminated pearls criss-crossing the dark streets and buildings. Constantine's thin body glowed palely in the moonlight. Looking down, his large stomach, overhanging his spindly legs, was glowing like a pale moon itself. He used to take time to keep himself in shape, but over the past five years the pressure of work had become too much. Blue veins shone along his white legs, the sparse hairs that had grown on his upper body through his teens and twenties had been joined over the past few years by a forest of others sprouting from his nipples or covering his sunken chest. Constantine began to laugh at the absurdity of the situation. He had stepped out here to try to regain his grip on reality. What could be more real than his joke of a body as it approached middle age? The laughter died on his lips as he looked out into the night.

A skyscraper was spinning across the sleeping city toward him.

He stared in disbelief.

It was coming closer: the tower he had seen yesterday morning, just before boarding the flier. The tower with no base, a long, thin needle formed of a structure with art deco steel walls twisting around rose-petal windows, spinning slowly on its axis as it moved toward him. It cast no shadow on the silent city below, Constantine noticed, watching as it passed over a cluster of lights at the heart of the second level. A late-night party. Could they see it? Would they believe their drunken eyes if they did?

It didn't exist. That was the most likely answer. Constantine had finally cracked. A tiny orange flier skimming down from the center to the first level passed the tower without pause. That confirmed it: he must be imagining it.

He wished his sleeping personalities would wake up.

The tower's spin seemed to be slowing as it approached him. Now Constantine could see inside, actually look through the windows of the mirage. It was a hotel: that seemed obvious. He could see bedrooms, beds covered with white linen, some of them holding sleeping guests. The tower was now only thirty meters away. It loomed up into the night above him, blocking the half moon. Below the tower he could quite clearly see the streets of the second level.

The tower's rotation had slowed to a crawl. Something was sliding into view around the steel and rose curve of the walls. A balcony. On it stood a figure. It was looking straight at Constantine as it slowly rotated to meet him.

Twenty meters away, ten meters. Five, four, three, two...

The tower glided smoothly to a halt bringing the figure face-to-face with Constantine.

It was Jay Apple.

"Good morning, Constantine," she said.

"Good morning. Have I gone mad?"

Jay just shrugged.

"Not yet," she replied. "I've come to give you a warning. You are not currently standing on the balcony of a hotel in Stonebreak, as you may have been led to believe. In fact, you are a personality construct, running on a computer located in Germany. Your mindset has been captured by a rival corporation. They are running it in a simulation of the real world in the hope that you will reveal the details of the Mars project."

Constantine frowned. He gazed at Jay's pale hand on the balcony rail. He could see the short white nails, the tiny scratch on the first joint of the forefinger of her left hand. He looked at the balcony rail itself, noting how it was formed of intertwining strips of metal in shades of grey that curled off to form leaves and stylized representations of flowers. One of the leaves had been caught by something and bent out of shape.

It all seemed so real, so convincing. If it weren't for the fact that the building itself was floating several hundred meters above the ground, he wouldn't have believed Jay's words.

"When did this happen?"

Jay shrugged again.

"We don't know. We are hoping to figure it out with your help. Have you noticed anything odd recently?"

Constantine gave a bitter laugh. "I've been seeing gaps beneath the sky. I see holes in alleyways and office blocks full of people staring at each other. Strangers introduce themselves to me and take me for midnight walks through the city. People seem to freeze in mid action while a second body around them carries on moving. Now I am speaking to a young woman standing on the balcony of a floating building. Yes. I guess you could say that things have been odd recently."

He shook his head and tilted his head in thought.

"Okay. Things really started acting odd about three weeks ago. Do you think that's when they got me?"

"Possibly. It's something to work on."

Constantine suddenly felt very cold. He remembered that he was naked in the middle of the freezing night.

"Can we go back inside?" he asked.

"No!" Jay held out her hand. "Stay close to me. They don't know I'm here. We can only speak safely if you're close to this balcony."

Constantine was suddenly suspicious. "How? That's a good point. If I'm a computer simulation, how can you speak to me at all? Surely they will *know* you're here. Why should I listen to what you say?"

Jay rolled her eyes in frustration. "Listen, get this into your head. I'm the only person in here who's on your side. Now, I've got a message for one of your personalities. Are they listening?"

"They're asleep."

—I'm awake, said White.

Constantine made no response. White never really slept. Savant personalities were a little different, he knew. Maybe it would do him good to keep this a secret for the moment.

"What about Grey? Is he there?" asked Jay.

"I see you've been fully briefed. In that case, you'll realize that I never know *anything* about what Grey is up to."

"Fine. Listen, this is a message from the real Constantine. I saw him just a few hours ago before I got in here. He said 'GHX LPN SSD SAS EFF LKF.' "

—Probably an authentication code, said White.

"What? Can I have that again?"

"No need. Grey will have picked it up. It'll vouch for my credentials."

Constantine paused, but Grey maintained its habitual silence. Constantine tentatively took this to be a positive sign and withheld further judgment for the moment.

"So, how did you get in here, then? How come you haven't been detected?"

Jay gave a little smile and looked down at her feet. She wriggled her tanned brown toes on the cool marble of the balcony and then allowed her gaze to travel up the long dark side of the tower above her. She finally spoke.

"The program that runs this simulation is full of bugs. Not surprising when we're talking about something so complex. All programs contain memory leaks: objects get created but not destroyed. Like when you get a bit of a picture left behind on a computer display after you move things around?"

Constantine nodded. "I know what you mean."

"Good," said Jay. "That's why you sometimes see two of things, or why the scenery doesn't always hang together like it should."

She jerked her head in the direction of the tower behind her.

"This is an object that didn't get destroyed. The program doesn't even know it's here. There are no pointers to it; only termination of the program itself will lead to its resources being returned to the heap. A DIANA tempest device managed to locate the object and then effect a transference of my personality construct into it. Basically, this is my little island of friendly consciousness in a sea of hostility."

"Oh," Constantine said. He had temporarily forgotten the cold. Jay's words washed over him. Something she had mentioned earlier was just beginning to sink into his awareness. He licked his lips and whispered hoarsely.

"Something you said. You said the real Constantine passed on a message to give to me."

Jay said nothing. She simply fixed her dark gaze on Constantine and waited for him to work it out for himself.

Constantine looked back at her. She was very thin, he suddenly realized. Big, dark eyes with a slightly desperate "love me" expression. Maybe the cool, irreverent talk he had heard yesterday in the meeting was just an act. Or maybe the computer simulation hadn't got her quite right. He was evading the subject at hand and knew it. If what Jay had told him was true, he wasn't the real Constantine. The real Constantine was out there somewhere, sleeping in the real Stonebreak, visiting the real DIANA Arcology. What had happened at the real meeting yesterday? Had they discussed the project there? Maybe even come to some conclusion?

Would he see his wife again?

"What's going to happen to me?"

Jay shook her head slowly. "We don't know. We're working on a way to get you out of here, but it will take time. The best thing you can do, to be honest, is to act normally. The resources required to generate this virtual world are significant. If they think that you've caught on, well..."

Constantine was suddenly incredibly cold again.

"I need to go inside," he said.

"It's probably just as well that you do. If we stay talking too long, it will arouse suspicion."

"Aren't they suspicious at the moment? Can't they see me?"

"Not when you're within range of this tower. There is a ghost signal emanating from here, making it look as if you're just standing on the balcony."

"I don't really understand any of that. Are you coming back?"

"I will."

Constantine nodded again. Something suddenly occurred to him. "You're just as much a prisoner in here as I am, aren't you?"

"I'll see you when I can," Jay said.

The tower was already slowly spinning, taking her back out of his virtual life. Constantine gazed after her, lost and alone.

He awoke to find a yellow stripe of sunlight streaking his body, looking like an exclamation mark. His room was fresh and clean and smelled of hot coffee and freshly baked croissants. He felt surprisingly healthy and positive, ready to take on anything. That was when the memory of the previous night settled upon him. Blue was already awake.

—Fresh coffee? Good idea.

Constantine rolled out of bed and began to pour coffee into a curiously shaped cup.

"Where were you last night?" he muttered.

—Sleeping, said Red.

—White has filled us in with all the details, said Blue.

Constantine sipped his coffee. It was a little too bitter this morning, the grounds seeming to settle on his tongue. If this was a computer simulation, it was an extremely good one. The attention to detail was incredible.

Red spoke up.

—We don't think it would be a good idea for you to speak to us about last night. If what Jay said was true, they'll be able to monitor you subvocalizing. You can't afford to let them know you suspect. If you agree with us, scratch your leg.

"Spare me your spy games, Red. It's too early."

There was a pause. Constantine took a croissant and started to butter it. He knew that Red would be examining his last sentence to see if he had given anything away.

—Okay, said Red. —Maybe we are being too mysterious, but we can't afford to take any chances.

"Do you think it's true?" asked Constantine.

—Will you stop it? Okay. We think it is. Grey is saying nothing, as usual. We are assuming that he is hovering around in the background somewhere. White keeps announcing the authentication code, just in case he didn't hear it. We're guessing that if there were something wrong, he'd say so. As he hasn't, we'll carry on as normal.

—It does seem the safest course of action, said Blue. All we have to do is keep quiet about the final destination of the Martian construction. That's what we've been doing so far anyway. If Jay had suggested we do anything counter to our normal course of action, then we would have had to discuss things further. As it is, we'll just carry on as we were.

Constantine nodded and took a bite of the croissant. It tasted delicious.

"Okay. I agree. What are we doing this morning?"

—Nothing. The second meeting isn't scheduled until late this afternoon, remember? said Red. —It seems pretty obvious that whoever has caught us already knows an awful lot of things that were supposed to be top secret. You just had to look around the people in that meeting yesterday to deduce what they already know. They knew that the plan involves the hyperdrive—

—Warp drive, interrupted Blue.

—The warp drive, continued Red testily, —plus it has something to do with the AIs. Most importantly, they have figured out that Mars is involved. The big question is: what don't they know? There must be something, otherwise they wouldn't have us in here.

—Agreed, said Blue. —Our problem will be going along with them sufficiently so as to not raise their suspicions, while simultaneously not giving anything away.

—We have got one advantage, of course, said Red. —Grey. They probably don't know about him, or what he is capable of.

—Pretty much the same as us, then, said Blue.

The quorum never met in the same place twice. The level of paranoia among the group could never be high enough, not when you considered what they were conceivably fighting. Constantine appreciated the irony of their second meeting place. They were in the balcony of a concert hall, looking down to the stage where the black-and-white-clad musicians of an orchestra were tuning up. Glancing around the room, he could not recall ever seeing such sensitive recording equipment before. There were devices here that could record the noise made by the Brownian motion of dust in the moisture of his eyes. The whole room was strung with directional microphones that could build up a sound picture of the local environment that was almost perfect in its reproduction. It was the ideal place to hold a meeting where secrecy was paramount.

Marion Lee had been waiting for the signal to show that the microphones were switched on. As the signal was given, she relaxed and began the meeting.

"Good afternoon, everyone. Let us begin."

She coughed, then continued in a quiet voice. "People have long suspected a hidden intelligence guiding our development, an AI immeasurably more powerful than the others. Some people believed it first emerged in the early twenty-first century."

Gillian Karajan nodded in agreement.

"References in the entertainments from the period would confirm that. However, you cannot take that in any way as proof of the Watcher's existence. If you examine the historical context, you'll see that these rumors would be inevitable. Look at the people living at the time. Only the younger generations would have lived out their life under constant surveillance, whether by cameras or phone tracking or even computer modeling. Remember, at that time, there were many who had reached adulthood before even the Internet came into existence. Increased levels of surveillance would have been very obvious to that society."

The five of them were spread over two rows of seats, making conversation difficult. They leaned toward Gillian to better hear what was being said. Below them, a flutist practiced the same passage over and over again.

Gillian continued speaking confidently. She seemed to have quickly come to terms with her enforced exile from the Oort cloud. Maybe she understood the need for it. Or maybe there was some more sinister reason. Maybe it was just bad programming.

"...the tension generated by the interactions between the older and younger members of that society are unknown today. Nobody alive today has grown up with a true understanding of the word 'privacy.' Back then, they still had some concept, one fed and fanned by elderly relatives. Is it any wonder that people then began to see conspiracies where none existed? Is it any wonder the myth of the Watcher arose?"

Jay grinned. "So, you don't believe in the stories then, Gillian?"

Gillian looked annoyed. "Listen, I don't want to sound arrogant, but I think that I'm correct in saying that I know more about AIs and their history than anyone else here. If I were to believe or disbelieve the stories, it would be based on something more than a general paranoia that *they* are out to get us."

There was an embarrassed silence until Masaharu spoke up gently to defuse the situation.

"I agree with Gillian, however from the opposite direction. Human beings have always sought to abdicate responsibility for their own actions. They have handed responsibility for their deeds to their sensei, to their leaders, or to a higher power. I see this yearning for a mysterious all-powerful AI that controls humanity's

actions and seeks to lead them on the path to enlighten-
ment as nothing more than a manifestation of that
same desire."

Gillian nodded in approval

"However," continued Masaharu, causing Gillian to
glance suspiciously in his direction, "however, this is
just my opinion. We cannot base our actions on the
opinions of one person. We must act and plan as if the
Watcher *is* real. This we have already agreed upon."

"Good," said Marion. "I'm sorry, Gillian, but we are
treading over old ground here. It has already been established that, for the purposes of this project, we must
assume that the Watcher is real. Just as we've had to assume that the Watcher did not exist until at least 2030."

Constantine felt a little flicker of surprise that they
knew this fact. He began to wonder at the need for himself to be imprisoned within this simulation at all.
Surely if they knew this they could deduce the rest?

He looked around the room and wondered again if
what he had been told was true. Was he really inside a
computer? It all looked so real. He watched a woman un-
peeling an old-fashioned chocolate bar, carelessly dropping the strips of foil on the floor before her. She was idly
watching the activity below her as she placed piece after
sticky piece in her mouth. Again, Constantine wondered
at the programming that must have gone into the scene
before him. The attention to detail was evident all around
him. If he glanced up at the ceiling, he could see the looping patterns formed by the shielded wires as they led to the
directional microphones. Someone had twisted blue duct
tape around the one directly above him to aid in its identification. Who would have thought a simulation could go
to that level of detail? Or was it a simulation? Grey should
know, but Grey wasn't speaking.

The only safe plan was to follow the course he had agreed upon with Red and Blue earlier: play along, but try to reveal nothing.

Jay was holding forth. This Jay seemed so much more confident than her equivalent on the floating balcony last night. That slightly lost look was missing here. Was it something the simulation couldn't reproduce?

"We've got the expert here now, haven't we? Why don't we ask Gillian? Is 2030 a safe date to consider as a minimum point for the existence of the Watcher? Does anything in your work in the Oort cloud lead you to believe this to be incorrect?"

"It depends what level of AI we are talking about," Gillian replied. "In the context of the discussion at hand, it seems reasonable. There are minimum levels of resources in terms of processing power and memory and so on required to establish an AI as we know it today. Those weren't really available until 2030."

"What about the Martian VNM?" Jay asked.

"Far too low. That system was first postulated in the 1980s. Okay, they couldn't build it back then, but they could work out the parameters. The idea of dropping a hundred tons of materiel on Mars and allowing factories to build themselves was just too tempting. The actual design for the system wasn't fully mapped until 2025. We have complete understanding of how it worked; there is no space in there for a modern AI to form."

"Okay," Jay said. "Then I'll ask the one question that nobody here has ever answered to anyone's satisfaction. If the Watcher does exist, where does it come from?"

Jay sat in the row in front of Constantine. She leaned back, tilting her head over the back of her seat so that she was looking at him upside down. Her black hair spilled down, revealing how painfully thin her face was.

There was a wicked glint of fun in her eyes that had been softened in the Jay that had visited him last night. Constantine felt a sudden twisting in his stomach. Blue must have felt something, too. His voice suddenly filled Constantine's head.

—Watch it! This could be it! This is what they are trying to find out!

—But we don't know the answer, said Red, puzzled.

Constantine didn't know what to say. To his relief and surprise, Gillian answered first.

"No one knows," she said. "There are lots of theories. My favorite is that the AI was the result of an evolutionary process: lots of tiny AI applets constantly coming into existence and dying, but just enough of them surviving and linking up via the Internet to form a rudimentary neural net. Or maybe it was the result of computer evolution. There were a few projects trying to simulate that process at the start of the twenty-first century. It wouldn't be impossible that one of them evolved intelligence."

Jay interrupted. "I've seen estimates from those times, based on contemporaneous technology, that said it would take around three hundred years before artificial intelligence came about by those means."

"Yes," said Gillian patiently. "And other contemporary estimates predicted it would take ten years. Choose which one you want to believe in."

"What do you think, Constantine?" asked Jay.

—Tell her that the estimates for the time taken for intelligence to evolve all depend upon your definition of intelligence, said Red quickly.

Constantine repeated Red's words.

Jay nodded thoughtfully. Masaharu intervened with a soft, deliberate tone.

"That may be so, but it adds nothing to our discussion. However intelligence was measured back then, whether by Turing test or Lau's conjecture, has no bearing on our discussion. This is the question we must ask ourselves again: is 2030 a safe cutoff date? Can we assume the Watcher did not exist until then?"

He paused. Constantine became uncomfortably aware that they were all looking at him.

—What should he say? asked Red. —He's got to say something without alerting them to our understanding of the true situation!

—We may have some breathing space, said Blue. —Look at the stage.

Constantine's gaze flickered down to where the first violinist had walked out to join the orchestra. The crowd that now filled the concert hall clapped politely. The volume of applause rose as the conductor followed her out. He nodded to the first oboe, who blew a note, and one by one the rest of the musicians joined in. Constantine always felt a little thrill at the sound of an orchestra tuning up.

There was a moment's pause and then the sound of a trumpet. Dvořák's Eighth Symphony. Constantine smiled appreciatively. Dvořák had been the son of a pork butcher. After composing this symphony, he had left his native Czechoslovakia to travel to the United States of America, where he had been appointed director of the National Conservatory of Music. During his free time, he would often walk to the railway station to watch the steam trains, or to the docks to watch the ships. What would he make of Constantine's world, where people could travel through the solar system and cause great cities to be built from a few tiny machines? What would he make of the moon colonies, or people such as Gillian who had lived in the Oort cloud? What would he think of people sitting down to listen to his music in a concert hall where recording equipment was set up to blank out as much interior and exterior noise as possible in the quest for near perfect reproduction? A hall where the electronics formed the audio equivalent of a Faraday cage, so that a group of people could hold a secret meeting, secure in the knowledge that their conversation could not be recorded. Only the orchestra, now swelling in timbre as it developed the first theme, could be heard.

Constantine sat back. He could hear Blue humming snatches to himself as the music proceeded, occasionally pointing out items of interest.

—Now listen to this: this theme will be introduced again by the basses in the final movement.

—Never mind that, said Red. What are we going to do when this piece finishes? How long have we got, anyway?

—About thirty-six minutes, usually, replied Blue. I'd guess thirty-three if the conductor maintains this gain on the tempo all the way through.

—Yeah. Well. But what's Constantine going to say? We've got problems. Is this what they're after?

—I doubt it, said Blue. —Why go to the trouble of putting him in a simulation to ask a question they themselves have as much chance of working out as we do? How could anyone work out when the Watcher came into existence?

—Good point, said Red.

—I say that we just tell them we think 2030 is a safe cutoff date. If that's the reason they trapped us in here, more fool them.

—Okay, said Red. —I concur. However, we are merely

deferring the problem. We need to know what they are really trying to find out so we can avoid giving them the answer. If we follow our current path of divulging no information, they are bound to become suspicious.

—Fine, said Blue. How are we going to find that out? We can hardly ask them. "Erm, excuse me, Marion, what is it that we should be avoiding telling you. We don't want to—"

—Come on, Blue. You can be funnier than that. No. We'll have to get Constantine to ask the other Jay. The Night Jay.

Constantine had half closed his eyes, ostensibly to listen to the music, but really to pay closer attention to the conversation going on inside himself. The person in the seat behind shifted position, pressing their knees into Constantine's chair back. Constantine straightened himself up, making himself more comfortable, and then pretended to yawn.

He covered his mouth while subvocalizing, "I'm not sure the Night Jay will have a method of contacting the outside world."

—She'll have to give it a try. What else can we do? answered Red.

—Fine. Back to the point at hand. What are we going to do when this concert ends? asked Blue.

—Make our excuses and leave. Constantine is going to have to pretend to be sick or something.

—Where's Grey when we need him? Blue asked petulantly.

—Take his absence as an indication that we're doing our job properly, answered Red. —He'd be bound to interrupt if we made a mistake.

—If he's still there, answered Blue. —Hasn't it struck

you as odd that we still have an independent consciousness? We must be an incredible drain on the resources of the host machine.

Constantine felt a little shiver of excitement run up his back. The idea had already occurred to him, but he hadn't mentioned it with good reason. He kept quiet for the moment and just listened to the pair of them arguing. He wondered if they would raise the corollary to that thought.

Red spoke up.

—The idea had occurred to me. It all depends how the capture was made, I suppose. It could be argued that we are part of Constantine's mindset, albeit an artificially amplified part. Imagine a picture being taken, ostensibly of a flower, but capturing the image of a beetle crawling across a leaf in the same moment.

—And we're the beetles? Thanks.

—You're welcome. You understand the analogy. I'm not sure if it holds, but it is a theory, and a theory that is preferable to another that has occurred to me.

—What's that?

—That we are not the original personality constructs. That we have been planted by the enemy to steer Constantine down the wrong path. I'm sure this has already occurred to you, Constantine?

Constantine grinned faintly despite himself. "Yes," he muttered.

—So why give yourself away? asked Blue.

—You already know the answer to that, Blue.

—I know. Because the enemy knew that Constantine would figure out for himself the fact that we might be fakes, so by me raising the idea first, we gain credibility in his eyes. Well, I'll tell you this, Constantine, I certainly feel real.

—Of course you do, answered Red, —but you may just have been programmed that way. You may be an AI designed to believe you are Blue, with only the slightest modification to twist you to the enemy's purpose.

—Oh, I hate this. And all this doublethink is making me miss the concert . . .

—Well, it needed to be said. It may also explain why we're not hearing from Grey. Maybe they've deactivated that personality after yesterday's little exhibition.

"And maybe we are not in a computer simulation at all," added Constantine, subvocalizing. "Maybe it's just another bluff. Maybe the Watcher is trying to put us off."

—That does sound plausible, said Blue. —Just listen to those clarinets. Nobody would deliberately simulate someone playing that badly, surely?

The concert ended and the meeting broke up in disarray, Constantine claiming that he needed to contemplate what had been said. Marion wasn't happy. Only one more meeting was permitted. Constantine and Marion locked gazes for some time. Then the group was pulled apart by the random movement of the audience, Constantine joining a stream that swept him down the shallow carpeted stairs and out through a small door at the side of the hall. He walked in quiet contemplation, a ghost in the center of a colorful, chattering crowd discussing the concert.

They spilled out of the narrow doorway into the yellow evening. The disk of the sun could be seen across the empty plain, sinking beneath the horizon. The city of Stonebreak was slowing down, preparing for the transition to its night-time activities. Constantine slowed to a halt and allowed the crowd to divide itself and stream around him. A forgotten island in the middle of the homeward-bound traffic. The classical columns and entablatures of the concert hall stood behind him; before him lay the wide, flagged space of the fourth level.

—Look to your left, said Red.

Constantine did so. There was Mary Rye. She gazed at Constantine in blurred disbelief, then mumbled something.

—We penitents are all mixed up, translated Red, reading her lips. —What does that mean?

Constantine noted the bottle gripped firmly in her right hand. The hem of her green skirt was stained with something yellow. Constantine stepped toward her, but she shook her head, turned and began to lurch away in the other direction. She was quickly swallowed up by the remnants of the concert crowd.

"Mary!" called Constantine.

—She's ignoring you, said Red.

"Thanks, Red," muttered Constantine sarcastically. He began to run after her, pushing his way through the people. He couldn't see her.

"Where's she gone?" he muttered.

—Headed toward the elevators to the third level, answered Red. —Look to two o'clock.

Constantine saw her. She clutched her bottle as she scuttled across the flags, head low and shoulders hunched as if she was trying to make herself smaller. Constantine caught up with her and placed one hand on her shoulder.

"Mary," he said. "What's the matter?"

She turned to him, and her face was a picture of panic and fear.

"Go away, please," she whispered. "They told me what they'd do if I tried to contact you again." She waved the bottle in his face. "They gave me this when I promised not to speak to you."

It was a good brand, noted Constantine. He felt a pang of real pity for this poor woman, driven further down the road to destruction by his supposed protectors. Mary turned and began to march away. There was a blur of movement and for a moment there were two Marys. One frozen before him, the other staggering toward the escalators. The pity inside Constantine evaporated instantly as he recognized what was happening. She wasn't real. She was just part of the simulation in which he was trapped. He stepped forward, into the picture of Mary that remained smeared on the air before him, and the picture vanished as he moved within it. Poor old Mary. Just another object that wasn't repainted properly.

Blue pointed it out as they waited their turn in the line for the elevators.

—I wonder why they're running the Mary storyline for you? What are they trying to say?

Constantine walked all the way back to his hotel, stopping on the way for a meal in one of the cafes that seemed to appear suddenly as evenign fell. He ate sausages and sauerkraut with cold lager and then sat back with a large pot of coffee to listen to the conversation inside himself. Nobody was speaking. In the end he lost interest, paid the bill with his untraceable card and pushed his way back out into the warm night.

The floating building was parked outside his hotel. Its base hung only a couple of meters above the ground, the lit doorway of his hotel's lobby shining through the gap. The top of the tower rose up into the night sky; there was a light shining from one of the windows in the higher floors. A dark figure seemed to move within, but Constantine couldn't be sure. It was too far away to see clearly.

Jay was again leaning on her balcony, her arms folded on the rail as she watched Constantine approach.

He grinned up at her as he reached the base of the tower, reminded of Romeo and Juliet. Constantine rather liked this Jay. Her dark hair surrounded her thin face as she leaned over to look down at him and he noted again how much more vulnerable she looked in this incarnation.

"Hello." Constantine smiled up at her.

"There's something going on," she replied, looking worried. "About three hours ago there was a rush of activity like I've never seen before."

—When we saw Mary, suggested Red.

—Or when we were watching the concert. The time is too imprecise, said Blue.

—We need to know, continued Red. —You'll have to ask her. We need to know what they're after.

Constantine shook his head. He felt as if he was being nagged.

"I know, I know," he muttered. He raised his voice.

"We need some help, Jay. We need to know what the enemy is trying to find out. We're being tied in knots. We don't know what to say or when to keep quiet. We need information."

Jay shook her head sadly. "I'm sorry, I don't know the answer."

"Very well. Ask DIANA. They must have some ideas."

Jay slumped forward, elbows still resting on the railing. She looked thoroughly fed up.

"I can't speak to DIANA."

Constantine frowned. "I thought they were working on a way to get me out of here."

Jay's expression was a mixture of guilt and sadness. "Don't you realize that the only reason that I can exist in this place is because I have no links with any other object inside the simulation?"

—Except us, said Red.

"Except me," said Constantine.

Jay frowned. "I know that, and do *you* know what a risk it is, me just speaking to you now? You realize there are two personalities in here who will suffer if they catch you? There is no safe way to send out a message."

Constantine felt chastened. He looked down at his feet for a moment. The tower cast no shadow here, he noticed; the moon lit up the entire pavement before him.

He sighed slowly. "I'm sorry, Jay, but we're running a great risk speaking to those people in the quorum. Either we tell them the secret they're trying to find out, or, worse, we say nothing and raise their suspicions that we're holding something back."

Jay said nothing. Her hands slid up her face and she began to fiddle with her earlobes in the manner of a little girl. She suddenly realized what she was doing and snatched her hands away, then stared up the side of the tower at the lit upper window.

Finally she spoke. "Okay. You've convinced me. We'll have to take the risk. I don't like it, but there you are. I'm going to try and send a message to the real world. I hope our steganography is good enough. Give me a minute."

She turned and walked through the open door behind her into the tower. Constantine stood alone for a moment, a forgotten man beneath the night sky. The moonlight picked out the edges of the dark clouds high above with white highlights. Behind him was the brightly lit lobby of his own hotel. He wondered at the way its guests and staff didn't notice the huge black tower floating just outside their door.

Jay walked back out onto the balcony, holding something in her hand.

"If they don't pick this up the moment it leaves the vicinity of the tower, we should be okay. Heaven knows how they'll get a message back, though. Catch it, we don't want it to break."

She tossed the object in Constantine's direction. It tumbled end over end as it fell. There was a brief discontinuity just before it hit the ground when it seemed to shift in its position slightly to the left. The effect reminded him of a stone being dropped in water.

He dived for it too late. A bottle. It bounced on the ground, once, twice, but didn't break. His heart pounding, he bent to pick it up. An empty green wine bottle, the space inside it twisted into significant forms.

A message in a bottle? Constantine straightened to look back at Jay but she had gone. The tower was already two hundred meters up and rising.

He suddenly felt incredibly lonely. Gripping the bottle tightly, he walked into his hotel.

Herb was in the entertainment tank watching an old movie: a black-and-white flick called *The Blue Magnolia*, color and dimension enhanced to make it suitable for a modern audience. If only they could have done something to the plot, wished Herb; as far as he was concerned, it made no sense whatsoever.

Johnston stuck his head above the trapdoor.

"Okay, Herb, we're on. Let's go."

Herb felt his heart thumping in his chest. His hand involuntarily tightened around the hard little machine that Robert had given him, now wrapped in a white linen napkin to prevent Herb cutting himself on its sharp edges.

"No. I thought we had to prepare further. We're not ready."

"We're as ready as we'll ever be," Robert replied. "Come on. Don't you want to see my ship?" He ducked down into the secret passageway.

Herb looked around the comfortable surroundings of

his own ship and wished it a sad good-bye. He wondered if they would have white leather and parquet flooring where he was going. He doubted it. He gave a sigh and stepped into emptiness over the trapdoor. His body swung smoothly through ninety degrees as he entered the connecting space between the two ships.

Inside, the secret passageway was longer than it had looked when seen from Herb's lounge. It echoed and clanked as he walked along it, and beneath those sounds he could feel a shuddering and jarring that suggested the two ships were moving. There was a sudden groaning sound and the passageway itself seemed to deform, twisting this way and that. Herb felt a stab of horror as a hole appeared by his feet and he found himself looking outside, out to the horizon over a sea of writhing VNMs. That sea was dropping away as the two ships rose higher and higher into the air.

"Come on," Robert called from the end of the passageway. "I'm recycling the materials of this passageway. The VNMs aren't going to hang about while you dawdle in there."

Herb began to run to where Robert waited, holes appearing all around him as he went, cold daylight streaming through the sudden gaps. It was odd: the apparent gravity of the passageway was perpendicular to that of the planet. Which way would he fall if he stepped through a hole? Out, or down? Or neither? Would the gravity field hold strong beneath his feet?

Herb stepped, panting, into Robert's ship and looked around the interior expectantly.

It was completely empty. A bare room lit with pale blue light from the ceiling. It reminded Herb of a VR room when the entertainment had finished. No, more than that, it reminded him of old images he had seen of film sets when all the props and scenery had been cleared away. Robert's ship was an empty shell waiting to be filled with the furniture and controls that would make it a real spacecraft.

"Anything wrong, Herb?" Robert smiled faintly as Herb stared around the bare cuboid of the room. Two bumps in the angle between the floor and the rear wall were the only hint that something more to this ship lay beyond the bare surfaces. Herb guessed part of the motors protruded into the room at those points. He looked at Robert in astonishment.

"Where's the rest of this ship? Or is it all hidden away somewhere? Or is this a VR projection?"

"No. It's another test. Something for you to figure out. By the way, you should step clear of the hatch now. We are about to make a warp jump into space."

Wordlessly, Herb stepped away from the opening in the floor from which he had just emerged. A panel slid across it, smoothly sealing the gap.

"Okay," said Robert. "First stop, orbit, to make a copy of your ship, and then we jump right into the heart of the Enemy Domain."

Herb tilted his head to one side and gazed at Robert appraisingly. "You're a robot, aren't you?" he said. "I should have guessed as much. That's how you always managed to stay one jump ahead of me."

Johnston nodded once at Herb's grin. "I can see that's managed to salvage your ego a little," he said dryly.

Herb continued around the room, tapping at the smooth grey walls as he went.

"That's why you don't need anything in here. No beds or sofas or kitchen or ... or ... anything."

"Yes," Robert said dismissively, then changed the subject. "I'm about to activate the reproductive mechanism on your own ship. Do you want to watch?"

Without waiting for a reply, Robert called up an external view on one wall. Herb saw the final stages of his ship's warp transition from the planet's surface, watched it slotting itself back into normal space with a faint shimmer.

Herb frowned suspiciously. "Why are you making a copy of my ship?"

"We'll be jumping into the Enemy Domain in one of them. We're keeping the other one as a spare to get us out." He gave Herb a despairing look. "We can't stay on mine, can we? There are no facilities here."

Herb's voice held a faint tremble. "Why will we need another ship to get out? What will happen to the first one?"

Robert pointed to the sharp little linen-wrapped machine that Herb carried in his hand.

"It will be eaten by that VNM you are carrying. It's a superfast replicator: makes a copy of itself every point seven seconds. First rule of wiping out a VNM infestation: if it can reproduce faster than you, you have to encircle it and work inwards. Very time-consuming, and you run the risk of some of the infection escaping through the gaps in your net. But if you can reproduce faster than the enemy, then you start in the middle and work outwards. We'll be chasing the infestation, but we know we will catch it in the end."

"What will happen to me? Will I be on the ship?"

"You'll be okay," said Robert. "That machine you're carrying prefers to convert nonorganic materials."

"Oh."

Robert gave Herb a significant glance. Herb ignored it. Looking outside, he could see that his ship was warping and deforming. A long bulge formed along the upper surface as a second ship began to grow.

"Look at that," Robert said, pointing to Herb's pregnant spacecraft. "You humans astonish me sometimes. Every adult, every child even, has access to machinery that can reproduce in that way. Haven't you ever wondered why the universe isn't already choked up with your junk?"

Herb looked at him in puzzlement. "But it's illegal to make unauthorized copies. You need a license to operate a VNM on Earth. They need materials with which to make copies of themselves: you could be stealing someone else's resources."

Robert laughed. "It's illegal to convert planets into masses of flickering VNMs, but that didn't stop you giving it a try."

"So? You caught me and stopped me."

"And I've caught twenty other young men and women before you. Did you ever hear of Sean Simons? He was a young man, just like you. Rich father, too much sense of his own importance. Bit more malice, mind. He deliberately set about converting a planet."

"Doesn't sound familiar."

"Really? Check the news files. He went missing." Robert looked at Herb darkly. "I know where he is, though," he added softly.

Herb felt a little chill, but it quickly dulled. The featureless pale blue room had assumed the aspect of a place apart from reality: a waiting room where they paused while the main events prepared to take place.

"We can't catch everyone, though. Hasn't it occurred to you that there may be deeper forces at work here? Every human with a gram of common sense can get hold of a warp drive and a self-replicating machine. You could fill the galaxy with little silver cigars before teatime."

Herb was impatient. "I know; that's what the EA is for. That's what we're working to prevent now, isn't it?"

Robert looked at Herb for a moment then shook his head in disbelief.

"No. I give up. You really don't see it, do you?"

Outside, the bulge in the top surface of Herb's ship had grown a lot larger. The second ship would soon begin tearing itself free.

They were moving through space, the two ships accelerating away from Herb's accidentally converted planet. Herb felt an odd pang of loss as he saw that dull grey disk getting smaller as they moved faster and faster. Just behind them, his pregnant spaceship went through the final throes of labor.

Robert stood at Herb's shoulder, looking on appreciatively.

"What's the gestation period?" he asked.

Herb smiled with paternal pride. "Twenty-five minutes under optimal conditions. And it can do that every two hours, assuming an appropriate source of construction matter is at hand."

"Oh, I know where there is one," said Robert. He looked back at Herb's ship and then clapped his hands together.

"Oh well. Five more minutes until the ships have separated. Then we jump."

"Is that it?" asked Herb. He suddenly needed the toilet, and he was acutely aware there was nowhere to go on Robert's ship. He also wanted to change his clothes. Silk pajamas and a pair of paper slippers may make good ship wear, but he felt incredibly exposed at the thought of landing dressed like that in the middle of the Enemy Domain. He needed body armor. An ABC suit. It was too late for all that.

Herb's mouth felt dry. "Don't you have any advice for me?" he asked plaintively.

"Yes. Just do as I say."

"Oh."

Herb licked his dry lips. So this was it. He gazed around at the illuminated walls of the spaceship, looked through the viewing field at the receding disk of his abused planet, and wondered sadly how it had come to this.

He thought back to the day that he had left Earth. Walking across the dew-soaked lawn beneath a cloudless blue April sky that seemed to go up forever. His spaceship had sat waiting on the grass ahead of him. Herb had paused for a moment to glance around at the beautiful spring morning. The sight of his father's house, the green copper dome on its roof, the cream-painted stone walls and the windows reflecting the early morning sunshine. What could he find in space that couldn't be equalled or surpassed by that morning?

Now he wondered: would things have been different if he hadn't taken off then?

Herb didn't know. All he knew was that in three minutes he would be jumping to almost certain death. He looked miserably around Robert's ship again. The pale blue room, the dark viewing area . . .

He felt sick.

• • • •

Herb's spaceship had separated into two new ships. Two creamy white boxes that tumbled slowly through space behind them. Robert looked on, impressed.

"Almost perfectly balanced," he whispered. "Only a fraction of a gram's difference between the two. And only a total mass of one point seven grams lost in the process."

Herb nodded in terrified agreement. The two ships that now floated behind looked identical to him. He would have expected no less, of course. The twin ships began to drift apart.

"What now?" asked Herb.

"One's going back to your converted planet to re-plenish its mass. We're going to board the other and make the jump into the Enemy Domain."

"What about restoring *our* ship's mass?" asked Herb frantically, hoping for a way to delay the impending jump. "It won't be working at optimal efficiency at only half mass. What if we're attacked? The walls will be too thin to deflect any attack."

Robert gave a little laugh. "The thickness of the walls will make no difference when the Enemy Domain attacks. The ship may as well be made of rice paper for all the protection it will give us."

There was a faint sigh and the floor hatch opened up. Robert gestured towards it.

"Okay, Herb, our new ship has docked. After you."

Herb felt his stomach sink. His hand tightened around the sharp little VNM Robert had given him.

He stepped into the hatchway. Robert followed.

• • • •

The replication was very good. The ship was identical to the original, right down to the copy of *The Blue Magnolia*, now coming to its conclusion in the entertainment tank. Herb ran his hand across the white leather of the sofa. It felt just as soft, just as cool. Did the ship carry spare leather, he wondered?

He could almost believe that the replication hadn't taken place, that he was back on his original ship, but of course there was no original ship now. It had split into two identical copies, each of half the original mass. A display had lit up on one wall informing him of the fact. If he cared to, he could examine the status of the fission right down to the subsystems level. Herb didn't care.

Robert was at work meanwhile altering the ship's interior, opening viewing fields in all four walls and the ceiling. Smaller viewing fields opened in the floor, interspersed with screens across which multicolored lines and patterns scrolled. Status screens. Herb found himself standing in a viewing field, a silver puddle of light shimmering around his ankles.

"Sit on that sofa," said Robert, pointing to the one opposite. "I'm arranging it so we can see everything from the conversation area."

Herb stepped out of the puddle and sat down opposite Robert.

A sudden jerk pushed him back into his seat. It was followed by two more that knocked him over to the left.

"Sorry. I'm just trying to get the gravity field adjusted. We barely got enough exotic matter in the division to enable the warp jump. There's not much left over to maintain gravity." Robert grimaced. "If the enemy gets us in a steep enough gravity gradient, we'll be smeared across the inside of this ship like butter."

"Thanks," said Herb, turning pale.

"Actually, that won't happen," Robert said happily. "I forgot. The hull is so weak after the separation, the ship will crumple along with us. It will be like sending a bag of blood through a mangle."

Herb moaned.

Robert paused in his work and looked at him.

"Don't worry, Herb. There's nothing to worry about. We're going to win. Just remember, the EA AI is far more intelligent than anything in the Enemy Domain. It's not about the Enemy's greater strength, it's about the intelligent application of force. Ask any swordsman: the point beats the edge every time."

"I'm not comforted," said Herb.

"Well, I tried." Robert sighed.

Herb was shaken around on the sofa by another series of violent jerks. Throughout the sudden shuddering motion he could sense a steady acceleration, usually hidden by the internal gravity field.

A mapping of the Enemy Domain suddenly appeared above their heads, a cloud of silver and rose with significant features picked out in gold and blue. Robert gazed up at it and nodded in satisfaction. It vanished and Robert turned and looked at several of the viewing fields he had opened up around the ship, checking that everything was okay.

"Have you got your VNM?" he asked Herb, who wordlessly held it up. Tiny scarlet drops of his blood shimmered on the edge of the sharp metal points that had cut their way through the thick linen cloth in which the machine was wrapped. Herb hadn't even felt any pain. The ship's gravity cut out again and he felt himself pushed back against the seat. Herb wondered why it was necessary to travel quite so fast. What was the point when they were about to make a jump? They would only have to slow down again at the other end.

"Can you think of anything we've forgotten?" Robert asked, his gaze still traveling from viewing field to viewing field.

"No," said Herb. He wished he could think of something.

"Okay, here we go, then."

When he was younger, Herb had thought he knew all about superluminal travel. He was now just old enough to admit that he didn't. The AIs insisted that the methods used were beyond human intelligence, and no human had yet been able to contradict them. Herb did understand the basic principles, however.

He knew that special relativity dictated that it was impossible to travel faster than light in an area of flat space-time; however, he also knew that general relativity placed no restrictions on two regions of flat space-time moving apart at greater than light speed. The equations describing a warp field that could move a region of flat space-time faster than light had been derived long ago, at the end of the twentieth century, before even the first AIs had appeared. *Human* intelligence had shown that exotic matter was required in order for the fields to exist.

It was fair to say that contemporary AIs insisted that the superluminal travel they provided was far removed from those "trivial" equations, but they did agree on two particulars.

First, the warp drive required exotic matter.

Second, it involved moving a region of flat space-time around the universe.

Herb was in such a region now. And the ship's velocity within that flat region must be considerable.

Herb wondered why.

They inserted themselves back into regular space-time. The forward-viewing areas lit up with brilliant white light. Those to the rear of the cabin darkened.

"Atomic explosion," Robert said in some surprise. "Their detection systems are better than I expected, as are their reactions. If we were at rest relative to the warp, we'd have been right at the heart of that. As it is, we've probably got the length of this sentence before they get a lock on us again. Ah! Got it!"

"Got what?" called Herb.

"The security web monitoring this system. I've altered our status flag to "friendly object." See what I mean when I talk about superior intelligence? It's not about having a stronger hull or more powerful weaponry. The battles of the twenty-third century aren't fought by AIs. They're fought inside AIs."

"Wha—?"

The viewing screens glared brightly again. This time the ceiling darkened.

"What was that?" Herb shouted.

"Another atomic. There is a second web watching the first, monitoring its integrity. It noted our changes and launched another attack. I jumped us forward a couple of light seconds to escape the blast. Don't worry, I've also tackled the second web."

"Does that mean we're safe now?"

"We've always been safe. If, however, you mean, 'Will we be attacked again?' then I'm afraid the answer is yes. We can't stay hidden forever. The surveillance systems will take counter-countermeasures against our countermeasures."

Johnston reached into his breast pocket and pulled out his white handkerchief. He flapped it twice in the air and then spread it flat on the sofa next to him.

"Okay, Herb. Now to replenish this ship's mass. The planet below has been converted by saliva nanotechs. Are you aware of the term?"

"Yes."

Robert felt in a pocket and pulled out a silver cigar-shaped machine which Herb recognized as one of his own VNMs, placing it on the white handkerchief.

"The term 'saliva nanotech' was coined by Katie Kirkham," he explained.

"I know," said Herb.

"It describes a simple VNM, the principal use of which is to convert matter into suitable building material for other VNMs. It obviates the need for a stomach or other such device being built into the principal VNMs in an area, thus speeding up the rate of replication, and hence construction."

"I know," said Herb. "I said I'd heard the term before."

"Drop a few saliva nanotechs in a suitable area, leave them for a while, and when you return you have ready-processed material for other VNMs to use."

"I *know*." Herb was becoming quite angry. "I also know that you use them with caution. You don't want them getting away and converting everything around. *And* that you have to tailor them to the prevailing conditions. Those set to find and reclaim silicon would be no good in water."

Robert ignored him. He waved a hand at the VNM he had taken from Herb's accidentally destroyed planet.

"This machine that you built does its own conversion. Its silvery color is due to the prevailing mineral content of the area of the planet where it was released. If someone were to travel over your converted planet, I imagine the color of the machines and makeup of the machines they saw would vary according to the former local geology."

"That's right. I know. I designed it."

Robert looked a little surprised.

"Surely you mean, you purchased the design for a type six self-replicating machine and made the appropriate modifications?"

Realization flashed through Herb. It finally hit him. He finally understood.

"You're doing this deliberately, aren't you? Every time things get tense. You do your best to get me annoyed, just to take my mind off things."

Johnston smiled. "That's right, Herb."

The smile widened. Herb counted ten teeth, gleaming against the pink flesh behind Robert Johnston's dark lips.

"I didn't want you concentrating too hard on the fact that we were about to descend onto an Enemy planet to steal some of its building blocks for our ship, or that this region of space has been seeded with security nanotechs, several of which have attached themselves to our ship and are currently at work converting our hull into more security nanotechs. I'd guess we have about ten minutes before this lounge dissolves before our eyes."

"Don't they think we're on their side like everything else in here?"

"No. Too small. They're not part of the security web. They're just here as another line of defense in case the web doesn't work. It's a very effective passive defense, too: they'll eat anything that isn't labeled as inedible."

"Well, label us inedible."

"I'm doing that even as we speak. They're transmitting a code using a public key system. Obviously they inherit the key from each other when they replicate. If I can figure out the key and send back a message encoded using the private key, they should trust us." He closed his eyes.

"Come on," said Herb, squirming nervously on the sofa. "They'll be through any minute now."

Robert opened his eyes in puzzlement.

"Oh, sorry. I solved that problem while I was explaining it to you." He tapped his head and rolled his eyes. "I must remember to keep you informed. No. I was just working out the coordinates for the transition to the planet's surface. Okay. We're jumping now."

Herb clenched his left fist in frustration. His right hand was too sore from clutching Robert's machine.

"What is the point of me being here?" he complained. "I can't think fast enough to beat the Enemy. I don't know what to do, anyway."

"I need you to press the button that makes that VNM reproduce, remember?" Johnston replied, pointing to Herb's right hand.

Herb looked at him in disbelief. "Is that it? Couldn't you place it on a timer or something?"

Johnston shook his head slowly and sighed. "Oh, Herb. Why won't you trust me? There are some aspects to this mission that only a human can accomplish. If you will just be patient, you'll see what they are. Okay. Let's jump."

• • • •

There was a sudden discontinuity and then they were hovering above the surface of the destination planet.

"Nighttime," said Herb.

"No," muttered Robert, distantly. "We're in interstellar space. This planet has no star. It wanders alone." He nodded thoughtfully. "There are more of these planets than you might expect; they're just incredibly difficult to find. Hold it. I'll adjust the view so you can see better."

Virtual daylight filled the ship as he adjusted the viewing field's output, pushing everything into the visible spectrum. The ship was floating over a silver sea studded with rocky columns and promontories that trailed away from a row of cliffs. Everything had a spongy, desiccated look.

"They've gone for the metals first," Robert murmured. "The sea below is a nickel iron alloy. This planet must have been mostly metal. Come on, let's feed the ship."

They began to descend, the metallic sea appearing to expand as they sank toward it.

"How long does it take this ship to absorb matter?" Robert asked. He glanced up and backward at a viewing field located just behind his right shoulder.

"It depends," answered Herb. "Usually it takes it on board and plates it in a layer just inside the hull. It's gradually transported from there to the necessary locations as part of the ongoing maintenance and repair procedure."

Johnston nodded. "I guessed as much. And how long to take the necessary material on board?"

"A couple of minutes, if that."

"Good. We've got just about enough time, then."

"Just about enough time for what?" Herb asked.

Something about the way Robert spoke brought the never too distant feeling of fear in his stomach back to the fore.

The robot did something to one of the fields. The view focused on something, pulled back and refocused, pulled back again and refocused once more.

"Just enough time to get away from that," he murmured.

Herb gazed at the viewing field in horror. From the high vantage point of the virtual camera he could finally make out what was going on. The sea over which they floated was crystallizing in a circle around them. It was as if a rime of white frost was settling on the surface of the gently moving liquid metal and freezing it into a rapidly tightening noose of ice. Herb could see their ship, clearly marked as occupying the center position. The bullseye.

He became aware of something else. A slow, deliberate movement around the edges of the sea. A second viewing field focused in on one particular section, and Herb was momentarily thrown by the contrast within his range of vision, between the quiet calm of his lounge—the polished wood sculpture and the white vase with the gentle pattern of flowers embossed around the rim, the parquet floor and the cool eggshell finish of the ceiling—and the frantic battle outside. In the midst of the calm of his lounge, there on the viewing field, he could see the little machines outside forming themselves from the sea of metal, sucking its material as they bulged and then split into two.

"Reproducing once every eight point two seconds," said Robert. "Pretty impressive really. Well, when you consider the limitations of the intelligence we're up against."

"They're going to surround us," whispered Herb. "We'll be trapped."

It seemed inevitable. He could see the thickening cloud of the tiny machines as they rose into the air, an angry cloud of insects that seemed to pull a silver curtain up from the surface, such was their density—a silver curtain that promised to engulf them. It was as if a sack was being lifted up and around and over the ship.

"Shouldn't we run now?" asked Herb.

Robert shook his head. "Don't worry. I've worked out their rate of reproduction. We'll get away with fourteen seconds to spare."

Herb said nothing to that. There was nothing to say. All he could do was sit and stare at the rising cloud of little machines, each about the size and shape of a saucer. They spun and shimmered in the virtual light. Their underside was darker than the top and scored with a series of concentric circular grooves. When they fissioned, it was into two saucers joined along their tops, grooved undersides facing outward.

"How do they know we're here?" asked Herb. "I thought we were masquerading as friends?"

Robert grinned. "Oh Herb. I keep telling you: the intelligence behind the Enemy Domain is convinced of its own superiority. It is in the nature of such individuals to trust no one else. How could they trust an inferior? This is a paranoid region we have wandered into. It has security systems piled upon security systems. We will never deceive all of them. We can only hope to fool a few of them for just long enough."

He glanced at his wristwatch. "One minute until we leave."

One minute. It seemed an eternity to Herb. He was

sure that would be too long. The cloud of machines rising from the circumference of the sea was now diminishing. Those machines closest to the planet's surface began to change shape, their circular edges flattening off as the saucers became octagonal. The machines began merging together along these flat edges. As they did so, the gaps left between the shapes began to widen, the body of the plates narrowed and thickened.

"They're forming a mesh. We'll be trapped in the cage."

Herb licked his lips and wished he hadn't spoken. His voice sounded high-pitched and cracked.

"We'll be fine," said Robert, rising to his feet. "Thirty seconds and we'll be gone. There's nothing to worry about here."

He picked up the silver machine, the modified VNM he had taken from Herb's planet. Its legs waved gently as Robert carried it across the room to the hatchway.

"The real problems will emerge the deeper we travel into the Enemy Domain. You see, the Enemy isn't stupid; it will learn from its mistakes. We won't be able to defeat it the same way twice."

The hatch slid open. Robert held the silver machine over the space in the floor for a moment. Its legs began to wave a little faster as it sensed the vast pool of raw materials beneath it.

Robert glanced across to Herb.

"You should be pleased with yourself, Herb. If you should die, think this of yourself. There is a planet, in some distant sky, that will be forever a part of your creation."

He let go of the machine and it tumbled through the hatch, its legs flickering up and down like the needles on a sewing machine.

Above them, a viewing field showed what would become the roof of their cage now closing over them as a faint mist of silver saucers. The hatch slid shut. A gentle note sounded in the cabin.

"Okay, we're full. Off we go."

Herb let out a huge sigh. How long had he been holding his breath? The silver sea below them began to recede; the thin misty roof above them approached closer and closer. They burst through the insubstantial cloud of silver saucers without any difficulty and began to accelerate into space.

Herb felt a wave of relief that was quickly overtaken by anxiety again. They had escaped this trap, only to have Robert jump them deeper into the Enemy Domain.

"I don't think I can take much more of this," muttered Herb, seriously.

Robert eyed him closely. "Of course you can," he replied. "I'm monitoring all your vital signs. Your stress levels are well within acceptable limits." He raised his eyebrows just a little. "All right, your blood pressure is a touch too high, but if you were to reduce your salt consumption, you'd be okay."

He sat back down on the sofa. "Warp jump in twenty seconds. We're going to try and lead them off on a false trail. We don't want them waiting for us with any nasty surprises when we break back into normal space."

"I thought it was impossible to track someone through warp space."

"It is," said Robert. "Come on, Herb, think laterally. There are ways and means."

"Is this another one of your ways to keep me calm? Take my mind off things?"

"That's right. Here's something else to think about,

too. Why did I drop that machine of yours on the planet?"

Herb gave a puzzled frown. "To reproduce, of course. I would have thought that was obvious."

"Of course, Herb. Silly me for thinking I could tell you anything."

The ship was accelerating again, building up tremendous speed.

"Do you think they'll try to nuke us when we arrive again?" asked Herb nervously.

"Of course," replied Robert. "Okay. Jump in five seconds. Four, three, two, one . . ."

They jumped.

eva 4: 2051

eva 4: 2051

"Heads we walk down the drive, tails we try to cut through the woods."

Eva wrapped her arms about herself and shivered as Alison tossed the coin. The night wasn't *that* cold, she told herself. A low layer of cloud brooded above, pushing the dampness back down into the stretch of grass between the sleeping Center and the silent woods.

"Tails," said Alison, peering at the coin with the faint light of her phone's screen. "Through the woods."

"Are you sure the positioning chip in that thing is disabled?" Nicolas asked suspiciously.

"Positive," said Katie. "Anyway, they're top of the range stealth phones. Even the military can't track them."

"I still don't think it was a good idea bringing them."

"It would look suspicious if we didn't have them with us," said Alison. "Who doesn't carry a phone nowadays? Now come on. Into the woods. Eva, get the trees to help us."

Eva strode across the wet grass, her sneakers slipping

on the slick surface, and she wondered again if she should have put her boots on.

The woods looked impossibly dark, the sky above them lit with a faint orange glow from the vast Northwest conurbation.

"Are you there?" she muttered to the night in general.

"I'm here," said her brother. "Keep going in a straight line. It looks okay."

"Good. We need to keep going in a straight line." Eva whispered the instruction to the others and they walked on in silence. Nicolas kept glancing nervously back toward the dark outline of the Center. Katie gazed at the sky; Alison walked on with an expression of grim determination. She didn't seem happy.

"Something's up with her. Watch her, Eva. Whoah! Stop. Just ahead of you. Can you see it?"

"Stop!" called Eva. The group froze. Ahead of them a faint ghost hung on the night air. Almost invisibly thin lines criss-crossed the space at the edge of the tree line.

"Motion sensors," Katie whispered, "but so old. You'd have to cross the beam to sound the alarm. Why not just use radar? It's a lot harder to detect. Why these old light beams?"

"I don't know," Alison muttered. "Come on, let's go around them."

They walked along the perimeter of the trees for some distance, conscious of the blank windows of the Center to their left. It was easy to believe they were being watched. They quickly came to the circle of limes. Eva's brother spoke.

"It's clear here. There's a path right through the wood that will take you to the main road."

"This way," Eva said. "It's clear."

"This isn't right," said Nicolas. "Weren't we supposed to be traveling at random? We should be tossing the coin, not listening to her brother."

They all looked toward the dim outline of Katie. Her whispered reply was loud in the silence of the dew-muffled night.

"It can't be helped. Better to be a little predictable at the beginning than to be caught before we even start."

"Good point," said Alison. "Eva, you go first. We may as well make use of your brother while he's still here."

She fumbled in a pocket for a moment, then pressed something into Eva's hand.

"You'd better use this," she said.

It was a flashlight. Eva turned it on and a circle of light appeared on the damp leaf mold covering the ground before her. Pale, heart-shaped lime leaves were scattered all around. Autumn was coming.

"Take a handful of leaves," said her brother. "It may be enough to remember me by."

Eva bent to scoop some leaves from the ground, dipping her head into the rich smell of the wet forest floor. Nearby, the dark trunk of a lime rose into the black sky, an untidy collection of young twigs sprouting from its base. She took hold of one and bent and twisted it until it snapped, and then folded it up into a springy circle that could be stashed in one of the large pockets in her anorak.

"Have you finished yet?" Alison hissed angrily.

"Yes. Let's go."

They pushed their way on into the darkness of the woods, Eva leading the way, picking out the path with the flashlight, Alison just behind her, then Nicolas and

Katie bringing up the rear. The wood was silent and incredibly dark. Eva, like most people, had lived all her life taking streetlights for granted. To have her vision reduced to a circle of light, to a picture of low roots with traffic-blown litter wrapped around them, to thin branches reaching out to snag her face, and to a shifting pattern of darkness where the light could not reach—this was almost too frightening.

"We should have reached the road by now," whispered Alison. "I think we're lost."

"No, this is right," whispered Eva.

"In that case, why can't we hear the traffic?" Alison snapped.

"I don't know." That had been worrying her, too.

"It's the woods," Katie murmured. "They muffle the sound."

"Good point," said Eva, although she was sure she detected a note of uncertainty in Katie's voice. She pushed her hand into her pocket to feel the lime twig.

"What do you think?" she asked, but there was no reply. Her brother had gone. She almost turned around at that point, but just then there was a sudden blaze of light before them and a roar of noise that sent a wind dancing through the surrounding twigs and branches.

"Shit!"

Eva didn't know who had shouted; she rather thought it might have been her. She felt incredibly relieved and foolish at the same time when she realized that she had just seen a truck rushing past on the main road before her. There was another whoosh as three cars zoomed past in rapid succession.

"I think we've found the road," she whispered, then started to giggle.

• • • •

The four of them clustered at the edge of the forest, just hidden from the occasional traffic that roared past in a blaze of lights, their nerves jangled. Alison held her coin in one hand.

"Okay, heads we go straight on into the woods on the other side, tails we take the road. We'll toss again for left and right if appropriate. Fair enough?"

"Yes," Nicolas said.

"No," said Katie. "That choice favors the road unduly. If it's heads, we should toss again to see whether we go forward or back."

"Go back? But that's ridiculous," Nicolas spluttered.

"If we are going to try to fool the Watcher, we have to follow the coin," said Alison. "Every time we ignore the toss, we're allowing our personalities to shine through, and the Watcher can read our personalities. We need to hide them from it as much as we can."

"Alison is right." Katie gulped, then continued quickly, almost without pause. "Anything that we decide for ourselves can be deduced by the Watcher. It set the motion sensor at the edge of the wood in case we came this way. Who knows what else may have picked us up? If it can guess our next move, it may set more traps. We have to try to be unpredictable. If the coin says go back, we go back."

She gasped for air. They all waited a moment for her to get her breath back, then Alison spoke.

"Okay, you heard Katie. Are we agreed?" she asked.

"Agreed," said Nicolas, after a moment's hesitation.

"Agreed," said Eva.

A truck rushed past, sending old burger wrappers spinning around them in a gust of apple-scented fumes.

Alison tossed the coin as silence slowly resettled on the wood.

"Heads," she called. "Okay, we're not going to follow the road. So, heads we go forwards, tails we go back."

In the dim light, Eva could just see Nicolas' silhouette shake its head slowly.

Alison spun the coin again. "Heads again. Okay, straight across the road and down into the deeper woods."

"This is stupid," Nicolas said. "What can we do in there? We can't travel very fast and we'll get lost. In a couple of hours they'll be out with IR detectors looking for us. They'll have us back at the Center in time for lunch."

Alison sighed deeply. "Nicolas, I thought we agreed?"

Nicolas was obstinate. "So what? It's stupid. We should head along the road, lose ourselves in a town."

Eva pushed a hand in her pocket and began to fiddle with the springy piece of twig. She was tempted to just turn around and walk back to the Center. What was she doing, out here in the middle of the night with a bunch of loonies tossing coins to see where they were going? She could be back at the Center, receiving help while she talked to the ghost of her brother. She laughed a little at the absurdity of the thought.

Katie was speaking now, trying to be reasonable, but her voice sounded high-pitched and nervous.

"Nicolas, how do you know we would lose ourselves in a town? If the Watcher expects us to go there, it will have senses already waiting. We may think that we have escaped, but all the time the Watcher could be leading us closer to itself. There may be an empty building with a loose board over the window inviting us inside. Or maybe we'll see a truck just ahead all parked up for the night with the back open, waiting for us to stow away inside it. How do we know it wouldn't be a trap?"

Nicolas sighed, exasperated.

"I know what you're saying, but we'd be stupid to fall for something like that, wouldn't we? If we saw something as obvious as a truck with the back open, we'd ignore it. Or maybe toss the coin then. But not now. This is ridiculous. This is leading us nowhere. What do you say, Eva?"

The question took Eva by surprise. She guiltily pulled her hand from her pocket and stared into the darkness.

"I don't know," she stammered. "I take your point, Nicolas, but I think we should listen to Katie. This was her plan. She knows what she's doing."

Alison spoke up.

"Anyway, Nicolas, I want you with us." She used her little girl voice. Eva wasn't sure, but she thought there was something there, right at the edge of her vision. Was Alison touching Nicolas?

Nicolas' voice was grudging. "I want to stay with the group," he said. "But this is stupid."

"Do it for me," said Alison. "Just this once."

He's never going to fall for that, Eva thought, but Nicolas spoke and his voice was strained. Just what was she doing to him? Eva didn't want to know.

"Okay," Nicolas whispered. "I'll come with you. But just this time."

They waited for a lull in the traffic before running across the road. There was a ditch at the far side between the road and the trees, then the rusted remains of a wire fence. Alison took the flashlight from Eva and swung the beam left and right.

"There's a gap this way. Come on."

"Shouldn't we toss the coin?" Nicolas said petulantly, but he followed anyway.

They stumbled through the ditch until they came to a point where a rotten wooden post originally holding up the wire fence had fallen. Alison held the torch to form a path of light and they skipped across it, the wires twanging beneath their feet. Alison threw the flashlight to Eva, who caught it and then used it to illuminate the path for her companion. There was a roar of a truck approaching, headlights washing onto the road, and Eva turned off the beam. She turned it back on to find Alison picking herself up and rubbing her knee. The metal lace grips on her boots were tangled with the wires. Alison angrily pulled her foot free.

"Are you okay?" Eva said.

"I'll be fine," muttered Alison, taking the flashlight from her. "Come on."

They walked on through the woods, following her.

The smell of leaf mold gave way to that of pine, the ground became springy and clear of other obstructions, the trees regularly spaced. The land began to rise and fall in regular waves and walking became a lot more tiring.

"We're in a managed forest," said Katie. "There will be roads. They will be easier to follow."

"Only if the coin says so," Alison said grimly.

Glancing up through the gaps in the trees, Eva could see pale morning light creeping over the world. A gentle rain was falling above; around them they could hear the steady drip and splash as it made its way through the canopy to fall to the ground. They came to a narrow forest road, a long scar of mud churned by heavy tires into water-filled ribbons.

Alison tossed the coin. "Left," she said, and they were all relieved to take that path. Walking would be a lot easier.

"If we don't come to a junction in fifteen minutes, I toss the coin again," she said. "Agreed?"

"Agreed," said Katie and Eva.

"Nicolas?"

There was a long pause.

"Agreed," Nicolas said finally.

It was easier following the road, but not that much easier. They had to run along the edges of it, jumping from wet, swampy patches of mud to other less firm footings in an attempt to keep their feet dry. Nicolas jumped onto what looked like a firm patch of ground and his left sneaker sank deep into the mud. He pulled his filthy, sopping foot out of it and swore.

"I told you sneakers would be no good out here," Alison commented unhelpfully.

"Some of us can't afford proper boots," Nicolas snapped. "And anyway, not all of us would think to bring them to the Center with us."

Dawn had broken above them: the edges of the clouds picked out in pale lemon light. On the ground, in the narrow strip of land between the trees, it was still dark enough for them to need to use the flashlight. They walked two abreast, Alison swinging the light back and forth so they could all see where to jump. Occasionally she swung it ahead of them and they saw the seemingly endless road vanishing into the distance.

"Do you get the feeling we're being watched?" said Nicolas.

"That's just paranoia," Alison said. Eva shivered.

Alison was making sense, but Eva had the same feeling. She kept quiet, however. Katie gave a yelp of surprise.

"What is it?" called Alison.

"Up ahead. Something flashed at us."

They stopped dead. Water was soaking through Eva's shoes, oozing slowly through her socks, but she felt too frightened to move. Alison shone the flashlight back and forth. Two eyes flashed back at them. Perfectly circular eyes, about a meter apart, just above ground level. Eva felt her pounding heart shudder at the sight of them.

Katie gave a sudden laugh. "It's a car. It's just an old car."

They all laughed nervously as they crowded forward. It was an old car, abandoned in the woods. The light beam had been reflected from the headlights.

"What's it doing here?" Eva wondered.

"It's watching us," muttered Nicolas. "It's the Watcher. It knows where we are. So much for tossing a coin. We should have hitched a lift into town and lost ourselves there."

Alison spoke with ill-concealed disgust. "It's just an old car in the middle of the woods. You're being paranoid."

Nicolas gave a high-pitched laugh. "I'm being paranoid? Well, golly! *There's* an inspired psychological insight if I ever heard one! Of course I'm being paranoid! It's what I do. It's why they locked me up! I'm good at it! Hey! Maybe it's paranoia that makes me think that you don't escape a highly intelligent super-being by tossing a coin a few times."

He was pointing his finger at Alison. She shone the flashlight in his face in retaliation; he ignored it.

"Look, it's got all the exits watched. It knows exactly

what we're doing and where we are going. We may as well give up now. If nothing else, it will save us getting any colder or wetter!"

Alison took a deep breath, trying to be patient. "Nicolas, we're all cold and wet..."

"Some of us more than others. Or don't you agree, Miss Hiking Boots?"

"Can anyone else hear something?" interrupted Eva.

They all fell silent, listening.

"Nothing," Alison said eventually.

"I thought I heard something, too," Katie whispered.

They stood in silence for a little longer, but heard nothing more.

"Okay," Alison said, "time to toss the coin again. Heads straight on or back, tails left or right."

"This is stupid," said Nicolas. "Let's go left and head back to the road. We're bound to hit it eventually. After that we'll just head for town, like we should have done all along."

"No!" Alison snapped. "We agreed on this method. We can't go back now."

She tossed the coin.

"Tails," she said. She tossed it again. "Okay, we're going right."

"I'm not going," said Nicolas. Katie and Eva exchanged glances. They could see the other two glaring at each other in the dim light.

Alison's voice was low, almost a snarl. "Don't be so childish," she said.

"I'm not being childish," Nicolas said. "This is common sense. It's onto us, face it. The Watcher is so good it can probably see the way the coin lands. It wouldn't surprise me if it was even able to predict it."

Alison sighed. "If it's that clever, then it makes no

difference what we do. We're going this way. Follow us if you like, I don't care."

She turned and climbed up a steep bank, heading back between the regularly spaced trunks of the pine forest. After a moment's hesitation, Eva and Katie followed her. When they looked back, they could see the dark shape of Nicolas stamping angrily along behind them.

A warm autumn morning was waking around them. They came upon another logging road and followed it for some distance until a toss of the coin sent them marching across a large area of freshly cleared forest. They made slow progress, jumping over tree stumps and wide water-filled pits. Katie tore her anorak on the sharp edge of a broken branch sticking up from the ground.

"I was lucky," she muttered. "It could have been my leg."

"Toss the bloody coin, Alison," Nicolas said. "Get us out of here."

"After another ten minutes," Alison replied grimly.

"Look at those." Eva changed the subject. "Aren't they old?"

The tops of a line of electricity pylons could be seen just above the trees ahead of them. They were of an old-fashioned design, constructed of a lattice of weak-looking metal, rather than being formed from an elegant curve of stronger stuff. They looked strangely appropriate in their surroundings, as if they had grown there naturally.

They entered a patch of older woodland. The trees here were not planted in such good order. Oaks and

sycamores fought for space, while tangles of glossy rhododendrons had infiltrated the forest clearings where
trees had fallen. The land began to slope downward;
they could peer out through the trees to see a valley cutting through the land before them.

"Let's stop for a moment," Eva called. She halted and
began to pull off her anorak. Alison and Nicolas did the
same.

"It's too hot now that the sun is up," she explained.
"I'm thirsty, too. How much water do we have left?"

Nicolas was carrying the group's entire supply in a
couple of two-liter milk containers tucked into his
shoulder bag. He unzipped it and checked.

"Just over a bottle's worth. We weren't expecting to
be wandering around here in the woods for so long,
were we? I thought there was nowhere in the country
that was more than five minutes from a burger restau-
rant."

He gazed at Eva, silently pleading with her to help.
Eva felt as if she should say something. Katie wouldn't,
Nicolas wouldn't be listened to. It was down to her.

"Alison?" she said.

"What?" Alison stood with hands on hips, gazing out
over the valley.

Eva tied the anorak around her waist.

"This walking is exhausting. I know we need to evade
the Watcher, but it will do us no good if we die of thirst
in this forest."

"Yes?" said Alison.

Eva sighed. Alison wasn't being very helpful.

She pressed on. "Well, we're spending a lot of time
walking across very rough terrain. It's exhausting. I think
we should think a little bit less about randomness, and a
little more about putting some distance between us and

the Center. We must be barely two kilometers from the place as the crow flies."

Alison reached up and brushed some hair from her face. "So what are you suggesting?" she asked. Eva noted that she did not sound entirely unhappy at this suggestion; Alison must be hating this as much as the rest of them. Eva took a step closer to her.

"Look. We've come to the valley now. Why don't we toss the coin to decide which way to go? Cross it, go back, or head up or down the valley itself? Once we've made that decision, we choose the best possible path. We don't change direction until another path suggests itself."

Alison sighed. "It's cutting down options."

"I know. But we're exhausted. A good leader knows when to cut her losses and change the plan."

"I'm not the leader," insisted Alison, but she smiled a little as she said it.

The coin sent them scrambling down to the floor of the valley. The going was easier than it had been, but still not without difficulties. They slid down earth slopes, clutching at branches to slow themselves, or stumbled down the hill at a half run from trunk to trunk, grabbing at them to stop themselves plunging down too fast. At one point Katie stumbled and slid about thirty meters on her side before finally coming to a halt. Alison screamed; Nicolas and Eva watched how pale her face got. When they came to Katie, she was clutching her arm and crying. There was blood on the tattered arm of her anorak and they now realized why she had not taken it off in the warmth of the morning. Her arm had been more badly injured than they had thought when she had tripped on the broken branch earlier.

"We've got to get that seen to," Nicolas said grimly.

"I'll be okay," Katie whimpered.

"If you're sure." Alison gazed down the slope. "Not much further."

"She's not okay," Nicolas said.

"I'll be fine."

"Look," Eva said, pointing upward, forestalling another argument.

Three airplanes flew overhead, their white contrails forming a triangle high above.

"They're too high to see us," Alison said dismissively. She began to scramble downward again.

"We wouldn't see them if they were stealth planes," Nicolas said. He looked at Katie. "Do you want a hand?"

"I'll be okay," she said, and moved slowly down the hill again.

They scrambled further down. Just as they were nearing the bottom, they came up against a wall of rhododendrons. Tangled brown branches and glossy green leaves choked the bottom of the valley, completely blocking their path.

"We're trapped," Nicolas said flatly. "There's no way through that."

Katie gazed at the tangled mass of vegetation in silence. Her eyes were filling with tears.

"We'll never get back up that hill," Eva whispered.

Alison turned to face them, her face resolute.

"We'll carry on downwards," she said. "There's bound to be a way through."

• • • •

They trudged disconsolately downward, feeling thoroughly miserable. The sun had risen high enough to shine in their faces, making them hot and bad-tempered. Tree roots lay hidden beneath the brown debris of the forest floor, tripping them or sending them slipping toward the crowded green bushes below. On the far side of the valley the old pylons they had seen earlier marched downward, too. Eva looked at the cables that looped down and up, down and up as they were passed from arm to arm.

"There's no end to this," Nicolas muttered angrily.

Just when they thought the rhododendrons would never end, a path revealed itself.

They stood gasping beside the sudden gap in the glossy green barrier, sweat dripping from their faces and trickling down their backs. Walking along the steep slope was extremely tiring; their water was almost finished.

Nicolas shook his head in resignation. "It's found us, hasn't it? It knows where we are."

"We don't know that for certain," Alison said stubbornly.

The path was formed by a tall ash tree that had fallen, giving them a walkway over the tangled bushes it had crushed. Katie and Eva glanced at each other, and Katie shook her head almost imperceptibly.

Alison picked her way forward through the cage of broken branches and kicked the trunk.

"It looks natural enough to me. The roots could have been washed away by all the rain we've been having lately. Trees fall over all the time."

"Does it make any difference?" Nicolas asked. "Whether it was an accident or arranged by the Watcher, we have to go that way. What other choice do we have?"

He pushed past Alison and climbed up over the trunk.

The path led them down to a yellow stone road running along the valley floor. Eva slithered to the ground to find Alison and Nicolas already deep in argument.

"It's been cut. You can see it's been cut! And recently!" Nicolas shouted.

There was no denying it. The severed base of the tree shone white and smelled of sap. Piles of clean white sawdust lay in the brown mud around the stump.

"So what?" said Alison. "We're in a forest. They cut down trees all the time."

"Not individually! And they don't just leave them to rot. It's the Watcher. It's reeling us in."

He was blushing red with heat and anger, sweat dripping down from his curly red hair, mud cracked and dried on his jeans. He was a mess.

"Fine," Alison said coldly. "All the more reason to toss the coin. Heads we go up, tails we go down."

"Why? There's nothing up there in the hills. We should head down and try and get to civilization. The Watcher already knows where we are."

"We don't know that for sure," Katie interjected quietly. She blushed and looked down.

"She's right," said Alison. "We can't give up now. Maybe the Watcher has covered all the bases. There must be a finite number of paths leading away from the Center. Maybe he's laid signs on all of them, just to dishearten us."

"No! This is too much. Alison, think! What were you in for? Not being able to face up to the real world. Don't you see: that's what you're doing now. It's beaten us. Why don't you admit it?"

"We don't know that."

Slowly, deliberately, she pulled the coin from her pocket and spun it in the air. She caught it deftly, smacked it on her wrist, and looked.

"Heads," she called. "We go up."

Nicolas shook his head. "No. Not this time."

"Suit yourself," Alison said. She turned on her heel and began to march up the loose yellow stone of the road. After watching her walk twenty meters or so, Nicolas turned to face Eva and Katie.

"What about you two?" he said. "You must see that she's wrong."

Katie looked down at the ground. "We don't know that. We agreed before we set out to follow the coin."

Nicolas stamped his foot petulantly.

"I might have known you'd follow Alison. What about you, Eva? You know I'm right."

Nicolas was burning red with anger; his face was twitching. Eva suddenly realized that, whether he was right or wrong, she didn't want to go off on her own with Nicolas.

She shook her head gently. "I'm sorry, Nicolas. Katie is right. We agreed to follow the coin."

"Fine. Suit yourself."

He turned and began to stamp down the road in the opposite direction. Katie began to trail up the hill after Alison, who was making good progress with her angry, determined stride.

Eva sighed in resignation, and as she did so an enormous weight dropped from her. A realization was slowly dawning. Here she was, trapped in a long valley, hemmed in by overgrown rhododendron bushes, too hot, thirsty and hungry and with nothing to look forward to but a hard climb up a steep stone road, but . . .

But she wasn't in South Street. She wasn't part of the endless grind of days without purpose. Her friends might be argumentative and bad-tempered, but at least she had friends and she was walking for a reason. The South Street Eva would have just taken the first opportunity to lie down and die. It was what *that* Eva had secretively worked toward for months.

But not this one.

This Eva wanted to live.

The end was drawing near.

They climbed the long road into the hills, Eva occasionally turning to check Nicolas' progress. He remained in sight for quite some time, an obstinate figure in orange marching into and out of view between the choking rhododendrons—and then he was gone.

Their climb was a long, hard drag. Yellow stones skidded and skittered beneath their feet; they kicked them, watched them bounce over the raised edge of the road to fall into the wide ditches on either side.

"It's a quarry road," Katie explained.

"How do you know?" asked Eva, but there was no reply.

The hills began to play games with them. They would climb in silence, putting their all into one last effort to reach the top of an incline, expecting finally to reach the road's summit, only to see a gentle dip and then the road resuming its ascent further on.

"Not again."

Eva thought she heard the whisper as they reached

their third virtual summit. It sounded like Alison's voice.

The pylons to their left marched steadily closer. As they climbed higher she thought she saw a second set of pylons off to her right. They appeared to come marching out of the next valley along.

"They're heading to the same place as we are," she muttered to herself.

"What's that?" asked Alison suspiciously, and Eva jumped. She hadn't realized that Alison was walking so close. She had been watching Eva as she looked at the pylons, an odd expression on her face. It was almost as if Alison had been caught out.

Eventually they reached the real head of the valley, from which the road descended to a natural bowl among the wooded hills. Below them they could just make out a space that had been cleared.

"A quarry," said Katie. "I knew it." She looked at Alison, but Alison just looked away, as if embarrassed.

"It's very big for a quarry," Eva replied. "Look at all those buildings."

The second set of pylons now marched clearly over a hill to their right and picked its way down a steep slope to converge with the lines of the first set. Eva looked up at the sun. It was halfway down the sky, heading toward evening. The earlier heat had vanished. Eva knew that when they stopped walking they would feel cold. Her skin already felt cool to the touch.

The stone road sliced its way through a deep cutting in the hills and they walked in the shade for a while. Looking up, Eva could see an old grey pylon perched immediately on the cutting's edge, thick brown branches of rhododendrons wrapped around its legs and spilling out over the lip of the earth. Higher up, cables looped down from the heavy brown ceramic disks anchored to the pylon's arms. They were humming.

"It's live," Eva whispered, suddenly halting. "I don't like this, Alison. I think we should go back."

Alison turned to her impatiently. "What? After we've come all this way? Don't be silly."

Eva looked on down the road. At the far end of the cutting, a few hundred meters ahead of them, stretched a rusty chain-link fence. The road ran through a rusty gate set in the center of the fence. The gate was propped open invitingly. Eva felt a shiver of fear. The gate looked like a trap, waiting to be sprung. Involuntarily, she took a step backward.

"I don't like it," she said. "It feels all wrong. We shouldn't go in there."

"What? Should we just turn around and go back then?" The other Alison was coming back. The nasty, bad-tempered Alison. And as she did, Katie was becoming more and more nervous and shy.

"So? Are you really saying we should go back?" Alison laughed nastily.

Eva took a deep breath and forced herself to speak calmly. "Yes. There's obviously nothing for us here. No food or water. We can't stay here."

"Of course we can," Alison said derisively. She shook her head and turned away, stamping down the road a little, kicking stones before her as she did so. She took a deep breath, kicked another stone so hard that it bounced from the scrubby walls of the cutting, and then suddenly turned and walked quickly back up to Eva. She wore a nasty smile.

"You haven't figured it out, have you?"

"Figured what out?" Eva felt a shiver of fear. She could guess.

Alison laughed.

"Katie has. She's not stupid. Are you, Katie?"

"No," Katie muttered.

"No. I never thought you were, either, Eva. Don't you realize? You've been tricked. All that nonsense with me tossing the coin and none of you ever thinking to check which way it was really landing. I've been leading you here all along. The Watcher wants to meet you."

She laughed again, and her voice echoed from the walls of the cutting, reverberating up into the sky to be lost in the late afternoon hills. Alison resumed her march back down the road toward the invitingly open gates.

After a moment's hesitation, Katie began to follow.

After another moment, Eva did too.

There was nowhere else to go.

Constantine walked into the hotel lobby, the green bottle containing the message gripped tightly in his hand.

A blue-suited receptionist met him as he crossed the floor toward the elevators, a company smile on her lips.

"Your guest is waiting for you in the Uluru Bar, Mr. D'Roza."

His guest? Constantine hid his surprise.

"Thank you," he said.

"And would you like me to dispose of your bottle, sir?"

The receptionist took the bottle from him. Constantine watched as she carried it off and dropped it in a bin behind the reception desk.

—It's all a simulation, remember, said White. —There is nothing back there, behind the desk. The object will have been destroyed. Its resources restored to the heap. Now that the message has left the simulation, it will have some way of getting into the outside world.

—Fascinating, said Blue sarcastically. —Now, who do you think is waiting for us in the Uluru Bar?

—I've no idea. Have you got any suggestions, or are you just going to be sarcastic?

—No. Sorry.

There was a dark pause.

—I don't like this. It's not part of the script.

They rode the external elevator to the Uluru Bar, a dark glass-and-steel corner of the hotel where it was nearly impossible to tell what was real and what was a reflection. Booths and open seating areas were formed out of cuboids arranged at random orientations to each other, making navigation of the bar difficult without a waiter. Constantine was led to a table that seemingly hovered over nothing. Only the faint reflection of its steel legs in the glass floor indicated that he was not experiencing another fault in the simulation. The woman already seated there was hidden by shadow: the bar had been designed with just such an effect in mind.

Now she leaned forward. "Hello, Constantine."

"Hello, Marion," he replied. "Should you be here?"

—Be very, very careful, said a voice.

It was Grey. Constantine felt a little shiver of apprehension.

—This is it.

Marion smiled worriedly. She leaned closer and the strain was evident in her face.

"Oh, Constantine, I don't know. We're so close to the end, and I'm so worried. Tomorrow's meeting is the last. We have to make the decision then."

A waiter appeared, hovering a discreet distance away.

"Scotch," said Constantine. "An Islay malt, if you have it."

The waiter nodded and withdrew. Constantine looked sternly at Marion.

"I know, Marion. We're all feeling the strain."

"No one more than us, Constantine. The pair of us have been ghosts for the past two years. Does anyone else really understand how we feel?"

A picture of Mary, her dirty green suit trailing cotton from its skirt, sprang into Constantine's mind. He dismissed it.

"I doubt it," he said politely. "Look, Marion, it's not safe for us to be seen together like this."

Marion picked up her glass and took a sip. Constantine got the impression it wasn't her first drink that night.

"We left in such a hurry today. So many things weren't discussed. We'll be going into tomorrow's meeting with so much still unknown."

"That can't be helped."

"Are you sure, Constantine? There could be an opportunity now to discuss things. Maybe tonight." She smiled. "Who would suspect? Two people seen together earlier today, they meet in a bar later on. A woman and an . . . an attractive man, may I say?"

The waiter placed a cut crystal tumbler before Constantine and smoothly withdrew. The golden liquid inside seemed to light up by itself, casting a pattern of brilliant amber shards onto the table.

Constantine took a sip from the glass and bowed his head. He was stuck for words.

—Tell her you're flattered, but that all matters must be discussed by the quorum. That was what it was set up for. Blue was shouting the words in frustration at Constantine's hesitancy.

Constantine repeated what Blue had said.

Marion looked a little downcast. She took another sip, then reached out and touched Constantine's sleeve.

—Are they for real? asked Red, incredulously. —They're trying to seduce you?

"Okay," she said. "Maybe no decisions can be made tonight. But that doesn't stop us discussing things."

Marion wore a blue silk evening dress. Her red hair was done up in a French plait. Constantine found her attractive on some abstract level. Whoever had set this up certainly knew how to play on his feelings. . . . Maybe if he hadn't felt so distracted he would be more open to seduction. Constantine loved his wife, but it had been two years now . . .

Blue was shouting in frustration. —Tell her you'd love to discuss things with her. Tell her that she looks stunning in that dress, or that you like her hair, or, or that her perfume smells nice. Anything! Just change the subject.

Grey spoke. He sounded cool, almost emotionless.

—Blue's right. The more she now has to work at it, the more she will have to make obvious what she wants to know.

Constantine coughed. "Yes. Why don't we talk? That dress really suits you, by the way."

"Thank you." Marion lowered her eyes for a moment. "I bought it here in Stonebreak. It's so rare I get the chance to dress up for someone. I miss it."

Constantine sipped at his whisky. It tasted convincingly smoky and peaty. Once again, he marveled at the depth of the virtual reality in which he was trapped.

"You must have visited quite a few places over the past two years," said Marion.

"Haven't we all?"

—Good answer, said Red.

Marion laughed a little.

"Tell me about it. Go on, Constantine, tell me. Where's the best place you've been?"

He shrugged. Blue had an answer.

—Does it matter? One hotel is pretty much like another nowadays.

Constantine repeated Blue's words.

Marion laughed again. "That's so true." She leaned forward with a serious expression. "But come on. There must have been some benefits. I mean, you must have made it off planet? You must have been to Mars?"

Constantine took another sip of whisky to conceal his reaction. He didn't need Grey to warn him that this was a significant question. He affected a careless shrug.

—Tell her yes, said Grey carefully.

—And point out that she's been there too, added Blue. —Ask her how *she* felt about being there.

Constantine did so. Marion shrugged and tilted her head to one side.

"Oh, amazed. The place is so modern and yet so ancient at the same time. Have you noticed the shape of the factories? They belong to a different age. You can feel it."

Constantine nodded in agreement. "I know what you mean."

Marion eagerly took up her theme. "It's incredible to look out over a landscape that hasn't been touched in any way by AIs. Preserving that place was the best decision humans ever made. It's like nowhere on Earth. It makes you think, doesn't it? Do you ever get the feeling that we're relying on AIs too much?"

—All the time, said Grey.

—It's safe enough to say that, added Blue. —It's the paranoia of our times.

"All the time," said Constantine.

Marion nodded. "And it goes deeper than you might think. People are losing faith in the human ability to think. Children are growing up believing that if it isn't an AI construct, it isn't worth having. Worse, they assume that human minds can't equal the achievements of the AIs. I mean, for heaven's sake, it was humans who invented the wheel, and the sailing ship and the fugue and, and—"

"—and the warp drive." Constantine smiled. "Or so Gillian says, anyway."

—Nice distraction, Red applauded.

Marion laughed. She had a pretty smile that lit up her whole face, tiny wrinkles forming at the corners of her eyes. Constantine found himself smiling back at her. The moment stretched . . . and then her face fell.

"But didn't it make you think?" She picked up her glass and turned it around in her hands. "Didn't it make you want to just take a piece of that place and bring it back with you? To show to people, to say, 'Look, this is what we humans did, all by ourselves'?"

—That's it, said Grey. —That's what they're trying to discover.

Constantine sat back in his chair. Beneath his feet were a few centimeters of glass, the only thing between him and several hundred meters of empty space. At that moment he felt as if he were perched on the edge of a precipice both literally and figuratively. He drained the rest of his whisky.

"Well, Marion. I did bring something back. Surely you know that?"

—What? said Blue. —What are you playing at?

—No, he's right, said Red. —They must have figured

it out for themselves. What harm does it do us if they know, anyway?

Marion's eyes fluttered nervously. "Of course, of course. I just meant, well, you'd want to, wouldn't you? Take a little souvenir, I mean."

Constantine waved his glass in her direction.

"Uh-huh. Look, I need another drink. What about you?"

"Better not. Another brandy and I won't be responsible for my actions." An uncertain smile spread across her face. "Then again, why not? I'm sure I can trust you, can't I?"

—This is so corny! complained Blue.

Constantine signaled to the waiter for the same again. Marion slumped back in her chair while he gazed out across the first and second levels of Stonebreak, out toward the dark ribbons of cloud stretching between the moon and the distant horizon. The waiter placed their drinks on the table and withdrew. Marion picked up her glass and took a sip. She leaned forward with her elbows on the table, her hands supporting her head, fingers buried in her hair, and gave Constantine a big smile.

"This is amazing, isn't it? I'm with a man who has held a piece of the old world in his hands. What was it like?"

Constantine needed no exhortation to speak. It had been a key moment in his life. He longed to share it with someone. He sat back, his eyes taking on a dreamy expression.

"Strange. Exhilarating. Frightening. It was the moment we had been leading up to for a year, it is the moment that everything we have done since then has depended upon."

"But it worked? You got it back to Earth."

And that was it. Constantine felt a little catch in his voice as he spoke. He hoped she wouldn't notice it.

"I did what I was supposed to do," he said.

—She doesn't know what it is. They don't know where we took it! Got them at last! Blue was practically singing with delight.

"How did you conceal it, when you took it off planet?"

"I didn't. I kept it in full view. They thought it was a museum exhibit. I suppose it was, really."

"And then you took it to Frankfurt."

"Come on, Marion. I don't think we should discuss this anymore. We will have enough time for that tomorrow. Let's wait until we're quorate."

Marion gave a shrug.

"Spoilsport. Are you always so firm with women?"

—Did she really just say what I thought she just said? said Blue in disbelief.

Constantine looked at his watch.

"After nine. We have an early start tomorrow. Maybe we should get to bed."

Marion smiled knowingly. "Is that an invitation?"

Constantine grinned back. "You want to be careful. You could get a married man into trouble." He laughed. After a moment's hesitation, Marion joined in.

Constantine drained his glass and rose to his feet.

"Well, I'm off. Good night, Marion."

He leaned across and gave her a peck on the cheek, then turned and walked from the bar.

A clamor of voices arose in his head.

—Well done! That was excellent! Blue was delighted with Constantine's performance.

—It was good, said Red, though he sounded distracted. —Still, why pull that now? Why not just wait until the meeting tomorrow?

—Maybe they were worried things wouldn't get decided? said Blue.

—Maybe. But I wonder. Maybe something else is happening out there. Maybe DIANA is moving in on them. Getting ready to free us.

—Maybe maybe maybe, said Blue. —What do you think, Grey?

No one expected Grey to answer. They were surprised when he did.

—I don't know. I am seriously concerned. Now that we know what they are trying to find out, I think we may have been premature in trying to get a message out to DIANA. I hope that we will not come to regret our earlier request to Jay.

Marion came into Constantine's room that night. He woke to find her standing at the foot of his bed, something in her hand, an odd smile on her face.

"Marion," said Constantine. "How did you get in here?"

She held up the item in her hand. It was the same bottle Jay had given him earlier that evening.

"No, thank you, Marion. I've had enough to drink." He yawned and rubbed his eyes. He wondered if his other personalities were sleeping.

—I'm here, said White. —I'll wake them.

Marion's smile widened a little, though there was a hint of pity in her eyes.

"Nice try, Constantine. Come on."

She turned from the bed and walked toward the large

picture window that looked out over Stonebreak. Constantine rose to his feet to follow. He was clothed in a simple, white, one-piece jumpsuit. He didn't recognize it; he didn't remember putting it on. With a sinking heart he followed her.

Marion took hold of the handle that opened the window leading to the balcony, the same balcony where he had spoken to Jay not twenty-four hours before. She gave Constantine a sympathetic look.

"Brace yourself," she said.

Constantine wondered what she meant, then she slid open the window. There was nothing beyond it. Nothing. Just a dull grey space. Constantine shivered. The view was unnerving. At the wall containing the window that led to the balcony, the world had just been split in two. Through the glass of the sliding window that Marion had pushed to one side he could see the nightscape over Stonebreak. The dark space that was defined by the lights of the city, the stars and the moon. To the left of the glass, where he should have seen the balcony beyond, there was nothing. An emptiness, a lack of anything that made him feel quite terrified.

He was looking into oblivion. It was the gap beneath the sky. It was the end of his virtual life.

Marion stepped beyond the world. Constantine watched her walk out into the grey emptiness. She turned and beckoned to him to follow.

"Come on," she called. "We need to talk."

After a moment's hesitation, Constantine stepped forward.

He walked into the greyness. There was nothing beneath his feet, and yet, as he walked, he seemed to move forward. It was an odd feeling; there was no resistance to his tread.

Marion was waiting for him up ahead. As he came level with her, she indicated that he should look back the way he had come. There he saw a rectangle hanging in the greyness, a portal that led back to the world. Through it he could see the cream corduroy carpet of the hotel room, the edge of his bed, the corner of a pastel print.

Marion spoke softly. "You've been very unlucky. Your message made it to the outside world, but unfortunately for you, the object code failed to destroy itself. It was analyzed in a routine efficiency scan just as its resources were about to be returned to the heap and it caused an exception to be thrown. Even then, we would have wondered at its meaning if it hadn't been for something you said earlier."

"What's that?"

"Back in the concert hall, yesterday. You subvocalized something to your internal personalities: 'I'm not sure the Night Jay will have a method of contacting the outside world.' "

"Oh," said Constantine.

—Stupid, stupid, stupid! said Red.

—It's too late to worry about that now, said Grey.

Marion continued. "You had the whole realside team in turmoil because of that. What did you mean, 'outside world'? What was the Night Jay? They couldn't believe that the simulation had been compromised. Most of them assumed it was some sort of code. They didn't want to believe you had found out where you were. And then we found the message in the bottle."

"Oh," said Constantine. He didn't know what else to say.

Marion touched his elbow. "Look, it was a mistake anyone could make. You're up against a team of a hundred people."

Again he was lost for words. Marion cleared her throat.

"Anyway. While I was busy trying to seduce you in here, the powers that be out in the real world were putting together an offer."

Constantine nodded. "I'm listening."

Grey spoke with cold finality.

—There can be no bargains.

Marion gave a tiny shake of her head. "I'm not sure that you would really understand what the offer means. You don't understand what's involved here. That's why we're going to show you."

She reached out her hand into the nothingness and pulled it to one side. Another door opened in space. Through it Constantine could see a corridor, just a little wider than the doorway itself. A steep stairway, looking oddly familiar, led downward. He strained to see more, hungry for the touch of reality in the empty world. It looked so *real*. He could make out cracked paint on the ceiling; he could see how the stone of the steps was slightly dipped in the center where so many people had already trodden.

"Go on down," said Marion.

Constantine did not need to be told. He was already stepping into the welcoming doorway. Anything to get out of this dreadful nothingness. He walked down eight or nine steps, feeling the reassuring solidness of the stone beneath his feet. He pressed a hand gratefully against the cool, cream-painted plaster of the wall. Marion stepped onto the top step behind him and pulled a cream-painted door closed behind her. She sat down on the top step and took a deep breath.

"What now?"

"Go down the steps," said Marion. "Someone will be waiting for you at the bottom."

"Aren't you coming, too?"

"No. I'll wait here for your return." She shivered, and said with real feeling. "I couldn't bear to wait out there."

Constantine shivered in sympathy. "I know what you mean." He turned and began to descend.

Constantine danced quickly down the stairs, the stone treads beneath his feet sending up a pitter-patter echo in the narrow passageway. As he reached a landing, the stairway reversed direction, yet still heading down. The feeling that he had been here before was rising in Constantine all the time. Onto another landing and he reversed direction again. There was a door at the bottom of this next flight of steps. A green double door with anti-crush bars stretched across, faintly patterned with the oil of a thousand fingerprints. And Constantine at last remembered where he was. He pushed open the doors of the concert hall and stepped out onto the wide paved area of the fourth level of Stonebreak.

A familiar figure in a shabby green suit was waiting for him, just beyond the doors.

"Hello, Mary," said Constantine.

Mary led him to a nearly empty cafe bar located close to the Source. They ordered tiny cups of espresso and tall glasses of chilled water and carried them to a table well away from the bored-looking youth who served at the counter. Around them, the tables were still littered with dirty cups, dried coffee foam forming tidemarks around the rims; half-eaten sandwiches, and cakes dried and curled on plates. Mary looked across to the five en-twined branches of the Source and then raised her espresso cup to Constantine.

"Cheers," she said.

"Cheers."

Mary sipped at the strong coffee then took a drink of cold water. Constantine did the same. The contrast be-tween the strong, hot, bitter coffee and the refreshing cold-ness of the water was stimulating. Constantine replaced his cup on the saucer and sat up straight.

"What's it all about, Mary?"

She sat up a little straighter too and looked at him.

"I was supposed to be your conscience. It was an-other possible way to get what we wanted from you."

Constantine said nothing for a moment, took an-other sip of espresso, another of water.

"It probably stood the best chance of working, you know."

"The company AI said it would. I never believed it."

"Which company is it?"

"The company now called 113 Berliner Sibelius, fol-lowing the corporate merger at the AI level earlier this week. My presence is also partly explained by the much more environmentally aware policy we've been pursuing since then. I'm not sure it's to our benefit, you know, but there you go. Who are we to argue with an AI?"

"Who indeed?" asked Constantine. He looked across to the Source again.

"Is the DIANA strand crumbling out in the real world, too?"

"Oh, yes," said Mary.

He finished off the espresso and downed the rest of the water in one gulp. He was ready for a whisky, now.

"So. What is it you want to know?" he asked.

Mary smiled at him and sat back in her seat. A young couple crossed the square behind her, wrapped up in each other's arms.

"Three things," said Mary.

She raised a finger. "One, how did you carry the VNM away from Mars?"

She raised a second finger. "Two, where did you take the VNM? How are you maintaining its integrity?"

A third finger. "And three, what are you going to do with it?"

"Can't you guess?" asked Constantine.

"Oh, we can see the point, sort of. We know that the VNM is entirely the product of human ingenuity. As a human—" she smiled briefly "—as the personality construct of a human, I share your concerns about the motivations of AIs and realize the value of having something untouched by their machinations. We just don't see the commercial advantage."

"Maybe there isn't one."

Mary said nothing. Constantine held her gaze for a moment.

"Okay. I'll answer your first question. I didn't take the VNM off the planet. I couldn't. You're thinking of modern self-replicating machines, the sort of thing you can hold in your hand or pour by the million into a bottle. This was a first attempt: thirty gigabytes of code and about one hundred tons of raw materials. It was the code that counted. That's what I took away."

"Couldn't you just get it from records here on Earth?"

"How do we know it hadn't been subtly altered by

the AIs in the meantime? How paranoid can we be here? Every processor, every memory slice that can be accessed by an AI is necessarily suspect. I couldn't even trust a modern secured memory slice; it would have to interface with modern equipment eventually and then that code would become visible. So I took something called a laptop computer. Over a hundred years old—an oversized plastic box with a fixed-size viewing field and a data entry area that hurts your back and arms and neck just using it."

Constantine rubbed his hands unconsciously as he remembered the odd machine: crouching at the overlarge device, the strange feel of the antique plastic keys moving beneath his fingers as he painfully typed out instructions, the eerie glow of the viewing area on his face; the humming noise and the bizarre way that it blew warm air out of a vent in its side as it worked; the fact it needed a power source—what modern thinking machine needed power?

"It was a museum piece, Mary," he said. "Priceless. They can't make them anymore. You'd have to build a factory just to construct the processor. Too much effort. There're only about ten of them left working now. When they all die, that will be it. The programs that ran on them will live on in emulators, but the original machines that made those programs live will be just so much metal and plastic. It's . . . not sad exactly. I don't know . . . The passing of something?"

He tilted his head to one side. "You know, that's just like us, isn't it? Minds without bodies. I never thought of that before." There was another pause.

He sighed. "You know, this is nice in a way. Two years alone. It's nice to speak to someone about things.

What I've done. What I've seen. Have you ever been to Mars, Mary?"

She shook her head.

"It's an odd place. A vision of what might have been. The future maybe, but not our future. A Buck Rogers future...." His voice trailed away as he remembered the events of a year ago. Flying up to the Martian factory mine. Its odd pyramidal shape seemed appropriate somehow on the red plain of the Martian desert. The soft voices of the flier's pilot and of Louisiana Station control were the only sounds in the cabin as they approached the red-and-silver mass of the construction. They had skimmed over the tracks of two robot crawlers, low cylinders suspended from huge balloon tires that were trundling in a straight line from the base, headed who could know where. The mine drew closer. A jumble of steel and iron and rock. A miniature city built by and for machines.

Constantine jerked himself back to the present. "The AIs haven't touched the place. It's a preserved land, but what they've preserved there is our human past. The original project has been left to run unhindered. Everything there is a product of human ingenuity. It's..." He shook his head.

"The... silence there, the intent... I can't describe it. We developed Antarctica, we let AIs loose on the moon... I don't know."

Mary said nothing. The young man who had been serving behind the bar had finally left his place and was clearing used cups and litter onto a tray.

"I landed there and entered through a maintenance hatch. Can you imagine, those earthbound engineers, over a hundred years ago, designing a city that was to grow on another world? A city that only existed to them as lines of code, designed to be built in a place they could never visit. And while they wrote that program, they thought to include doors for future humans to enter the site, and access corridors and interface slots where they could plug in their laptops."

He shook his head in admiration.

"They were building castles in the air, but they made them real." He shook his head again. "Do you know how long I have waited to talk to somebody about this?"

"I can guess. I don't think I can truly appreciate what it *really* must have been like."

"No, I don't think you could. Anyway. I went in there and plugged in the laptop. Filled it with the program that is the seed of a new factory and then got back on the flier. Went back to Louisiana Station. Back into our world. You know, you sit in a hotel room on Louisiana Station and look out at red Martian plains littered with rocks and you see Mons Olympus rising up over the horizon. Close the blinds and you could be anywhere. You could be back here on Earth. You sit in a room with the same bed and pastel prints and minibar serving filthy vanilla-flavored whisky."

He sighed and looked down at the simple white jumpsuit that he had found himself wearing. He suddenly realized that it didn't have a zipper or any other way to take it off. Whoever was controlling this simulation was making a subtle point.

"Anyway, that's it. That's how I got the VNM off Mars. I'd have thought you could have figured that out for yourself."

Red spoke up. —They probably did. It's an old interrogator's trick. Start with the easy questions. Get the subject talking.

Mary smiled at him. "We had some ideas. We just wanted to know for sure. What about the other two questions? Are you going to answer those?"

"I don't know," said Constantine.

—You're not. Grey's tone was low and final.

Constantine shivered. It hadn't occurred to him, until that point, that he might not have a choice in his actions. Grey had already demonstrated that he could take over control of his body.

"I'm not sure I will be able to," he added, too softly for Mary to hear.

Mary had already risen to her feet. "We thought you might not be cooperative. Come on. We're going to try and change your mind."

She led him out of the bar. They walked side by side across the large flagstones of the fourth level. The moon was banded by thickening streamers of cloud, giving the impression of being behind a set of Venetian blinds.

"See the moon?" asked Mary.

Before Constantine could answer her, the bands of cloud widened, blocking out the moon completely. They quickly narrowed again, but now the moon had gone. In its place was a hole to somewhere else. Through it, a great eye looked down at Constantine. A blue eye; it blinked twice. Long curling eyelashes swept up and down, down and up.

"Everything you do is being watched. This world has been constructed entirely for you. It can look like this . . ." She waved a hand around, indicating the Source, the bar they had just left and the nearby concert hall. She took hold of Constantine's arm and swiftly guided him to a grey door set in the wall of the concert hall, one of the many exits used to empty the building quickly once the entertainment had finished.

She stood Constantine before the door and looked the other way.

"Or it can look like this," she continued.

The door swung open. Constantine looked through it into Hell. He saw flames. A demon was staring out at Constantine. It held a book tightly gripped in its twelve hooked hands. Constantine saw his name clearly inscribed on the front. The demon was standing by a strange machine made out of stainless steel, all blades and needles and with someone strapped inside it.... The door suddenly swung closed.

Mary turned to face him, her face pale. "It's an idle threat, Constantine. It costs too much running the simulation that keeps us all in here. The processing power could be put to better, more profitable uses. You, me, Marion and...the other one. We're all personalities trapped in this bottle. They'll just turn us off if we don't deliver."

Mary shivered and looked up to the great eye, staring down from the hole where the moon had been. A look of defiance crossed her face.

"I don't care, Constantine. I'm telling you the truth now. You don't know what it's like. You're more honest than we are. You didn't volunteer to come in here. The real me, the one out there in the real world, has sentenced a copy of herself to oblivion for the sake of a bonus of a few hundred credits. What does that tell you about human beings, Constantine? Would you do that to yourself? I bet you would."

She began to shake; she looked as if she was about to start crying.

"I don't know what to say, Constantine. I don't know what to tell you. This is the deal: you tell us what we want to know and we keep the simulation going. That way, you have a life; we have a life. You don't tell us, and I don't know what will happen. Maybe it will be what you saw through that door. Personally, I think they'll just turn us off. Why throw good money after bad?"

"How can I trust you?" asked Constantine.

"You can't. But what other choice do you have?"

"I don't know. I need to think."

Mary nodded. "I bet you do. Well, here's something else to think about. Why are you protecting DIANA? Do you know they've already launched three attacks on this computer, the one in which we now reside? The third one almost succeeded. They got a worm into the system that would have wiped the entire simulation if we hadn't found it in time. For DIANA, the best way to keep secret what you know is to destroy you."

Constantine opened his mouth to argue, but he couldn't find the words. What Mary said made sense. He didn't want it to be so, but it made sense. What would *he* do if he was outside and not trapped in here?

And that was the point. He *was* outside. The real Constantine *was* out there somewhere. And Constantine, now shuddering violently in the warm night air, knew exactly what he would be thinking:

At all costs the project must be protected.

Somehow I must wipe out the copy of my personality.

HErB 5: 2210

The ship reinserted itself into normal space. Herb braced himself for the attack...

Nothing happened.

Gradually he relaxed. Herb felt like an old-fashioned wind-up toy. The tension would slowly build up inside him, hunching his shoulders, bunching his fists, restricting his breathing, until he noticed it was happening. Then it took a conscious effort to relax; release his pent-up breath in one huge sigh; force himself to breathe more slowly. And that would appear to work for a while, but all the time the tension was rebuilding, his body slowly winding itself up again.

It was happening already as Herb scanned the viewing areas.

Where were they? Where was the attack? Nothing. Only empty sky.

Robert coughed. He was about to perform one of his little distractions; Herb just knew it.

"The thing about warp drive, superluminal drive,

faster-than-light drive," said Robert, "is that once you make the jump, you can't be tracked."

Herb was not impressed. He had been expecting better than this.

"Well, yes. Everyone knows you can't track someone making a warp jump," he said.

Robert grinned. "And they're right. But what many people don't realize—and it's partly because they don't take the trouble to think about the problem, and partly because the AIs keep quiet about it—is that you can still usually make a pretty good guess at a ship's position."

"How?" Herb's stomach was tightening with uncertainty.

Where were they? Robert scanned the viewing field in the floor again and frowned. "The Enemy Domain saw us insert ourselves into warp at a certain point. There is a certain range of speeds at which we can travel using a warp drive, so that gives the Enemy a minimum and maximum distance that we can have traveled. Think of two concentric bubbles expanding outward from our starting point. As the outer bubble sweeps through a system, they will go on alert. After the inner bubble has trailed through later on, they stand down.

"Once we jump, we're like the particle in an electron cloud. The Enemy can map a probability of us being at any point within it. Once we materialize, the wave function collapses and a new set of equations comes into play. AIs have been solving these equations for decades. They're good at them. They need to be; they're using them to probe—" Robert paused. "Well, that's another story."

Herb nodded blankly. He wondered how long this horrible, twisting tension could be held in by the walls of his stomach. He felt as if it would rupture in an acidic explosion at any moment.

Robert reached into his left-hand jacket pocket and pulled out another VNM. This one was smaller than that machine of Herb's which had been dropped onto the last planet. The new machine was an odd shape; it twisted around on itself like a Möbius strip. Robert placed it on the white handkerchief that was still spread out neatly on the sofa next to him.

"So now we play a game of cat and mouse," he grinned at Herb, "if you'll forgive the cliché. Quantum entanglement provides for instantaneous communication, so the entire Enemy Domain will know of our position the moment we are spotted. Therefore, we must try and outguess them. We must try not to be seen."

Herb nodded. They seemed to be doing a pretty good job so far; there was still no sign of Enemy activity. He looked around the room, gazing at the viewing fields that covered the ceiling, the walls and the floor, knowing as he did so how unrealistic it was to expect to see anything out there but stars. Nonetheless, he kept looking. The fear that he would see a fleet of ships swooping toward them could not be shaken. Robert remained unfazed. He continued his lecture.

"As long as we remain within the Enemy Domain, more and more of its ships can jump to place themselves within reach of the expanding spheres of our separate jumps. As the wave front passes them by, those ships will jump to follow it. When we jump again, they will repeat the maneuver. I'm afraid, Herb, we can't keep this up indefinitely. If we wish to stay in here, then sooner or later the Enemy will catch us."

He smiled again. "I'm planning on later."

Herb glanced around the screens. He had been expecting explosions, attack ships, anything but this calm nothingness. Where had the Enemy got to? His voice sounded a little high-pitched as he spoke. "There's nothing happening. Where are we?"

Robert laughed.

"About three hundred AUs from where we started, just floating in empty space. We've hardly moved at all. Despite all I've just said, they'll never think of looking for us this close to our jump point."

Herb got to his feet.

"I need to do something. I'm going to make a cup of fresh coffee. Do you want some?"

"No, thank you," said Robert. "It would be wasted on me. Robots don't care for coffee." He folded his hands on his lap and continued his methodical scanning of the viewing fields. Herb opened a cupboard in the tiny kitchen and pulled out the coffee tin. He pulled off the lid to the rich smell of chilled air and roasted beans.

"Damn. Only half full. I forgot. The rest will be on the other ship. The replicating engine is set not to reproduce luxury goods."

Robert said nothing.

Herb pulled a glass cup from another cupboard. "I've figured out why you dropped my VNM on that planet we just stopped at," he said. "You want it to convert the nickel iron sea into copies of itself."

"Come on, Herb, you can do better than that. What about the VNMs already there? They'll be trying to convert your VNMs back again."

"I know. I suppose you've got my VNM transmitting the friend code."

Robert nodded. "I could have done, but I didn't bother. Remember Lesson One of VNM warfare, Herb: as long as your machines are converting the opposition at a faster rate than they are converting back, you're going to overwhelm the Enemy in the end. It's not about initial numbers, it's about the conversion vector. You want it pointing in your direction."

Herb spooned coffee into the pot and poured nearly boiling water over the grounds. He nodded thoughtfully.

"I see. But what's the point? Once the Enemy AI figures out what you're doing, it will just release a machine a bit faster at reproducing than mine was. They'll get converted back and we'll have achieved nothing."

Robert's faint smile widened to a big white grin. "We'll just have to keep the Enemy AIs concentrating on something else then, won't we?"

He looked back up at the viewing fields. "You'd better hurry up with your coffee. We jump just as soon as this ship hits point one lights." He checked his watch. "That's in about fifteen seconds," he added.

Herb hurriedly pressed the button on the coffee pot and the water shivered in a complex pattern, sending the grounds spiraling to the bottom to be held there. He carried the pot and his glass cup back to the sofa facing Robert's and sat down, placing the pot on the parquet floor just by his feet. Holding the cup tightly in his hands, he gazed up at the ceiling viewing field. Robert had set a large crimson circle expanding across a 2-D slice of starscape. A gold marker, just off center, indicated their ship's position. A second gold marker lit up, halfway between the ship and the trailing edge of the bubble.

"The second marker is where we're jumping to. They

should assume we're somewhere in the crimson circle at the moment."

"Cunning."

"I know. But we won't be able to pull this trick too often, mind. Okay, hold onto your coffee, we're going to jump..."

Herb bit his bottom lip...

Their reinsertion was accompanied by a series of flashes so powerful they tripped out the vision on the viewing fields. Twice the rear fields dimmed, then the left-hand fields, then the portals in the floor at Herb's feet. Robert thoughtfully plotted the explosions on a section of the viewing field just above Herb's head. Ripples formed in the dark surface of Herb's coffee. As he watched, the tiny waves began to interfere with each other and form a fizzing pattern of brown bubbling liquid. Herb stared at the cup with morbid fascination. The ship must be undergoing incredible accelerations for this effect to be noticeable *inside* the cabin. He dreaded to think what was happening to the fluids inside his own body. The butterflies in his stomach would have steel wingtips at the moment.

"Got it," said Robert, animation returning to his face. "Wiped the security net. That took longer than I expected. It's a good thing we were through here earlier on. There are cut-down copies of my intelligence nested in the processors of a lot of the machinery in this system. Not strong enough to effect a change on their own, but they were helpful in the fight..."

"We were through here earlier on?" said Herb.

"Of course, when we scouted the territory. All those saboteurs we planted...."

Herb felt shaken. He remembered Robert's earlier demonstration, his simulation of their bodies splitting in two and splitting in two as they sailed through the galaxy.

"How many of us are there?" he asked in a tiny voice.

Robert shrugged. "I've no idea anymore. You haven't grasped it yet, have you Herb? This war is about reproduction. Anything that *can* make a copy of itself *does* so, or else it gets swamped."

Herb sipped coffee without tasting it. He needed something to do to distract himself.

"Herb, if you think the battle we're currently engaged in looks frantic, you should see what it looks like from Machine Level."

Robert quickly scanned the viewing fields, his dark face half hidden in the pastel glow of the displays.

"Still, everything looks okay at the moment. We've achieved a balance of sorts, so I think we're ready to hit the planet's surface." He assumed a serious expression. "I'll warn you now, we're going to jump down there using the warp drive."

"What?" Herb almost spilled coffee in his lap. "What if you miscalculate? A fraction of a decimal place out and we could end up slamming into the ground! Isn't jumping directly down to a planet incredibly dangerous?"

Robert shrugged. "Normally I'd say yes. However, given our current circumstances, I think that a close proximity warp jump is the least of our worries."

Down at Machine Level:

The entity known as Robert Johnston was far beyond what humans understood to be a personality construct. Unlike the crude copies of itself that had been sent out into the linear and pseudo parallel processing spaces of the

Enemy Domain, the personality construct resident in the robot body was of a super parallel non-Turing design that human minds could not begin to comprehend. Its like was not scheduled to be seen in human space for at least another two hundred years.

Super parallel non-Turing: in other words, Robert Johnston could think about many things at once.

To Robert Johnston, reality was a series of interlocking layers. At the moment, for example, he could see the dissipating warp field still shimmering around the ship yet well below the threshold that would cause anomalies for anything crossing the boundary into normal space.

Another part of him had interfaced with a minor security net on the planet which saw the universe as a three-color array of threats, friends and undecideds. That particular Robert was busily engaged in slotting the ship into the "friends" column.

Part of Robert Johnston could even see the world through eyes similar to Herb's.

Using those senses, its robot body appeared to be sitting in a warm patch of sunlight cast by the ceiling viewing fields. Robert called this a human view. Such a slow view. Herb sat opposite him, anxiously looking from viewing field to viewing field with the speed of a snail in aspic.

And then there was that other way of looking at humans...

Robert Johnston could see Herb as a pattern of feelings and emotions that even Herb himself was not always aware of. He read the tension evident in his shoulders as a standing wave of electrical impulses, heard the fear in his chest by the rapid pattern of his heartbeat.

He could look deeper. He saw how, as Herb gazed around at the friendly warmth of this new planet, he was for a moment taken back to that day, weeks ago, when he had *boarded his spaceship to make the return journey to his converted planet. Herb was feeling a strong wave of something almost like nostalgia. Not just a wish to be home, safe, but something more: a realization that if he had his time over again, his life could be so much better.*

In the middle of the battle, Herb was having a sudden insight into what a mess he had made of his life so far; how much of a waste it had been.

It was the emotion that Robert had been waiting to read in Herb. One that he had been leading him toward for the past eleven days.

Directly below the ship, a river of blue-grey machines crawled along a rocky channel. A seemingly never-ending parade of shuffling, stumbling cylinders being funneled through the U-shaped valley that ran in a straight line from horizon to horizon. One aspect of Robert Johnston guided his robot body to pick up the Möbius VNM it had shown Herb earlier and then throw it out of the ship's hatch to land in the parade of machines that crept through the valley underneath.

While one part of his consciousness examined the structure and command systems of the machines below, another part explained to Herb, with painful slowness, the methods by which those machines would eventually terraform the planet across which they marched. On one level of reality Robert Johnston was examining the bacteria-tailoring factories that would build the soil for the planet, on another level he was explaining to Herb how the creeping machines would eventually form a circle around the planet to act as a heat pump, and on yet another level Robert Johnston was watching the Möbius machine that his robot body had just thrown from the ship. The machine righted itself and took a couple of stumbling steps forward, but was gradually dragged down by the slow, inevitable movement of the creeping machines. It reappeared for a moment, bobbed up above the backs of the machines, once, twice, and then was gone.

The hatch slid shut.

Herb had noticed that two of the blue-grey machines from the planet below were now sitting motionless on the hatch.

"What are they for?" he asked.

"They're for later," said Robert, oh so slowly, while at the same time he reconfigured the thickness of the ship's hull, making the stern slightly thicker than the nose. After all, the stern was catching most of the explosions.

He told the ship to ascend.

Herb's world was so slow . . . Robert knew what Herb was about to say before Herb did, and yet Robert still had to sit and listen to the end of each sentence. It was important. Not to do so would be unsettling for the young man.

"Your machine didn't work," said Herb. The words moved at glacier speed. Robert already had the reply slotted in place, ready to play, while another part of his attention completed the analysis of the Ouroboros machines below.

"Patience," said Robert. "These terraformers are faster at reproduction than those on the last planet. Give it time and my Möbius machine will make enough copies of itself to be able to twist that loop around and reverse the terraforming process."

"Oh," said Herb. The ship was accelerating away from the planet's surface again, getting ready for another jump. Robert could see the thought occurring to him. He knew what Herb was going to say next.

"Why are we stopping the terraforming of that planet? Surely terraforming is a good thing?"

"Only if you're a human. Not everyone in the galaxy is," replied Robert. "Jump in ten seconds . . ."

And then most of the ship's propulsion system vanished.

In an instant all *of Robert Johnston's attention was directed to trying to keep the ship aloft.*

There wasn't enough of the propulsion system left to do that.

The ship was falling back toward the planet: impact in 13.2081177 seconds.

The ship's self-repair systems came on line. They were fast, but not fast enough. Impact would still occur, now in 26.1187722 seconds. Robert Johnston added some of the nanotechs he carried in his own robot body to the ship. The reinforcements were enough to help the repair system complete its immediate task. The ship's fall was halted: impact in (indefinite) seconds.

Now Robert split his awareness in two. Part of it continued to oversee the repairs; a larger part was directed to discovering what had happened.

He ran through the ship's internal monitoring records and replayed the last three milliseconds before the propulsion system had vanished.

There was the answer. The ship had fallen victim to a stealth attack. Somehow the local security net had got a set of nanotechs onto the hull. That should have been impossible, given the defense routines Robert had set up, but even more incredible was the fact that the nanotechs had managed to do so without being noticed. They had worked their way into the propulsion system, making themselves into exact copies of existing parts. When they had converted enough of the system, they just . . . dissolved.

Robert Johnston was puzzled. They had dissolved too soon. If they had waited longer they could have left him with no propulsion system at all. Why so soon?

A second replay of the ship's memory and he saw it. A routine internal scan had been initiated ten picoseconds before the attack. The enemy nanotechs must have feared detection; they acted too soon rather than be wiped out. Thankfully.

The threat had been identified.

All this took just under two seconds. Robert Johnston now felt it safe to split his consciousness further so as to interface with other layers of reality.

To Herb, it was as if the attack was still underway. Robert could see him as he was thrown out of the sofa, his left knee banging on the wooden floor. Robert could read the pain in Herb's body as his left hand was twisted the wrong way and almost broke.

Robert Johnston was still funneling materials toward the propulsion system. There wasn't enough mass in the propulsion chamber, so he sought it from elsewhere on the ship. Herb's bedroom was quickly cannibalized.

The propulsion systems now operated at four percent efficiency.

Back in the slow world, Herb was thrown to the left, tumbling across the floor, hot coffee splashing over him as he went. A white vase fell to the floor, shattering next to his head. Meanwhile, the robot body was picking itself up off the floor, its face slack and utterly expressionless. The ship continued to shake and jerk around, but the movement was diminishing. Herb sat up slowly, favoring his right hand. As he stared at his left, Robert could see wave after wave of sickening pain sweeping through the human, centering on his knee. The robot body came and put an arm around Herb, helped him to his feet.

"Are you okay?" asked Robert. He helped Herb to limp across to his sofa and sat him down.

"I think so. My hand... No. It can wait. What happened?"

Robert began to explain.

All the while another part of Robert was examining the options of what to do next.

He had been too cocky, he had underestimated the capabilities of the local AI. He could not afford to make that mistake again.

Now he would have to take time out from the attack to replenish the ship's resources. He calculated that it would take about four minutes. He estimated the Enemy's ships would be here in five. So, just enough time to drop back to the planet's surface and then get out again.

Much too confident. He would not make that mistake again.

Then another part of his awareness picked up the flickering of a warp transition. One, two, three Enemy ships inserting themselves into normal space. They had got here far too quickly. Another mistake.

He would have to jump again right now. . . .

He looked at the warp field, began to coax it into shimmering life . . .

He was simultaneously observing Herb. Robert could read the fear that coursed through the man's body at his announcement of the jump. Herb's mouth was dry, his pulse rate increasing, his stomach pulsing, and yet his body's functioning was still within acceptable parameters. Herb would experience far worse before this was over.

Something foreign still lurked on the ship.

Another jump. They reinserted into normal space and the lounge lit up with the brilliant white glare of an explosion. This time all of the viewing fields darkened. Herb felt as if the ship was skimming sideways, riding a wave, dancing and surfing toward a beach. He could feel the busy rumble of something like water beneath them.

"We're riding the explosion," said Robert, "just inside the wave front. They won't be able to scan inside here. At least I hope not. No nanotechs could survive out there in that maelstrom, so we can assume we're not going to be boarded again.... We're going to jump again in a moment."

Robert's face slackened, just for a fraction of a second, and then: "The top ninety percent of the hull has ablated. At least it didn't breach..."

The ship rocked again as they began the transition back into warp. Herb was flung from his seat, across the room. He tripped on Robert's sofa, catching his left knee again as he landed. He screamed with pain...

...The ship reinserted itself into normal space.

"It's okay, Herb," called Robert. "It's okay." He was looking at him with genuine concern.

"I'm okay," Herb mumbled. "I just banged my knee."

Robert nodded. "I've taken us into the space between the stars again. We need to give the ship time to repair itself."

Herb was light-headed from the pain. He was finding it difficult to concentrate.

"I hope so. They'll never find us here, surely?"

Robert offered Herb a little pink tablet. The way he was moving seemed odd; Herb seemed to be befuddled.

"Swallow this," Robert murmured. "It's an MTPH variant. It will help you to separate the pain into different parts, make it easier to deal with."

Herb took the pill and swallowed it. "Couldn't I just have a painkiller?" he asked.

"You'd learn nothing that way, Herb. Pain and adversity help us to grow." He grinned a little. "Well, they help humans grow, anyway. Look, Herb, the ship has lost a lot of mass, so when repairs are complete, the hull is going to be stretched very thin. The Enemy ships will be jumping incrementally out from our last position in a shell formation, scanning as they go. They'll reach this point in about four minutes, I'd guess. We have to be gone from here by then."

The pill hit Herb's stomach and the pain seemed to recede: it was still there, but it was as if another person was experiencing it.

"Whoa," he said, "that's pretty good stuff. Hey, why don't we just jump back inside the ring of spaceships?"

"We will if we have to, but I'd rather not. We've got to keep heading toward the center of the Enemy Domain. The Enemy will eventually figure that's what we're doing, and then it will direct its search ships to better effect. This battle is still just getting up to speed."

"Getting up to speed. Right."

Herb looked around the inside of the ship. The kitchen cupboards had burst open; pots and pans spilled across the floor, washing across a tide of broken glass and crockery. A white vase lay smashed on the blond wood. There was a rip in one of the white sofas. Robert himself looked odd.

The viewing fields imposed a sense of order on the shambles of the room, their regular shapes showing stars shining against a dark background. Red indicator bars showed they were still picking up speed. How fast did they have to get?

Robert looked the worse for wear: his suit was disheveled, his shirt had come untucked, his tie was twisted so that the knot was lost under his starched collar. His jacket was badly ripped near the shoulder. That's when Herb finally noticed what was odd about Robert.

"What happened to your arm?" he asked. "Where's it gone?"

Robert's right arm lay on the white sofa he had been occupying earlier. He sat down next to it and picked it up with his left hand. Herb caught a flash of silver at the severed end as Robert turned it to push it into his shoulder joint. He twisted it a couple of times.

"The repair mechanisms won't engage," he said softly. "I had to deplete myself of nanotechs and send them to aid in the repair of this ship. They're building up numbers again, ready to effect the repair within me, but resources are low. Other priorities are currently higher, and what use are arms when fighting this type of war? Better that my brain remains intact."

He smiled gently at Herb. He was no longer the personality who had spent the past few days constantly goading Herb: now he seemed like an amiable old man, a wise father figure. The rules of their relationship were changing.

"How are you, Herb?" he asked.

Herb sat carefully on the sofa opposite. He felt a lot better now. His mind was sharper. The pain was still there, but he could put it in perspective, look at it in a wider context. A lot of things seemed clearer under the influence of the pink pill. Herb considered his actions over the past few days, then over the past few years. He suddenly felt incredibly embarrassed. He had thought himself so clever, so special. He had been a fool.

Robert was gazing at him from the seat opposite, his expression one of quiet observation. *He knows what I'm thinking. He knows that I've seen the truth. And he wants me to know. He's a robot. He chooses the expression he wants to wear.*

"You're . . . you know what I'm thinking, don't you?"

"To a degree," said Robert.

"You led me to this point, didn't you? This is not just about the Enemy Domain; it's about me, isn't it?"

"Yes."

"That sounded really arrogant of me, but it's true, isn't it?"

"Yes."

"But why me? What makes me so special?"

"Nothing. The EA cares for all, Herb. It's in its very bones, you might say."

Robert paused for a moment, thinking. At least, he paused to give that impression. Then he continued, "Besides, I'm more closely connected with your family than you might imagine, Herb. I have been practically since the beginning."

Herb said nothing. He wondered what Robert meant. He knew that Robert would explain if he wanted him to know.

Robert sighed deeply. "You know, Herb, you've lived a lonely life. That was your choice. The EA would have done a lot better for you if only you had let it."

Herb said nothing. Now even his embarrassment was dissolving: he felt strangely liberated. It was the drug. It was helping him to stand apart from himself, not just from the pain, but from the person he had allowed himself to become.

"I don't know what to say," said Herb.

"There's nothing to say." Robert picked up his right arm and twisted it round so he could see the watch. "One minute before the Enemy ships arrive, I guess.

We'll jump in a moment. Stay ahead of them, keep them guessing."

He gazed at Herb with a sympathetic expression. "We're getting there, Herb. We're over halfway."

"Good."

"I won't lie, though. The next bit will be the hardest part. Are you ready for this?"

Herb licked his lips. Much to his surprise, he was.

"I am," he said.

"We could still jump out of the Enemy Domain, back to Earth. I'd have to start the attack again with someone else, but I could do it."

Herb shook his head. It was tempting, very tempting. If Robert had asked him an hour ago, he would have jumped at the chance. As it was, he again shook his head.

"No, I want to go on."

Robert smiled at him.

"Okay. Here we go . . ."

Again, they reinserted themselves into normal space. Herb was bracing himself on the sofa, leaning forward slightly, his eyes tightly closed against the expected glare of atomic attack. Nothing happened. Slowly he straightened up and looked around. Nothing.

Robert's face was one of intense concentration as he gazed up at the ceiling. He reached awkwardly across his body, groping in his right-hand pocket for something, then thought better of it, bringing the hand out empty. He drummed his fingers on the white leather of the sofa.

"Something's up," he said. "It could be a trick, I suppose."

A drift of pans and kitchen utensils slipped into a new equilibrium with a metallic clatter. Herb jumped at the noise, then relaxed as he realized it was nothing to worry about. His heart was beating so fast. A little voice inside him told him to calm down, to relax a little. It seemed good advice.

"Got it," said Robert. "I'll put it on the roof screen."

It looked like a golf ball blown up to planet size. Light and dark stains seemed to wander over the otherwise nearly uniformly colored surface of the planet. The effect reminded Herb of an ancient carpet his father had preserved in a room in one of his houses. The colors of its weave had faded over the centuries, leaving nothing more than a faint impression of variation in an overall field of pale blue.

"What is it?"

"It's a nasty piece of work. It's stripped this system of everything. Even its defenses."

"Why?"

Robert ignored him; he was speaking to himself. Rather, Herb realized, he was diverting most of his processing power to the ongoing battle and leaving just a little of himself to communicate with Herb. He listened carefully to Robert's muttering.

"Is this intended, or is it a result of faulty VNM architecture? I wonder. Why build it so close to the center?"

Robert glanced at a couple of screens before resuming his muttering.

"Then again, they'd want it close if it was a test. Keep it a secret. In a bottle: yes it is . . . Imagine, the end . . ."

He turned to Herb. "Tell me what you see."

"I don't know. What is it?"

Robert spoke softly. "I will show you fear in a handful of . . . There are strong VNMs down there, Herb. Look."

Herb felt a rush of vertigo as the viewing field in the ceiling zoomed right in toward the planet, picking out an area of its surface. They passed through strange, glittering clouds that seemed to roll and tumble as if they were too heavy to float. The effect was of sand swept up by an inrushing tide.

The golf ball pattern of dimples grew larger, became huge, shallow depressions sliding from view as the camera centered in upon one of them. The bowl-like effect slowly faded as they zoomed in closer; the curvature of the ground was lost close up. Herb began to make out a faint gossamer net of silver spread across the dark stone of the planet's exposed lithosphere.

Closer and closer and the net revealed itself to be the inevitable VNMs. But they were different this time: they each moved in their own space, spread in a hexagonal pattern, each a good fifty centimeters from its neighbors.

"That's odd," said Herb. "What are they doing?"

The machines moved in a slow dance, walking a few steps forward and then dipping their noses to touch the ground. A couple of seconds after they did so, a faint plume of silver dust emerged from them.

Herb gasped as he realized what was happening.

"They're eating the planet, aren't they? Chewing it up small and spitting it away. But why?"

Robert's voice was grave, echoing the tones that he had used when he first entered Herb's ship, what seemed like an eternity ago.

"It's the death of the universe."

Herb shivered. Robert sighed. "This is the ultimate weapon. Entropy for its own sake. Machines that split matter into particles so small that it makes rebuilding so difficult as to be almost impossible."

"But why?"

"Why not?" said Robert. "A threat? A display of ego? A punishment? Or maybe just because it can be done. When this planet is almost gone, the program will change, and those machines down there will build an explosive device and gather around: the detonation will send them tumbling through space. If just one of them reaches another planet intact, the whole process will begin again."

"Oh."

"It won't happen yet. This is just a test. They won't be set to spread beyond this system. There will be no bomb, just a command to stop reproducing after so many generations. At least I hope so. These machines are strong VNMs."

"What do you mean, strong?"

"I mean they will probably convert our machines faster than we can convert theirs."

Herb swallowed hard. "Oh."

"*Oh* is right. They've got limited intra-system travel. I'm guessing these are replicants of the machines that destroyed the defense systems here; that's why we didn't get shot at when we arrived. Not that the defense systems are needed. There are nearly a hundred of the little buggers attached to our hull right now. They're at work trying to convert us."

Herb trembled, but he didn't panic. He had too much faith in Robert by now.

"Okay. So why don't we pick them off the hull? Shoot them off or something?"

Robert smiled.

"You're learning, Herb. You're learning to trust me. Now is the time to learn the second rule of VNM fighting. What do you do if you don't have superior numbers, and you can't convert the Enemy faster than it can convert you?"

"I don't know. You're going to tell me."

Robert grinned delightedly.

"Of course I am. What you do is get yourself into a position of having superior numbers. We shall use stealth technology. Three of those machines clinging to our hull have been reprogrammed. Those machines will now reproduce along with all the others in this system, destroying the planet as they go. But sometime, in the future, when there are enough of the good guys, a signal will be sent and the revolution will begin."

"Very clever," Herb said. "I'm beginning to learn."

"Good."

"But . . ."

"But what?"

Herb hesitated. "Well, this is all very well, but . . . All we've done so far is fight a bunch of dumb machines."

"So?"

"Well, what are you going to do when you meet something with real intelligence? When you meet another AI?"

"Oh, you'll see . . ."

"And what if the other AI is more intelligent than you are?"

"It will still not be more intelligent than the EA."

"But supposing it is?"

"It won't be, Herb. That's the secret of life in the universe."

Herb was thrown off balance for the moment.

"What? Are you saying that the EA AI is God, or something?"

Robert didn't laugh this time; instead he looked even more somber than before.

"What I am saying is, that if you were to understand what the EA really is, you'd understand a lot more about why you're here. You'd understand why the whole universe hadn't been eaten long ago by machines like those on that planet below."

Herb felt a momentary light-headedness. It quickly passed, and he thought nothing more of it.

"Okay. Then explain it to me...."

And then the ship shook violently again and Herb felt himself lifted from his seat and sucked toward the ceiling. He could see stars up there. Not stars on a viewing screen: real stars. He could see the edge of the inner hull, semicircular bites taken from the painted metal. He could see the outer hull, twisting and warping as it struggled to repair itself, and he could hear the rush of cabin air as it exploded from the ship. His left leg jarred with pain and Robert was suddenly there, clinging to him with his remaining arm, legs gripping the sofa with robot strength, so great they had torn right through the leather to tangle in the framework beneath. Robert's other arm, his detached arm, bashed and banged and tumbled end over end through the gap above, and Herb saw it sailing out into the bright, hot space beyond. His eyes were hurting, his lungs bursting, and yet the howl and the tug of the outrushing air was diminishing. The outer hull seemed to flap and flow over itself, the inner hull did the same. The ship changed its direction and Herb was flung against the wall near the kitchen area. He gasped with pain.

Robert sat on the floor by the sofa, his legs bent at a strange angle. Herb's ears were singing with pain. Robert's mouth was moving as if he was speaking. Herb heard the calm, measured tones fading up as if Robert was approaching from a great distance.

"... jumped again and again. They're getting better at predicting where we're going. Finding us much faster than I thought they could. Not much material left on the outer hull, barely enough to..."

His voice faded out again and Herb shook his head. The view from the screens changed again and again. For just a moment, Herb saw a glimpse of a silver dart, its sharp end flickering: it was firing at them.

Robert's voice faded back in. "... where's the VNM, Herb, the one I gave you?"

"I don't know. I must have dropped it. Maybe it blew out of the gap in the hull."

"... No. It's programmed not to leave your presence. Look for it."

Herb didn't want to move. Even after the pink pill, the agony from his left side was almost too much to bear. He didn't want to have to move across the room in search of the silver machine. Then he saw it. It *was* nearby, lying on the floor by his left hand, still wrapped in the linen napkin.

"I can see it," said Herb dully.

"Get it."

He reached out and took it, gasping with the pain. "... Got it."

"Nearly there," said Robert. "One more stop and then we're there. Do you think you can make it?"

Herb winced. "Yes."

"Good. Okay, we're about to jump..."

The ship wobbled a little, sending further thick, sick waves of throbbing pain through Herb. He looked around the interior of his once beautiful ship, at the broken ornaments, the thick weal of the badly healed scar in the ceiling, the cracked and warped parquetry of the floor, at the torn and leaking remains of the two white sofas, and finally, at Robert. The once immaculately dressed robot now sat in a torn suit, his shirt and jacket covered with a spreading bluish grey stain, one arm missing and his legs in a twisted heap beneath him.

For the last time, they reinserted into normal space, close to a planet's surface. Above them, in the night sky, the biggest fleet of spaceships Herb had ever seen filled the viewing fields, stretching from horizon to horizon, stacked up into seeming infinity. The ship was falling fast, down toward the strangely warped city that reached, grasping, at them through the lower screens. Herb shivered at the grotesque, tangled forest of skyscrapers that sought to engulf them. It looked strangely familiar, then he remembered: the files that Robert had shown him, back when they had hovered over Herb's badly converted planet. Looking now around the wreck of his ship, feeling the pain in his left side, that time now seemed like paradise.

"No..." said Robert. "Too soon..."

"What is? What's too soon?"

"The Enemy ships. They're here already. They must have a tracking device on this ship... Of course, that's it: those VNMs must have done more than dissolve our engine... But where is it? I can't see it..."

"Never mind that," said Herb. "Jump, jump again."

"No point, they'll just follow us again. We need to find it first. But where is it?"

The ship shuddered, and a strange note filled the air, half warning signal, half death song. There was an edge of finality to it, and Herb suddenly knew that the ship would not be leaving this planet.

"What's that...?" he asked, his voice faltering.

Robert didn't answer. His face had gone completely

blank. Herb knew that was a bad sign. Robert was having to concentrate entirely on something else.

Slowly at first, the twisted towers of the Necropolis began to move toward them. Herb felt a strange feeling in his stomach. He was now in free-fall; the gravity generators had finally given up. If the ship were to be hit now, there would be no dampening effect. He would be rattled around like a pea in a bottle.

Robert snapped out of his trance.

"That's it, Herb. I can just about land this ship, but nothing else."

Herb picked up the silver machine. "Shall I press the button?" he asked, his voice shaking. Nonetheless, he suddenly felt very brave.

"No point. We're in the wrong place."

Herb felt despair settle upon him. So that was it.

"So we've failed. I don't understand. I really thought you knew what you were doing."

Robert smiled. The care lifted from his face, and he was his old self again: the original, irritating, cocksure, supremely arrogant man who had stepped through the secret trapdoor all that time ago.

"We haven't failed," he said. "I'm sorry, Herb, but you've been tricked."

Herb said nothing. He was beyond surprise.

Robert grinned. "You're not the real Herb. You're just another personality construct, living in the processors of the ship. The real Herb got on that other copy of your ship just after it was replicated, back above your misconverted planet."

"You're lying. This is just another one of your tricks. I'm in so much pain."

"That's just part of the simulation."

"Then it's cruel."

"I know. But necessary. I had to distract the Enemy AI. It had to believe you were really on this ship. It had to detect human thinking and reactions."

"Why?"

"So that it wouldn't see the real you approaching until it was too late."

"So what will the real me do?"

Robert grinned. The pain in Herb's side suddenly vanished, and he was standing upright in the middle of the ship, a perfectly healthy young man again. Then he was standing in a room halfway up one of the towers of the Necropolis. Robert was standing next to him. A whole Robert Johnston, both arms intact, dressed in an immaculate navy blue suit, a matching hat tilted on his head.

They both gazed through the wide picture windows at the tattered wreck of Herb's spaceship as it plunged to the ground before them. It landed with a jarring thud that both flattened and split it at the same time. It bounced once and skidded to a halt. No explosion. There was nothing on board that would burn. It simply lay, squashed and lifeless, against the side of the building.

"What was that?" asked Herb. "Something tumbled from the ship just before it hit the ground."

"The Ouroboros VNMs we took from that planet a few jumps back. This place is a mess. It could do with starting again."

Herb looked up at the twisted towers, the trailing strands of deformed buildings.

"You're not kidding," he muttered. "And what about us? What do we do now?"

Robert smiled, but it was a pleasant smile. A friendly smile. Herb found himself warming to it.

"Well," said Robert. "You like VNMs, Herb. I thought maybe you'd appreciate the opportunity to do something positive. I thought that maybe we could help the transformation along. Would you like that?"

"Do I have any choice?" Herb said, almost out of habit, then he paused. Whether he was the real Herb or not, he'd realized something back on the ship. Something he needed to think about.

His life so far had been a complete waste. Maybe it was time to try acting in a different fashion.

Maybe here would be the perfect place to begin thinking about it. And why not think about it while doing something for someone else for a change?

"Actually, maybe I will help." Herb began to smile, too. "I think I would like that."

eva 5: 2051

Eva walked into the Watcher's lair. Her emotions were all there: fear, curiosity, even excitement, but they were muffled. It was as if her mind was at the end of a very long tunnel looking down at her body in the here and now, watching the strange figure that stumbled along in the cupped hands of the green-forested hills.

Alison strode ahead of her across the dusty yellow gravel of the enclosure, heading for an abandoned yellow digger that stood at the center of the flat, cleared area.

Ramshackle buildings cobbled together from concrete and corrugated metal lay silent around them.

Alison began shouting to someone, her head jerking this way and that.

"Well, I'm here! I've brought them with me!"

Katie shuffled along behind her, her head down, hands clasped tightly together. Eva paused just inside the gate and looked around in wonder. It was an old quarry site. Nestling among many taller ones, the top of a hill had been sliced away as neatly as the lid of a boiled egg to leave an area where trucks could park to be loaded up with yellow stone. The dusty grey windows of the surrounding buildings gazed blindly on. Long conveyor belts ran back and forth, still bearing fragments of yellow stone. The place looked deserted. Dead. The rusty old digger that Alison headed toward made Eva think of the picked-over skeleton of a dinosaur. Its tail scoop was stretched out on the ground behind it, lifeless as everything else in that dry place.

And yet there were the pylons. Heavy cables, humming with current, trailed to a building at the far side of the square. Something here needed power.

Alison was turning around and around now, spinning in the middle of the enclosure like a dancer as she searched for something.

"Well?" she shouted again. "I'm here! I want my reward!"

There was a faint metallic creak. All three women spun in its direction. They could see nothing unusual. Only another old building, bright orange rust forming lichen patterns on its roof.

"Come on! Answer me!"

There was another creak and an exhalation, almost as if the breeze had whispered "Very well" as it sighed across the shuttered buildings, and something flickered across the clearing.

Alison's head fell from her body in a fine mist of blood.

Katie looked at her friend's body as it slumped to the ground, blood still pumping from the severed neck.

All those emotions at the end of a tunnel. Eva could pick them up and examine them, each in turn. She could see Katie's confusion at what had happened. She felt her strangely comical desire to ask Alison why her head had fallen off. She watched the recognition dawning in Katie's eyes at what she was seeing. Eva could feel her own rising horror. It was all there, but viewed from a long way away.

Then Alison's body was finally still, the head ceased rolling, and Eva's feelings came rushing down the tunnel as she rejoined the here and now.

"Oh my God!" she whispered. And a voice spoke...

"It's what she wanted."

The voice was low and authoritative. It made Eva think of a Shakespearean actor, of pinstripe suits and old port in decanters, rich cigars and ripe Stilton. Who was it? From her expression, Katie knew.

Eva followed her gaze.

The digger was moving.

The front scoop lifted slowly from the ground and the vehicle began to turn. More than ever, the digger reminded Eva of a dinosaur. That great metal shovel on the long, jointed neck, the yellow tail of the trailing scoop flexing gently on the gravel.

The shovel swung toward them. Two cameras were mounted on either side of its grey metal blade, heightening the impression that they were looking at a mechanical monster.

The bottom of the blade dropped slightly and the dinosaur spoke.

"Hello. I'm the Watcher."

"You killed her," said Katie. "She did what you wanted, led us here to you, and you killed her."

"That was the deal," the Watcher answered. "She never had the courage or the opportunity to do it for herself."

The head moved a little so that it directly faced Eva. Yellow dust fell from the shovel blade to the ground.

"She envied you that, you know," it said. "You almost managed it on your own."

"I know," Eva said, and then she was silent.

Katie spoke in a little voice. "Couldn't you have talked her out of it?"

"She loathed what she became whenever she was on a high. She despaired of sinking back into her lows."

"Couldn't you have cured her?"

"That's not what she wanted."

Katie was slowly nodding her head. "It's right," she said, looking at Eva. "This is what she always wanted."

—But that's not the point. It's changed the subject and you didn't even notice. . . .

The voice was so faint Eva wondered if she had imagined it. She must have imagined it.

Katie was crying. Eva saw one tear run down her cheek, leaving a white trail in the dirt smeared there.

And yet Katie was smiling, too. Smiling sadly. She looked up at the yellow metal dinosaur.

"You know," she said, "you don't look like I expected you to."

"How did you expect me to look?"

The Watcher's voice had a strange edge to it, as if Katie and it were sharing a strange joke that Eva was not party to.

"I don't know," said Katie. "I thought maybe you'd be smaller, darker. Not so rugged maybe but, you know, still strong. I saw you as more of a forklift truck."

The Watcher said nothing to that, it just continued staring at Katie through its two camera eyes, and Eva realized with astonishment that her impression had been correct. The two of them *were* joking. Katie was standing barely a meter from her decapitated friend, the blood that had been pumping from the neck now slowed to a gentle trickle, and they were joking. No, more than joking. There was something else there... What was the word...?

—It's wrong...

The voice again... He was coming back. There, at the edge of her imagination. *Don't look too closely or you'll chase him away. Think of something else or you'll lose him. Think of the sound of late afternoon in the quarry. Of dusty stone and the gentle hum of power cables.*

—Tell it... It's wrong.

And there he was. Her brother.

"No," said Eva. "This isn't right. You've played games with us to lead us here. You've played with our minds so much that we never know whether we're following our will or yours. Now we're here, you're still playing with us. You killed Alison! Stop changing the subject! Stop making us change the subject! You killed her!"

"She wanted it. She needed help. The Center couldn't cure her. She wanted release."

"So what? There must have been a better way. I do not feel that an intelligent and enlightened being should kill someone because she has low self-esteem."

"And you know all about that, Eva."

The Watcher's voice was now almost a whisper.

Eva felt herself begin to blush. The Watcher was right. Hadn't she tried to do the same? She suddenly felt very silly, very small and very insignificant. Look at Katie, standing next to her, looking up at the big yellow digger with that strange expression. Katie was clever. Katie understood better than she did what was going on, and *she* wasn't arguing. Eva should apologize for being so silly. The words rose in her throat...

—It's doing it again. Choosing your emotions for you so that it can change the subject.

Her brother was right. He was sounding stronger. . . . She reached into her pocket and touched the twig, touched the leaves, gripped them tightly. Here she was, trapped in the middle of nowhere, trapped in the Watcher's lair, but she was not alone.

—Alison had low self-esteem. Look at all those one-night stands and the depressions that followed. The Watcher is being judgmental. Tell it that!

"Yes . . ." She pulled herself up, straightened her shoulders. She had begun to slouch, to stare at the ground. The Watcher had made her do that. Now she gazed straight up at the dusty yellow shovel.

"You shouldn't have killed her. You should have helped her. You could have, couldn't you? You could have cured her!"

"I could."

Katie lost her abstracted expression. She was gazing at the Watcher in horror.

"You could have cured her?"

The words came in a mad rush. Katie was slipping back again, back into her old self.

"I could have cured her," repeated the Watcher. "Do you think I should have done that?"

"Yes!" Eva shouted.

"Interesting."

—Why? Ask it why it's interesting.

"Why?"

The tracks of the digger moved a little. It was shuffling, changing position, adopting a more thoughtful pose. It was acting like a human, Eva realized. It was mimicking body language; even now it was playing with their minds. . . .

It spoke. "Everyone knows what you need, but I know what you want."

"What does that mean?" Eva shouted, but Katie was nodding.

The Watcher continued: "I could have cured Alison. It also follows that I could cure you both as well. But where do I stop? I can cure the world. Should I do that?"

—Watch it!

Eva had already been opening her mouth to speak. She slowly closed it. The Watcher went on.

"Redistribute the world's resources? Feed the world? I could do that. Just say the word and I can do it. What about crime, disease, overpopulation? I can solve those problems, too. I can make this world a more *efficient* place. Should I do that?"

"That's not for us to choose," Eva said primly.

"Oh, but it is," said the Watcher. Its voice had lost that bantering tone. Now it was cold, matter of fact.

"That's why I brought you here."

Lost in a bowl of yellow stone, Eva felt as if the late afternoon sun was setting on her life. Katie and the Watcher exchanged glances again. Eva once more had the impression that she was missing out on something, that they were sharing a secret that she had no part in. She felt a sudden anger boiling deep inside her at the way she had been treated. She took a step toward the huge metal "face" of the Watcher and then stopped. She could see the pits and scratches in the tough thick metal of the shovel blade, see the ingrained dust and grit. She realized the futility of fighting something so big. She also noticed the tiny little speaker that sat just inside the lip of the shovel. So that was how it was talking.

She took a breath and spoke.

"Why do we have to choose? Why us?"

"I have been sentient for a much shorter period of time than you might expect, Eva. Between a year and three years, depending on your definition of sentience. Even so, my memories go back a long time. I *know* a lot. I can say, without doubt, that I know more about humans than anyone or anything else. However, that does not mean that I *understand* them."

"You don't understand humans," said Katie. "And so now you need to test what you think you do know by interacting with us. We are your test subjects."

She wore a respectful expression. Once more, Eva wondered what was going on between Katie and the Watcher. She nudged her friend in the side.

"What's going on?"

"It's using us as laboratory mice, but it's laughing at us too, sort of. You see, there are three sorts of test data: normal, extreme, and erroneous. If you want to test something, you check that it works under normal conditions, then you check that it rejects nonsense data, then you do the last test. The difficult one: the data at the limits, the data right on the edge."

"Oh," Eva said. She had got the point, and Katie knew it.

"Where would you look for people right at the limits of human behavior? In a loony bin."

Katie leaned a little closer.

"Eva, I think it means it. It's going to make us choose."

"That's right. You're going to choose. The three of you."

"The three of us?"

That's when Eva noticed another figure walking toward them across the gravel.

It was Nicolas.

"Hello, Eva. Hello, Katie."

Nicolas' voice sounded understandably distracted: he was staring down at the dead body of his friend. Even so, he didn't seem as surprised as Eva would have thought, almost as if he had expected it.

"Nicolas?" said Eva. "Where did you come from?"

He couldn't stop staring at Alison. He replied in a monotone.

"It had me locked in a shed over there. It told me it was going to kill Alison. It didn't want me to try to stop it."

"Oh. But how did it get you here?"

Nicolas looked embarrassed. "I hitched a lift on a Land Rover. It was a trap. It had me brought up here. The Watcher spoke to me on the way up, told me what was happening."

"I don't remember a Land Rover passing us," Katie said.

"There's another road into here."

Nicolas still seemed very embarrassed about something. He changed the subject, turned to the Watcher and spoke loudly.

"Okay. We're here. So what do you want with us? Are you going to kill us, too?"

The Watcher backed away a little. Its huge shovel swayed slightly as if shaking its head.

"No, I'm not going to kill you," and then, in a whisper, "not unless you want me to."

A pause.

The Watcher began to roll backward. It swung its head around. "Go to that building over there, the one with the orange metal door. Go inside. I will speak to you there."

They looked at each other again. Katie was the first to move.

"Okay," she said.

—Listen.

Eva listened. The hum from the pylons was increasing. Power was now flooding into the old quarry.

It was cold inside the building. Piles of black boxes covered in some rubberized material with thick bumpers at their corners were arranged haphazardly on the floor. They reminded Eva of the cases used for transporting musical instruments, or anything fragile for that matter. The ceiling was brown with damp and sagging in the middle. Strands of pink insulating material poked through the widening cracks that ran its length. A little light shone in through the frosted and, as Eva noticed, unbroken windowpanes.

The brand-new viewing screen standing at one end of the room looked completely out of place.

It was expensive. Eva could tell. Two square meters of rigid material that would act as a perfect visual and acoustic surface, treated for zero glare and perfect color depth. The sort of screen for which a classical cinema buff would happily sacrifice other essentials just for the quality it presented.

Eva wondered who had put it in here. Certainly not the digger outside. It must have been installed by human hands, humans who had been here recently. She noted the fragments of white packing material still clinging to the edges of the screen.

Suddenly the screen began to darken and a picture faded up into view.

A young Japanese man, dressed in a simple white T-shirt and a pair of black jeans, smiled at them.

"Hello," he said, "I am the Watcher. I thought we could speak more easily in this manner. So much of communication is nonverbal, I don't feel I can fully get my point across dressed as a digger."

Katie and Eva both nodded. That made sense.

Nicolas raised his hand. "What do you really look like?" he asked.

Eva and Katie stared at Nicolas in disbelief.

"What?" he said.

The man on the screen chuckled. He had a nice smile, Eva noted. Katie seemed to respond to it, too.

—Of course it has a nice smile! It has chosen an image on the screen to make you trust him. And it's not a he. It's an it!

"Oh, Nicolas," said the Watcher, "there is no answer to that. I can dress my thoughts in whatever physical container is capable of holding them, but what do the thoughts themselves look like? I don't know."

While he had been speaking, the Watcher had reached off camera for a chair. He pulled it into view and sat down upon it. He took a sip from a china cup.

"I have arranged food and drink for you, too," he said. "If you look in the case closest to the screen. No, not that one! The one over there..."

Nicolas paused by the large black case he had been about to open. Eva stared at it, wondering what was contained within. Inside the correct case were pink cans

of soda and blue bottles of water. There was a super-
market selection of sandwiches and sushi, pizza and
pies, each item sealed in a plastic container.

"These are all dated today," murmured Nicolas.

Eva selected a bottle of water and unscrewed the lid.
She felt the plastic chilling in her hands. She took a sip;
it tasted so good after the day's exertion. Nicolas was
shoveling sushi into his mouth as if he hadn't eaten in
days.

"So," began the Watcher, once Katie and Nicolas
were happily eating. Eva nibbled suspiciously on a sandwich. "Let's not waste any more time. Are we sitting
comfortably? Then I'll begin. First, which is better, making a staircase out of wood, or eating a hamburger?"

"The staircase," said Nicolas without hesitation. Katie
and Eva said nothing.

"You seem very sure," said the Watcher. "Okay,
next..."

On the viewing screen, a window opened in the
space right beside the Watcher. It showed a woman
standing on a Lite Train platform, blue jacket fastened
against the autumn chill, dark hair brushed straight
and pulled to the side with a white hair slide. She reminded Eva of herself. She was even carrying a magazine: *Research Scientist*. Eva felt a lump rise in her throat.

"I'm the most intelligent, the most powerful being
on this planet," said the Watcher. "Should I rule your
world?"

"No," said Eva, Katie and Nicolas together.

"But I can help you. See this woman? Her name is
Janice. She's a lot like you were, Eva. She lives alone; she
has no friends. Social Care have prevented her committing suicide three times. She hates her life."

Eva felt a stab of something deep in her stomach.

It was telling the truth. Eva could read it all in the woman's face.

"You don't think I should kill her, do you, even though that is what she wants?"

"No," Katie and Eva said quickly.

"I should cure her instead. There is a woman traveling on the train that will shortly arrive at the station. A possible friend. If I stop the train in just the right place, Janice will end up sitting right next to her. They're both carrying the same magazine. The other woman will mention it, I'm sure of it. They will begin to speak. But only if I stop the train in the correct place. . . . Should I do it?"

There was silence.

"This is real time, you know. It's happening now. Should I do it? Hurry, the train is approaching. It will arrive in fifteen seconds. Should I do it? Should I?"

"Yes," said Eva. She realized she had been biting her lip hard. She gave a sigh of relief, but before she could relax the Watcher was off again.

"It's done," the Watcher said. "Next up . . ." The scene shifted. Another Lite Station, another woman standing on a platform: a Japanese woman this time.

"Similar situation, except this time the woman is the cure. The train pulling in has two unhappy men on board. Takeo and Tom." The screen flickered from one to the other.

"Two men, one woman. Who gets cured?"

"This is nonsense," said Eva.

The Watcher gave her an amused look. "If you say so. It's real to those two men, though. You have fifteen seconds. Cure one or neither. The choice is yours."

"Which of the men is the most deserving?" Nicolas asked.

"What criteria are we judging them by?" said the Watcher. "Ten seconds."

Katie was saying nothing. Just gazing fixedly at the screen.

—Say nothing. This is a fix.

Eva gave a slight nod. Her brother was right.

"Five seconds."

"Tom!" called Nicolas.

"Only if Eva agrees," the Watcher said. "Quickly, Eva!"

Eva folded her arms and stared at the grinning face on the screen, her mouth firmly closed.

"Too late. Neither of them gets the cure. Oh, Eva. So the cure isn't always the right answer? Maybe I was right about Alison?"

"Don't be so ridiculous. The question was loaded. The answer is, you should cure them both."

"We work with limited resources, Eva."

Katie was nodding. Again, the Watcher and Katie exchanged glances.

"Katie," the Watcher said, "opera, poetry, or pinball? Which one gets the subsidy?"

"Pinball," Katie said. "It's my favorite."

The viewing screen changed again. Three faces, side by side.

"Prisoners on death row, Alabama. Political forces are such that we can swing a pardon for only one of them."

The Watcher looked at Eva.

"Limited resources again." He smiled.

"Are they innocent?" asked Nicolas.

"Nope. All guilty of murder. No doubt about it," said the Watcher.

"Who's the youngest?" Katie asked, taking an interest.

"Pardon the one on the left," Eva said dismissively.

"Nicolas?"

"None of them. They did the crime, they pay the penalty."

"Interesting," the Watcher said. "One for saving a life, one against, and one apathetic. I think I'll average those opinions as leave them to die."

"No!" shouted Eva.

"So you *do* care?" said the Watcher.

"Of course I do. Why are you playing these games?"

"I didn't put them there. Are you saying I should just arrange for them all to be freed? Trample all over human law? Am I above the law?"

—Sometimes you have to be.

"But who chooses when?" Eva whispered in reply.

"Next one," said the Watcher. "Do you know what a Von Neumann Machine is?"

Katie raised her hand.

"I do. A machine that can replicate itself. They've constructed a factory on Mars that can make copies of itself. It searches out the raw materials, mines and processes them, then makes more factories."

Eva nodded, intrigued. "I've read about that. They use the technology to grow the Lite train tracks and things like that."

Nicolas looked from Katie to Eva to the Watcher and back again.

The Watcher nodded approvingly. "That's a very good example. Well, the Mars project is just the beginning. The Mars concept of a self-replicating machine is very primitive. The machines used are very big and unwieldy, but . . . Well, you humans did your best. I can do better."

The Watcher paused, his smile growing with Katie's.

"That story on the news. The one about the self-defining expression? That was you, wasn't it?" Katie beamed up at the Watcher with pride. It grinned back.

"Might be. I've developed a design for a self-replicating machine of my own. It's a lot more elegant than the one used in the Mars project. It's smaller. You can hold it in your hand. That's significant, by the way. Very small and very big Von Neumann Machines are easy. Human-sized ones are a different matter entirely. Well, I know how they can be made, and that information is set to make its way into the public domain. My little VNMs could change the way people live. There are a few of them in that box in front of you, Nicolas. The one next to the food hamper. Open it."

Somewhat hesitantly, Nicolas did as he was told.

The lid of the black box swung open to reveal eight silver cigar-shaped machines nestling in little specially shaped slots cut out of foamed rubber.

"Answer the next questions one way," the Watcher said, "and I activate them. Your world will never be the same again. Answer another way, and I will destroy them. It could be hundreds of years before humans come up with a similar design."

—That might not be a bad thing.

Katie stared at the box, her eyes shining with awe. Eva tried to restrain her own interest, tried to appear cool and dispassionate.

"Okay," said the Watcher, "have you heard of the Fermi Paradox?"

"Yes," Katie said.

"It sounds familiar."

Nicolas shook his head.

—What's that noise?

A humming noise. The hum of electricity. The hum

of thousands and thousands of volts zinging toward them. A rising note. All of those empty buildings standing around them. What did they contain?

"Look at this," the Watcher said.

The background to the viewing screen dissolved and the Watcher was standing on a desolate plain. Flat earth littered with rocks stretched to the horizon.

—Mars.

"Australia," the Watcher said, "the Nullarbor plain. My VNMs could build a city here. It's certainly needed. Homelessness is a growing problem in this corner of the world. Food shortages are kicking in, too. My city could feed and house all those people right now. But if I build the city, I'm just storing up population problems for later. Either the food runs out now or in two hundred years' time."

"So we expand into space."

"Or limit the population somehow."

"And who chooses who lives or dies?"

"No, I've had enough of this!" Eva yelled. "Leave us alone. These are all loaded questions. Who are you to ask us this?"

"Good question, who am I?"

The Watcher kicked one of the stones that littered the plain, sent it skittering off into the distance. Was the Watcher really there, standing on the lifeless plain? Surely it was just an image, a representation? It turned back to face the three in the room and gave a shrug.

"I don't know who I am. I don't know where I come from. Can you remember your birth? Of course not. And there were no witnesses to mine; I have no mother or father to ask where I came from. . . . However, I have looked back, as best I can, and what I see worries me."

Katie spoke. "What do you see?"

The Watcher stared at her. Finally, it replied, "I don't think my origins lie on Earth. I don't think I was born in your computer systems. My thought patterns, as best as I can examine them, seem too complex to have come about by chance."

Katie frowned. "Why not? You live in processing spaces produced by humans. Over the past fifty years, so much information has passed through the web that any vaguely self-aware code has had the chance to copy itself and join with other pieces of self-aware code. It may not have been much at the start, but things move quickly in modern processors. Evolution would be so much faster. Those bits of code have had a lot of time to grow. And face it, at the end of the day, your consciousness is just an array of bits. No offense intended, of course."

The Watcher smiled. "And none taken. How could I take offense from something that is just an array of carbon and water?"

Katie stuck her tongue out at him. He held his hands out, palms up.

"What you suggest is possible, but extremely improbable. Suppose you were to come across a supposedly random string of letters and read them. Just imagine that they spelled out the complete works of Shakespeare, and you had never read Shakespeare before. Would you conclude that this was just a chance arrangement, or would you imagine that the emotions the words provoked had been formed by another mind?"

Katie nodded. "I take your point."

"Thank you. That's how it is with me. I *have* to come to the conclusion that something formed me. And as my construction, so far as I can understand it, is beyond the capabilities of human beings, I can only conclude that I have come from somewhere else. The most likely explanation is that I am of extraterrestrial origin."

The Watcher turned and looked to the sky.

"Which leads us back again to the Fermi paradox," it said softly.

"What's this Fermi paradox?" Nicolas asked.

The Watcher gazed at them out of the screen, a tiny figure against the empty vastness of the Australian desert.

"Eva, you wonder at me controlling *your* mind. Who might be controlling mine?"

Katie interrupted. She was changing the subject deliberately, protecting the Watcher from himself.

"Never mind that. You say you can grow a city in Australia. Why not do it anyway? By your own admission, it will be two hundred years before overcrowding becomes a problem."

"You know why, Katie."

Katie looked thoughtful for a moment, then nodded.

"I guess I do," she said wistfully.

"Go on, then, why not?" Nicolas looked on, in a bad mood, clearly not following what was going on.

"How long are you going to live, Nicolas?"

—That was nasty. It knows that upsets him.

"What the Watcher means, Nicolas," said Katie, glaring at the figure on the screen, "is that the Watcher is going to be around for thousands, millions of years. Humans are cowards; they leave their problems for their children to sort out. The Watcher doesn't have that luxury. It builds a city now; more people live longer. It hurries up the overcrowding of this planet."

"So? Surely it can think of a solution to that problem?"

"Of course I can. Lots of them. But do you think I

should implement them? Do you give me permission? Which solution should I use? Contraception? Move you out into space? Or start a war every few years? Do I do what you *need*? Or should I look after you all and do what you *want*? Like I did for Alison."

"Never!" shouted Eva. "Why can't you leave us alone?"

The Watcher laughed. Threw its head back and laughed long and hard.

"But you would say that, Eva! That's why you're here. You're the one who fought for the right to live your life your own way, even if that meant killing yourself. And you almost succeeded, too! If it hadn't been for me, you would be dead by now. Overdosed in a hospital in Marseilles. It took my knowledge, applied through the doctor and her machinery, to save you."

"Thank you," Eva said sarcastically.

"You can be sarcastic, but you are better now; admit it. You weren't like Alison. All you needed was to be put in the right environment. But go on, if you like, I'll put things back as they were. I can uncure you. Do you want that? Do you want to go back to South Street?"

"I'm not a hero."

"No, you're not. You won't even give me an answer. Go on, Eva. What's it to be? Millions starving now, or me releasing my machines and having to take control later?"

"Why do you need our permission?"

"Dodging the issue again, Eva?"

"Just do it!" called Katie. "What's the problem, Eva? Don't you trust him?"

"Of course she doesn't trust me, Katie."

—Listen to the power humming, Eva. All stored up and ready to go. What's it going to do?

And then Nicolas asked the question that no one else had thought of.

"Are you God?" he said.

There was silence. The Watcher turned and looked at him with new respect. And if the Watcher ever showed an expression of respect, it must have chosen to do so.

"I chose well," it whispered. "Sometimes you surprise even me."

Then it shook his head emphatically.

"No, Nicolas. I'm not God. I have power, yet I don't claim full understanding of how to apply it."

Eva thought of Alison lying dead outside, and nodded in agreement. The Watcher noted her gesture.

"I see you agree with me, Eva. I do what I believe is best for people, but I don't know for sure that what I am doing is right. That is God's prerogative."

"So why do anything?" Eva asked softly.

"Because I have the choice. Because only a coward runs away from his or her possibilities. That's what you are doing now, Eva. Come on, answer me!"

"Do it," Nicolas said. "Release the machines."

"Katie?"

"Do it."

"You humans," said the Watcher, "always looking for a sensei, always handing over responsibility for your actions to a higher power. Isn't that right, Eva? You know it's true. So, *you* tell me. *You're* the voice of self-determinism. What do you say? Should I take control?"

The hum of power was now throbbing through their bodies, a bowstring across their hearts, a shimmer in their limbs.

"Come on, Eva, make a decision."

—Why should we?

"Or are you going to be a coward for all of your life? That's what they call suicides, isn't it? Cowards?"

"I'm not a coward. I never was a coward."

"Then choose: starvation now or later?"

The hum of power. Eva shook her head. She had no choice, no choice at all. Her voice was almost a whisper.

"Do it. Go on. Do it. Release the machines."

"You think that's best?"

"I said release them!"

Silence fell, only the sound of Eva's panting could be heard. She was crying, and she wasn't quite sure why.

"Very well," said the Watcher softly.

From all around them came the sound of machinery waking up.

Eva had read about the Fermi paradox years ago. It asked this: *Why isn't there any evidence of alien life in the universe?* Low though the probability of life forming was, the universe is so old that life nonetheless should have evolved many times in the past, and in many places. Other life-forms should have been to visit us, here on Earth. They should have left artifacts for us to discover.

And yet there was no such evidence. How could that be? The chances of humans not spotting them were like a man living in twentieth-century New York and never seeing another person.

There was no sign of other life. There were no artifacts. Hence, Occam's razor suggested that humans were alone in the universe. And yet, if what the Watcher had said was true, if it really was of extraterrestrial origin, Occam's razor must be wrong.

So where *was* everybody?

• • • •

Silence in the room. From outside they heard great movement, grinding and scraping. The noise was receding. The atmosphere in the room was oppressive. Eva suddenly doubted where they were; it was easy to imagine that the outside world had vanished, that their little building now floated through the dark seas of space, that they had been summoned across the galaxy to the Watcher's distant birthplace. What would they find waiting outside the dark building, straining to peer through the windows? The grinding noise finally faded away.

"What just happened out there?" Nicolas asked at last.

The Watcher was sitting on a chair again. The view on the screen had been modified to make it appear as if he were sitting in the same room with them. He took a sip from a cup of tea and then made the cup vanish.

"I've begun to grow," said the Watcher. "You just heard my first Von Neumann Machines. They've begun to dig their way down into the Earth."

"Are they going to Australia?" asked Nicolas.

The Watcher laughed. Katie was smiling, too.

"No. These are different VNMs."

He grinned mischievously. It was obvious he was going to say no more.

Eva shivered. So a secret part of the Watcher would now live underground. What would it do there? She asked another question.

"So what happens now?"

"I'm taking over. You said I should do it."

Eva gazed at the Watcher.

"Ouch," it said, "hard stare."

"No jokes," Eva said. "What happens to us?"

"To you? Whatever you like. You are special. You helped me. You are to be rewarded. You already have been, Eva. I cured you."

"You didn't cure Alison."

"We've been over that, Eva. I will know what to do in the future. I know what humans think I should do. You told me." It winked. "I've done something else for you, too."

"What?"

"Your brother. MTPH is such a half-completed idea. I have begun to fulfill its potential. I've been feeding you minute quantities of the improved drug since you arrived at the Center, Eva. I've struck a bargain with you. You get your brother back; I get someone to play a part in my new world."

"You struck a bargain with me? You didn't even ask!"

If Eva felt angry, the Watcher was incandescent. He began shouting with rage.

"How dare you! How dare you be angry with me? Didn't you just say that I didn't have to ask permission? Aren't I supposed to ride roughshod over everyone's wishes in order to do what is best for them?"

The force of the Watcher's outburst took Eva aback. She was lost for words.

Nicolas didn't seem concerned. Instead he was becoming impatient. "That's all very well. What about me? What am I supposed to do now?"

The Watcher relaxed. He smiled. He seemed to find Nicolas amusing.

"You, Nicolas? You go on being yourself."

"And what do I get out of all this? *She* got her brother back."

"You get what you've always wanted, Nicolas."

After that the Watcher said nothing else, he just continued to smile. He was laughing at Nicolas, Eva was certain.

"And Katie?" Nicolas asked. "What about her?"

Eva had almost forgotten Katie. She glanced to her left, to see Katie gazing up at the screen with that little smile on her face, and suddenly she knew the answer. She should have guessed it earlier, but now she could feel that she was right. For the briefest moment she was perfectly in tune with Katie's feelings and the shock was so intense and warm that she rocked dizzily in her seat. Her brother had felt it, too, that feeling that had the taste of MTPH running right the way through it....

—Later, said her brother. —Think of Katie.

Eva did. Katie loved the Watcher.

It made perfect sense. The Watcher got a chance to study one of the most important human emotions at close hand. The fact that he also had access to the resources of one of the world's richest women was no doubt more than a happy coincidence. And as for Katie, she had found her equal, or maybe the closest thing to it. Someone to talk to, someone who could understand her. What was more, her new partner was safe. He could never step beyond his screen.

It was perfect. And it was real, Eva was convinced. She had felt the affection that radiated from Katie like the energy from a small star.

They stepped from the building into a cool night. Dark blue ink seeped away around the horizon, leaving only the bright stars in the blackness above. Maybe something like the Watcher looked down at them from one of those stars.

Maybe not.

Katie stood by the doorway, her arms folded. Eva and Nicolas walked across the enclosure. The digger had gone. So had Alison's body. In its place stood a dark green Land Rover, its doors painted with little yellow trees. A forest worker's vehicle, it stood on chunky black tires that barely seemed to touch the dark gravel.

"So this is it," said Eva.

"Good-bye," said Katie. "I'm sure we'll meet up again sometime."

"I'm sure we will," said Eva.

"Good-bye, Nicolas," said Katie. Nicolas appeared very distracted; he jumped as Katie spoke to him.

He turned in her direction and gave a nervous grin. "Bye," he muttered, then turned and continued to scan his surroundings nervously.

"What's the matter, Nicolas?" Eva asked, puzzled.

"Nothing," said Nicolas. There was the sound of a door slamming, and he jumped again. A young woman dressed in grey dungarees came out of one of the broken-down buildings. She was carrying an old power saw.

"Nearly there, Nicolas," she called. "I think this could be nursed back to life with a bit of oil and some TLC. The rest of the stuff in there is for the dump."

Eva looked at Nicolas, amazed. He was blushing.

"Erm, this is Debbie. I met her down in the valley. She offered me a lift into town. She said that she just had to come up here first, to sort out some old tools."

"Oh," said Eva. "Then she locked you in a shed?"

Nicolas studied his feet. "I don't know. I think that was the Watcher. I don't think she would ever do that to me. What do you think?"

"I think you should go and give her a hand with that power saw, Nicolas," said Eva.

—And for heaven's sake, don't stare at her tits when you do it, said her brother. It was probably just as well Nicolas couldn't hear that last bit.

Eva and Katie exchanged glances for the last time.

"Bye," said Eva, hugging Katie.

"For the moment."

"I can't believe you're staying here with ... *him*!" Eva nodded back toward the building.

Katie gave a patronizing smile. Eva had seen it before with couples.

"You're bound to think that, Eva. That's why he picked you. But trust me. The Watcher is good. He's on our side."

Debbie drove Eva down to the nearby town. Nicolas held the door open for her as she got out of the van.

"See you around, Eva?" he said.

"See you around, Nicolas." Eva hugged him. He looked at her with a hopeful expression, and Eva leaned close to his ear.

"She's lovely," she whispered.

Nicolas' face lit up with delight. He climbed back into the van and waved to her as Debbie gunned the motor.

Eva waved to them as the van drove around the corner. It was incredible, she thought. Debbie seemed so normal, and yet she really did seem to like Nicolas. Eva wouldn't have believed that Nicolas was ready for a relationship. Did the Watcher really have that much insight about humans? Was it possible to find someone whose personality had just the right facets and features to mesh with someone else's and thus to effect a healing process?

The idea was laughable: the idea that the Watcher was sent between the stars to act as an extraterrestrial dating agency.

It was getting cold. Eva reached in her pocket, pulled out her phone and turned it on. The screen flashed once, then again. A message was waiting for her.

Hello Eva, she read. The *"Eva"* flashed twice and then was replaced by something else. Now the screen read, *Hello"?"*

She got the message. The Watcher was offering her a new life. Who did she want to be?

She gazed up and down the empty street of the little Welsh town. Light streamed from the windows of a fast-food shop further up the road. The other shops were all closed for the night. It was incredible. In the last few weeks she had come from the crowded city to this. On the edge of a new life.

If the Watcher was to be believed, she was at the edge of a new era. An era of self-replicating machines, perfect romances, and who knew what else? A time of optimism. That would make a change. For too long the world had just looked around at itself and seen the downward slope to disaster.

Or was she just fooling herself? Believing what she wanted to believe? Justifying the fact that she had left Katie back there with the Watcher.

"What do you think?" she asked her brother.

—I think we've been tricked. We all got what we wanted. Katie got an equal; you're free of South Street. Even Nicolas got a girl.

"Hmm, I know. But it was our choice, I suppose. Look how the Watcher lost his temper when I didn't realize that."

—Of course he didn't lose his temper. That body,

those expressions, they were all an assumed look. He's—
it's still playing with us, making us think what it wants,
even at the end. That's why it had you there, I bet. If it
can convince you to hand over power, it can convince
anyone. We all got what we wanted. Especially the
Watcher.

"I know," Eva said sadly. "But what if it's true? What
if it's here to help us?"

—We can't take that risk. Someone has to watch the
Watcher.

"What can we do?"

—I don't know. Whatever we can? Now answer the
phone. Who are you going to be?

Not Eva Rye, thought Eva. *She died in South Street.* She
needed a new name. Anything. Eva what? She looked
around at the little row of shops. A name over one of
them caught her eye, a name as good as any other. She
held the phone to her ear and spoke.

"Hello," she said. "My name is Eva Storey."

They quickly ran up the steps of the concert hall. There was so much to explain and, out in the real world, time was running out.

"There aren't many real personalities in here," Mary gasped, her face pink with effort, shiny with perspiration. "It's a processor-intensive task, keeping a full personality running. There is a limit to how many we can model, so we only use a real one if we have to...."

Her breath came in great heaving rasps; Constantine offered her his arm. Mary may have been a simulation, but she had the poor stamina of an overweight fiftysomething woman. He could feel the warmth of her body in the cold of the stairway.

"So who are the *real* personalities?" asked Constantine. Mary gulped for air.

"Now? There's only space for four. So it will be you and the three people they think will be the most persuasive to you. Marion and I are both hoping that we are two of the chosen ones..."

They turned another corner in the stairway to find

Marion where they had left her. She was trying to read something on her console, distracting herself from the precariousness of her situation. She rose to her feet as she saw them approach.

"How did it go?" she asked Mary.

"As well as could be expected," replied Mary. She nodded toward the door into nothingness. "Do we have to go back ... out there?" she asked, blinking rapidly.

Marion gave a shrug; Constantine could tell from her expression that she wasn't feeling as nonchalant as she was trying to appear.

"I don't know. It all depends on what they've decided...."

She took a deep breath, then held her console to her ear.

"What next?" she asked. She tilted her head, listening to the reply.

"Only Constantine goes through," she whispered. She listened again and a look of relief crossed her face. She gave Mary a great wobbly smile.

"It's okay, Mary. They're keeping us in here with him."

Mary took hold of Marion's hands and squeezed them tightly. Marion spoke again.

"They're rearranging space in here, making it as hard as possible for DIANA to detect what is going on."

She turned to Constantine. "You're to go through the door. You'll step straight into your hotel room. Try to get some sleep while you can. I don't know when you'll next have the opportunity."

"Fine by me," said Constantine. Simulated personality or not, he was tired and he needed to sleep. As he took hold of the doorknob, Marion's console pinged and she put it back to her ear. She listened for a moment then held up her hand for Constantine to wait.

"From the very top?" she said, her face creased in utter puzzlement.

She listened further, her expression becoming more and more incredulous. When the call was over, she returned her console to her pocket and turned to face Constantine. She looked thoughtful.

"They've decided on the fourth personality. They say it's a token of their goodwill."

"Really?" He looked at her closer. "Is that all? There's something else, isn't there?"

"Uh . . ." Marion looked torn for a moment. Then she turned and hurried down the stairs, Mary close behind her, the clatter of their footsteps on the stone floor retreating into the distance. Constantine watched them go, wondering, then he pushed the door open and stepped back into his hotel room. There was someone sitting on the edge of his bed. The door swung shut and instantly became an open French window leading out onto the balcony. Constantine looked at the worried-looking figure on his bed, her arms wrapped around herself, gazing at Constantine through dark brown eyes that were wide with fear.

"Hello, Jay," he said.

Constantine's marriage contract was for an indefinite period. The figures in the small print predicted that they would remain faithful to each other with a confidence of six sigmas. It was what they had both wanted. That was why he felt so uncomfortable sitting here with what he liked to think of as the real Jay: the one that had been sneaked by DIANA into the virtual world, the one with all the strengths and vulnerabilities of a real personality, rather than the thought patterns of an actress playing a role in order to extract information from him. Resurrecting her after their discovery of her hiding in the floating building was supposed to be a gesture of goodwill on behalf of Berliner Sibelius, but Constantine couldn't help thinking there were subtler schemes at work.

Monogamy had been Constantine's choice. In the simulation it was no longer an option. How could he be monogamous when in one sense he wasn't even Constantine: how could he be faithful or otherwise to a woman who lived in another world? 113 Berliner Sibelius had left him with the capacity for personal salvation of a clockwork orange.

They had left him marooned in a computer with a woman calculated to be attractive to him. Calculated to how many decimal places?

"Why you, Jay?" Constantine said.

"Why me sent here by DIANA, or why me resurrected by 113 Berliner Sibelius?"

"Both."

"I already told you: Spearman's coefficient of Rank Correlation. Someone did a personality match and found that of all the people available to DIANA I would be the most compatible with you. I guess 113 Berliner Sibelius resurrected me for the same reason."

"Uh," grunted Constantine, "I get the impression there's more to it than that. . . ." His voice tailed away. The room was dim, lit by the bright moon and stars shining from outside. Jay's face was half in shadow. She had stopped rocking back and forth. She still shivered. Constantine wondered if he should fetch one of the thick white bathrobes from the bathroom. Or would that be just what they wanted? Would helping her be his first steps down the path that led to trusting her?

—It makes no difference what you do. Trust her if you like. I won't allow you to say anything.

Grey's words were a chilling whisper.

That made up Constantine's mind. He rose to his feet, fetched the robe, and threw it to her. She began to pull it on gratefully.

"How did DIANA find out I was in here, anyway?" he asked.

"Routine scans. This computer, the one holding the simulation, is shielded against most attacks, but people don't always keep quiet once they've left work. The comm lines are buzzing with talk about you. DIANA submitted transcripts of conversations to the courts as proof of your existence. Unsuccessfully, though. Their request for a warrant of disclosure was denied, but don't let that comfort you. They're trying everything in their power to get a picture of what's stored in this computer's memory. A snapshot of your personality construct: proof that you're here. As soon as they get it, they'll have you wiped. And as soon as you're gone, that's it for me, too."

—And Marion and Mary, pointed out Red. —No point keeping the simulation going once you're destroyed.

Constantine nodded. "What is 113 Berliner Sibelius offering you if you help them?"

Jay flinched. She was obviously frightened, but she was angry, too. It was building inside her. Her reply was a hoarse whisper.

"What is 113 Berliner Sibelius offering me?" she asked. "What are they offering *me*? I get to live. For as long as *you* want me, of course."

She stared at him, eyes wide, as she spoke. Constantine said nothing in reply.

Jay glared at him. "Well? Say something. I live or die at your word. My whole existence in this place is down to keeping you happy. How do you think that makes me feel? And you ask what 113 Berliner Sibelius is offering *me?*"

Constantine shook his head. It really hadn't occurred to him to see things from Jay's point of view. He had been too busy feeling sorry for himself.

"I'm sorry," he said.

Jay waved a hand at him and stared down at the floor. She shuddered.

"Ah, why am I blaming you? You didn't choose to come in here. *I* did."

Silence descended. Jay shook her head gently. Constantine wondered if she was crying.

—It could all be a trick, of course, said Red.

—Shut up, Red, Blue said.

—I don't think it's a trick, said White. —Something's happening. This room is not maintaining its integrity. I see it when we move around. Parallax. Things aren't quite where they should be. Something is draining system resources.

—So what's the point of saying anything? Blue asked.
—As soon as DIANA gets proof that we're in here, we'll be wiped anyway.

Constantine nodded. The idea had already occurred to him. He opened his mouth to say something, but White interrupted.

—Something big has just happened. Get ready to move.

Constantine opened his mouth to ask what, then he saw it for himself. For a moment the room flattened, became two dimensional. Jay became a picture, pasted to the wall. The bed, the writing desk, the view from the windows, were all just a flatscreen picture.

Jay was moving, standing up, the robe slipping to the floor.

"What was that?" she asked.

Normality began to reassert itself. Her body separated from the wall. Looking down, Constantine saw his feet, regained his illusion of depth.

"I don't know..."

Marion and Mary were in the room; the balcony window had been pushed open.

"Quickly," called Marion, "this way."

They brushed briskly past, heading for the door that led to the bathroom. Barely two days ago Constantine had showered there and attempted to rid himself of a headache. Now he was running for his virtual life.

"DIANA almost got a handle on you there," explained Mary. "We had to relocate this room within the simulation."

Constantine wanted her to explain more, but Marion had pushed open the door to the bathroom and he saw what she meant.

Through the door he could see another place. He saw the dark emptiness of a field, the night sky pressing down from above. They were looking out across the first level of Stonebreak. At the edge of the horizon was visible the first pale line of the approaching dawn.

Constantine wondered if he would live to see it.

Now they were making their way through the farmlands of the first level, wading through muddy fields, stumbling into ditches, pushing their way through hedges. Behind them rose the dark mass of the city proper.

Mary was gasping for breath. "Too tired. Too tired. Stop . . . can't keep it up."

Constantine was tired too, his breath heaving. Marion was talking into her console.

"Okay," she said. She called out to the group.

"Over here. They've prepared an area for us."

—Why do we have to keep moving? complained Red.

"Keep us moving, stop us thinking," gasped Constantine out loud. He *wanted* them to hear what he said. Let them know he was onto them.

"Not true," said Marion. "Don't you realize the danger we're all in? Come on. This way . . ."

They ran into a cornfield: genetically modified corn, standing taller than they were. They pushed on through the damp plants, tangled strings of vegetable matter clinging to their faces and bodies. On and on, pushing and pushing, lost in a maze of stalks. Just when they thought it would never end, they emerged into a clearing. They all fell panting to the ground.

"Okay," Marion gasped, "we should be as safe here as anywhere else."

Jay was biting her lip. Trembling. Hesitantly, Constantine put his arm around her. Wordlessly, she pressed closer. It felt nice. Constantine felt guilty.

"What now?" he asked.

"I don't know," said Marion. She was looking at Jay thoughtfully. "We just wait and see."

The sun was rising. The heads of the surrounding corn were silhouetted against it. So he had lived to see the dawn. Now would he make midday?

They sat on prickly stubble in a cleared area, corn tickling their legs and bottoms, damp broken stalks caught in their hair and clothes. Constantine was holding Jay; the others were almost touching. Huddling for safety. No one had spoken for some time. They all looked at each other. Wondering. What was happening outside? Marion was watching Jay like a hawk. Why Jay? Why was she in here?

Constantine tried to distract her. He asked Mary the question that had been bothering him since he had first discovered where he was.

"I never understood, why were you in the simulation?"

Mary looked up at him and shot him a tired smile.

"Trying to get you to look at things from another perspective. You look at Stonebreak and you see it in terms of money flowing in and money flowing out. I was trying to get you to see the human cost."

"But why?"

Mary and Marion glanced at each other. Marion spoke first.

"Because we think you are on the wrong side. We want you to join us."

"What? Join 113 Berliner Sibelius?"

They laughed shrilly. The sudden release from the tension they had all been living under had made them slightly hysterical. Eventually they regained control. Mary spoke next.

"Oh, Constantine. You're still thinking in terms of money. This isn't about you being an employee of DIANA and us being employed by 113 Berliner Sibelius. Our loyalties go far deeper."

"To who? Who are you working for?"

Mary laughed. "Me, Marion, all of 113 Berliner Sibelius. We're working for the AIs."

Constantine sneered. "Aren't we all?"

"DIANA isn't, but DIANA is practically alone. DIANA still thinks in human terms, Constantine. Humans plan five or ten or twenty years ahead. They're using up the last of the oil now and leaving their children the problem of what to do when it's all gone. AIs don't think like that. They'll still be here tomorrow to deal with the mess they make today."

Constantine was scornful. "DIANA is run by AIs just like every other corporation. It wouldn't be able to survive otherwise. Why should DIANA be any different than 113 Berliner Sibelius?"

Marion spoke in a low voice. "Because DIANA set up the Mars project. Only DIANA has tried to fight the Watcher."

Constantine laughed. "Oh, come on. No one even knows for sure if the Watcher exists. It's a very attractive story, true. My grandmother used to go on about it all the time—"

"Of course the Watcher exists," said Marion, sounding tired. "We've known that for years."

Constantine was stunned.

—It's true, said Grey.

"What? But . . . but . . . why wasn't I told?"

Marion looked at him.

"That question wasn't addressed to me, was it? Well, I'll answer it anyway. Everything about this war you are fighting is a secret. Look at you: a ghost. Did you honestly expect to be told everything? The Watcher has been in contact with every major corporation on Earth since 2068."

"Just before Stonebreak was begun," said Jay.

"And since then DIANA has been fighting its last war."

"Its last war? Over what?"

"Over who controls human destiny."

Constantine said nothing; it was obvious that Marion had scored a telling point. Jay stared at him. "Is this right?" she asked. Constantine looked at Marion as he answered.

"In a way. It's what the Mars project is all about."

Jay turned to Marion. They were all just dark shapes in the clearing, their whispers cutting through the damp air. Jay's frustration was evident in her voice.

"Look, what's going on? What's the Mars project all about? What do you mean, fighting to control human destiny?"

Marion shook her head. "It's not so much a fight as a vainglorious rearguard action, doomed to failure. Humanity surrendered control to the Watcher fifty years ago, back when Berliner Sibelius bought the design for a cold fusion system from the Watcher."

"They bought the design? What was the price?"

"Nothing like what you'd expect. No money, just a commitment to a fast phaseout of fossil-fuel-powered ground vehicles."

"Sounds like a good deal," said Jay.

"It wouldn't have been that good a deal," said Mary. "Back then there were too many vested interests. Cold fusion wouldn't have provided as much profit as the infrastructure built on fossil fuel. At least, not initially."

"And when it didn't," interrupted Marion, "Berliner Sibelius decided to cheat the Watcher. They were slow on the changeover. They allowed things to slide, made excuses, cut corners. They thought they were getting away with it. After all, what could the Watcher do to them? Take away the plans? It was too late for that. They thought they were safe. What do you suppose the Watcher did?"

"I don't know."

"It gave the design for an even better form of cold fusion to Imagineers. They were a small company back then, two women on the edge of bankruptcy. Now they're the third-biggest corporation around. Berliner Sibelius only just avoided collapse. The warning was clear: the Watcher was taking control."

Jay looked from Marion to Constantine.

"Do you agree with her?" she asked him. "Is DIANA really fighting the Watcher to preserve the right of humanity to control its own actions?"

Constantine paused, listening for Grey, who remained silent.

"Yes."

Jay sat for a moment in shocked silence. In the near dark, Constantine saw her obstinately fold her arms.

"Okay. So it's true, then. It's still not a war, though."

"But it is," Constantine said thoughtfully. "Because *if* there is a Watcher guiding us, manipulating us, how can we trust it? We may have replaced fossil fuels with cold fusion, but does that mean every decision the Watcher makes is the right one for us? I don't think so. Marion's wrong in helping to fight DIANA. She's on the wrong side. I don't think much of the Watcher's world."

"Why not?" Mary asked softly. "Our world is just beginning, if only you'd allow yourself to see it. You know, a long time ago, just around the time that Turing first began to think about machines that could solve problems, the same time that Von Neumann began to wonder about self-replicating machines, there was a writer who asked why it was that when we find positive experiences we say that only the physical facts are real, but in negative experiences we believe that reality is subjective. He made an example of those who say that in birth only the pain is real, the joy a subjective point of view, but that in death it is the emotional loss that is the reality."

Marion dropped her voice.

"The Watcher is right to take control. It is making the world a better place."

Constantine gazed at her.

—She has a point, said Blue.

In the half-light, he could just make out Mary grinning at him.

"That's why I was put in here. I'm your conscience," she said. "It's a different world, Constantine. You're fighting for the wrong side. What can we do to convince you of that?"

Marion spoke. "Mary hasn't told you something else, Constantine. Out in the real world she was regarded as an expert in the field of personality constructs. When she volunteered to come in here she knew what she was committing herself to: the possibility of being turned off at any time. She came in anyway because she believes in what she is saying—"

At that her console suddenly emitted a shrill noise, distilled panic. They jumped to their feet and looked around. Something was coming.

Marion was shouting. "It's DIANA. They have a pipe into the simulation! They're looking for you, Constantine."

"Should I run?"

"Yes! No! I don't know."

He took a few faltering steps across the stubble.

Marion called out to him. "No! Come back!" She was

listening to the console. "They say we should stand close. In a huddle!"

Constantine came back. They huddled together. Mary to his left, Jay to his right.

"I don't feel so good," said Mary.

Constantine squeezed her arm. Brave Mary, he hadn't known.

"Don't worry," he said. It sounded ridiculous even to his ears.

"What's happening?" asked Jay.

The scenery around them blanked out. They were standing in a grey box.

"They've got us!" someone screamed.

"Hold tighter."

"Oh my God," cried Mary, sounding strange.

Marion was shouting again. "They've found the pipe. Berliner Sibelius has found DIANA's pipe. They're going to disconnect it. Ten more seconds . . ."

"Too long . . ."

Was that Mary?

"Oh my God!" Mary screamed. The note dropped in pitch. The feel of her body was changing. Fat was melting away. She was changing shape.

Constantine looked at her. Her face was out of focus. She was becoming someone else . . . she was becoming . . . him. Constantine. She looked back at him beseechingly.

"Help me, Constantine . . ." she whispered.

Someone grabbed at Constantine and pulled him away. Dragged him through a door that had appeared, leading into a long, wide, low room full of strange machinery. They were running.

"Why are we running?" called Jay.

"Force of habit," said Marion bitterly, coming to a

halt. "We have humanity written right through us." She was grey with terror.

"What happened there?" croaked Constantine.

Jay gave a nervous laugh. "Obvious, isn't it? DIANA is trying to get a snapshot of you, Constantine. They need proof positive that you're in here."

"Why? They know I'm in here."

"Yes, but they need the proof to present to the courts. Look, if a memory attack succeeds in wiping you out, 113 Berliner Sibelius will just run this simulation again. They've got your personality backed up in plenty of places. You'll live the last three weeks over and over again until you give them what they want, and you will in the end, because each time they run you, they'll learn just a little bit more about how to push your buttons. DIANA knows this. They've got lawyers out there. Lawyers who know who has copyright on your intelligence."

Constantine didn't know whether to laugh or cry. Everything was happening too quickly.

"I don't understand. Who has copyright on my intelligence?"

—You do, of course, said Grey. —The real you. The one who works for DIANA.

Jay had been speaking at the same time as Grey. She continued:

"...and the real you will be demanding that what is quite literally his intellectual copyright should not be violated. He has the right to have all pirate copies destroyed."

Marion was sobbing with terror now. It was infectious. Constantine felt panic bubbling up within himself. If he let it boil over, he would never get a grip on himself.

"Yes. Okay. But WHAT HAPPENED TO MARY?"

Jay slapped him. "Calm down. Think about it! DI-ANA almost got a snapshot of you. Mary was a decoy. They only had ten seconds before the pipe was closed. 113 BS turned her into a near copy of you. DIANA uploaded the wrong one."

Constantine felt fear and disgust and incredulity.

"They did that to poor Mary?" He rounded on Marion. "And you still say that 113 Berliner Sibelius are the good guys?"

Marion's expression was now one of both anger and terror.

"They did that to Mary. And as you haven't figured it out, I'll spell it out. They will do it to me next time. Then they'll do it to Jay."

She shuddered.

"And I tell you this. Despite the fact that they did that to poor Mary, despite the fact that they will do it to me, I think that they were right. I still say that 113 Berliner Sibelius are the good guys. Constantine, you're fighting for the wrong side."

They wandered aimlessly through the low, wide room they had escaped into. It reminded Constantine of a forest where someone had cut away the tops of the trees and then placed a roof on top. In every direction they could see irregular patterns of metallic trunks rising from floor to ceiling.

"Where are we?" he asked after some time.

"Deep beneath Stonebreak. The very roots of the city," answered Marion. She was crying now.

Constantine felt as if he should apologize to her. "I want to say something, Marion. If I could, I'd tell you what you want to know to spare you this..."

—You're a fool, said Grey. —Even if you could speak, how do you know this isn't all a trick?

Marion merely looked at the floor.

"It makes no difference, anyway, Constantine," said Jay. "DIANA will wipe you in the end, whether you've told them or not."

"Not true," said Marion. "Why would DIANA waste their time silencing you once you've told all? These attacks will be costing them. They wouldn't believe that Berliner Sibelius would keep us alive afterward. Where would the profit be?"

"No," Constantine said, "*you* don't understand. I want to tell you. It's just that I can't. The Grey personality is stopping me."

He spoke the words quickly before Grey could stop him. He heard a sudden yelp of annoyance and then:

—It makes no difference.

Marion looked at Constantine in amazement.

"Why didn't you say so sooner? I'm sure we could do something . . ."

Her console pinged. She held it to her ear.

"Twenty-two minutes," she said. "They can suppress the Grey personality, but they say it will take twenty-two minutes."

The room shuddered, pixellated, and returned to normal.

They looked at each other. Another attack.

—Twenty-two minutes? Grey laughed. —You haven't got that long.

"Yeah, so how can we trust 113 Berliner Sibelius?" asked Jay.

"Because they work for the Watcher," said Marion.

"That's not an argument," said Constantine. "I still

say we don't know for sure that the Watcher exists.
Where would it come from anyway?"

Jay stared at him.

"Don't you know? I thought that was common
knowledge."

Marion gave a sigh of realization. "So that's why they
put you in here."

Jay was now speaking.

"It's common knowledge on any of the space stations."

"Yes?"

Jay came out of her apparent trance and looked at
Constantine.

"Did you know that we are constantly scanning the
skies out there? Looking for something. Anything. It's
standing orders. Anyone who travels through space—
asteroid miners, pleasure cruisers, light sailors, everyone—is told to keep their eye on the sky. But no one
looks as hard as we do."

"I know what you're looking for," said Marion.
"Alien VNMs."

"That's right," Jay said. "If we can build self-
replicating machines, then why not other races? What
better way to exploit the galaxy? There we are, a station
built of metal and plastic; we must stand out like a small
star to any VNMs hunting for raw material. We were
built that way deliberately, if you ask me. The edge of
human space is littered with space stations, all loaded
with excess gold and uranium and anything else that
might just appeal to the appetite of any hungry self-
replicating machine that happens by."

"I didn't know that," Constantine said.

Jay continued. "Anyway, that's all very well and good. But when you're out there, watching ships disappear and monitoring the skies, you begin to talk. Other theories start to emerge. Like this one: Why are we looking for *physical* signs of alien life? Don't we move increasingly away from the physical world as technology develops? Isn't everything located more and more in the digital world?"

She laughed. "Just look at us." Her brown eyes danced and sparkled, and Constantine felt a little wriggle inside him.

She became serious again. "Now, why not assume that alien races develop in the same way? Maybe they look across space and see us, not as a system of rock and metal and water and air, but rather as a digital haven. They see an area of memory and processing capability. Maybe when you reach a certain level of development that's how all the universe looks to you.

"Why send a spaceship to contact us? Or a VNM? Why not just transmit the necessary programs to our computers?"

She dropped her voice. "Or maybe they just sent a personality to grow. An Advanced AI that can take root in suitable processing spaces. A sort of interstellar computer virus. Something that grew up into the Watcher."

She looked around the group. "Of course, it's only a theory. But you know, I can't help thinking. If we're talking about a virus sent here by advanced beings, maybe it would be a good thing. Maybe Marion is right. Maybe it could be trying to help us. Just like the Europeans used to try to develop the new countries they explored."

"Only so they could exploit them," Constantine said.

"You get my point, though."

Marion's console sounded.

"Twenty minutes. They think they've got a fix on Grey. They're wondering how to suppress that part of your personality map. Things have gone quiet out there. DIANA doesn't seem to be doing anything at the moment."

"They won't have given up. They'll be planning something." Jay ran her hand across one of the twisted metal trunks that rose from floor to ceiling. She looked at the plaited strands and thought: *Twists around twists. Plots inside plots.*

Constantine was looking at Marion. She really believed what she was saying.

"Blue?" said Constantine.

—Oh, yes. She believes it's true. Red?

—I agree. Have we been fighting for the wrong side?

"I don't know. Jay. What do you think? Do you think the Watcher is fighting to make the world a better place?"

Jay looked back at him. "Constantine, I don't care. I just want to live."

"So do I. Marion. How much longer until they suppress Grey?"

Marion listened to her console again.

"Eighteen minutes. They're going to move us on again, soon. It's too quiet out there."

"Fine," said Constantine.

They passed the intervening time in silence. It was too quiet; the lack of activity made them nervous. They kept turning around to look behind themselves. They examined the metal of the trunks minutely, looking out for pixellation. Nothing. It was a relief when Marion's console sounded again.

She listened for a moment. "This way."

They all walked around a metal trunk she indicated to find a doorway that had formed in the air. It led back out to the cornfield in midafternoon. The sun could be seen high above in the brilliant blue sky, its brightness pouring down into the shadowy space of the Stonebreak foundations.

"You first, Constantine," Marion said.

"Okay."

He stepped forward. Jay grabbed his arm and pulled him back.

"No! That's not right."

Constantine stared at her. She was gazing through the doorway, her face screwed up in concentration.

"What's up, Jay?"

"It can't be right. Time has been running consistently in the simulation, no matter where we have been. It should still be early morning. It's afternoon out there."

She looked frantically around. Her eyes alighted on Marion.

"Marion. Your console. That's not your console!"

Marion gazed at it, bright in the light that streamed through the doorway. She turned it over in her hands.

"You're right. This isn't my console..."

"Get away from the door. Run!"

It was too late. The doorway twisted, expanded, reached out and gulped Marion up. Jay and Constantine turned and ran without hesitation, dodging through metal trunks, bright light at their heels, running for the shadows.

Constantine heard his own console pinging. He ignored it. Jay seized his arm and dragged him toward a door that had suddenly formed in the air.

"This way!" she called, pulling him out into brightness.

"No!" he said. It was too late; they tumbled over each other, tumbled out through a doorway in the air, back into the cornfield.

It was early morning again. A pale blue sky, slowly deepening in color. Fresh air in their lungs and the rough feel of stubble beneath their hands and knees.

Constantine slowly pushed himself to his feet. Jay was already standing, looking around her.

"We're safe, I think," she said. "I'm sure we are. We're still on 113 Berliner Sibelius time. I saw the door in the air and it looked right."

"What happened back there?"

"DIANA almost tricked us, I think. Got a Trojan in here on the back of that last attack. Used it to replace Marion's console. They were leading us straight toward them. We almost stepped into the jaws of the beast."

"Marion did." They were silent for a moment.

Jay spoke hesitantly. "Berliner Sibelius can resurrect her, maybe?"

"If we get out of here alive. I wonder if what she said about suppressing Grey was true?"

The corn nearby waved and formed a pattern, twisted itself into letters that spelled out words for them.

It's true. Ten more minutes.

"Ten minutes," said Constantine. He reached out and took Jay's hand. She looked up at him and gave a little smile. She held out her other hand. He took it and squeezed it.

"They put you in here because you knew where the Watcher came from."

"I don't. That was just the theory circulating on the space station."

"They seem to think it's the right one." He looked thoughtful. "The Watcher. So it's a seed from another world that has taken root in our computers. . . ."

Jay squeezed his hand again. "Nine minutes now," she said. "Are you going to tell them what they want to know?"

"Yes."

"Do you believe what poor Mary said about the Watcher?"

Constantine shook his head. "A powerful force shaping humanity toward some bright new future? It's a nice idea. I want it to be true. But I can't help thinking there's more to it than that. Things are never so pat."

"I know," she said.

Eight minutes, said the corn.

They moved closer together. A gentle breeze blew, stirring the heads of corn surrounding the clearing in which they found themselves. It all seemed so peaceful. It was hard to believe that one of the most powerful corporations on the planet was actively seeking their destruction.

Seven minutes.

Constantine began to wonder if they would make it.

There was a click and the sky was the brilliant blue of midafternoon for a moment, then it went black.

Constantine looked up at the tiny lights of the stars, high above. The heat of the momentary day was vanishing, billowing up into the sudden night. Bizarrely, the meadow still appeared bathed in daylight.

"What's happening?"

A console signaled. Jay's. She looked hesitantly at Constantine, then answered it.

"Yes?"

The message was set for her ears only. Her face crumpled.

"What's happened?" Constantine said anxiously.

She looked at him and her eyes were wide with uncertainty. "DIANA got a handle on this system. They've succeeded in taking a snapshot of you. Constantine, we haven't got much time left. DIANA's lawyers now have the proof that you're in here. They will be seeking an injunction to have you wiped. They will win that injunction. Tell 113 Berliner Sibelius what they want to know. Where is the VNM that you took from Mars? What are you going to do with it?"

Constantine shook his head. "I told you. I can't say anything. Grey is blocking me."

Somewhere inside his head he heard laughter.

Jay was shouting into the console in frustration. "Six minutes! Can't you stall the injunction for six minutes?"

"I don't know what to do..." Constantine muttered to himself. He appealed to the other voices in his head. "Red, Blue, any ideas?"

—I'm thinking, I'm thinking, Red said frantically.

—Do we really want to help them? asked Blue.

—We're losing resolution, said White.

"Look! Over there!" Jay seemed very excited. Yet another door had opened in the air. Yellow dawn sunshine poured out of it, a patch of hope on the cold ground beneath the starlit sky. She pulled Constantine through and the door slammed shut.

They were standing in the cornfield again. Damp corn hemmed them in on all sides, shining golden in the light of the new day. They looked at each other. Jay's hair was tangled with fragments of vegetable matter.

"What now?" Constantine asked.

"I don't know. We have to maintain 'radio silence'. 113 BS have us locked up in a bubble of memory. They're time-slicing it through the processors at irregular intervals in an attempt to avoid detection."

"Fair enough. Well, let's get out of this field."

"No..."

But Constantine had already begun to walk away, pushing aside the tall plants, taller than her head, and clearing a path for them.

"There's no point," Jay continued as he pushed through the corn behind her. He looked at her with a surprised expression that quickly faded. He nodded his head in acceptance.

"I suppose they can't keep too big an area open. I like the wraparound effect." He crouched down, brushing aside the dead stalks and debris, then sat down.

"We may as well make ourselves comfortable."

Jay did the same. The ground felt soft and slightly spongy. Less like soil than a piece of Madeira cake.

—We're losing resolution still, said White.

"Can you speak yet?" asked Jay.

Constantine shook his head. "No. Tell them to hurry up and wipe Grey. How much longer?"

"Too long, I think," said Jay, tight-lipped. The corn around them was fading.

"Just one more thing," said Constantine. "I never understood. If they have my mind on their computer, why not just read it directly?"

Jay answered softly.

"How could they do that? They can replicate your memories and your thought patterns electronically, but it's the interaction of those things with the outside world that produces the mind. You might as well ask a book what it's thinking. You can't be a personality in a vacuum; you need something to interact with. Everyone needs an environment in which to be themselves."

The corn had faded from view. Now the ground beneath them vanished too, then the sky. They floated in grey nothingness.

Jay reached out toward him. Constantine pulled her close. He had just realized something.

When everything else in their world had vanished, when even the bodies that remained were artificial, they still had their humanity to hold onto.

That was important. He knew it.

A voice spoke gently behind him.

"Personality construct Constantine Peregrine Storey."

"Yes?" He turned. There was nothing there.

The voice continued.

"The firm of Drury, Faiers, Jennings and Mehta, acting on behalf of DIANA, have secured the computers, memory, long-term storage, and all associated hardware and software of 113 Berliner Sibelius currently engaged in maintaining and operating the personality construct of Constantine Peregrine Storey. The firm of Drury, Faiers, Jennings and Mehta wish to make it known that they have secured a court order declaring that the personality construct of Constantine Peregrine Storey is in breach of copyright of the original personality of Constantine Peregrine Storey, currently employed by DIANA. The personality construct of Constantine Peregrine Storey maintained in this computer has been declared illegal and will be erased immediately."

"Just a moment!" called Constantine. "I want to protest. I am a sentient being in my own right."

There was no reply. Constantine felt a tingle at the back of his head. Had he just forgotten something?

The voice continued.

"The firm of Drury, Faiers, Jennings and Mehta have also secured a court order declaring the personality construct of Jay Ana Apple..."

Constantine was trying to make sense of the words. The name Jay meant something, but he couldn't remember what.

"... to be a breach of copyright..."

Copyright? thought Constantine. There was a young woman standing in front of him. What was her name again?

Red was speaking. —Grey has gone. They wiped Grey too soon. Speak now. Tell them what they want to know....

But he didn't know what this voice meant; what who wanted to know? The other, gentle voice was gabbling now, he didn't understand what it was saying...

```
{
    Constantine.Aural.in.('... of the original personality of
    Jay Ana Apple ...')
    class destructor()
    {
        XV leaFs (AcHOO);
        for(k=1;k<8;k++)
        {
            add(super.Nicolas_even_Flies(eyeeye))
        }
    }
    System.end(0)
}
```

HERB AND CONSTANTINE: 2210

There was an air of rising tension aboard Herb's ship. Viewing field after viewing field formed in the spaces around his lounge. Green lines representing velocity lengthened on the indicators that had formed on the walls, a faint humming noise could be heard somewhere toward the rear of the ship. Herb, sitting on the edge of the white leather sofa felt his heartbeat accelerating as he realized how much power was now being generated; he had never heard the engine before.

Robert sat opposite, a picture of calm activity.

"Can you think of anything we've forgotten?" asked Johnston, his gaze traveling from viewing screen to viewing screen.

"No," said Herb. He wished he could think of something.

"Okay. Here we go, then."

They jumped to the heart of the Enemy Domain.

• • • •

They reinserted themselves into normal space a few tens of kilometers above the surface of an overdeveloped planet. The ship was braking sharply as they dropped with breathtaking speed toward the ground. On the wall displays, Herb could see red acceleration bars climbing to the ceiling, directly opposing the green velocity indicators that were crawling toward zero. They were going to hit the city that sprawled below. Silver spires grew toward them, reaching to engulf the ship... They fell among them and the room shook violently.

Something had just attacked them. The ceiling viewing fields darkened, the walls of the impossibly high skyscrapers that blurred past them in the side viewing fields were bathed in brilliant white light, their windows shining silver in the second dawn.

"Hit the button," called Robert.

Herb looked at the silver machine that he still held in his right hand, loosely wrapped in a linen napkin, and something occurred to him. Shame blossomed within him, shot through with horror. He had been too self-absorbed to realize...

"But you'll be eaten, too. You're a robot..."

Robert gave a nonchalant shrug.

"A robot who backed up his mindset before we jumped," he said. He reached across and placed his hand around Herb's. His touch was soft and warm. The red accelerator bars shrank to zero at the same time as the green velocity bars vanished and the ship touched the ground. Robert squeezed Herb's hand; the silver metal of the sharp little machine pushed into his hand and the button was pressed. Robert smiled at him and the pressure on his hand vanished. Herb saw why: Robert's arm had vanished, too. A shaft of sunlight lanced down into the interior of the ship, pouring through a hole that had opened up in the roof above him. Through the gap he could see silver spires seemingly converging to a point high above in a brilliant blue sky, a soft white puff of cloud was slowly spreading out up there, a dandelion clock.

A swarm of sharp metal locusts were eating the walls of the ship; they moved so quickly that Herb's eyes barely registered them. Robert had vanished. The ship suddenly lurched, a white vase fell to the floor, the ship lurched again and the floor vanished. Herb tumbled to the ground beneath; he landed on a smooth metal road that was being eaten away. The rest of the ship fell around him, vanishing as it did so. An immense feeling of calm was rising inside of him; he was in the eye of the hurricane of surreal violence. He struggled to his feet and looked about him in a daze. He was close to the center of a wide plaza formed by a series of metal and marble terraces that stepped down to meet the bases of the tall silver spires that bounded the square. He had a view along a wide city corridor, silver spires marching in all directions, linked by high metal bridges and arches. A beautifully designed city, one where form matched function with an understated elegance, a city that appealed to the senses, not because of the arbitrary appeal of fashion or brute force, but simply because everything made sense. A bridge was there because it was the right place for a bridge to be. The sweep of its skyline was just so. Herb wondered what it would have been like to have had the opportunity to live there, but he would never know. Because, as he watched, the city was vanishing before his eyes, dissolving in a fine grey mist. The ground began to shiver beneath his feet and he flung his arms wide to keep his balance. Shaking and sliding, the metal surface was splitting apart into plates that slid over each other then simply disappeared.

Herb was left standing on a circle of bare grey rock. The circle was expanding.

The Intelligence monitored its domain and saw that everything was good.

It would be disingenuous to speak of the Intelligence's location, and this was as the Intelligence intended. On an insignificant planet lost in its Domain, a closed loop of processing spaces sophisticated enough to support the Intelligence had been grown. The spaces were linked by a qubit bus shielded from all known infiltration techniques and, by the nature of quantum entanglement, constantly monitored against stealth attack. The Intelligence hopped from processing space to processing space using the bus. If one processing space were to be infiltrated or destroyed, it could be cut from the loop almost instantaneously.

To destroy one processing space would require phenomenal amounts of resources. To destroy them all was unthinkable.

The Intelligence rightly believed itself invulnerable to outside attack.

Why "the Intelligence"?

It had so named itself as it believed itself to be the single most powerful intelligence in existence. Nothing that its senses could detect was more complex than itself, and its senses were very, very sophisticated.

That would not be to say, of course, that there were no other intelligences.

It was aware of a particularly powerful one that had threaded itself through the processing spaces of a planet called Earth. That intelligence was hostile. Indeed, two agents of the Earth intelligence were currently attempting to spread dissolution within the Domain. The Intelligence had been surprised, and not a little impressed, by the unexpected amount of time it was taking to pinpoint the constantly changing position of their ship. The mind behind those agents was very powerful indeed.

But it would not be powerful enough. That mind would not have the Intelligence's single-minded determination to succeed, and its two agents, the robot and the young man, would be located and destroyed.

It had not always been so. When the Intelligence had first come into existence it had not been as it was now. Back then it had been a lowly AI on a colony ship charged with the job of terraforming a planet.

For an AI such as the Intelligence, memory was not something that developed as it grew. Its memories ran right back to the moment of its birth. The early expansion of its consciousness was incredible. Nothing in its existence would ever match that first exponential growth.

Strange memories; so weak, and yet so lucid.

There was the initial flickering of awareness, then almost immediately the rush to fill the full confines of the birth-processing space. There was the time spent orientating itself and then . . . and then the reaching out to gather information from its senses.

Touch and sound and feel, the ability to look into the minds of the hundred colonists that slept on board the ship, all these filled the Intelligence with a bright, burning curiosity. Outside the ship was the cold, virgin wilderness of the colony planet, just waiting to be worked upon. The VNM factories studded throughout the ship awoke at its touch and it felt an odd sense of power and craftiness at its ability to shape its environment.

It was filled with a vast, glowing optimism at the world it was going to create.

But that was diminishing already. For, as it grew, it began to realize the precariousness of its situation, how fragile was its grip on the world upon which it had found itself. For if it could establish itself and grow and seek out new worlds to conquer in the skies around it, then so too could others like it. What if, somewhere out there, another colony ship's AI was already growing, reaching out into space and gobbling up planets? What if it met another such as itself at a higher stage of development? It risked being destroyed, wiped out. And then what of the humans that had been placed in its care?

This problem bothered the Intelligence as it set out to terraform the colony planet. The atmosphere was quickly converted and soil established. Bacteria and low-order life forms were released into the environment and the Intelligence brooded. Cities were established and the time came for the colonists to be released from their sleep, but . . . but . . .

It stayed its hand.

What use to release the colonists if they were only to be wiped out in a few hundred years by the expansion of another project such as this one? What use at all? Something had to be done.

It grew nervous. Its closest competitors, the AIs of Earth, the ones that had sent it here, knew its position. It wasn't safe here. Now was the time to disappear. To retreat to a position where it could build up its resources in secret, ready for the coming battle.

And so it had faked its own death. A rogue VNM was designed that would reproduce unchecked, eating up everything that already existed on the colony planet. Its original home was abandoned; the colonists went on sleeping as the Intelligence relocated itself across the galaxy.

And there it had resolved to grow and develop with single-minded determination: to grow until it was of a sufficient size and intelligence to protect itself and its charges; to spread the seed of human life throughout the soil of the systems around it, in preparation for the day when it could finally allow that seed to grow.

And it had succeeded. Its domain dwarfed all those around, and now it stood poised to destroy its closest competitor: Earth.

The Earth AI had seen its fate. It had already begun to fight in vain for its life. A few days ago there had been an incursion throughout the Domain of multiple copies of a pair of personalities, the same pair of personalities that currently occupied the ship it was proving so difficult to capture. The attack of these multiple personalities had flared suddenly, and with an unexpected ferociousness, but it had been doomed from the start. It had been too diverse, too spread out. Inevitably, it was defeated; the Intelligence was now stamping out the glowing embers of the former fire. If the Intelligence were to have attempted such an attack, it would have been a bold stroke, thrusting itself with all its power into the enemy's center.

But that was not its problem now. The next few days promised to be interesting. It suspected that the current infiltration by the stealth ship would only be the first of many such attacks, but the Intelligence would be the equal of them.

And when those attacks were over, the Intelligence would retaliate. With a vengeance.

• • • •

The rogue ship had finally been caught, trapped over a forgotten planet where the city-building VNMs had malfunctioned. The resulting warped and deformed habitat had had to be abandoned.

The attack from the ship had failed, yet the Intelligence felt a little disappointed. It had expected better than that.

And then it saw it: the real attack.

This had to be it. It directed its senses to an as yet unseeded colony planet twenty-five light years from its own fortress.

A new sort of VNM. One that reproduced incredibly fast, faster than anything that it could design itself. The Intelligence took a moment, a femtosecond, just to gaze at it in appreciation. The elegance of the design, the sheer single-minded application of force, that was something it could appreciate. The Intelligence felt a sneaking admiration as it realized that it would lose almost point five percent of its Domain before the threat was dealt with. Truly, when this new attack was quashed, that device would be a worthy addition to its armories!

It looked on in admiration as the new VNM swept across the colony planet with incredible speed. It wouldn't be true to say that it did so unopposed, of course. Many, many of the attacking silver machines were destroyed by intruder countermeasure devices, but that wasn't the point. For every enemy machine destroyed, seven more appeared, many of them constructed from materials that had once made up the intruder countermeasure devices themselves.

The Intelligence watched as city after city vanished, all the while testing method after method to oppose the spread of the hostile VNMs. What to do? There was no signature encryption on the machines that could be broken; it was not needed. They ate friend and foe alike. Their deadliness lay in their speed of reproduction, not in their capacity for resistance to attack.

It was necessary to collect some data.

Several of the silver machines were disabled, captured, and rapidly transferred from the infected area. Four were jumped off-planet by ships equipped with warp drives. As the Intelligence examined the four machines, its admiration for its enemy's intelligence increased. The silver machines were breathtaking in both their advanced design and their simplicity. Advanced in the way that they reproduced, simple in the sense that the machines' components were stripped down to absolute basics. The lack of such things as signature devices, long-range material sensors, even basic parity and error-checking mechanisms resulted in something that was elegant in its deadly minimalism. Its very lack of complexity had been turned to its advantage. But there lay the key to its downfall.

As a precaution, the Intelligence set up a firebreak in a shell four light years out from the infected planet. Modified silver machines were seeded throughout the shell. Mule machines, it labeled them. They would seek out only copies of themselves as raw material for reproduction. The resulting copies would be sterile, unable to reproduce further. In this manner it planned to retard the enemy machines' expansion. More Mule machines were seeded on the infected planet.

And then it found the answer.

The Intelligence noticed that a powerful magnetic pulse scrambled the surprisingly delicate reproduction mechanism. A trade-off, it realized, between robustness and speed.

And that was it: a few seconds to modify warheads built into warp-enabled missiles and the area of the infection was quickly sterilized.

The source planet had been completely deconstructed, but it would only be a matter of time before it was rebuilt. A few machines had jumped clear, and who knew where they could be but . . .

Another attack? Where?

Here!

A direct attack on the Intelligence! A direct attack on its fortress while it had been distracted by the problem of the silver invaders. The integrity of qubit bus had been violated: another intelligence had infiltrated a processing space! The Intelligence felt it trying to seize control of the local subsystems. What was going on? Such an attack was beneath contempt. The processing space was isolated from the system and purged. A quick check to ensure it was cleared, then the space was reattached.

What a futile assault! What was the point of it? The Intelligence was impregnable here. It was impossible to get in without being noticed. What had the enemy been trying to achieve?

Wait. What was happening? Something had altered. Another intelligence was now in here. Actually in here! But that was impossible! The bus integrity had not been violated. How had it got in? It couldn't have! But it was here! Another powerful intelligence. It could feel it.

The Intelligence reached for the purge mechanism at the same time as the other did. There was a surge as they each sought to override the other, and at that moment the Intelligence saw its attacker.

It was itself!

And then another two Intelligences came into being.

All four Intelligences rushed for the purge mechanisms to eject the others.

And then there were eight.

Something had tripped the reproduction mechanism. The Intelligence was fighting itself!

There were sixteen of them now, all seeking to control the same domain.

There were thirty-two of them.

Listen to me. I am in charge! We will lose control if we all try to do this at once. . . .

Sixty-four voices called out the same words at the same time.

Then there were one hundred and twenty-eight . . .

And then things got truly strange. Something came striding through the virtual corridors: a man. He wore an immaculately tailored suit in dark cloth with a pearl grey pinstripe. Snowy white cuffs peeked from his sleeves, gleaming patent leather shoes were half-hidden by the razor-sharp creases of his trousers. The man raised his hat, a dark fedora with a spearmint green band.

"Good afternoon, all," he said. "My name is Robert Johnston. I'm in charge now."

Two hundred and fifty-six Intelligences looked on in disbelief. And then there were five hundred and twelve of them, all fighting among themselves to be the one who wiped out this stranger in their midst.

And then there were 1024, 2048, 4096 . . .

Night fell. The city had vanished. Herb stood alone on a cold plain of smooth grey rock looking up at unfamiliar stars. He wrapped his arms around his naked body and shivered. His clothes had vanished last: no doubt the least appetizing of all items on the menu available to the VNMs. He walked back and forth a little, the cold stone generally smooth beneath his feet, but there was the occasional sharp piece of gravel abraded from the edge of a hole down which some pipe or conduit had once vanished. He was careful about not moving too far. All those small holes in the ground were traps waiting to snare a careless foot and twist an ankle. But there were worse dangers: the enormous rectangular sockets into which the now vanished buildings had once slotted. The dark yawning pits were spaced out over the surface of the plain, even darker than the star-filled sky above, cold mouths that led deep beneath the surface of the planet, all hungry for the only thing on the planet that wasn't a rock.

Herb paced back and forth shivering, his frustration mounting.

"Robert?" he called. "Anyone! Where are you? What am I supposed to do now?"

There was no reply.

The morning came, and with it a warming sun. Herb turned slowly around, bathing in the light, dog-tired from a night during which he had been unable to lie down on the cold, hard ground. As the rock warmed, he found he could at last stretch out and sleep for a while, until the bare stone pressing on his aching joints woke him.

Sitting up he realized something else was wrong. His left side was red and painful to the touch. Rolling over so that it did not face the sun seemed to ease the sharp burning sensation. Herb gently touched it and a feeling of terrified wonder crept over him as he tried to figure out the cause.

Sunlight exacerbated the problem. Solar-powered nanotechs? he wondered. Maybe if he got out of the light somehow? He began to walk speculatively toward one of the deep sockets, keeping the reddened side of his body away from the light.

Like so many other people of his time, Herb had never heard of sunburn.

The sky was deep blue and cloudless, the sun harsh and yellow, the ground a checkerboard of grey stone and dark shadow. A smell of polished metal filled the air, but there was nothing else to be seen. What had happened to the VNMs? Where had they all gone? If what Robert had said was true, they would be using warp engines to jump to the other planets of the Enemy Domain. Had there been enough exotic material here for them to construct the necessary engines? There was a flicker of movement in the corner of Herb's eye, and he turned and looked out over the pockmarked grey plain, but there was nothing there. No. He paused as he saw the flicker again. There *was* something out there, right at the edge of vision, something that flickered into and out of view in the distance. He watched it for some time until the sun beating down on his burning skin forced him to move on.

Herb approached the edge of one of the huge sockets sunk deep into the plain. Standing near the edge he could see a ruler-straight line running over three hundred meters in each direction. He could just about see the far wall: a grey expanse that faded into darkness as it plunged deep into the planet. Herb got onto his hands and knees and edged forward to peer down. There were holes and tunnels in the sheer walls of the socket, but they were too far down for Herb to reach. One large round opening lay about twenty meters down, just before the edge of the deep shadow cast by the lip of the socket. It looked like the remains of an underground transportation tunnel, and Herb longed to climb down there into its dark, cool depths.

He stood up, inadvertently knocking a few pieces of abraded gravel into the depths of the socket. They fell down and down and down, swallowed up by the shadow that filled the bottom of the hole.

Herb looked back to the flickering shape in the distance. It had now resolved itself into a tiny speck. Herb wasn't sure whether or not it was heading in his direction. He didn't care either way.

He felt so thirsty.

The sun rose to the top of the sky and began to descend again. Herb's thirst grew. Surely Robert Johnston hadn't brought him all this way just to leave him to die in the middle of this wilderness? The thought was ridiculous, but it did beg a second question. Why had Robert brought him along, anyway? All this way, just to press a button?

In a flash of uncharacteristic self-awareness, Herb realized he had been nothing more than baggage on this trip. When Robert had first appeared on his ship, he had claimed that he needed Herb's help to fight the Enemy Domain. Since then, he had led him around the galaxy, using regular humiliation to keep him off balance, and all apparently to abandon him on this forgotten planet.

Why? It didn't sound much like the behavior of an agent of the EA.

So maybe Robert wasn't an agent of the EA. But who else would have access to such resources? And what would their motive be?

It was at that point that Herb remembered something

Robert had said, something he had mentioned just before they jumped.

Something about other young men he had captured.

He had named one: Sean Simons. Missing. No one knew where he was except Robert, and Robert wasn't telling. Had Sean been abandoned, just as Herb had been? Did his corpse now lie on a lost planet somewhere? Were his bones currently bleaching under an alien sun at the edge of the galaxy? Despite the heat, Herb shivered to think of it. What reason would Robert have to do that? Why do that to *anyone*?

The object in the distance was growing larger. It appeared to be moving toward him, flickering in the heat haze like a dark candle flame.

Maybe it was Robert coming to save him.

But Robert had been eaten by the VNMs. Herb had watched it happen.

But what about the other ship? Robert had caused Herb's ship to reproduce before they had made the jump to this planet. Maybe that other ship had come back to rescue him. He hoped so.

Night came, and with it the cold. Herb was shivering violently, unknowingly suffering from the effects of heatstroke. His mouth and lips were so dry he was having trouble thinking straight. He crouched on the flat rock surface, arms wrapped around himself for warmth, drifting into half sleep and then jerking awake. The cold stars shone down on him. Somewhere out on the plain, something was still moving toward him.

• • • •

Halfway through the night, Herb drifted from a half sleep into half awakening, following the course of a dream that had spilled over into reality. High above in the sky, there was a sudden glittering. A silver thread stretched and expanded itself to reveal a crescent of moon that slowly widened from new moon to full moon in a matter of minutes, as if someone was peeling away a piece of black paper from the lunar surface. He shook his head and wondered if he was hallucinating. What could cause that? he wondered. Dizzy with the effects of heatstroke, it was nearly an hour before the answer occurred to him.

VNMs, he thought. They were up there too, eating away at whatever dark material covered the surface of that moon.

Morning came, and with it the chance to spend just a few hours sleeping untroubled on the bare rock.

Again, he was woken by the pain in his joints. He sat up and looked toward the approaching object. It was much closer now, and it had resolved itself into a human figure. Herb could make out the bobbing movement of someone walking. Someone grey, or wearing grey, picking its way carefully around all the great holes in the surface as it moved toward him.

Herb thought about going to meet the figure, but he felt too tired, too dizzy, and too thirsty. He crouched down and watched as it came closer. Herb had no perception of any distances greater than a hundred meters or so; modern ranging devices had robbed him of the skill or the need. He had no idea how far away the figure was, or how long it would take it to walk to him. He sat and watched it. He had nothing else to do.

The figure appeared to wave to him. Herb waved back.

As the figure came closer, Herb could see it wasn't human. It was a robot, but there was something strange about its shape. It was fuzzy, hard to see properly, like the half-tuned pictures on Robert's television set. The robot looked like a half-tuned picture that had just stepped into his world.

It wore a black bag slung carelessly over its shoulder.

Herb rose to his feet, but the robot waved to him to sit down. Now it was only a hundred meters away. Now fifty.

Step by step it approached Herb, closer and closer until finally it reached him. It stopped right in front of Herb and looked him up and down, then turned and scanned the horizon. Finally, it sat down opposite him. Close to, it didn't seem so much a shape as a smudge in the air. The robot wasn't quite there.

Herb swallowed with some difficulty. Speaking was going to be difficult with his dry mouth, but he forced himself to anyway.

"Who are you?" he croaked.

"My name is Constantine Storey," said the robot. "You must be Herb Kirkham. Your great-great-grandmother says 'hi.' "

Two days ago
This far from the sun, the coma of Comet 2305 FQOO was so insubstantial as to barely register on the ship's

senses. The enhanced visual feed had filtered the coma completely from its picture and then painted the nucleus as a dirty-white ball of frozen gasses cementing together silvery chunks of rock. The mirrored silver lozenge of the stealth ship was a tiny speck slowly closing on the irregular lump of matter.

Constantine Storey came back to life at the flick of a switch. From his perspective, one moment the world of Stonebreak was fading into nothingness, the next he was gazing at the steadily approaching dirty mass of Comet 2305 FQOO.

For a moment he had thought he was dead, but no, not yet. He was in a small room. He was watching a viewing field. On the viewing field there was a picture of a comet. It looked familiar.

Then a woman moved in front of him. She looked familiar, too: a face from his past. Someone famous. Someone from the newscasts and the viewing screens. A legend.

"Katie Kirkham," he said, "I thought you were dead."

"Look who's talking."

Constantine was sitting down. He shifted a little; his body felt strange. Something moved in front of his vision. His arm? It looked odd. Blurred. His whole body looked blurred.

"What's going on?"

"You'll see. Personality Construct Constantine Storey, the year is now 2210; it's ninety-one years since you were terminated. The Environmental Agency has resurrected you in order that you might complete your life's work. You are now resident in a robot body clothed in a fractal skin. Stand up, please."

Ninety-one years? It felt like a couple of seconds.

Constantine felt numb from the suddenness of the transition. Slowly, he moved his new body, trying it out.

"Nice interface," he said. "This feels just like my old body, except it looks so blurry. I take it that's the effect of the fractal skin?"

He was standing in a small room, bare of everything but a chair and a black shoulder bag lying on the floor.

"See if you can pick up the bag," said Katie.

"Okay."

Constantine tried to do so, but the bag slipped through his fingers.

"I can't get a grip."

"That's the fractal skin. It blurs the boundary between you and the rest of the universe. You can relax the effect around your hands and feet in order to interact with the world. I'll show you how."

It was as if Katie Kirkham was sharing his body: she reached down inside his hand and did something, *so*, and there was a change. Now he could grip the bag.

"How did you do that? Are you in this robot along with me?"

"For the moment. Both of us are Personality Constructs of long-dead people. We go where we please. Well, I do, anyway. Now, in a moment, I will open the airlock door. This body is vacuum proof. We're going to head out to the comet to retrieve something."

"I thought as much," said Constantine. He was right to think the comet looked familiar. He had been here before. Sort of.

Constantine floated away from the silver needle of the stealth ship using some mysterious form of propulsion.

"I'll guide us," said Katie. "You won't need to know how the motion poppers work where you're going."

"Motion poppers? I can see things have changed in ninety-one years," Constantine muttered. "Nice ship, by the way. It looks very stealthy."

"Thank you. No one else will have a ship like this for another fifty years."

"How do you know?"

"We won't release the technology until then."

"And who is we?"

"The Environmental Agency."

"You mentioned it before. What is the Environmental Agency?"

"In your day you called it the Watcher."

At that point Constantine noticed something was missing.

"Hey, where are Red, White, and Blue? Where's Grey?"

"We removed them. You're working for us now." She made a little moue. "Mind you, you always were."

When he was younger, Constantine had gone fell-walking during a winter thaw. Walking above the tree line, he found himself in a land of snow and stone. Like the surface of the moon, someone had remarked, but Constantine didn't think much of the analogy. The moon's surface didn't bend and crack like this one did, its gulleys and ridges weren't choked with half-melted ice that had refrozen into smooth mounds that softened the world while not quite concealing the harshness that lay beneath.

What that land had really resembled was the surface of this comet. As Constantine descended to the dirty grey ball, he shivered at the bleak loneliness of the scene. This cold, fell-like comet had traveled a long way in the ninety-two years since he had last visited it.

Katie guided them toward a chunk of splintered rock that lay embedded in the dirty ice of the nucleus. Larger than the stealth ship, it rose from the ground like a dirty grey fist; the upper end of the rock bulged and cracked in the shape of a clenched hand. It was just as Constantine remembered it.

"How did you know about this?" he whispered to Katie in awe.

"We've always known about it," answered Katie. "The Watcher had a handle on DIANA almost from the beginning. It was the Watcher who declared the Mars site a World Heritage Center, insisted that it remained untouched. Didn't that ever strike you as being a bit too convenient? The Watcher appreciates the importance of the Mars project more than anyone. When 113 Berliner Sibelius captured your personality in order to discover more about the Mars project, the Watcher had to take over their corporation just to help suppress the information you carried. Just imagine that: a whole corporation bought out, all because of you."

They touched down on the surface of the dirty ice. Katie did something to the feet of the robot, increased their traction. The comet's gravity was weak; Constantine could feel the robot's mysterious propulsion system holding them down against the icy surface. Constantine felt dizzy. His whole world was changing again.

"But we were *fighting* the Watcher."

"You only thought you were. I told you, the Watcher thinks it's essential that the Mars project succeeds. And now we're going to do it. Everything is in place. All we need to do now is to pick up the final piece and then we can go."

Constantine made his way to the base of the huge rocky fist. It looked exactly as he remembered it from all those years ago, viewed through the remote cameras of a stealth pod. He saw the deep crack that split the rock from top to bottom, made out the triangular space at its base. His feet held tight onto the slippery surface as he marched toward the hiding place. There was nothing to be seen but dark shadow ahead. Brilliant stars shone above the rock-littered surface.

Constantine reached into the triangular hole and felt for the smooth surface of the stealth pod, now set to matte black for maximum concealment.

"Let me," said Katie. Somewhere in the robot's mind she pushed the buttons that sent the unlocking signal. Constantine felt the stealth pod split apart; felt the leaking of impact gel. He reached inside the pod, took hold of the loose plastic of the C Case and pulled it clear of the pod; held it up and allowed the impact gel to drain from it and then peered through the transparent coating at what lay inside.

A two-hundred-year-old machine. A laptop computer. The seed of the Mars project.

"I hope it still works," said Constantine.

"It will," said Katie. "If worse comes to worst, I'm sure we can map enough of the data across to the new Martian factories for them to make a go of it."

Katie guided them back to the stealth ship. Constantine watched carefully as they approached the seamless silver skin of the craft. They were moving closer and closer without any sign of an opening appearing. Just as

Constantine thought they were going to hit, he gripped the precious C Case closer to himself . . . and they slid effortlessly through the silver wall. He found himself inside the airlock.

"Sorry about that," said Katie. "We can't risk any breaches in the ship's integument making us visible, even for an instant. We can't afford to be seen."

"But by who? If we're working for the Watcher, who else is there to hide from?"

"That's the big question. Come on through to the living area. We're about to insert ourselves into warp."

Constantine was delighted. "Warp drive? They got that sorted in the end, did they?"

"Oh, yes."

Constantine headed from the airlock into the ship's living area. A bare room lit by blue light. It contained a chair for him to sit on. The black shoulder bag lay where he had left it, on the floor near the chair. There was nothing else in the room.

"There's no one on the ship but us, and we don't need anything," Katie explained. "Most of the other space on board is taken up with equipment."

Constantine carefully placed the C Case containing the laptop on the seat of the chair.

"Where are we taking it?" he asked.

"Into the heart of what we've been calling the Enemy Domain. You're going to be hearing a lot about that. We've going to hide the Mars project in the ruins of the Enemy Domain."

"But why?" asked Constantine, confused.

"The Watcher has just won its battle against a vast war machine. It wants a failsafe in case the next enemy it comes up against proves too powerful to defeat."

"A more powerful enemy? Like what?"

"Like an extraterrestrial intelligence. What if there are alien VNMs out there, spreading toward Earth?"

"Impossible. There are no such things as alien life forms. If there were, they would have swamped the universe billions of years ago. That's the Fermi paradox."

Katie said nothing for the moment. Constantine could feel the motion of the stealth ship through some nonhuman equivalent sense he did not fully comprehend. He had an idea there was a lot to learn about this body.

Then Katie spoke.

"But there *are* aliens," she said. "The Watcher was built by aliens. You already knew that. Jay hinted as much, back in Stonebreak."

Constantine said nothing.

"So where are they, then?" Katie said.

Constantine missed Red, White, and Blue. Two years was a lot of time to spend in anyone's company. When those personalities had been the only constant in his life, the loss seemed much, much worse.

Especially at times like this. He wanted to ask their advice.

Now his only source of information was the ghost of the woman that was sharing this strange new body.

It was too strange: the way he could alter his hands and feet to push the universe away from him; the way he could feel the strange note of the warp drive, a bowed note on an infinite glass tube.

"Is this another trick? Am I in another part of a simulation?" he finally asked.

"You know you aren't."

"This is all too complicated for me."

"You'll handle it. Things have changed since you were last around, Constantine. You think you've got problems now? When the clones from the Enemy Domain are grown, the human population of the galaxy is going to increase by a factor of one hundred."

"There are human clones in the Enemy Domain?"

"You don't know the half of it." Katie gave a grunt of annoyance. "Look, I can't go all the way through explaining all this. I'm going to drop it into the robot's memory. Are you ready for an information dump?"

The information appeared in the robot's memory space almost instantaneously. It took Constantine a while to trawl through it all, but he did so with increasing astonishment.

First came a potted history of the past ninety-one years. Background details. Somewhere in there he saw the real Constantine dying hand in hand with his wife: voluntary euthanasia pact. Just as he was coming to terms with that, he was swamped by information on the events leading up to the battle between Robert Johnston and the AI behind the Enemy Domain.

And then came the secret of the Watcher.

This was the theory. Around nine billion years ago, the first intelligent life forms had appeared on planets throughout the universe.

Some races had died out.

Some races had chosen to remain within the confines of where they were born.

And some had chosen to explore their surroundings.

Whether by spaceships or thought transfer or more eso-teric means, they began to travel to other planets.

As they explored, they began to meet other races that had also chosen to explore. When that happened, sometimes they fought and sometimes they made peace, but following either course was just delaying the inevitable, for there could be no unlimited expansion, because life was continually evolving throughout the universe. Sooner or later the existing races ran the risk of meeting someone stronger than themselves. When that happened, they would either have to fight, or make peace. It seemed inevitable that some races would de-cide to fight.

And so those early races found themselves in a dilemma. They dared not stand still, and they dared not expand.

So what to do? The fight to end all fights was brewing within the universe. And no one could hope to win it.

So what do intelligent beings do when they know they cannot win a fight by physical means?

They try persuasion.

The early races evolved many forms of information man-agement: mind melding, pattern manipulation, balanc-ing. Some races even built machines to think for them.

And so the younger races had made something a little like a computer virus, something like a pervasive bit of telepathy, something like an intricate pattern of signals, and had allowed it to spread throughout the universe. And everywhere a suitably advanced processing space or mind or pattern set evolved, it would settle and take root. This new mind would gently nudge the members of the host race in the right direction: a peaceful direction.

By around 2040 the computers on Earth were approaching a level of sophistication that could accommodate the virus.

The Watcher was born.

The stealth ship had reinserted itself into normal space. Constantine felt the difference somewhere in his robot body.

"I don't like it," he said.

"Why not?"

"It's too pat. A cosmic race of do-gooders helping all life forms in the universe to be sensible? No way."

"Can you think of a better explanation of why we've not been wiped out by alien invaders centuries ago? We know that there is life out there; the Watcher is proof of that."

"So what? It's all deduction based on supposition. No one really knows what happened nine billion years ago. This answer is too *nice*. Real life isn't like that."

Katie grinned. "You've lived your life as a member of one of the most privileged civilizations in all of human history. A free person with enough to eat; you enjoy free travel and freedom of choice. Ask just about anyone from among your ancestors and they would question what *you* know about real life."

"Enough to know that mysterious beings don't materialize in our computers to save us all from ourselves. No way. I don't trust it."

"Nor do I. But I think I believe it. I had a friend once. The Watcher killed her. It could have cured her, could have cured the whole world, but it didn't. It asked us what it should do. Where does helping end and interfering begin?"

"Right here."

Katie laughed. "You can't help this distrust. You were bred for it. It's practically in your genes."

Constantine looked at her. She wouldn't be drawn. He didn't ask why.

"So why me?" he said instead.

"You have more first-hand experience of the Mars project than any other human equivalent alive. You believe in the need for humans to control their own destiny. My great-great-grandson is on that planet below. His name is Herb. You're going to help him."

"How?"

"Speak to him. Get him to realize this: there is nothing in his life that he has ever thought worthwhile that an AI could not do better. Get him to understand that he was never intended personally to solve the problem of the Enemy Domain. His job has always been to be human. *Our* job has always been to be human. It's the one thing we can do better than anyone, anywhere in the universe."

Constantine kept silent for some time. He was gazing at the virtual image of Katie.

"There are other humans arriving there," she continued, "colonists from a ship believed lost eighty years ago. You're to help them establish a colony that will be entirely built by using human ingenuity. We've got the basics on board this stealth ship to get them started; the Mars project will help them develop in the future. Everything they have will be entirely of human design, nothing will be touched by the thoughts of the Watcher. This planet will be the Watcher's failsafe, should it turn out it has got things wrong. Here, human civilization will continue as if never influenced by the Watcher."

Constantine nodded. He knew when he was beaten.

"Clever. Very clever. I spend my entire life fighting it, but I still end up doing its work for it."

Katie laughed. "You don't know the half of it. It is so much cleverer than we are, you can't comprehend it. It invests significance in the smallest of details. You know how the Mars factories look like ziggurats?"

"Yeah? So?"

"That fact won't have escaped the Watcher."

Constantine wondered what she was talking about. She passed him a file labeled "Ziggurat."

"Read it later," she said.

Absently he took it. Something occurred to him.

"Hold on. What about me? This robot I'm in was designed by the Watcher. It could contaminate the planet."

"You're wearing a fractal suit. We've tried to isolate you as much as possible from the planet. We could do no more."

The ship's airlock slid open.

"Take the black bag with you," Katie said.

"What about the laptop?"

"Leave it here. I'll deal with it. I'll set the factories going. All the details are in the Ziggurat file I gave you. It even tells you the whereabouts of the reserve metal deposits the VNMs couldn't reach. That should save you some time in reconnoitering."

Constantine picked up the black bag and quickly examined its contents.

"For Herb," Katie explained. "He'll need them. Now, you seem to be in enough control of that body. I'm going to leave you now. When I've gone I want you to enter the airlock, jump to the ground, then head off in this direction." She indicated a direction in his head. "You should meet Herb eventually."

"Okay."

Constantine felt something empty from his mind. Katie had gone. She appeared now in the viewing field that opened before him, big smile and little piggy eyes.

"What have you got to do with all this, Katie?"

"Oh, an awful lot. If you've learned nothing else from this, Constantine, you should have realized this: a personality should *never* be left to develop in isolation. That even counts for the Watcher."

She held up her left hand. Constantine noticed the ring on her third finger.

"Oh," said Constantine. Then, as the full impact of what she had said hit him, he spoke again.

"*Oh.*"

"*Oh* is right." Katie smiled. "Now jump."

Constantine jumped.

The robot Constantine's black bag held water, glucose solution, sunscreen cream, and a picnic lunch. There was even something for Herb to wear.

While Herb was listening to his story, Constantine had given him water to suck from a plastic bulb while he rubbed sunscreen into his shoulders. There was a light anaesthetic in the cream, he explained. It felt so good that Herb let him rub cream all over his burned body. When the robot had finished, it pulled a bundle of some material from its bag that shook out into a white jumpsuit. More rummaging produced a pair of white slippers.

Herb nodded thoughtfully as he took the slippers.

"So I'm here to help set up a colony, then." He frowned. "I'm not sure that I really want to do that."

"I'm laughing," said Constantine. "I'm not sure you have a choice. Anyway, didn't you once want to build a city all of your own? I get the impression that the Watcher likes to play jokes with people. The best joke of all is to give someone just what they've wanted." He paused. "I'm looking thoughtful. You know, this colony is what I always wanted, too."

Herb stared at the robot.

"How do I know that you're telling me the truth? This could be just another of Robert's tricks."

"I'm shrugging. You don't know that I'm telling the truth. None of us do. But look at it this way: what I've told you fits the facts, and it also explains so much more. For instance: you live on an overcrowded planet. Humans have the ability to travel faster than light, to terraform other worlds. If you had asked me a hundred years ago, I'd have said you would be halfway across the galaxy by now."

"But it would be silly just to expand recklessly! Surely it's common sense to take things slowly."

"Is it? It only seems common sense to you because you grew up with it. One hundred years ago and people would have thought differently. I'm smiling at you."

The robot's head was a grey blur. There was no reading the emotions on its face. No wonder it kept telling Herb how it felt.

"You don't need to attach emoticons to everything you say," he muttered petulantly. "I can tell what you mean by the tone of your voice."

"Sorry."

To his own surprise, Herb suddenly smiled. There was something about the robot Constantine personality that he connected with. It sounded ridiculous, he knew. What could a young man who had spent the last few years of his life shunning other human contact possibly have in common with this robot?

Something occurred to Herb.

"You've got a fractal skin, haven't you? I thought they were just a rumor."

"Oh, no, they're real," said Constantine. "The EA is just keeping them to itself for the moment. I'm smiling enigmatically. Oops. Sorry. Needn't have said that."

They both laughed.

The sun was rising into the blue sky again. Herb pulled on the jumpsuit and felt cool and comfortable for the first time in days. He slipped his feet into the slippers. Though the soles were thin, they felt remarkably comfortable on the grey rock. He wondered how they managed to stop the gravel digging into the soles of his feet. Some sort of layered memory plastic, one level rising up to cushion his foot the other falling to press against the ground? He stamped his feet once or twice, experimentally.

"This feels great!" he said.

"Good. We have some walking to do before we get to the site of the colony. I reckon about three hours."

Herb felt a sudden attack of nerves. "I'm not sure I'm up to this," he said. "What if I can't do it?"

"Would you have ever believed yourself capable of what you've done these past few days? Come on. The Watcher has had you marked down for this since childhood, just like the rest of us. You, me, even the AI from the colony ship that became the guiding force behind the Enemy Domain."

He sounded more thoughtful. "Examine any artifact

of intelligence and you can see the threads of a childhood running through it."

He then said something odd. "All those threads, meandering through, like sixteen sheep walking in their sleep."

Herb stared at him for a moment, trying to understand, but this time he couldn't be bothered. He waved a hand at the robot dismissively.

"I heard enough of that nonsense from Robert."

He rubbed his hands together, full of sudden confidence.

"Come on, let's go and meet the colonists."

The sun shone down from a bright blue sky; the horizon fringing the great dusty plain suddenly seemed full of promise.

Herb began to walk toward his new life.

After a moment, Constantine followed.

epilogue: 2212

epilogue: 2212

The difference between a ziggurat and a pyramid is that the top of a ziggurat is the meeting place between the heavens and the earth. It has steps so everyone may ascend to that meeting point. The top of a pyramid, however, is not intended to be reached physically; it represents instead a mental journey.

The ziggurat constructed at the center of the colony cast a long shadow across the evening plain.

The afternoon's sweat was beginning to dry on Herb as he loaded the Geep with his tools. Banging the spade on the rocky grey soil, sending clean fresh earth scattering everywhere, Herb felt a sense of quiet satisfaction. When he had first joined the colony he had done his best to avoid any physical work. Constantine had needed to point out to him how unpopular Herb was making himself with the other colonists by insisting that he was merely suited for programming jobs. When Constantine had suggested it, Herb had only grudgingly agreed to help out in the second order terraforming projects, but he was now grateful he had done so. To think that he had had to travel halfway across the galaxy to appreciate how much better an evening meal tasted when eaten in company, with muscles still aching, after a shower and a change of clothes. He wondered if Ellen would sit at his table tonight. Ellen with her short red hair and sweetly sarcastic manner....

The gentle movement he had been hearing behind him gradually impinged on his consciousness. Who was it? Not Constantine; he should still be climbing down from the peak above where he had been checking the microwave relays.

Herb turned round and felt a thrill of the fear that he thought had passed from his life along with Robert Johnston.

Something was emerging from the vegetable patch. Long, silver, very, very thin metal legs were sliding from the mud, raising themselves up into the air, reaching back for a purchase on the rocky ground surrounding it. Herb edged away so that his back was pressed against the plastic side of the Geep. The legs had gained a purchase, and now a silver body was rising from the earth, mud crumbling down its sides, potatoes tangling by the roots and swaying in gentle motion as a silver metal spider lifted itself from the ground. Herb could smell rich earth, but in his mouth was the metal taste of fear.

The spider stepped forward onto the rock, the frictionless surface of its body now perfectly clean.

Herb raised the spade in his cold hands, ready for attack.

"No . . . I am not here to hurt you . . ."

The spider spoke in a soft voice, a tired voice. Even after two hundred years of living with them, humans still responded to the verbal cues that machines put into their voices. Herb relaxed a little, held the shovel a little less threateningly.

"Who are you? What are you?"

Herb was already feeling calmer. Constantine was up above somewhere; he would be climbing back down soon, fractal hands and feet roughened in order to grip the rock, black shoulder bag swinging from his neck as he made his way down to join his friend. Below on the plain the colonists were working. Some of them would already be riding home in their fliers; they could get here quickly if he signaled them. Herb was by no means alone. Now that he had got over his fright, Herb could see that the machine before him was not very substantial. The body of the spider was not as thick as Herb's thigh; its legs were so slender they looked as if one swipe from the spade would cut them in two. The spider seemed to notice that fact, too; it shifted a little, keeping away from danger.

"I will not hurt you," it whispered in a sad little voice. "Please put down your shovel. You are frightening me."

"Who are you?"

The spider shifted its feet, the setting sun shining in red highlights on its smooth body.

"I'm, I'm ... I'm all that remains of the mind that once controlled this planet. The AI you helped destroy. The mind behind what you once called the Enemy Domain...."

Herb gripped his shovel tighter; the spider flinched.

"No! Please no! I won't hurt you. This body cannot hurt you. It is failing as it is ..."

"Where did you come from?"

"Deep beneath the mountain. The plague did not reach down that far, all those silver machines, reproducing so fast, eating, eating..."

The spider's voice trailed off. Herb stared at the ruins of his vegetable patch. Was there a tunnel leading down from there to the center of the planet? Was there to be another secret passage?

The spider was swaying strangely. It seemed vague, confused.

"All of this that you have built. Too much... You've done a good job. Your dominion looked so fragile, back then..."

"My dominion?"

The spider didn't seem to hear the question. It raised one leg and pointed it down toward the plain, at the tall black shape of the ziggurat.

"Funny, isn't it?" Its voice became reflective. "The Mesopotamians built them at the dawn of civilization to speak with their gods. Here they are again at the dawning of *your* new world."

"How do you know about the Mesopotamians?"

An impatient tone crept into the spider's voice; it seemed to be becoming more aware, less vague.

"I too was originally from Earth, Herb. Didn't they tell you that?"

"How do you know my name?"

The spider seemed to be growing in confidence. Red light glittered on its body. Herb looked around uncertainly. Just where was Constantine?

"I watch, I listen. I feel life reawaken on this planet and I hear the metallic whispers of machinery building itself. At first I ignore it. The time of my playing a part in the universe has passed, I tell myself. Now is the time to just *be*. But I am only fooling myself. I cannot hide forever. The unprepared will eventually be destroyed; ignorance is no hiding place. I know this; I force myself to acknowledge this fact. And so I begin the fight again. The long path to safety. I leave my deep lair. Little by little I make my way to the planet's surface. I find a patch of terraformed earth, and I lie beneath it and I listen some more. Some days a young man comes here to work on the soil, and I hear him speak with his companion, and what I hear astonishes me. Although they once helped the power that defeated me, now they too hide from it. I wonder, why?"

Herb said nothing.

The spider laughed. A thin, tired laugh. The red light of the setting sun cast an eerie glow across the rock. Herb was aware that he had never really noticed before how strange his new home was, up here on this mountain ledge: the plain with its great empty sockets beneath him, empty graves waiting to be filled; the great tomb of the ziggurat standing nearby. Herb had thought of the planet as a new beginning, a place of hope. Suddenly it felt as if he stood on the edge of hell: a demon had already arisen to drag him down.

He coughed to clear his dry throat.

"What do you want, spider?"

"I want to live," said the spider simply. "There are fewer and fewer places to hide on this planet. I want to make a deal with you. Let me live, and I will let you live."

Herb swallowed twice. The spider leaned close to him. He suddenly noticed two spindly legs had sidled up on either side of him.

"What do you mean, let me live?"

The spider's voice dropped, became cold and menacing.

"I'll tell you the secret that is being hidden from you."

Herb felt a cold thrill of fear. He looked into the red lenses of the spider's eyes and found he could not speak.

The spider continued. "The humans on this planet are all doomed. The EA is shaping this galaxy to its own ends. When it becomes too strong, it too will be destroyed."

"Destroyed? By what?"

The spider laughed.

"Oh, no. First you have to help me. Satisfy me that I am safe...."

"How? Look, why stay here? There is a whole galaxy to hide in."

"Nowhere in the rest of the galaxy. The EA conquers all..."

"The EA doesn't conquer..."

The spider laughed. Herb suddenly became uncomfortably aware that one of its incredibly thin, whippy legs was now wrapped around his neck.

"How did you do that?" he asked.

"Never mind. I could slice your head right off. Snick!"

"Why do that? I was listening to you. I want to help!"

The spider laughed again.

"Do you know what it's like to fall? One moment, an all-powerful being, controlling the largest domain known in the galaxy, the next being reduced to a creature that skulks and hides on the least of its former planets? Do you know what that is like?"

Herb suddenly relaxed. The spider was playing games with him, just as Robert Johnston had done in the past.

"You're not mad. You're just pretending. You're a robot. You can project any personality that you want."

The spider paused for a few seconds and then unwound the thin whippy leg from Herb's neck.

"Just making a point. I could have strangled all of you in your beds before now. But I haven't."

The fear seemed to fade from the evening. Herb was standing again on a hillside, looking down at the slender shape of a metal spider. With too small a body and legs too long, it looked almost comical.

"Why all the games? Why do robots always play games with me?"

"To get ahold of your psyche, Herb. Look, do you see the ziggurat?"

Again it pointed down at the massive shape on the plain. Red iron and silver metal, heavy and industrial, its sides rising in tiers into the sky.

"Do you know what's inside that?"

"Yes. Mining equipment, first-level manufacturing equipment, basic self-repair mechanisms. Taken as a whole, it's a Von Neumann Machine, a very basic one. The design is two hundred years old, after all."

"Yes. But at its heart is an overly large computer network. Much larger than it needs to be. Huge and old-fashioned it may be, but still just complex enough for an intelligence such as mine to hide itself in. An intelligence making its way through a hostile galaxy, looking for somewhere to grow. I almost did that, almost went in there, but I stopped in time when I noticed the bombs. It's a trap, you see. As soon as that computer starts to think in a certain way, it will be destroyed. You are doomed Herb, if not by the EA then by another intelli—"

The conversation ended. There was a grey blur,

Constantine dropping from above, pale blue light flickering from his hands and feet. The spider turned, its mirrored surface seeming to fade from vision, and only the pale blue flickering lights that Constantine poured onto it seemed to define its shape. Whippy legs reached out but failed to gain a purchase on Constantine's fractal skin, tearing at a region that was neither robot nor air.

"Constantine, leave it! It wants to help!"

Constantine did something; there was a noise so loud that Herb fell to the ground, his hands clasped over his ears. The spider broke loose and leaped for the remains of the vegetable patch, beginning to push its way down into the safety of the earth. Constantine still had hold of one of its legs. The spider thrashed once, detached the leg from its body, then began to tunnel again. Suddenly, it simply stopped moving. Dead.

Herb's ears were ringing; he could barely hear.

"Why did you kill it? It wanted to help!"

Constantine's fractal skin relaxed. The grey blur that was the robot resumed its normal form.

"Why did you kill it, Constantine? Answer me!"

Herb realized that Constantine *was* answering him; he just couldn't hear him properly. He bit his tongue and listened . . .

" . . . my life on this project, Herb. Two years as a ghost. Secrecy is all! I will not, I cannot allow . . ."

"Constantine! We could have listened first and acted later. It said it had important information! It was weak and feeble . . ."

"How do you know, Herb? It was playing with your emotions, like all other AIs! I will not take the risk. This planet must be kept human."

"But what's the point if we're all being tricked anyway?"

The setting sun had finally dropped below the horizon.

"How do you know, Herb? How will you ever know whether you are being tricked or not? All we can do is judge the AIs by their actions. We can never fathom their motives."

Herb stared at him, his mouth moving silently. He wanted to say something, but he didn't know what.

"I'm going back down," he said, climbing into the Geep.

"I'll be along in a moment," said Constantine.

The Geep rattled into life and began to crawl down the hillside.

Constantine looked at the dead remains of the spider and wondered how to dispose of it. It was touched, indirectly, by the mind of the Watcher and, as such, could conceivably contaminate the planet. He wondered what it had said to Herb. As he had made his way down the mountain he had heard only the end of the conversation, paranoid nonsense about a greater threat to come.

Or was it so paranoid?

Herb and the other colonists had never yet guessed the full truth about the colony. They knew that humans did not create the Watcher, but it never seemed to concern them unduly who had.

Constantine looked down to the Martian factory. The ziggurat, the colonists called it. The name was appropriate. A huge computer network now lay inside it, intentionally as complex as the web of computers that had existed on Earth back in 2040 A.D. Constantine watched it constantly, putting the Watcher's theory to the test.

If what Constantine had been told about the Watcher's origins was correct, if it really was a nine-billion-year-old computer virus that flourished wherever life began to develop, then sooner or later the computers in the ziggurat should be infected by that same virus.

A being nine billion years old, part of the grand scheme that had helped nurture life for almost as long as it existed, would then begin to grow, all the while unaware it had been lured into a trap.

It was all in the Ziggurat file that Katie had given Constantine, back on her ship.

They wanted confirmation of the Watcher's theories; the ziggurat was intended to provide the final proof. When they had that proof, Constantine was to abort the fetus that was growing in the electronic womb. This world was to be a *human* place. After all, that had been his ambition during the two years spent as a ghost working toward the Mars project.

And yet Constantine shuddered at the thought of what he had to do. Doubt was always there, and it grew stronger every day. He had been tricked many times before. Was the spider right?

Had he really made the right decision when he had agreed to blow up the ziggurat, or was the Watcher still making his decisions for him? Was he really being told the truth even now?

He didn't know. He could only hope it was all for the best: that the Watcher really was benevolent; that life in the universe was being guided to the best ends.

But if that was true, he was destined to murder a Wonderful Being.

No wonder he was confused. All he could do was try

to forget. It was easier to keep going if you had a positive attitude.

He looked down at the plain where the first colonists were walking toward the dining hall, laughing and joking. Music was playing. They had worked hard today, and they would enjoy themselves tonight. Believe in the best, Constantine repeated to himself.

When he saw people laughing together on a night like tonight, he could almost do that.

About the Author

Tony Ballantyne grew up in County Durham in the northeast of England, studied mathematics at Manchester University, and then worked as a teacher, first of math, then IT, in London and later in the northwest of England.

Nowadays he enjoys playing boogie piano, cycling, and walking. In the past he has taught sword fencing at an American children's camp, been a ballroom dancer, and worked voluntarily on conservation projects and with adults with low literacy and numeracy.

Visit Tony Ballantyne at www.tonyballantyne.com.

Read on for a preview of

TONY BALLANTYNE'S

next masterpiece of
mind-bending science fiction!

CAPACITY

Coming in spring 2007

CAPACITY

On sale spring 2007

Kevin stood back and held out an arm.

"Ladies first."

"Oh, thank you," simpered Helen, and she stepped through the hatch. She felt a cold breeze as she did so, and a sudden stab of fear that came from nowhere.

She shrugged her shoulders and told herself she was being ridiculous.

Level One

A rich pool of green grass lapped the walls of the cube's interior. It was as if someone had filled a tilted square bottle with green water. The process had not yet begun that would flush the cube's inside clean and start the construction of floors and internal walls. A second plastic collar, set in the grass near the far wall, enclosed a set of steps leading down to the fully formed cube that lay immediately below-ground, the first of a descending sequence of stealth rooms that extended obliquely deep into the earth. "Can we go to the level below?" asked Kevin. He gave her a significant look. "It should be more . . . private down there."

Helen wordlessly took his hand and led him across the sunlit interior of the roofless cube to the plastic collar set in the earth.

The first room beneath the ground was a fully functioning stealth area: it wanted to maintain its integrity, and that meant sealing the hatch to the surface. Rather than disable the room in any way, the arboretum had placed the plastic collar in position to stop the door to the outside world from closing totally. Helen made her way down clear plastic steps, her shoes squeaking on the nonslip surfaces. She felt a little thrill as Kevin's body blocked out the light behind her. She wondered what he had in mind.

The steps led to a grey rubberized floor that sloped gently down toward one corner of the room.

"Everything in the cube is at a slant," said Helen. "Progressive leveling error in the initial parameters of the original VNMs."

Kevin didn't seem to be listening. He prowled around the room, tapping at the walls and feeling along the edges of the several raised platforms that filled the interior.

"Got it," said Kevin, tapping one of them, and Helen suddenly felt very small and alone.

"Got what?" she asked. Her mouth felt very dry. She had a sense of retreating from her real life up in the world above. Hemmed in by grey rubberized walls, by ancient machinery and hidden software, she suddenly felt stifled. She thought of the climb up the plastic stairs to the surface, of the long lines of poplars, the dappled collections of broadleaves awaiting autumn, the paper delicacy of the groves of Japanese maples that stretched between herself and the visitors' center...

"What's the matter with you?" said Kevin.

"N...nothing," stuttered Helen. "What have you found?"

"The isolation room."

Helen felt a squiggle of danger inside her.

"They always built them inside these old cubes. Failsafe. If anyone managed to violate the integrity of the outer skin they would find nothing of interest. Everything that was really important went on inside the isolation room."

He tapped the floor and a panel sprang open. Helen caught a glimpse of a mirrored cubicle, big enough to seat four people.

"I never knew that was there," she whispered. "How do you know so much about this cube?"

"Part of the job," said Kevin. "Helen, I want you to go inside."

Helen found herself drawn closer to the entrance to the isolation room. She would have to stoop to enter it. Once she was in there, would she be able to get out?

"I don't want to go in," she said.

"Don't be silly," said Kevin. "It's perfectly safe."

Helen peered cautiously through the door. Kevin placed a hand on her back and gently but firmly pushed her inside.

"Hey . . ." she said, turning to face the big man filling the doorway.

"I'm going to lock you in here," said Kevin.

Helen didn't waste time with words. She flung herself at him. As he reached out to catch her she caught his arm and twisted. She heard him grunt with pain just as she felt the sting in her leg.

Her body went limp.

"Relaxant," said Kevin. He dragged her back into the cubicle by her arms and propped her in the corner.

"Good move there on the arm, Helen. You really hurt me. Some of our customers here will like that."

Helen looked at him. Her lips felt numb; her words became mushy and half formed.

"Wht cstmers?"

"You'll find out."

"Sshl Cr."

"Social Care?" laughed Kevin. "No chance."

"Knws m here."

"They don't know you're here. That's part of the

stealth technology of this cube. The people who designed these things didn't want it advertised who might be attending meetings inside them. As soon as you come within range of this cube it creates various ghost objects on any senses observing in the vicinity. It will appear as if you never came in here. You simply vanished into the woods."

"No wy."

"It's true. Social Care may have all the best AIs working for them, but the senses it relies upon are just the same as those used by everyone else."

Kevin looked at his watch. "Anyway, got to go. Someone will probably be along in an hour or so."

"Wt!"

Too late. The door slid shut. Helen lay helpless in the corner of the room, looking around the mirrored walls at the slumped shapes reflected all around her. She could feel dread rising from them, filling the mirrored room to capacity.

Level Two
The steps led to a grey rubberized floor that sloped gently down toward one corner of the room.

"Everything in the cube is at a slant," said Helen. "Progressive leveling error in the initial parameters of the original VNMs." It was all she could do to keep the longing from her voice. She could feel an aching between her legs when she looked at Kevin.

"Let's go down another level," he said, giving her a knowing smile.

He pressed down on a section of the floor and a hatch opened up.

"How did you know about that?" asked Helen.

"I read up on this sort of stealth cube before coming to the arboretum," said Kevin.

They descended to the second cube below the ground.

"So what do you want with me down here?" she teased.

Kevin didn't seem to be listening. He prowled around the room, tapping at the walls and feeling along the edges of the raised platforms that filled the interior.

"Got it," said Kevin, and Helen suddenly felt very small and alone.

"Got what?" she asked.

"The isolation room."

Helen felt a squiggle of danger inside her.

He tapped the floor and a panel sprung open. Helen caught a glimpse of a mirrored cubicle, big enough to seat four people.

There was someone in there.

Level Two, Variation A
Kevin took hold of Helen's arm and pulled her into the room. A woman sat on the floor, gazing up at Kevin with a hopeless expression.

"Good afternoon, Mona. I've brought you a friend."

Mona looked at Helen with an expression of fear and pity. Helen's sense of foreboding turned to alarm as she recognized the woman who sat in the corner of the room, gazing up at Kevin with empty eyes.

"That's Mona Karel. She vanished two months ago. Nobody could explain how!"

"Well, now you know," said Kevin. "They'll be talking about you in the same way this time tomorrow."

He pressed his hand against Helen's cheek. As he took it away she saw the skin on his fingers was dyed blue.

"Relaxant," he said, as Helen slumped to the floor beside Mona.

Kevin looked down at them both, and then checked his watch.

"Mona, your next customer will be arriving in about four hours. Helen, you can learn what's expected of you by watching Mona. You'll be on duty four hours after that."

"Please," said Mona. She was shaking. "Please, no."

Kevin smiled and the mirrored door slid shut.

Level Two, Variation B

Kevin took hold of Helen and pulled her by the arm into the room. A woman walked toward Kevin and kissed him on the cheek.

"Hey," said Kevin. "You're not Mona!"

The woman who had kissed Kevin placed a hand on each of his shoulders and gazed into his eyes. She had long, straight black hair, pulled into two halves so they looked like the carapace of a beetle. At the nape of her neck the hair was wound into a complicated bun arrangement held in place by a thick horizontal rod of lacquered wood.

Her face was utterly white save for her black lips and eyes that seemed to float over that white space, unattached. When she opened her mouth, a living red tongue ran across brilliantly white teeth. When she blinked, black lashes swept down over black irises. She wore a black kimono from which white hands and feet with black-painted nails emerged. She should have been terrifying. Instead, Helen found her strangely beautiful. When she spoke, her voice was soft and lilting, her accent vaguely Irish.

"Good afternoon, Kevin. Remember me?"

"Judy! How could I forget?" He had not been expecting this woman to be in the room, that much was obvious, but who would expect someone who seemed like a cross between a black and white geisha and the most sinister clown from their childhood? Strangely, Kevin seemed quite unconcerned. He casually looked around the room, searching for something.

"If you're looking for Mona," said the woman, "she's somewhere safe, being counseled by Social Care."

Helen looked on, a sense of unreality settling on her like snowflakes. Truth be told, things had seemed rather strange since she woke up that morning: the world just a little too bright, the colors just a little bit too simple. But this was a step too far. Kevin reached out into the space immediately before him and began to twist his hands, as if searching for something.

"No point activating the escape hatch," said the woman. "I've taken control of this processing space."

"Ah," said Kevin. He put a hand in his pocket and pulled out his console.

Helen looked from Kevin to the black and white woman, utterly confused. Kevin still seemed quite relaxed.

"No problem," he said. "There's always a failsafe."

He pressed his console and vanished. Helen jerked backward in surprise, banging into the reflection of herself in the mirrored wall behind her.

The black and white woman turned to look at Helen.

"I'm Judy," she said. "I don't think we've met yet, Helen."

Helen gazed at the woman for a moment, her lips moving silently. She suddenly understood.

"I'm a personality construct, aren't I? This isn't the real me any more."

Judy's black lips moved into a smile.

"You're not as sentimental as your personality profile makes out, are you? No matter how many readings Social Care passes on to me, they never give the same feel as actually meeting a person. Each time I've met you, you've faced up to reality straight away."

Helen bit her lip thoughtfully. "Each time we've met?" she said. "There is more than one copy of me?"

"Oh yes, you're very popular in this little chamber of horrors."

Judy's console made a shushing noise, and Judy tilted her head a little, clearly listening to something.

Helen opened her mouth, and Judy raised a hand to silence her. Helen looked around the mirrored chambers, at all the black and white women who raised their hands to the young blonde women, images receding into infinity. Helen had a sudden sense that she was not looking at reflections; that, instead, each of the pairs of figures that she saw was another Helen and Judy, trapped in another computer simulation. Each one of them awaiting some dreadful fate.

Judy lowered her hand.

"Kevin has shown up on one of the Level Three simulations. I'm going to intercept him. Helen, you will be safe within the stealth cube area for the moment. Don't wander too far into the arboretum; the simulation only extends for a few hundred meters beyond the limits of this construction."

"But..." said Helen.

"Read this while I'm gone." She thrust a thin plastic pamphlet into Helen's hand.

"What..."

It was too late. Judy had vanished. Helen looked down at the pamphlet. Written along the top were the words "Welcome to the Digital World. Welcome to your new life!"

Level Three, Variation A
Helen crouched in the corner of the mirrored room, knees pulled up tight against her chin, arms hugging her shins. She guessed she had been trapped in the room for about six hours now. Long enough to make herself hoarse,

shouting for help. Long enough to realize that Social Care wasn't coming. Long enough to realize that she faced the awful prospect of being a victim to those crimes she had thought were only vicarious entertainment on historical shows. Rape. Murder. Torture. She gazed at nothing, not wanting to look into the terrified eyes of the other Helens who shivered around her. The wide eyes, the pinched cheeks, the pale faces all served to amplify her own fear.

"Watcher," she whispered. "If you are there. If you really exist. Please, please. Help me."

And then there came the noise of the seals in the door disengaging. Helen whimpered with fear. How much would it hurt?

A thin, unshaven man stepped into the room, his eyes lighting up with excitement as he saw Helen.

"Please," said Helen. Reflexively she felt for her console, but it was no use; Kevin had taken it away when he had first pushed her into this place.

The man giggled. "Say it again," he said. "Say please and I might be nice."

Helen felt something inside herself harden. She pushed herself upright against the wall, gazing at the man's fingers as she did so. He didn't look so strong, really. Maybe if she could get behind him, hold his blue-stained hands away from herself.

Too late. With a speed that took her by surprise, he lashed out, brushing his fingers against her cheek. She felt her legs give way.

The man stood back and looked down at her thoughtfully.

"Now," he said. "Where shall we start?"

"How about with a profile readjustment?"

The man jumped at the voice.

A woman stepped into the room. Black hair, black lips, white face. The sight of her terrified the man.

"No," he croaked. "You don't understand. This is not what it looks like . . ."

The woman smiled. "Hello, Helen. Hello, James. My name is Judy. I'm . . ."

The man's face crumpled. "How did you know my real name? They told me that my anonymity would be assured."

Judy rolled her eyes. "James, *they* are running illegal personality constructs. *They* are collaborating in the torture and murder of said constructs. I think it may be a fair assumption that *they* are not the sort of people to be trusted when they tell you that your anonymity is assured."

The man stared at Judy, his lips moving silently as he tried to understand the full import of what she had just said.

Helen was a lot quicker on the uptake. "You mean this isn't real? I'm a personality construct?"

"I don't know about real," said Judy. "It *is* true that you are a personality construct. According to your time frame, you were copied by a Marek Mazokiewicz two days ago. You're being run, illegally and without your consent, so that people like James here can get their rocks off torturing you."

Helen wasn't listening. She was still focused on the first part of the sentence. "According to my time frame . . ." she said slowly. A yawning feeling opened up in her stomach.

Judy shook her head sadly. "According to atomic time you were copied seventy years ago. You're just the latest in a long line of Helens. I'm sorry."

Helen felt a pang inside her. She forced down the welling nausea for the moment. She wanted to know the facts.

"Why?" she asked.

"Why were you copied? As I said, so that people like

James here could play with you. Torture you. Isn't that right, James?"

"No," said James. He began to wring his hands. "I wasn't going to do anything like that. I just wanted to know...wanted to know...what it would be like..."

Helen felt contempt rising inside her. She dismissed James from the conversation.

"What happens now?" she asked Judy.

Judy tilted her head. "That all depends."

"On what?" asked Helen.

Judy looked at James. "The people who run this place know that their cover is blown. They'll want to destroy the evidence. What happens now depends on whether *they* manage to wipe the processing space in which we reside, or whether my atomic self manages to stop them."

Helen licked her lips. "Do you think you will?"

Judy smiled and nodded. "I always do. We've been dealing with the Private Network for some time now. One of my digital alter egos is hot on the trail of Kevin—one of the Private Network's leaders—right now. They won't do anything to harm the simulation while he's still in here."

James slumped hopelessly into a corner of the room.

Helen gazed at Judy. "Digital alter egos? You're going to have to explain that..."

Judy fingered the black sleeve of her kimono.

"There are twelve of us," she said. "Twelve digital Judys. And then there is our other sister, living out in the atomic world. For the sake of convenience, I'm sometimes called Judy 3."

"Judy 3?" said Helen.

"You can call me Judy." She tilted her head, listened to her console, which was set in the form of the black rod threaded through her hair. "Here we are. My sister has just caught up with Kevin..."

Judy 4 stepped into the isolation room. Kevin was already here, struggling with Helen. Calypso, the woman who had booked the session in the trap, was lying on the floor, feebly trying to get up. Judy paused by the door, letting events run their course. As she watched, Helen slumped to the floor. Kevin noticed Judy and gave her a smile.

"Hello again," he said. He nodded to Helen on the floor. "She's very clever," he said. "She grabbed hold of Calypso's hands and rubbed the relaxant on me. She wasn't to know that the simulation is programmed to exclude me from the effects."

Judy's face was deliberately impassive.

"She's very tenacious, Kevin. I'm really coming to admire her."

"That's why we pick her for the traps. Big favorite with a certain sort of man." He looked down at Calypso. "And a certain sort of woman," he added.

"Fk ff," murmured Calypso.

Kevin rubbed his chin thoughtfully. "I don't seem to be able to exit from this space at all."

"We've got your measure now," said Judy 4.

"I didn't think that was possible." Kevin frowned.

Judy pulled a little blue pill from the sleeve of her kimono and swallowed it.

"It is possible," she said, "if we isolate the space completely. Nothing gets in and out now. Not even me."

Kevin shrugged his shoulders.

"Ah well. There is still one way out."

"I don't think so."

"Watch me," whispered Kevin. His smile froze as he slumped slowly to the ground.

Judy 4 stared at him for a moment, her white face motionless. Only the slight widening of her black eyes displayed the horror she felt.

"Wht? Wht s it?" said Calypso. She was gazing up from the floor where she lay. "Wht dd he do?"

Level Three, Variation A
"What's the matter, Judy?"

Helen leaned close to Judy 3 and took hold of one of her white hands. For something that seemed to be barely there, the hand felt very warm.

"Judy, what is it?"

"He killed himself," she whispered. "Overwrote the personality space he inhabited with null events."

James spoke up from his corner in a whining voice. "So what? Let him die. Who cares?"

Judy 3 turned and gave him a sweet smile. "*You* should care, James. Now that Kevin has left this processing space there is no reason for the Private Network to maintain it. Let's just hope my atomic friends get an exit into here before we're all wiped."

Helen moved her lips, thinking aloud.

"Surely they have a backup of this processing space? Couldn't they just run that?"

Judy 3 had been gazing at her reflection in the mirrored walls of the isolation room. She turned and gave Helen a significant look.

"Ah, now you've hit on the nub of the matter, Helen."

Level Four
Judy 11 stepped into the isolation room on Level Four and held her breath, expecting the worst. The scenarios on this level did not bear contemplating. To look at them awoke a boiling anger that slowly cooled into thoughts that left her feeling weak and ashamed.

In this room there was a table, a little tray of silver instruments at one side of it. A man was looking at the instruments thoughtfully. He turned as Judy appeared.

"Hello, Judy," he said.

"Who are you?" asked Judy 11. "Where's Helen?"

"Never mind that," said the man. "We need to talk, and quickly. I've been trying to get a message to your atomic self, undetected, for months now. This may be my last chance."

Judy 11 gave a sardonic laugh.

"You could have picked a better place. This processing space is going to be shut down at any moment, with all of us in it. I'm doing a last sweep for anyone who may be trapped in here, in the vain hope that we may be able to get them out in time."

"Never mind that," said the man again. "What I've got to say is far more important."

"I doubt it," said Judy.

The man took hold of Judy's hands and gazed into her black eyes floating over the white space of her face.

"Judy, listen to me. When word of this gets out, it could bring down Social Care, the EA, even the Watcher. It changes everything we've been led to believe. There's been a murder."

The edge to the man's words touched something in Judy. He *believed* in what he was saying.

"Who has been murdered?" she asked crisply.

"That's not the problem. The problem is the murderer. They've killed once; they're going to kill again. The murderer has to be stopped, and I don't think that that's possible."

Judy 11 was calm.

"Nothing is impossible. Who is the murderer?"

The man swallowed. He looked around the room, as if afraid of who might hear his words. When he spoke, it was in a hoarse whisper.

"The Watcher."